THE TWELVE KINGDOMS

ROSE WOLFE AND THE TWELVE KINGDOMS: BOOK ONE

DANA A. CALDWELL

THE TWELVE KINGDOMS

Mystic Mongoose Books

Published by Mystic Mongoose Books (LLC)

Cover design by MiblArt

Map by Saumya Singh (@saumyasvision/Inkarnate)

To every version of me who tried and failed.
At long last, our dreams are becoming a reality.

TABLE OF CONTENTS

AUTHOR'S NOTE

Due to large amounts of fantasy violence, gore, and brief scenes of torture, this book is not recommended for readers under the age of fourteen. A full content guide can be found by scanning this QR code:

For your convenience, a glossary and pronunciation guide has been provided at the back of the book.

Happy reading,
Dana A. Caldwell

MALECARE
DARV
DEVIL'S CANYON
ELATIRE
MARSTAFF MANOR
AVONSHERE
BRENNATE
DEL HERA
SYBIL
THE MADORIAN ISLES
ALEDDAI
CAVBRO
MADORIA
NICIA
MYDOR
DARIA
VAERA
THE
THE ISLE OF GORDA
NORTH SOREN
SOREN
SOUTH SOREN
THE SIBELINE ISLES
THE TWELVE KINGDOMS

PATRIKOS
PIKBRIE
THE BORVIAN ISLES
THE IVRODE RIVER
CHESS
HOLFETINE WOOD
RUDANE
ELWRITE
MEDEA
LUCIA
NEMETH
FAELANDS
VARGO
SHAB

PART ONE

PROLOGUE

Blood shone in the moonlight, glittering on skin and blade alike—as though a bag of rubies had been torn, and the precious gems scattered across a scene of smoke and ruin. But there was nothing precious about this place. The crimson drops were no more than blood drying on the bodies that littered the street, their flesh torn and their mouths ajar with the ghosts of their final screams.

Guided by the moon's pale light, I made my way through the smoldering remains of a village. Dwindling flames lapped at the charred frames of homes, devouring the memories they once held. Not even an hour ago, this place stood, a steadfast haven.

Then, the creatures came. Those horrid, soulless shadows of beings bound to *her* command. They fought, I ran, and it all *burned*.

I walked alone through the carnage. My stinging eyes glazed over the array of corpses as their lifeless faces faded into distant memories. After two years of living in the heart of war, the practice was second nature. You live, you love, and they die. All that's left to do is forget.

The smoke thickened, smothering my senses and sending sharp pangs through my lungs. I pushed forward, covering my mouth and nose with my hood, only to stop in my tracks the moment the haze cleared.

An ache carved through my dulled heart as I gazed at the blackened remains of a cottage. *My home. Destroyed again.*

The scorched remnants of the floorboards splintered and snapped as I stepped through the doorway. My boots left prints in the ash that covered the ground like sand on a beach. A small fire burned in the corner, the flames creeping toward a fallen painting with a cracked frame.

No.

I threw myself forward with a cry, landing hard on my knees. I was fast, but not fast enough. The flames licked the canvas's edge, flaring as the paint ignited.

I flung my cloak over the burning mass, frantically beating until the fire faded into smoke. With a shaking breath, I uncovered the painting. The edges were browned, but that didn't matter. My gaze was locked on the family that stared back at me. *My* family. Happy, loving, and together. Only two years had passed since the painting's creation, yet everything had changed.

Where was my mother, a beautiful and fair elf maiden with the points of her ears peeking out from her dark waves? Where was my father, tall and blond, with the greenest eyes in the Twelve Kingdoms? And their daughter? That little girl of ten years with a bright smile and innocent eyes. Where was she?

Gone. They were all gone.

Fresh tears stung my eyes as I rolled up the painting, shoving it into my satchel. I'd been that girl two years ago. I'd been happy and loved. *But now...*

I closed my eyes, taking in a deep breath of smoky air tainted with the stench of death. I couldn't even pretend this was a dream.

I brushed away a tear, ignoring the ash and blood that stained my pale hand—and now my cheek. How had I ever thought I could finish my mother's fight? I wasn't a leader or protector, I was a little girl broken by war. No, not just broken, *destroyed*. Robbed of my birthright, my parents, and my home. Yet I had believed I could win this and restore my family to the throne.

I opened my eyes to the glint of silver—the tip of an object peeked out from the ashes. With trembling fingers, I dug, grasping at cold, curved metal. I knew what it was before I could even pull it free.

Fresh tears pooled as I stared at the crown in my hands. How many days had I seen it resting on my grandfather's head? How many seconds had it sat on the head of my father before it was knocked away? And how many hours had I spent clutching it and crying, knowing that it was the only piece of him I had left?

I brushed a shaking thumb over the three star-shaped diamonds set into the dark metal, sapphires on either side. An emblem of my family, once a source of comfort and pride, now pain etched in the sky above.

An inhuman scream pierced the air, carried on the icy wind. I dropped the crown with a shudder, clamping my hands over my ears.

No, no, no. Already, they had returned. I covered my mouth to smother my cries as my mind raced with thoughts of their claws, slick with scarlet. They were Natalia's creatures, bound to her twisted mission. Forged to kill, with blood as black as their master's soul.

I could try to outrun them, but it wouldn't matter. Natalia would never be satisfied until I was lying among the corpses. Until I was as dead as my mother and my father and everyone else who stood in the way of the throne.

A hollow sob slipped through my fingers. A dead girl, that's what I was. And the dead don't cry. No… the dead *survive*.

I raised my hand, my gaze transfixed on the sapphire ring on my forefinger. With the moonlight reflected just right, I could see the design carved into the small stone. The head of a wolf sat within a crescent moon, gazing out at a trio of four-point stars. My family's crest. Once upon a time, it flew proudly across the Kingdom of Avonshere, proclaiming our power. Now it was forbidden, cast aside by everyone in the kingdom, including me. The ring was a brand that marked me as Crown Princess of Avonshere. It could be the death of me, or it could be my escape.

I slipped the ring off my finger, my voice cracking as I spoke.

"Dead girls don't cry."

Natalia wanted me dead, and I would give her what she wanted. Tonight, I would die.

When morning came, my ring would be found on the finger of a child's skeleton, charred beyond recognition. A silver crown would lie by the skull, and those who found it would know the princess's fate.

They would not bother to search for evidence beyond what was before their eyes, nor would they notice the girl who slipped into the forest. They would be too busy spreading the message to everyone in the kingdom: Rosara Wolfe was dead.

FIVE YEARS LATER…

THE HUNTRESS

A crisp breeze blew through the forest, rustling the red-speckled branches above me and sending a shiver down my spine. I let out a sharp breath, adjusting my grip on my bow; I should have known better than to leave my cloak behind.

Today marked the beginning of the harvest season. While the forest grew more and more vibrant, the temperature would plummet, slowly dragging the Kingdom of Chess toward rime—a season of ice and snow. I'd thought I'd have a few more days until the cold settled over Chess, but the goosebumps lingering beneath my shirt told me otherwise.

Biting back a sigh, I continued my walk through the forest. My one goal was to catch something good for dinner, and I was failing miserably. Squirrels skittered across branches while wrens and sparrows glided through the treetops, but none were big enough for tonight's meal. The entire town of Rudane was gathering to celebrate the first day of harvest, and it was up to me to provide meat for my family's stew.

I kept my gait light, doing my best to avoid stepping on dead leaves. The creatures residing in Holfetine Wood were well aware of the threat posed by hunters such as myself. At the slightest hint of danger, they would run or hide amid the brush, becoming all but invisible to the human eye. However, I did have a slight advantage, considering my eyes were only half human.

Last night a storm had blown through Rudane, knocking down branches and fences and sending the forest's inhabitants into hiding. The weather cleared around midnight, but the ground had yet to fully dry. My prey could run, but not without leaving a trail.

I scanned the forest for signs of disruption. *There.* A trail of bent grass led through the bushes. Kneeling, I pushed aside branches to reveal a string of teardrop-shaped hoofprints etched into the damp ground.

Perfect.

With the tracks as my guide, I followed the deer's path. They went straight for a while, then stopped before the river.

Biaht. I bit my lip to keep the curse from slipping out. The deer must have crossed the river, and if I wanted to catch it, I'd have to cross as well.

I eyed the flowing water with disdain. Last night's storm had nearly doubled the water levels, raising the usually ankle-deep river to my knees. That, coupled with the cooling temperatures, kept my feet planted on the bank.

Disappointment settled over me as I shouldered my bow. Three hours of hunting, and I had nothing to show for it. But, it wasn't entirely my fault. I had never seen Holfetine this quiet before. Once the storm cleared, the forest's inhabitants should have come out to forage. Yet the forest remained still, almost as if something kept the creatures in hiding. But what?

A snap broke through my musings. My gaze shot to the opposite side of the river, where leaves shook—not from the wind, but from a slim girl weaving her way up the tree. She passed a patch of bare branches, allowing me a glimpse of pale skin and fiery curls.

I groaned. "What are you doing, Megs?" I muttered as my friend settled on a branch thinner than her arm. Far below loomed the unforgiving ground, littered with rocks. It wasn't unusual for hunters to take advantage of the elevation and camouflage provided by the forest, but Megs possessed a reckless sense of invincibility gained from sixteen consequence-free years of life. Her recent ascension into adulthood left me more concerned than ever for her safety.

I took a step forward, ready to intervene, when something large and gray shifted, drawing my gaze and taking my breath in one fell swoop.

A wolf stood, lapping at the stream, her coat flecked with silver. Although her eyes were gentle, her body was woven with strength. Beautiful, dangerous strength that made her a deadly enemy. *Or a loyal friend.*

In my mind the golden eyes turned blue, and the silver coat shifted to white. My throat tightened. All I saw was her. Dozing by the fire, playing with the pups, resting her head in my lap, *lunging*—

A gasping breath broke free as I fell against a tree. *Zevre.* Her name echoed in my head, but I refused to let it leave my lips. I clenched my jaw, fighting to push the memories down. Then the faintest click reached my ears.

I froze. *Megs had a crossbow.* My eyes landed on her, barely visible through the foliage. *No.*

My heart pounded. Each beat brought back another memory of my childhood and my wolves. Nausea swept over me at the thought of them with arrows in their necks.

In a single motion, I drew back my bowstring and let loose an arrow, sending it flying toward the wolf—and right between her ears.

The wolf started, her eyes meeting mine for a split second. She took off, disappearing into the brush.

I released a slow breath as my mind settled and my fear faded.

"Rose!" Megs's voice came from the tree, followed shortly by her red curls and poncho-wrapped body. She dropped to the ground, an understandable pout on her lips.

"I had the wolf in my sights!" Megs exclaimed as she waded through the river, kicking water up to her thighs. Her poncho fell from one shoulder, dragging in the river behind her. Reaching the bank, she held out her hand.

"I'm sorry," I said, pulling her onto dry land. "I didn't see you there."

Megs frowned, crinkling her freckled nose as she tugged off her poncho. Though it fell just below her waist, the risen tide and dragged end left her with a half-soaked sheet of wool. Muttering obscenities, she attempted to wring out the heavy material before tossing the damp garment over a low tree branch.

"Did you catch anything?" I asked. Maybe if I moved the conversation along, she would forget about the loss of her prey. *Because Megs never holds grudges.* I nearly rolled my eyes at the thought.

"A couple of rabbits." She used the least soaked part of her poncho to dry the twin daggers she kept strapped to her thighs. "Most of the traps were tripped by the storm. Hertz went off to check the fishing poles while I went out in search of the most beautiful, sleek, and silver—"

"I get it. And I'm sorry for scaring the wolf."

"I'm just sorry you missed." Megs returned her daggers to their sheaths. "But don't worry, I'll find a way for you to repay the debt." She grinned up at me, her green eyes sparkling with mischief. Sweeping her damp poncho over her shoulders, she set off into the woods.

I glanced back at the bushes the wolf had disappeared into. *You're lucky I care.* Megs Mohler was one of my closest friends and the human embodiment of a malicious pixie. Not only would she stand by her word to make me pay, but our three-and-a-half years of friendship had given her all the tools she needed to ensure her victory.

"Have you decided what you're going to wear tonight?" Megs asked as we walked through the forest, dead leaves crunching beneath our boots.

"Not yet."

She shot me a disdainful look. "You're hopeless."

"You're too invested in this. The Harvest Festival isn't some extravagant ball. It's neighbors gathering and asking Layona to bless the coming harvest. That's hardly an excuse to force your mother to make you a new gown."

"Just because she's the Divine Lady of the Fields doesn't mean Layona doesn't care about appearances," Megs pointed out. "She might even appreciate the effort and give us an even *more* bountiful harvest. Kingdoms know we could use one."

A soft *hmm* was my only reply. In this case, it was better to keep my opinions silent. "Where did Hertz say he'd meet us?" I asked, diverting the conversation.

"By the old oak," she replied. "And I see what you're doing."

"Oh, come on." I protested, bumping her with my elbow. "You have to admit—your priorities are a bit skewed in this instance. By all means, look pretty, but you asked for your dress to be draped in pearls!"

"*Dripping* in pearls," she corrected. "And *Modir* would have done it, too, if it weren't for the Madorian queen being a cleming who won't trade with the land kingdoms."

"Soren still trades in pearls." The words slipped out without a thought as maps and trade routes flashed through my mind.

"Soren overcharges." She shook her head, annoyed. "It's all so silly. One little mermaid sword goes missing centuries ago, and we're still left without affordable pearls!"

I pressed my lips together, my pace slowing as I fought back a retort. That *little mermaid sword* was one of twelve, blessed by the divine guardians who saved the land from the Dark War and helped establish the Twelve Kingdoms. Madoria's severance from the rest of the kingdoms might not be justified, but it wasn't without reason.

"Forget about the pearls," I said, falling back into step with Megs. "Just think about Hertz's cake."

A grin spread across her face. Even she had to agree that the most elegant of dresses were worthless compared to our dear friend's baking.

"Fine, you win." She gave my shoulder a playful punch. "Race you to the oak."

Without waiting for a reply, she took off running, leaving me to chase after her. Leaves crunched beneath our feet, the noise sending squirrels skittering up trees. We slid to a stop at the base of a massive oak tree clinging to its last few leaves of green.

"Cheater," I teased.

Megs grinned, breathing heavily as she leaned against the thick trunk. Her emerald eyes followed the leaves as they fell.

"I miss the calescent season," she said. "It's so pretty and green, then everything dies."

I frowned. "That's morbid."

She shrugged, staring off into the forest.

A figure dropped out of the trees, landing nimbly before us. Megs yelped, scampering back. My hand shot to my quiver, my fingers brushing against the feathered fletching, only to stop when I saw the figure's familiar face.

"Eris?"

Eris straightened, shoving her tangled hair out of her eyes. A chorus of butterfly-like liposas nestled themselves into a crown-like shape on her head. As a tree nymph, Eris blended into nature, with textured skin that shifted between green and brown and antlers protruding from her knotted locks. Despite her wild appearance, her gentle eyes would reveal her kind nature. But not today. Today, they were filled with mad, unrestrained fear.

"Are you all right?" I asked, reaching out.

She recoiled, her eyes darting about. "Something's coming. Something dark and… and evil."

"What is it?" I asked, my heartbeat picking up.

The nymph's eyes widened, scanning the woods. "It's already here," she murmured, sniffing the air. "Don't you smell it?"

"Smell what?"

"Death." With a cry, she scrambled up the old oak tree, disappearing as her skin shifted to match the bark.

Megs turned, her lips parted, and her copper brows furrowed. "*What* was that?"

"I have absolutely no idea."

"Kingdoms, she looked insane!" she exclaimed, her confusion shifting into an awkward laugh. "All that talk of evil. I mean, that's all it was, right? Talk. Nymphs can't sense danger coming… can they?"

"I don't think so." Even so, wisps of worry grew, nervous spirits flitting within my stomach.

A branch snapped behind us. With a synchronized shout, Megs and I spun, facing a tall, dark-skinned man with closely cropped hair and broad shoulders.

"Hertz." I let out a sigh of relief.

"Are you two all right?" he asked, looking between us.

"Fine," Megs replied. "We just heard a noise and assumed it was some incarnation of evil coming to kill us."

Hertz stared at her. "Right…" He turned his attention to me. "Catch anything?"

"Nothing. You?"

He held up a bloody sack. "Some rabbits. We'd have more if not for the storm—it took out four traps *and* blew away all the fishing poles."

"Rack!" Megs swore, earning a frown from Hertz.

"We're not done yet," I reminded her. "There are still a few traps left to check. Maybe we'll get lucky."

The sun rose high overhead as we ventured through the forest, checking the remaining traps. Our catch grew to include a total of five rabbits and three squirrels. Only one trap remained: a deadly instrument invented by Megs, and approved by no one.

I'm not entirely sure what I was expecting as we made our way toward her latest bad idea, but it certainly wasn't a giant buck sprawled across the path, a short arrow in its neck.

Megs let out an excited laugh at the sight, racing ahead to examine her prize.

I stared at the crossbow-style weapon she had mounted on a tree. *It actually worked.* Her idea of running a string along the known deer path and connecting it to small crossbow's trigger sounded mad. But I couldn't deny the results. Her trap had succeeded. The buck had pushed against the nearly-invisible wire and sent an arrow into his own neck.

"You're going to shoot someone one day," I warned as she restrung the trap.

She waved me off. "Yes, yes, I know. This trap will go horribly wrong and wind up shooting some innocent hunter's kneecap."

"It will," I insisted.

"Not if they are smart enough to look where they walk." She flicked the string, sending the short arrow flying past her nose.

Hertz and I exchanged a defeated look. By now, we knew which arguments were worthwhile and which were as productive as fighting a stone wall.

"Let's go. I've got skinning to do today." Megs hoisted the deer onto her shoulders, wobbling under its weight, which likely matched her own.

"And a festival to attend." Hertz caught her as she began to tip backward. He took the buck from her, trading her the sack of rabbits.

"Rose and I were talking about that earlier," she said after a quick word of thanks. "And how the Kingdom of Madoria is full of waterlogged sults who are too prissy to handle proper trade."

"Language, Megs," Hertz said.

"What? They're sults. Racking, little Biaht-bound sults."

I couldn't help but laugh, earning me a disappointed look from Hertz.

"You too?"

I held my hands up, still laughing. "I wasn't the one who said it."

"You're encouraging her."

"Megs doesn't need my encouragement. She has a big enough ego to carry on for years."

"You are aware that I'm standing right here, right?" Megs said, hands planted on her hips—a commanding pose somewhat spoiled by the bloody bag of rabbits hanging by her knees. Not that I could judge her, considering I had dead squirrels dangling from my belt.

"Yes," I replied. "We are."

She spun with a toss of her hair, leading us onward.

"You know," she called over her shoulder, "there's nothing wrong with being confident. Or with voicing my opinions."

"There is when it involves unsuitable language," Hertz noted.

She scoffed. "What are you, a priest?"

"He's the head priest of the temple of bread and cake," I quipped.

He shook his head, smiling softly.

Megs laughed. "Instead of animal sacrifices, they sacrifice—oh, dead deer!"

"What?" I asked, taken aback by her sudden shift.

"Dead deer," she repeated, one hand covering her mouth, the other pointing to a fly-speckled carcass a few feet ahead of us. The deer's side bore deep scratches and a portion of her neck had been ripped out, leaving a gaping wound matted with blood.

"What do you think did this?" Megs crouched beside the carcass, examining the scratches with a stick.

"Perhaps a bear," I suggested.

"It wouldn't have left the organs untouched," Hertz pointed out. "Besides, that doe looks strong. It seems like unlikely prey."

"And it's fresh," Megs added. She sat back, still studying the carcass. "Strange."

I stepped closer to inspect the wound. The injuries on her side were clearly claw marks, but her ripped out throat seemed more like a bite. Oddly, the size of the wound implied the biter's jaw was small, like that of a human.

My eyes flicked back to the set of slashes... *four* slashes, to be exact. Four claws. One tucked against the palm, the rest begging for blood. It had only taken one swipe to slaughter the deer. That's when it bit into the twitching corpse, tearing out the throat with its human jaw—now filled with teeth, sharp as an executioner's blade. But the creature hadn't continued the feast. It couldn't. It had been called back into formation.

I drew back, my gaze locked on the wound as paralyzing fear gripped my chest.

"I guess that's the great evil."

My heart jumped into my throat. "What?" I croaked.

"The evil Eris sensed," Megs explained. "She said she smelled death, and here we have a fresh carcass, ripe for the smelling." She grinned, climbing to her feet. "We're safe and sound once more."

With a smile, Megs started off toward Rudane, Hertz following behind her. I tapped my bow nervously, my gaze trailing across the grizzly scene.

You're being ridiculous, Rose. Deer are slaughtered every day. It doesn't mean a thing.

My eyes fell on a dark splatter staining the grass like ink that fell from a quill's tip. But it wasn't ink. It was blood.

My heart raced. *It can't be... they can't be here. She believes I'm dead. She can't have sent them.*

"Rose! Are you coming?" Megs called.

"Yes." I tore my gaze from the black mark, hurrying to catch up with my friends.

Surely I hadn't seen… *it.* The mark could have been deer's blood that dried darker than usual. Or something spilled by a fellow hunter. It didn't have to be an omen.

I took in a deep breath, letting the harvest air quell my frantic heartbeat. The branches rustled overhead, carrying the ghost of Eris's words.

It's already here.

THE HOME WITH THE GARDEN

It was midafternoon by the time we returned to the dusty streets of Rudane. After dividing the day's catch, we parted ways, agreeing to meet in the town square that evening.

All around, the villagers busied themselves with preparations for the coming celebration. Carts filled with straw and pumpkins rolled by, stirring up the dirt that dusted the old cobblestone road. Women hung banners from their window sills and hooked garlands on the eaves of their roofs while children dashed about underfoot, laughing and playing.

I sidestepped a pack of children, ducking into the front yard of a modest, single-story cottage, guarded by a waist-high wall of stacked stone. With a thatched, sharply slanted roof, the wooden walls stood strong despite years of wear. A little herb garden grew by the fence, the wilting remains of perennial flowers clinging to their existence below the windows. To a passersby, the house might seem abandoned, especially sitting in the shadow of the apothecary beside it.

The apothecary thrived as a staple of Rudane's charm. Though it was just as old as the house, it felt alive with candles burning in the windows and its stone-rimmed door always unlocked. My family, or host family as they truly were, ran the apothecary with Anne Crowborne, who was both the village healer and Megs's aunt. She and her husband lived above it with their sons, Derek and Simon.

I opened the creaky front door of the Estmar house and stepped inside. A fire crackled in the hearth, quenching the abandoned feeling and filling the room with a warm, smoky scent. Cerise Estmar bustled about the kitchen, preparing a stew.

A smile spread across my face. "Good afternoon."

"Oh, Rose!" Cerise exclaimed, setting aside a bowl. "How was the day's catch?" She returned my smile as she brushed strands of mousy hair from her sweaty forehead, then wiped her hands on the striped apron tied around her curvy waist.

"Two rabbits." I dropped the sack on the table before moving to the washbasin.

"Oh, good." She pulled out a cutting board and began to chop a carrot. "You should see Lili. She's been preparing for the festival for an hour now."

"I thought she was at the apothecary." I rinsed my hands off, leaving traces of dirt in the water.

"Anne gave her the day off for the festival."

A fresh grin flicked across my lips as I dried my hands. Lili had been apprenticing at the apothecary for almost a year now. Her focus and determination to follow in Anne's footsteps and become a healer were unrivaled. The only reason Anne would allow her off early was if Lili was too excited to focus, and I had a feeling that her enthusiasm had little to do with the festival itself.

"Rose, you're back." Ronan Estmar limped into the kitchen. After a quick greeting to his wife, he settled down into a chair, stretching his bad leg out in front of him. "How was the forest after the storm?"

"Not good. It blew away all the fishing poles and damaged several traps."

"Biaht." Ronan swore, rubbing his knee. It had been years since he sustained the injury, yet the pain continued to flare, often keeping him sequestered in the house or the apothecary. Although I hated to see him hurting, I couldn't help but be grateful for it; when Ronan was injured, the Estmars were robbed of their sole provider, forcing them to rely on the kindness of their neighbors to keep them afloat during the rime season. Three more seasons came and went, and the desperate family had no choice but to take in a stranger whose only tribute was her ability to use a bow. The arrangement was only meant to last a few months. After that, I would move on. But his leg never fully healed, and three years later, the Estmars thought of me as a second daughter.

I took a seat at the table across from Ronan. "Megs's new trap managed to take down a buck."

"Well done, Megs," he mused, absently scratching his beard. "That girl never fails to amaze me."

"I'll be amazed if she doesn't kill anyone."

He chuckled softly, his smile highlighting the wrinkles forged by long days working beneath the sun.

Cerise cleared her throat, cutting off our conversation. "We have a festival to prepare for. Ronan, I need you to watch the stew, and, Rose, dear, you must get dressed. And tell Lili that we leave in an hour."

Leaving the couple in the kitchen, I made my way to the room that Lili and I shared. Unsurprisingly, both our beds had been covered with the contents of our closet.

"Lili?" I called, hanging my bow and quiver on the hook behind the door.

Liliana Estmar's beaming face popped out of our wardrobe. "You're back!" she exclaimed, tossing another dress onto the pile before hopping down. Her bare feet landed on a discarded cloak. "I've been looking for something to wear."

"I noticed."

Her cheeks flushed with excitement, her eyes sparkling as she surveyed the dresses before us. "They're all so beautiful," she said, clasping her hands before her. "I can't decide which to wear."

"Well, you'll have to choose soon. Your mother says we have an hour."

Her eyes widened, and I laughed.

"Don't worry. You'd look beautiful in any of these."

"Still, I want tonight to be perfect." She sighed, fingering the sleeve of a dark-green dress. "Is that silly?"

My smile softened. "No." I picked up a periwinkle dress and offered it to my adoptive sister. "You should wear this one."

"You think so?" She held the dress to her chest, examining herself in the mirror. The light-blue color and soft embroidery complemented her delicate features, and we had the perfect belt to highlight her slim waist.

I stepped forward, resting my hands on her shoulders. "It's perfect."

Lili smiled at me in the mirror.

In another life, we could have been true sisters. Our skin was the same, untanned white, though her straight hair was a much lighter shade of brown than my own wavy locks. Even so, it was easy to pretend we were blood. That was until I looked into her eyes. The entire Estmar family had been blessed with eyes as blue as a cloudless sky. Beautiful and clear, they reminded me of ones I had seen a long time ago: eyes that glistened with gold inside the blue. That gold had come into my own eyes, cutting through my green irises like molten rivers. It was a small detail, but one I couldn't forget. No matter how much I loved Lili, she would never truly be my sister.

"Oh!" Lili gasped, snapping me out of my reverie. "We still need to find you a dress."

She rummaged through the pile, holding up gowns in various shades before we settled on one of dark-red linen.

I dressed, and she led me to the small vanity we shared. There wasn't much need for primping in a farming village like Rudane, leaving us with little more than a mirror, a box of hairpins, and a small collection of ribbons.

"I can't wait for the festival." Lili twisted my hair into a bun and secured it with a decorative pin. "The music, the dancing…" She sighed wistfully, her eyes momentarily growing vacant before snapping back to reality. She stepped back. "Done."

I turned my head, examining my hair in the mirror. Pretty as the updo was, its tightness gave visibility to the sharp points of my elven ears. I tugged on my hair, loosening it as much as I could without the bun falling out.

Perhaps I was being overly cautious. The Kingdom of Chess had a long history of rejecting and even waging war against magic. Though they had eventually made peace with it, the blood of the past had not been forgotten, and few magical beings cared to step across the border. It was like a dog chasing its own tail. Since the fear had died out, no one had been taught how to detect magical races. However, because of the overwhelming persecution, magical races rarely came to Chess, leaving small towns like Rudane blind to the most obvious signs of magical beings. To them, my ears were a soon-forgotten oddity. After three years, I'd grown fairly comfortable showing them off, but with Eris's mad warning echoing in my head, I refused to take the risk.

With my ears properly concealed, I traded places with Lili. I ran a brush through her silky hair as she babbled on about the night to come.

"…And then we'll feast on ham and chicken, and afterward, he and I will dance."

"And *he* is?" I teased, knowing exactly whom she spoke of.

"Nobody." Her eyes shot to her lap. She bit her lip, sneaking a glance in the mirror.

I stared her down, fighting back a smile.

"What?" she said defensively.

"I just think that you and Derek will look lovely on the dance floor."

Her cheeks flushed. "I didn't say 'Derek.'"

I smiled, tucking a silk flower behind her ear. "You didn't have to."

CHAPTER THREE

THE HARVEST FESTIVAL

The sky had darkened with streaks of orange visible against the horizon as we made our way through the streets of Rudane. Paper lanterns cast patterned shadows across the cobblestone road and provided a warm, yellow glow as we reached the candlelit square. Already, a crowd had gathered, their attire ranging from everyday garb to fine vests and gowns.

Megs stood among the crowd, surrounded by her parents and young, triplet brothers. Her dress might not have been dripping in pearls, but the off-white color provided a simple elegance. Diamond-shaped cutouts ran down the long sleeves, giving the gown a dash of her rebellious spirit. Her mother, Bette, hovered by her side, adjusting the tie on the gown's woven belt.

I caught Megs's eye and waved her over. After a quick exchange with her mother, she made her way to where I stood with the Estmars.

"So, what do you think?" Megs asked, giving me a twirl.

"You look wonderful."

She beamed. "*Modir* almost didn't finish in time. It was supposed to have embroidery, but she was too busy with Princess Freya's new gown." She sighed. "Don't you ever wish you were a princess?"

I wish I weren't. The thought remained silent, and I said, "I'm happy where I am."

Megs rolled her eyes. "Sap," she teased. Her attention shifted to the gathered crowd. "Have you seen Hertz?"

"He should be here already. His cake is out, see?" I gestured to a massive, three-tier cake decorated with falling harvest leaves, each one hand-carved out of chocolate and painted to create an ombre effect. "He's probably with Donna."

"Hertz and Donna," Megs mused. "Rudane's sweethearts."

"Jealous?"

She scoffed. "I'll have you know, I am on the brink of a very serious romantic entanglement with Caleb Fawley. Look at this." She glanced around before drawing a small pouch from her pocket. With a tip of the pouch, iridescent, orange crystals spilled into her palm.

My eyes widened. The crystals glowed in Megs's hand, their color shifting like a crackling flame. *Magic.*

"Where did you get those?" I hissed, moving my body to better block the crystals from view.

"Calm down." She poured the crystals back into their bag. "Magic isn't forbidden anymore. These are pyrix crystals imported from Pikbrie—Caleb found them at a market in Torsto."

I know what they are. I pressed my lips together to keep the words in and pulled Megs away from the Estmars. Summoning a calm tone, I asked, "Why do you have them?"

She stared at me as though I were a fool. "My invention!"

I held her stare blankly.

She sighed, slipping the pouch back into her pocket. "You know how awful it is to write out long letters? The ink smudges get on your fingers, and then you have to trust the letter boy won't deliver it during a rainstorm or else the whole thing will be ruined, and your hours of work will be for nothing."

"When has that ever happened to anyone?"

"Well, once my invention is complete, it will never happen again. Instead of having to write out long, messy letters, you speak into this little sphere I've created. The sphere will transcribe the message, and at the press of the button, it will pop out"—she waved her hands—"and appear as though written in thin air."

"As wonderful as that sounds, you seem to be forgetting that you're not a witch, and you're certainly not an Ekeider—you have no magical prowess whatsoever."

She held up the bag of crystals. "Why do you think I got these? I don't need power of my own. I'm just manipulating the magic that exists in the stones."

"You can't mess around with magic, Megs. It's dangerous."

"They're just rocks," she said with a shrug. "And it's not like I'm creating a weapon. It's a simpler method of communication, not a kingdom-destroying box of curses."

"Just be careful. Please."

"I will." Megs agreed, but her tone was careless. She didn't understand how easily a mistake could turn deadly.

I clenched my fists in my skirt, ready to continue the argument, when the town bells began to toll, signaling the feast to begin. I glanced at Megs, who was already headed for the tables that had been arranged in a square—three rimmed with benches, one bearing piles of food, and a large space in the center for dancing.

With a heavy breath, I pushed out my fear and annoyance and drew in the scent of the feast. Turkey rose above all else, but hints of spiced potatoes and meaty stews slipped through the gaps. I wasn't done with the argument, but I could set aside my concerns for one night.

As I took the empty seat left between Lili and Megs, I noticed Hertz laughing with Donna, their hands joined. Beside Donna sat her father, Percival Branburn, the Town Master of Rudane. He watched the tables fill, slowly spinning his wooden mug with his thumb and forefinger. The same handleless mug sat before every place setting.

Once everyone was settled, Percival stood, facing the town with a smile. "Welcome, friends and neighbors," he began. "For six months we have worked the fields, sowing our seeds so that we might one day reap the rewards. And, friends, that day is dawning. Once more, we are called to harvest, and once more we turn to a higher power to make our bounty plentiful.

"Chess has always had a strong connection to the divine guardians who watch over our kingdom, and tonight it is our connection with Layona, the Divine Lady of the Fields, that we honor."

He raised his mug. "In this cup is the fruit of last season's harvest. I now invite you to take your own." We all picked up our mugs filled with ale fermented over the past nine months. "As we drink, let us offer Layona our gratitude for past seasons of success as we humbly ask her blessing on this year's harvest. To Layona!" he declared before draining his mug.

"To Layona!" We echoed him, following suit. I threw back the ale, enjoying the sweet, fruity taste.

Percival set down his mug and raised his hands high. "Let the feast begin!"

Cheers rang out, mixed with scraping, as the benches were pushed back. I joined the crowd swarming the buffet and snagged a bowl of stew, a cut of turkey breast, and a sizable slice of Hertz's cake before returning to the table, nearly tripping on one of Megs's brothers as I found my seat. Megs slid in beside me, a teetering tower of food on her plate. Dropping it onto the table, she got to work, tearing into a chicken leg with her fingernails, her nose scrunched with focus.

For a while, the town ate in near-silence. Conversation melded into a low hum, occasionally broken by a loud laugh. Then Megs leaned forward and asked the Estmars, "Did Rose tell you about the dead deer we found in Holfetine?"

"Why would you bring that up over dinner?" Bette asked, shaking her head at her daughter.

Megs swallowed the final bite of her meat before replying, "Because it was odd."

"What's so odd about a deer killed in its natural habitat?" Ronan asked.

"It was clawed to death," she explained. "The throat was ripped out, but the organs were left alone, so it couldn't have been a bear."

"That is strange." Ronan tapped a finger against his cup, his brow furrowed. "Perhaps a mountain lion migrated."

"If it were a mountain lion, we'd have heard reports from nearby villages," she countered.

He raised a finger in agreement and would certainly have continued the conversation if not for Bette tossing down her napkin.

"Let this conversation cease!" she exclaimed. "We are to be thankful, not dour."

"You are absolutely right," Cerise said. "Tonight is for celebration." She stood, holding out her hand to her husband. "Shall we dance, my love?"

Ronan rose to his feet, a smile on his lips. "If we must," he teased.

Hand in hand, they took to the open floor. The band took the cue, a folk ballad rising from their instruments' strings. Cerise and Ronan spun about, graceful despite Ronan's injured leg. The smiles on their faces brought one to my own.

"Now who's jealous?" Megs asked, her chin propped on her interlocked fingers and her bright-green gaze fixed on me.

"I like seeing them happy," I replied. "It makes *me* happy."

She rolled her eyes, popping one last bite of a roll into her mouth before climbing to her feet. She held out her hand. "Come on. Let's find you a dance partner."

"I'm all right here."

"Not an option." She grabbed my arm, attempting to pull me off the bench.

"Megs!"

"*Rose.*" She dragged the word out, dropping my arm and looking me dead in the eye. "Do you really want to sit and watch all night?"

I opened my mouth, but no words came. Megs wasn't simply encouraging me to dance; she wanted me to chase what Cerise and Ronan had. Companionship, romance, *love.* As wonderful as that sounded, it was impossible—I told too many lies and had too many secrets haunting my shadow. My relationships were doomed before they began.

Megs rolled her eyes. "Ugh, fine. You can sit out this first dance. But I will return, and I will find you a partner."

"I don't doubt that."

I waited until she was safely in the arms of dark-eyed and dashing Caleb Fawley to leave the table, wandering to the edge of the dance floor where Lili stood. She wobbled on her tiptoes, peering around the wave of swirling skirts. Her eyes searched the crowd until they landed on a familiar head of brown curls.

I smirked, sliding into place beside her. "Derek's looking quite dashing tonight, wouldn't you agree?"

"I suppose." She toyed with the fringe on her shawl.

I fought the urge to scoff. Did she really think I couldn't see her feelings for him? After three years of her denial, it shouldn't have shocked me. Especially since she'd been oblivious to Derek's reciprocation of her affections since before I'd arrived in Rudane.

"You should ask him to dance," I suggested.

Her cheeks flushed. "Why would I want to do that?"

"It's merely a thought. I'm sure there are plenty of girls who would dance with him if you don't want to."

"No, I'll do it," she said quickly, pulling her shawl tight around her shoulders.

"Then *go*." I pushed her into the crowd.

She froze for a moment before making her way across the square to Derek. After a short conversation involving rapid hand movement on Lili's end, he took her hand and led her to the floor.

They faced one another with stiff backs and straight arms. Though they followed the dance's path, every step was awkward, second-guessed before it was taken.

That's all right. They can get where they need to go. All they need is a little push.

I held on to the thought, letting it grow. My magic awoke within me, like a flower lifting its head to greet the sun. It reached out, its power merging with my command. No word was spoken nor gesture made; the thought was all it took. The spell engaged, causing Lili to stumble and fall—right into Derek's arms.

The pair flushed as they regained their balance, settling closer than before.

A smile flicked across my lips. *So easy.* The tingle of magic lingered, my fingers itching for more. I clenched my fist, cutting off my power. No one in Rudane knew what I was, and I intended on keeping it that way.

Megs strolled toward me, a fresh cup of ale in her hand. "Look at those two… Young and in love. Isn't it beautiful?"

I raised an eyebrow. There was a game at play here. "What do you want, Megs?"

"To demand payment," she said. "You took away my wolf pelt. Some may seek vengeance by taking away something of yours, but I'm feeling generous. I'm going to give you something."

"Give me what?"

"A dance. With *him*."

I followed her gaze to a man on the other side of the square. He appeared to be close to my age, with black hair that fell in a jagged line above his shoulders and fair skin that stood out amid the sun-tanned farmers around him.

"Go talk to him," Megs said.

"I am not—"

"Ah, ah, ah!" She held up a hand, sloshing droplets of ale onto her sleeve. "You owe me. Besides,"—her voice fell to a whisper as she leaned in—"you can't see it from here, but he has a scar beneath his eye." She grinned. "That makes him mysterious."

"Or a fool."

"There's only one way to find out."

I held her gaze for a moment longer before snatching her cup of ale and draining it in a single gulp. Glaring, I shoved the empty cup into her hand. "I despise you."

She beamed. "Have fun!"

I cannot believe I'm doing this. My regret deepened with each step I took toward the dark-haired stranger. A strong part of me advised running in the opposite direction, but I wouldn't put it past Megs to chase me down and physically drag me over to the man. At least this way I was in control of my potential humiliation.

Steeling myself, I approached, opening my mouth to speak. Then his eyes fell on me, and the breath left my lungs.

As Megs had described, a scar ran down his cheek, just below his eye. What she hadn't mentioned were his actual eyes, midnight blue with silver splitting his irises like bolts of lighting. They were unmistakable. And gorgeous.

"Rose Bennai," I blurted, holding out my hand.

The man took it, kissing its back as though I hadn't just forced an introduction like a madwoman.

"Animo Terrot," he replied.

"Yes. But I don't believe we've met. Not before tonight, anyway." *Kingdoms, what am I saying?*

Animo smiled. "Would you care to dance, Miss Bennai?"

"Yes," I replied, my words no longer forced by Megs.

"Wonderful."

Animo slid my hand to his arm and guided me to the dance floor as the violins' music rose in a new song. He stepped back, bowing and once more kissing my knuckles before pulling me close. Despite his soft touch, a sort of restrained strength lingered beneath the surface.

"How long have you lived here?" he asked, seemingly oblivious to the way his proximity made my heart race.

"Three years." I forced myself to focus on the conversation and not his hand resting on my waist.

"Interesting." He guided me through the steps of a country dance, yet his movements held a courtly air. "What drew you here?"

A smile flicked across my lips. "I was going to ask you the same question."

He raised a brow, his silence goading me to continue.

"In all my years living here, I've never seen another elf."

Animo faltered, almost running into the couple beside us. They shot us a glare, then spun away.

He regained control of the dance, yet his posture remained stiff. "How did you know?"

"Your eyes." My gaze locked with his, drinking in every twist of silver.

He let out a scoffing laugh, shaking his head. "Of course." He spun me before continuing. "I forget about them more often than I'd care to admit."

"I don't think I ever could," I replied, returning to his arms. "Especially in a place like this."

"On the contrary, this is exactly the kind of place where you forget. You get used to the humans that surround you, and you forget that you're not like them."

I glanced at where Lili danced with Derek. "Is that so bad?" I asked quietly.

"Sometimes." Animo paused before adding, "We seem to have moved off topic a bit. I believe you were complimenting my eyes."

"I was *commenting* on your eyes."

"Close enough."

I smiled, shaking my head. "Why don't we move past talk of your eyes and on to something far more interesting?"

"Such as?"

"Why you came to Rudane."

"That," he said, "is a very long and complicated tale."

"I have time."

His dancing slowed. "Then perhaps we should go somewhere more private and…" His voice trailed off as his gaze fell onto something behind me.

"Is everything all right?" I glanced over my shoulder, expecting some kind of trouble, but found nothing but smiling, laughing faces.

"I'm afraid I must leave you," Animo said, stepping away.

"What? Why?" I asked as he guided me off the dance floor.

"It's nothing of concern. Merely business I must attend to." He took my hands in his. "But I will see you again. And perhaps then I can tell you my story."

"I'd like that."

He smiled, his gaze falling to our clasped hands. Dropping one, he raised the other to his lips, brushing a soft kiss against my skin. "Until then." He drew away, our hands sliding apart as he slipped into the crowd.

I sank against the table, a smile lingering on my lips as I watched him walk away. The dance was only meant to appease Megs, but something stirred within me. Something warm and oddly nervous.

"You can thank me anytime." Megs appeared at my shoulder, her cheeks flushed and her green eyes sparkling.

I dropped my smile. "Why would I possibly thank you for throwing me into the arms of a stranger?"

She scoffed. "Oh, please. You have eyes."

I utilized said eyes with an annoyed roll. She wasn't wrong, but I had no intention of admitting it.

Megs plopped down onto an empty bench, leaning forward. "I saw your face. You enjoyed dancing with him." She smiled. "This is *good*, Rose. Years from now, we will look back on this night as the night you two first fell in love."

I laughed aloud. "I shared one dance with him. And as far as I'm aware, at no point in that dance did I lose all of my wits."

"Wits or not, I know what I saw." She paused for dramatic effect. "Sparks."

"You know what, you are absolutely right." A mocking edge cut my voice. "There were sparks, so many sparks. And you know what? I think you introduced me to my soulmate. Animo and I are going to get married and settle down to raise our children."

"How many?" she asked. I shook my head, tired of the charade. "You're right, I should guess. Let's see." She scrunched her nose, thinking hard. "You will have two, one boy and one girl. Oh! Since I introduced you, that means you have to name the girl after me."

"Yes, but I'm still fairly mad at you, so you will be reduced to second-name status."

"That's rude."

I shook my head, my gaze falling onto the dance floor. Straw skittered across the cobblestone as women spun, their skirts flaring, then falling as they returned to their partners' arms. Memories, sweet as the scent of ale, revolved in my mind. I wasn't one for dancing with strangers, but Animo had been different. Perhaps it was the fact he was an elf or simply the ale pulling me into fantasies, but dancing with him had left a mark—one I didn't want to fade.

"Good evening, ladies," Hertz said, joining us on the bench

I greeted him with a smile. "Your cake was delicious."

He laughed "I'll have to take your word for it. By the time I made it to the table, it was all gone."

"That's too bad."

He shrugged. "I can make more anytime. Besides, tonight was wonderful without it."

"Lots of dancing with Donna?"

"Plenty. What about you? I thought I saw you on the dance floor, but I didn't recognize the man you were with."

"His name was Animo," I replied. "He's in town on business."

"What business is there in Rudane?"

Megs mumbled, stretching out on the bench, an arm draped over her eyes and a discarded cloak balled into a makeshift pillow.

"What did she say?" Hertz asked.

I grimaced. "It's probably best we didn't hear."

He nodded in agreement, then asked, "Will you see him again?"

"I believe so." *I hope so.*

Cheers erupted from the dance floor as the fiddle rose in a jaunty tune. Through the tightly packed crowd, I caught sight of a man, his limbs flailing wildly. Only one person in town danced like that: Olstaff Hestr, the local innkeeper, a man notorious for performing absurd and crowd-pleasing dances.

A smile burst across Hertz's face, and he shot to his feet. "We can't miss this. Come on, Rose."

"I'm all right."

His expression turned incredulous. "But it's the harvest jig! Olstaff works for months to ensure each year is better than the last."

"And if you keep trying to convince me, you're going to miss it." I nodded at the cheering crowd. "Go!"

With one last teasingly disappointed head shake, he raced off.

I lay my head back with a smile. It truly had been a lovely night. I snuggled against the tabletop, my eyelids fluttering before shutting completely.

Applause broke out, followed by calls for an encore. They didn't want this night to end, and neither did I. Animo's face floated to the front of my mind. The weightlessness of dancing with him, the promise of another meeting, and those *eyes*. It was silly to allow this single fleeting interaction take up so much thought, yet that didn't stop his starlit irises from encompassing my imagination as the sounds of the Harvest Festival faded into darkness.

WAKING NIGHTMARE

The Woman in White stood beside me on the dark balcony. Moonlight caressed her silvery-white hair while the wind whipped about her skirt, revealing bare feet, nearly as pale as her dress. Her face was ageless, but her ice-blue eyes carried the weight of ancient memories as she gazed out at a sea of sharp, snow-capped mountains that dropped off into a deep canyon.

My lips fell apart. I'd seen those mountains before. Not daring to breathe, I turned, my gaze locking on the turrets that pierced the night sky like obsidian blades.

"Malecare." The wind stole the word the moment it left my lips. Fear knotted my stomach. This was her fortress, buried in the icy heights of Devil's Canyon. A castle of death, stolen like the very throne she sat on. No one came out of Malecare alive. Not even my mother.

"You must be careful."

My gaze snapped to the Woman in White. She stared straight ahead, her hands resting on the balcony rail. "The time has come," she said, her voice distorted as though an invisible wall divided us.

"'Time'?" My mind grasped at her words as though they were fleeting flakes of snow. "Time for what?"

The woman's chin fell as she raised her hand to touch the iridescent pendant that lay on her chest. Her sleeve slid down, revealing a circle of angry red marks rimming her wrist.

My brow furrowed. There was something strange about her. Something that gnawed on the deepest crevices of my memory, yet I failed to find the source.

Her head snapped up. "This isn't right."

"What do you mean?"

An angry wind kicked up, blowing strands of dark hair into my eyes. The Woman in White stepped back, clutching the pendant as though it were the only thing keeping her upright.

"I shouldn't be here. I—" For the first time, her eyes met mine. Her gaze shifted, and although I couldn't explain why, I was certain she recognized me.

She stepped forward, holding out her hand. I stood transfixed as she raised it to cup my cheek, her cold fingers sending a shiver down my spine. With her gaze locked on mine, she uttered a single word: "Run."

The word was a starting flag to my body. I raced through the only door I saw, emerging in a gaping chamber of black granite laced with web-like veins of silver.

A pair of doors slammed shut. Then another. I spun around, my gaze landing on every point of escape only to find it sealed. Fear crashed down on me like a meteor, falling, burning, and destroying everything it touched.

Somewhere, a woman screamed. She was in pain. Was she dying? I needed to help her… I needed to help her, but I couldn't.

A memory split my mind. Cobblestone cracks caked with crimson. Like a river all dried up. A body drained of life.

With a scream-like sob, I dropped to my knees, covering my face with my hands. Something warm and wet seeped through my skirt. I lowered my hands, my gaze falling to the floor, now coated with blood.

Horror ripped through me. I tried to stand, only to slip, falling into the puddle. My muscles tensed as I writhed to escape. Blood drenched my body. I squirmed and sobbed but the ground held me like quicksand. If I had the breath to scream, I never would have stopped.

Scraping reverberated through the chamber, like an assassin cutting off my cries. A shaking mess, I crawled onto my hands and knees, my palms leaving prints in the blood. My eyes darted about the empty room, searching for the source of the noise. Voice trembling, I spoke, "Natalia?"

The name echoed as though it were carried by the voices of ghosts. They screamed it at me: the name of the murderer, tyrant, and queen.

A crash split the air. Shards of glass rained from above. I screamed, covering my head with my hands. They peppered my skin, slicing my flesh before falling and shattering against the blood-soaked floor, the crimson fluid now black as ink.

A cold voice echoed from the back of my mind, sharper than the glass that pierced my skin. It was a voice I had heard so long ago. A voice that I had done everything to forget:

"Rosara Wolfe, it is time to die."

I shot up, sweat covering my skin and Natalia's name on my lips. Obsidian was gone, replaced by wooden walls and knit blankets. My muscles relaxed in a full-body sigh as I twisted my fingers into my blanket. *It was just a dream.*

With a shaky breath, I lay back against my pillow. I must have been carried home after the festival—my red dress was tangled around my legs, and Lili slept in the bed opposite me.

Closing my eyes, I willed myself to sleep. Tomorrow would come and my nightmare would end. Only, my mind wouldn't quiet.

Sticky blood haunted my palms and screams lingered like a torturous song as the Woman's voice carved itself into my mind. *Run.*

I kicked the blanket off of me, sitting up with a huff. How was I to sleep after *that?* That nightmare had awoken every fear I'd buried. Natalia would find me. Her minions would tear through my home and drag me back to her fortress to meet the same fate as my parents.

I shoved my hair back, my fingers catching on the knotted remains of my updo. Why was I never free?

I curled myself into a ball, letting my head rest on my knees as I stared out the window. Dark clouds hid the stars, leaving only the moon's faint outline to illuminate the town. All was still. All was silent.

A flash of shadow on a distant roof pulled my gaze. My pulse spiked. I raced to the window, pressing my face against the glass, but once more, all was still.

Unease rose within me. Dreams, shadows, blood… was this a sick coincidence, or was Natalia—*No.* I forced the thoughts to halt. *She believes I'm dead. She's* won. *There's no reason for her to run about chasing ghosts.* So why had I heard her voice in my head?

I closed my eyes, resting a hand on my racing heart. *It's just a dream… it's just a dream… it's just a dream…* I chanted the words like a prayer in my mind. *It's just a dream… It's just a dream…*

It's already here.

Eris's warning. I was caught in a circle of signs toppling over one by one, and behind each was an unmarked grave for a girl twice buried. My dress clamped my body like a shackle.

Feverishly, I stripped it off, letting the night air cool my skin before changing back into my hunting garb. A sense of comfort washed over me as I laced my boots. From the worn-down knees of my brown pants to the stretched seams of my bodice, every part of this outfit conformed to me. It was *mine.*

After a quick check to make certain that Lili was asleep, I crawled under my bed. The first night I'd arrived, I'd pulled up a loose floorboard and carved a little hole in the dirt so I could hide the things I brought from Avonshere. Now I withdrew a small, wooden chest from its depths.

The chest's perfect square shape boasted simplicity yet elegance, my family's wolf-and-moon crest engraved on the lid. It was a symbol of power, turned one of rebellion, worn only by our followers, the Ardent Pack. I brushed my fingers over the engraving as memories of love and pain washed over me. For nearly two years my mother had led the Ardent Pack. She fought Natalia with every breath in her lungs, but it wasn't enough. And neither was the Pack.

I closed my eyes, blocking out the darkest memories as I pressed my thumb to the simple stone on the box's front. In my mind, I saw the stone's color shift from white to red as the blood magic lock engaged.

Six generations. That was how long this chest had been in my family. Enchanted by a fairie, it had passed from one queen's hand to another until landing in the possession of my mother. That was where the line of queens ended.

I opened my eyes, my finger still pressed against the lock. Each time the box changed hands, the enchantment was altered to add a new owner. I was never officially inducted, but when I was a little girl, I learned that sharing the blood of my mother—and all the Wolfe queens who came before—was enough to grant me access.

Back when the days were golden, I would sneak into my mother's quarters and open this very chest. I would lift the lid, excitement blossoming within me and diamonds dazzling my eyes, glittering as bright as my future.

Now I raised the lid, revealing a velvet interior as dark and dull as my heart. Only two items remained inside the box: a portrait with charred edges, folded into a small square and a silver dagger with a sapphire embedded in its pommel.

I wrapped my fingers around the dagger's hilt, its cold steel sending a chill through my body. With trembling fingers, I pressed my lips against the sapphire, kissing the memories it held. My grandfather gave the blade to me when I was six years old. From the moment I touched it, I treasured it, never allowing it to leave my side. I wore it during lessons and kept it tucked under my pillow as I slept. It even hung over my ballgown when I stood beside my mother and father on the day of their coronation. Somewhere in my mind, I believed that it would protect me.

Fool. Get out of your head!

I snapped the box shut, wincing at the sound. I needed to focus. If Natalia knew that I was alive, I would already be surrounded by her creatures. Five long years had come and gone, and the past was the past, gone in a rush of smoke. I was *safe*.

An inhuman scream echoed in the night, cutting into my very soul.

Lili sat up in bed, rubbing her eyes groggily. "What was that?"

No. It can't be. The dagger slipped from my hands and onto my bed. *Kingdoms, don't let it be.*

"Rose?"

"It was nothing." My voice cracked on the words. "Just a coyote."

She'd believe my lie. Why shouldn't she? She had never heard that scream before.

I climbed to my feet. "I'll take care of it." I slung my quiver over my shoulder, then tossed a glance back at Lili, who had pulled her sheets up to her chin. "Everything will be fine."

My promise satiated her, but a voice stirred in the back of my mind: *It is time to die.*

CHAPTER FIVE

HUNTING MONSTERS

A cold wind bit against my skin. I shivered, rubbing away the goose-bumps that rose beneath my shirt. A thick fog covered the cobbled road, lit only by the faint moonlight. Banners still hung from windows, but the shutters were latched with only darkness slipping through their cracks. Had the whole town slept through the scream? Or was it all in my head?

Every part of me stood on alert—my body tensed and my eyes darted about. I kept an arrow nocked as I walked, my footsteps soft and quiet. *I'm not the only one who heard it. It woke Lili, which means it's real.* The thought should be terrifying as they could only have come for me. But I refused to be a scared little girl again. Now, I was a huntress, and they were my prey.

The sound of footsteps brought me to a halt. Someone was approaching, just around the corner. The steps were too heavy to be a monster, but Natalia always sent human captains to guard her creatures. I raised my bow, stepping out to meet my attacker.

"Woah!" a boy with warm-brown hair and a ghostlike splatter of freckles shouted, nearly dropping the lantern he carried. From his belt hung a sword, its hilt covered by the loose, white sleepshirt he wore.

I exhaled sharply as I relaxed my bow, partly relieved, partly annoyed. "It's just you."

Derek Crowborne stared at me, his usually cheerful, green eyes now wide with panic and rimmed with sleep deprivation. "Of course it's me!" he yelped. "Since when do coyotes wear boots?"

"I thought…" I shook my head. "Never mind."

"Have you seen it?" he asked, looking around. His curls stuck out at awkward angles; he must have rolled right out of bed.

"Not yet." I shouldered my bow, continuing my walk down the foggy street. "So, you think it's a coyote?"

He jogged a few steps to catch up. "What else would it be?"

"Perhaps a hog," I suggested lamely. My eyes jumped through the shadows, waiting for something to lunge at us, ready to kill.

"A hog?" he scrunched up his nose.

"It could have broken loose from a nearby farm."

"Maybe…"

I cast a sidelong look at him. Why was he out here? He wasn't the type to hunt down a wild beast. If not for his position as a blacksmith's apprentice, I doubt he'd even own a sword. Why, *why* had he chosen tonight to test his courage?

"Whatever it is, we'll take care of it," I said finally. Derek nodded.

"Well, well, well, look who it is."

I jumped at the sight of Megs walking along a line of barrels. She hopped down, flashing a grin as bright as the torchlight glinting from her daggers' hilts. Like Derek, she had dressed in a hurry, pulling a pair of pants over her nightdress.

"Come hunting, have we?" She ruffled Derek's hair playfully. He frowned, swatting her hand away. He was only a few months younger than his cousin, but she never let him forget it, especially now that she was of age.

"What do you think it is?" he asked, changing the subject. "I think it's a coyote, but Rose says it's a hog."

"It could be either or neither." She grinned mischievously. "Perhaps the nixies have come out to play."

He glared at her. "Don't do that."

"Do what?" she asked, her eyes glittering. She'd spent the better part of last summer crafting an elaborate scheme to convince him that evil forest spirits had taken up residence in Holfetine Wood and were luring people away by playing the violin. It had been amusing at the time, but thinking of chilling stories—even false ones—threatened to sever the final strand of my sanity.

"Megs," I warned, "now is not the time."

"You're tense," she said, falling into step beside me while Derek trailed a little ways behind.

"I wonder why."

"It's just some animal."

I pressed my lips together, tightening my grip on my bow.

She looked about. "Although I suppose it is strange that we're the only ones out here."

"Not really." Derek jogged to reach us. "After you two fell asleep, some of the men brought out the stronger drinks and things got... *indulgent*."

"Are you telling us that *everyone* in town is drunk?" I asked.

He shrugged. "More or less."

Megs let out a cross between a scoff and a laugh. "Kingdoms, I hate I missed it."

"Your mother had you carried away the moment the first cork was pulled. And the Estmars left nearly as quickly." Hints of sorrow rippled across Derek's face.

I caught Megs's gaze—she must have seen it too. But a horribly familiar glint radiated in her emerald eye.

"You know who we should be worried about?" she began.

"Us, if we don't get moving," I said, attempting to threaten Megs into silence with my eyes.

Derek looked between us, his brow furrowed. "What did I miss?"

"Rose has a gentleman pursuing her."

I scoffed. "You *forcing* us to dance does not count as *pursuit*."

"Wait until tomorrow," she said. "You'll see pursuit."

"I sincerely doubt it."

"Disrespectfully, I disagree." She brushed past me, leading the way through town.

I shook my head. Megs could think whatever she wanted. There was not a chance in any of the Twelve Kingdoms that Animo would pursue me in any way, shape, or form. It had been one dance, that was all.

He did say that you would see him again. The hopeful voice rose in my mind. *But maybe that was just a formality. Then again…*

I caught myself. *Curse it all.* This could be my life, lilting and careless, full of opportunity. I could have a future. But no, I knew my future. It was wrapped in shadows and paved with blood. Animo had no place in it.

"Are you all right?" Derek asked, his head tilted in concern.

"Fine," I replied. "Simply tired." Tired from the dancing, anxious from the scream, and irritated by my friends' sudden enthusiasm to hunt monsters.

Megs stopped before the bell tower where the road broke into three paths, each concealed with shadow.

"We should split up," she said.

My stomach plunged.

"What? Why?" Derek's panicked voice asked the question I couldn't.

"To get this done sooner." She snatched a pair of dark lanterns that hung from a nearby doorframe. "It's the middle of the night, Rose isn't telling me anything of interest, and I would like to get some sleep." She took Derek's lantern and used its flame to light a piece of straw that, in turn, lit the dead lanterns.

"We'll search for an hour and then meet back here," she said, stamping out her makeshift match. "Whoever kills it gets to keep the pelt."

Derek took a step back. "I'm not so sure—"

"You'll be fine," she insisted, shoving a lantern into his hand. "Take that road,"—she pointed at one of the dark streets—"I'll take that one,"—she pointed at the street opposite—"and Rose can take that one." Her finger settled on the middle street.

Claws of doubt wrapped around me, yet I said nothing. What excuse did I have? Megs would never stand down if I said this was a terrible idea. If anything, she'd run into the darkness faster.

I sighed, taking one of the lanterns from her. "Be careful," I warned as we separated.

She glanced over her shoulder, a mischievous glint in her eye. "When am I not?"

BLOOD IN THE SHADOWS

M y lantern cast flickering shadows across the wood and stone buildings as I walked, turning the most innocent of things into a ravenous beast prepared to strike. An involuntary shudder raced through me as I rounded the bend.

A crash sounded. I jumped, thrusting the lantern forward to cast its light into the shadows.

"Hello?" I took a tentative step forward. "If someone's there, I would suggest you come out."

A flowerpot fell from a windowsill, smashing into pieces against the cobblestone. I dropped the lantern. Glass shattered as I nocked an arrow against my gloved forefinger.

"Last warning."

A fuzzy ball about the size of my fist leaped down, landing beside the broken flowerpot. It waddled over to me, its feet barely visible beneath its thick fur and its big, golden eyes blinking in the torchlight.

I groaned, lowering my bow. It was just like a brownie to pick the worst of times to cause trouble.

The brownie cooed, joining its friends in a fluffy pack.

I sighed, bending to pick up the broken lantern. Shards of glass littered the cobblestone, reflecting the flame's light. Only… *what is that?* I picked up a piece of glass, holding it before the candle. Something red and sticky coated its edge.

My body tensed as I gathered the broken lantern, using its light to follow the faint path of blood. Thick drops ran alongside footprints, and then handprints joined the trail.

I picked up the pace, practically running as the drops grew bigger and bigger, accumulating into a puddle.

I came to a halt, my heart lurching as I stared at the face-down body that lay in the road. *It's not Megs or Derek,* I reminded myself. They'd gone the other way, and the entire Estmar family was safe at home.

But Hertz could be out here. Not to mention Animo. Had I fallen so far that the mere act of dancing together was the same as signing a death warrant?

There's only one way to know. I knelt before the body, and then cast my eyes to the sky. *Please.* There were no other words added to my silent prayer.

I rolled the body over. *Olstaff.* His throat had been clawed out, his chin and shirt slashed and doused in blood and bits of organs. I jerked back. My foot slid in the puddle of blood. Throwing out my arms, I caught myself.

Summoning all the courage I had, I leaned in close, examining his wounds. His chest had been torn apart by claws, *four* claws. No bear, no hog, nor any wild animal could ever have done this. These wounds… they were the mark of a monster.

I pulled a long shard of metal from Olastaff's grasp. Black liquid, like ink, tinted the edge. He must have grabbed the closest thing to defend himself. But even armed he was defenseless against her creatures.

A sharp screech erupted from the shadows.

The shard fell from my grasp, clattering to the ground. I raised my eyes, meeting a hollow, lifeless gaze reflected in the distant candlelight. My hand slid to my discarded bow.

The creature stepped out of the shadows, revealing its grotesque features in full: pale-gray skin hung limply from its bony frame, along with tattered remains of clothing. The monster bared its razor-sharp teeth dripping with fresh blood.

I let loose an arrow before the creature could move. It fell with a scream and a splash of black blood. I had seen and killed its kind before. A shade—one of Natalia's soulless minions, born of dark magic and twisted to obey her every command. I had seen them slaughter cities, devour the innocent, and tear apart the bodies of those still loyal to the name of Wolfe.

A choking scream came from the nearby butcher's shop. I rushed inside, bow at the ready, only to come to an abrupt halt. A man stood above the twitching corpse of a shade, its blood splattered across his shirt and skin. Strands of hair as black as the blood that coated the wooden floors fell before his eyes. He stared at the dying creature, his sword dripping with its inklike fluid, then drew the blade across his pant leg, leaving a dark stain.

I lowered my bow.

"Animo?"

Animo's head snapped up, his eyes meeting mine. "It's dead."

"I can see that."

"You don't seem surprised."

"Neither do you."

I studied him with narrowed eyes. He had traded his more formal clothing from the evening before for a worn shirt and pants. Not sleepwear like Derek and Megs wore. Almost as if he knew he wouldn't be getting a peaceful night's sleep.

He was the one to break the silence, his midnight eyes staring into mine as he spoke. "Rosara Wolfe."

In a flash, my bow was drawn and pointed at his head. "Who are you?" I demanded, my heart beating like an executioner's drum.

Animo held up a hand. "I'm not here to kill you. I was sent to keep you safe."

"Sent by whom?" I tightened my grip on my bow, my knuckles white as I awaited the answer.

"Not who you think." He gestured for me to lower my weapon. I didn't move. "Rosara—"

"Stop calling me that," I snapped, desperately searching for a way to keep my lies alive. "She's dead."

"That's what you told everyone. But you escaped. You *survived*. You've been gone for five years, dead if you like. But now it is time to go back."

Back.

Back to Avonshere. To the ruin of my family's reign. To the land where I had buried all that I loved.

My voice shook, but my words were firm. "You'll have to kill me first."

Resignation fell over Animo's face. His hand slid to the hilt of his sword. "I don't want to do this."

"Then stand down."

"I can't do that any more than you can," he said, his eyes begging me to put my bow aside. Slowly, he removed his hand from his sword. "I won't fight you."

"That makes this a lot easier."

Animo ducked as I let loose an arrow. Its iron head plunged into the wall behind him. Before I could nock another, he swept my leg, knocking me to the ground. The bow fell from my grasp.

I scrambled to my feet, snatching the nearest weapon I could find—a meat cleaver. Spinning, I brought the cleaver down. It met Animo's sword in a clash of metal, splitting in two and leaving me defenseless once more.

I reached for an arrow, but Animo caught my wrist and twisted my arm behind my back. I threw myself into a roll, freeing myself from his grasp and leaving us both sprawled out on the floor. Scrambling to my feet, I snatched a knife from the counter. Within a breath, I pinned Animo against the wall, my knife pressed to his throat.

"Think it through," he warned, glancing down. He had a carving knife poised below my ribs.

I slit his throat—he slits my lungs.

"I am not the enemy tonight," he said, though his blade told a different story.

"Why should I believe you?" I asked, pressing my blade harder against his skin.

Before he could answer, a hollow scream resonated from outside.

"You don't seem to have a choice." With a sharp exhale, he tossed his knife away, letting it clatter against the blood-soaked floor.

Just like in my dream.

"Doubt me if you will," he said. "But your friends are hardly prepared to take on an army of shades. If you want to survive the night, you'll have to trust me."

I hesitated. Animo knew my name. As far as I could tell, he was the one person in Rudane who could force me out of hiding. With a single flick of my knife my secret would die with him.

Or—he could be one of many who knew my identity, and killing him would invoke their wrath. My secret would be spilled, and, later, my blood. Rose Bennai would rest in the same grave as Rosara Wolfe.

Both options made my skin crawl. But only one saved my friends.

I lowered my blade. "How many are left?"

"I've taken care of four already," Animo said, his tone focused. "They're moving in ones and twos, and there's no sign of the captain."

I nodded. Every battalion of shades was composed of fifteen members: fourteen shades, and one human captain, submissive to Natalia.

"They're determined. Either you die, or they do." He paused before adding, "I have a feeling they'll do a better job of checking the body this time."

I retrieved my bow and stepped back out into the street. My broken lantern flickered, its glow reflected in the pooled blood.

"Did you know him?" Animo asked, gesturing to the body as he picked up the lantern.

"His name was Olstaff," I replied. "He was a good man."

Animo nodded. He seemed strangely accustomed to the sight of death, and I found myself curious to know what sort of life he had lived.

"We shouldn't linger," he said.

"I can't leave him like this." I pulled a canvas cloth off of a pile of hay and draped it over Olstaff—the best I could do to provide his body dignity.

"Where are your friends?" Animo asked.

"We separated near the bell tower."

He frowned.

"It wasn't my idea," I muttered, adjusting my quiver.

"They shouldn't be out here alone. We need to find them before the shades do."

"Follow me."

I led him down the street to the fork before the tower as the bells tolled with the third hour.

"It's been nearly half an hour since we separated," I said. "Megs and Derek should be back soon."

Minutes ticked by. I paced the road before the bell tower, watching the adjacent roads for any signs of my friends' return. I clenched my jaw.

They're taking too long.

A woman's scream split the night.

"Megs!" I sprinted down the street she had taken. The dark path turned, revealing a frozen figure, lit by a fallen lantern. Ahead loomed a shade, its empty eyes glinting with malice.

I released an arrow, and its head pierced straight through the shade's.

"Megs!" I grabbed her by the shoulders, turning her to face me. "Are you all right?

"Rose…" Her hand clamped around my arm, her nails digging into my skin. "There's—there—" She looked back at the gray corpse.

"I know," I said. "I *know.*"

"What is that thing?"

"It's called a *shade.*"

"Where did it come from?" she demanded. "Why are they here?"

"It's a long story," I said as Animo joined us, his sword drawn. "I'll explain later. Right now, we need to find Derek and get you to safety."

Megs looked about, and the color drained from her face.

"Rose, get her back!" Animo shouted, surging past toward a dark alley. Megs shrieked as he slashed through a lunging shade. Three more appeared behind them, their claws raised.

"What is happening?!" she screamed.

I nocked an arrow, felling a shade with a headshot as Animo stabbed another in the chest. With a quick draw, I sent an arrow into the final monster's throat.

"Megs! Rose!" Derek ran toward us from the direction of the tower. "I heard screams. Someone found a body—" His eyes widened as they dropped to the shade's corpse.

"Stay back," Animo ordered.

"Who are you?" Derek demanded.

"There's no time to explain." I pushed Megs and Derek between Animo and myself. "Stay behind us, and everything will be all right."

"But—"

A shriek drowned out Derek's words. Another followed it, and then another. Shades were closing in all around us. Their hunched forms detached themselves from the shadows as they bared their bloodstained teeth.

"Hold fast," Animo said.

I aimed my bow at the nearest shade. With a steadying breath, I released.

The shade screamed as my arrow tore through its flesh and it collapsed to the ground. Its pack charged with howls of fury. I loosed arrow after arrow, each one finding its mark.

Behind me, steel sliced flesh as Animo battled our foe. A cloaked figure stepped out from a shadowed alley, his gaze as vacant as that of the monsters he led.

"Captain!" I called, alerting my companions to his presence. I released an arrow, which he dodged with ease. Cursing, I drew another from my quiver.

The captain surged forward, his sword raised. My next shot skimmed the side of his head, drawing blood. I scarcely had time to register my small victory before he was on me.

Animo pushed me to the side, meeting the captain's sword with his own. The clash of metal rang out as they exchanged heavy blows. I turned my attention to the shades, my stomach twisting at the sight of pale corpses littering the street, their inky blood slicking the cobblestone.

Someone shouted—I spun to find Megs throwing a shade to the ground.

She danced back toward where Derek hovered in a half-crouch, ready to run at any moment. The fallen shade reached out, slashing at Megs's ankle. She screamed, tumbling to the ground. Derek grabbed her, pulling her along as she crawled away from the monster.

"Megs!" I reached for an arrow, only to find an empty quiver.

The shade leaped on top of her, slapping Derek away with the back of its hand. Megs kicked wildly, but her hands were pinned.

I dragged Derek away from the shade, drawing his sword as I hauled him to his feet. I plunged it into the beast's skull. It screamed, coughing blood onto Megs's face.

She gave a cry, squirming out from underneath the twitching body. "That's disgusting." Her eyes widened. "Rose, behind you!"

I spun to find a shade's face inches away from my own. With a flash of silver, the head fell away to reveal Animo standing behind.

"Are you all right?" he asked, breathing heavily. Specks of black blood coated his face and shirt.

"I'm fine." I took Megs's hand, pulling her up.

"That was deranged," Derek said, clearly rattled. "Those things were every-where!" He shook his head, wandering through the array of bodies.

"There will be more," Animo said, catching my eye. "If not now, then soon. It's not safe for you here."

Megs screamed, pointing to where Derek stood, blood trickling from the corner of his mouth and a sword protruding from his stomach. He fell, his body sliding down the blade—the bloodied captain hunched behind him. Megs attempted to run forward, but I held her back, my grip tight on her shaking arms.

The captain raised his sword, his eyes wild. Animo lunged forward, driving his sword into the captain's chest. He threw the captain down, drawing his sword back before landing another blow—this time through the head.

The captain's body twitched and then stilled, his hand falling limp against the cobblestone. Megs broke free of my grasp, rushing to Derek's side.

"Derek—Derek, talk to me." Her voice shook as she pressed her hands against the wound. Despite her begging, his eyes remained closed and his breathing ragged. Megs glanced up as I knelt down across from her. "We need to stop the bleeding and—and get him to Anne. She'll know what to do. Right?"

I opened my mouth, but the words refused to form.

Her lip trembled, her green eyes glistening with barely contained tears. "Rose?"

I looked over my shoulder at Animo. He watched me, his gaze holding the question I was too afraid to ask. *Is this secret worth his death?*

I reached out, moving Megs's hands off of Derek's wound and replacing them with my own. Closing my eyes, I called on my magic. I didn't need an incantation—I had cast this spell a thousand times. With a single touch, I could feel every part of the wound: the broken skin, the pierced organs, the blood flowing free throughout Derek's body. I felt it all, and I could mend it.

Warmth flowed through me as I focused my magic, releasing it like a breath. The power spread through Derek, knitting his flesh together and healing everything the captain's blade had damaged. His breathing grew steady, and his body relaxed into a painless sleep.

"What—how—?" Megs's wide eyes met mine, carrying a thousand questions.

I climbed to my feet, slowly backing away from her. "I'm sorry."

"For what?"

"For all of this." Unable to bear looking at her for a moment longer, I turned on my heel and ran into the night.

CHAPTER SEVEN

BEAUTIFUL DREAMS

Megs had seen me use my magic.

I had to. Derek would have died if I hadn't. But by saving his life, I had destroyed my own. Even if I could convince Megs to keep my secret, it wouldn't matter. Derek had been stabbed—his organs split in two. By now, she was sure to have taken him to the apothecary and told Anne everything. The worried mother would ask questions that could only be answered with the truth: I was not who I claimed to be. Every day I had spent with these people—every happy memory—was a lie.

The sun was hours from rising, yet Rudane was already waking. Bloodshot eyes darted about, searching for an explanation to the ruckus that woke them. Whispers flitted and several times I caught the word *body*.

Derek said that one had been found. Was it Olstaff, or had the shades taken another innocent life in their pursuit of me?

I squeezed my eyes shut, letting a tear slip out.

It had been a dream, this life, a beautiful dream of friendship and happiness. But sooner or later, all dreams must end. Eventually, the sun rose, and there was nothing to hide the nightmare of reality.

With a sigh, I opened my eyes to find myself standing before the Estmar house. My *home*. My dream.

A light burned in the corner of my vision. Not in the Estmar house, but in the window of the apothecary next door. Cautiously, I approached and peered through the glass.

Derek sat on a bed, still wearing his bloody shirt. Beside him sat Lili, a flickering candle in hand. I couldn't hear what they were saying, but judging by her blank stare and his hands waving in stablike motions, he was explaining what had happened. He lifted his shirt, revealing healed skin.

Lili's eyes widened. She reached out to touch where the wound had been, only to jerk her hand away when she realized what she was doing.

Avoiding his eyes, she babbled about something, brushing a strand of loose hair behind her ear. After a moment, her posture softened. Whatever she said next was surely sweet and real.

He smiled at her, and she at him.

My heart ached as I watched them. Lili would look for me, wanting to tell me everything about that moment, but all she would find was an empty bed.

"Rosara."

I flinched at Animo's voice. He watched me from a few yards away, by the Estmar's fence.

I sighed, allowing myself one last look at Lili before joining him. "Don't you have anything better to do than follow me around?"

"No."

I folded my arms. "What do you want?"

"To see if you're all right."

"I'm fine."

We stood in silence for a moment before he said, "At the festival, I promised to tell you why I came to Rudane. It was to find you, Rosara. After tonight there's no denying it, Natalia knows you're alive. I don't know how, but she does. Which means that this is only the beginning. She'll send as many legions as it takes to bring back your head."

"I know. That's why I'm leaving."

"To go where?"

I glanced back at the shadow of Lili in the apothecary window. "As far away from here as possible."

"That won't protect them," Animo said. "Natalia knows you were here. As far as she's concerned, the only way to ensure you've left is to burn this whole place to the ground. Just like Darvyn."

Fury flashed through me. "Don't you *dare* speak of Darvyn! You have no idea what happened that night."

"I know that for two years, the hope of Avonshere was kept alive by your mother and the Ardent Pack. Then it burned with that village."

I shook my head. "Avonshere's hope died with my mother."

"It died with *you*. But it can be resurrected. If you return now, you will have the support of an entire kingdom. They will follow you." He paused before adding, "Until the very end."

I winced at the words. They were the mantra of the Pack. A mantra of death.

"I'm not committing suicide for a kingdom that's already fallen," I said. "The Ardent Pack was destroyed. Natalia won. It's over."

"It's not over until one of you is in the ground. She'll come again. She'll *kill* again."

"That's why I'm leaving. I'll lead her away. Let myself be seen in remote places where no one will be hurt. Then I'll disappear forever."

"That's not good enough."

I pursed my lips. "What do you want of me?"

"I want you to be the person you are meant to be." He stepped closer. "You were born to sit on a throne. I can help you get there."

Sit on a throne?

I couldn't feel my heartbeat. Was it still beating, or had the mere suggestion killed me? If I so much as put a toe across Avonshere's borders, I would die. How could Animo possibly expect me to sit on the throne?

A shaky breath slipped out.

"Rosara—"

"Don't," I said, raising a trembling hand to stop him.

"I—"

"No." I turned away.

He caught my arm. "You have to face this," he urged.

I tore my arm out of his grasp. "I don't have to face anything. I am not Rosara Wolfe. I am Rose Bennai, an orphan girl who lives in Chess. I'm not a queen, and I never will be."

"So you're going to hide." A mixture of shock and bitterness swept across Animo's face. He shook his head. "Just like you did all those years ago."

I clenched my fist, tempted to punch him in the face.

"I survived," I said, my voice shaking with restraint. "You have no idea what I went through to gain this life. A life that's as good as gone now."

"Not if you dethrone Natalia."

"I won't."

"Then say it," he demanded. "Say that you don't think about Avonshere. Tell me that memories of what you lost—of what you still have to lose—don't haunt your dreams. Say that you can turn your back on a dying kingdom without batting an eye or say that you will be queen." He drew a ring from his pocket, holding it out to me.

My breath caught at the sight of the Wolfe crest carved into the glittering sapphire. I hadn't seen the ring since I slid it onto the finger of a skeleton five years ago. My throat tightened, the scent of smoke wafting through my mind.

"How did you get that?" I whispered.

"Does it matter?"

I shook my head, biting down on my lip.

"I can't force you to do this," he said, his voice softening. "But people are dying. Natalia is unfit to rule and she will destroy Avonshere unless someone stops her. You are the heir to the throne. Your kingdom needs you."

He pressed the ring into my hand. I shuddered at the feeling of steel against my skin.

"I won't go back. I *can't* go back." My gaze met his. "I'm sorry."

He nodded sadly. "As am I."

I wanted to say something, but the words fell dead on my lips. Nothing could change the past.

I offered Animo the ring.

"Take it," I urged when he didn't move. "Give it to the next queen. Someone who can do the people of Avonshere good. Let her save them, not me."

He shook his head. "I can't do that."

"Then leave, but know that I won't be following."

With a sigh, he took the ring. "That's why I'm sorry." His eyes flicked past me, and he gave a slight nod.

A weight hit my back, latching on as a black hood fell over my face. I fell backward, landing on my assailant. Hands pinned my wrists to the ground. I thrashed about, screaming, only to inhale a sweet-smelling powder. Dizziness swept over me as coughs wracked my body. Voices swirled and darkness pulled me under.

PART TWO

FRIENDS AND PRISONERS

Sunlight warmed my skin, covering me like a blanket. I groaned, rolling over to bury my face in the pillow. My body longed to sink into the mattress and never resurface, but my mind knew better. The harvest season had begun, leaving a mere three months until the rime season hit, killing crops with ice and snow. As my household's sole hunter, it was up to me to venture into Holfetine and bring back enough meat to maintain us through rime.

With a heavy sigh, I dragged myself upright. My body fought against the motion, sending waves of faint nausea through me.

How late did I stay out?

I rubbed my eyes, forcing them to open. A bright room met my gaze, lit by a large, square window on the wall opposite me. I froze. This was not my bedroom.

"That son of a—" I shot to my feet, only to drop back onto the bed as dizziness swept over me. Breathing deeply, I sat there, my back hunched and my hands planted on the mattress. Memories of last night flooded my mind, followed by anger.

Animo had insisted that he had come to Rudane to help me, and then he *kidnapped* me. Was he completely mad?

Rubbing my aching temples, I took in my current confines—a simple bedroom with plain stucco walls and a single table in the corner. The room resembled an inn, but Animo couldn't possibly be foolish enough to carry an unconscious woman through such a public place. It had to be a private residence of some kind.

I stood—much slower this time—and faced the door. Before I'd passed out, I'd heard two voices, so Animo must have a partner. If my assumption was correct, there was at least one more person in this house, maybe even on the other side of my door.

With a huff, I shoved loose strands of hair behind my ears. Cold metal brushed across my cheek.

What the…? A shackle-like cuff, etched with strange symbols was clamped on my wrist.

"Runes," I muttered, running my fingers over the symbols. *Dwarvish* runes, if I wasn't mistaken. Why would Animo lock me in a chainless restraint? Did he think that by making me feel trapped he could pressure me into returning to Avonshere?

Smoke wafted through my memory, and my breath hitched. He was wrong. No amount of captivity could make me go back.

Pushing down the memories, I took in a sharp breath of fresh air. *I will not walk into another trap.* The door was too much of a risk, leaving me with only one option—the window.

Keeping my footsteps light, I made my way across the room and gave the glass pane a push. It swung open with ease. I leaned out, peering down at a cobbled alley lined with undivided sandstone houses. There was almost no gap between the wall's smooth stones, which was unfortunate, considering the eight-foot drop below me.

Kingdoms, don't let me fall. I swung my legs out the window, awkwardly twisting my body as I eased myself down. My foot felt about blindly until it landed on a thin lip of stone. Muscles tense, I slid my hand down the wall, searching for a grip.

Biaht! My fingers slid right off the smooth stone. Gritting my teeth, I shifted my grasp on the windowsill, lowering myself as best I could. It still wasn't far enough. A drop from this height and angle risked injury—broken limbs or even a cracked skull.

I bit back an angry cry as my arm began to shake.

"Need a hand?"

I flinched, nearly falling off the wall.

"Woah! Be careful!" the same male voice called, his tone as distressed as I was. "Okay, there is a crack to your right. Do you see it?"

My cheek rubbed against the rough wall as I turned my head to find a crack running down the side of the building, an arm's length away.

"I see it." Channeling all of my strength into my right arm, I pushed off from the window, shoving my left hand into the crack and leaving my legs dangling. Bits of rock ate at my fingertips as my muscles trembled.

The man yelped as I slid my feet against the wall. Finally, they hit a ledge.

"Ahh! Please, please be careful," he cried.

I pressed my lips together as annoyance bubbled within me—most of it misdirected anger drawn from my aching arms.

"Curse it all," I muttered. Planting my feet against the wall, I kicked off, half-jumping, half-falling toward the street. The man yelped again as I twisted my body around. I landed on the balls of my feet and propelled myself into a roll.

My shoulder slammed against the ground as I tumbled, the hard stone jarring my joints until I came to a stop, crashing into a barrel.

A small hand helped me up. "Are you okay?"

"A little bruised, but I'll be fine." My eyes fell to the sun-tanned dwarf who stood beside me. The light wrinkles around his eyes suggested he was in his mid-forties. He had a rugged appearance with a low mohawk, black diamond earring, and a rough scar where his right ear should have been.

"Did you lock yourself inside, or do you just like climbing out windows?" he asked.

"It's… complicated."

"Hmm." The dwarf watched me, his catlike pupils mere slits in the sunlight. "You know, I could help you out if you'd like. My house is only a few blocks from here, and from the looks of it, you need a place to get cleaned up."

"What—?" I looked down, only to find my shirt splattered with black and red blood. *Biaht.* "I killed a hog last night."

He held up his palms. "I'm not here to pry, just offer help." After a pause, he extended a hand. "Ketchnoori of Family Runix. You can call me Ketch if you'd like."

"Rose." I shook his hand.

"Well, Rose," Ketch began. "My offer remains if you need a place to… take care of the hog's aftermath."

I hesitated. Rarely was it smart to follow a stranger into their home. Though Ketch's smile made him seem like a friend, a closer look at his appearance left him with a more suspicious label: several scars ran across his face, one on his eyebrow, another on his chin amid a thin layer of stubble, and a third across his crooked nose. Even more incriminating was the blocky tattoo on his neck that read *030921*. That number was a brand, a *prison* brand.

"If you don't want to, that's fine," he said, reading my silence. "You just seemed to be in a bit of trouble, and well… I know the look."

My hesitation faded. I *did* need a place to clean up. And stumbling across a dwarf could be the stroke of luck I needed. If he could translate the runes on my cuff, I might actually be able to understand Animo's intentions.

"A place to clean up would be wonderful," I replied. "Thank you."

He held out a welcoming arm. "Right this way."

I followed him through the foreign streets, taking a series of dizzying turns that left me more lost than before.

"How much farther?" I asked as he led me down a shaded alley.

"Right here." Ketch stopped before a door peeking out from the sandstone wall. He opened the door without a key and led me into the living quarters. Travel supplies spilled out of bags carelessly tossed on the sofa and a stack of used dishes covered most of the table.

"Make yourself comfortable," he said, taking one of the bags from the sofa and tossing it onto the ground with a concerning clank of metal. "I'll see if we have anything less bloody for you to wear." He wandered upstairs, his footsteps echoed by light creaks of the floorboards.

I tentatively took a seat on the couch, my hands folded in my lap and my back straight, barely touching the pillow. As kind as Ketch seemed, I was uncomfortable to be alone in the living room of a complete stranger.

It's fine. Just relax. I leaned back, and something hard pressed against me.

What is that? Brow furrowed, I moved the pillow. A sheathed sword, far too long for Ketch to carry comfortably, lay on the couch. Picking it up, I examined the pattern of thorny vines that wound their way around the hilt. Along the cross guard was etched the word *Bathril*.

My breath hitched. It was a name in Aesin, the language of elves. This sword—this beautiful, powerful piece of steel—belonged to an elf.

Biaht.

The front door opened and in walked an elf whose pretty face was not nearly enough to gain amnesty.

Animo's eyes widened slightly at the sight of me holding his sword.

I unsheathed the blade, raising it in defense. "Kidnapper."

"I apologized."

"For *kidnapping* me!"

He sighed irritably and shut the door behind him, sliding the deadbolt into place. "You think you can outrun Natalia, but you can't. She'll find you, and she'll kill you. Only, this time, your death will be meaningless."

"How many times do I have to tell you? I don't care."

His expression darkened. "Your kingdom will die. Your *people* will die."

"They're not my people anymore. And I'm leaving." I marched forward, but Animo kept himself planted firmly in front of the door.

"Move," I ordered.

"No."

I raised his sword. "I'll make you."

"No, you won't." He grabbed my wrist, twisting it so that I dropped the sword. Spinning me, he pulled me against him—my back pressed to his chest and his grip tight on my arms.

I squirmed, but he held my arm up, forcing me to look at my shackled wrist.

"This is a restrictor cuff," he explained. "Those runes keep you from accessing your magic. So before you attempt anything foolish, I would consider your odds of beating me in physical combat."

I elbowed him, finally breaking free of his grasp. With a toss of my falling braid, I faced him with a glare. "What do you think this will accomplish? Do you expect to threaten me into compliance?"

"I expect you to stop letting your people die!"

My left hook met his jaw. His head snapped to the side, and he stumbled just enough to grant me a clear path to the door. Before I could make a run for it, someone sighed behind me. "I see we've skipped to the violent part of the afternoon," Ketch said, looking between me and Animo, whose hand was pressed against his face.

My glare landed on the dwarf. "You liar." I flung the words at him with all the fury I possessed.

Ketch held up his hands in defense. "I never said I *wasn't* responsible for kidnapping you. We really do want to help. Starting with fresh clothes. Animo,"—he turned his attention to the elf—"Rose needs a less bloody change of clothes, and nothing I found upstairs will fit her."

Animo's gaze flicked over my outfit, taking in the blood and dirt. "Fine." He marched over to the cluttered couch and began rifling through the bags.

Ketch ambled over to me, a somewhat sheepish expression on his face. "I feel I should apologize."

"You can try," Animo said loudly. "She won't care."

I rolled my eyes.

Ketch continued, ignoring Animo. "I'm sorry that I tricked you. I wouldn't have done so unless it was necessary."

I folded my arms. "I'm sure you felt that way."

He opened his mouth to reply, then seemed to think better about it.

"Here," Animo said.

A bundle of cloth struck my head before falling into my arms. I pulled the pieces apart, holding up a white shirt and brown vest, both of which appeared to be Animo's.

"This isn't going to fit me," I said.

He shrugged. "At least it isn't covered in blood. You can change in the bedroom." He gestured to a door next to the staircase.

Since I had no available way of escape, I obeyed, allowing myself the slightest hint of defiance by locking the door. I had a feeling Animo could break it down without so much as a sweat, but I wasn't going to give up what little power I had left.

I changed out of my bloody hunting clothes, pulling on Animo's oversized shirt. It hung well below my waist, but I managed to salvage the outfit by stuffing the shirt into my pants and belting the vest to form a sort of tunic.

I was about to return to the main room when muffled voices seeped through the wall.

"You couldn't resist, could you?" Animo asked.

"I thought they were real dragon eggs," Ketch protested. "And if I had been right, then doing nothing could have led to absolute chaos."

"And instead you saved... what was it?"

There was a pause before Ketch said, "Sculpted clay."

"Of course. And while you were out freeing the clay eggs, Rosara went ahead and walked out the front door."

"Actually, she climbed out the window. Apparently, this place is too run-down to have more than three working locks."

"But the other windows are secured, aren't they?"

I didn't hear Ketch's reply—I was already out the very unsecured window. As soon as my feet hit the cobblestone, I took off running, barrelling past villagers as I cut down as many sidestreets as I could without looping back to my captors.

A final turn stopped me dead in my tracks: a massive river raged before me, dividing the kingdoms of Chess and Lucia. A bridge wide enough to fit five carriages at a time connected the two. I had seen it, but only from one side.

My gaze fell to a sign that read: *Crossing to Chess, one quarter-mynet.*

"No," I breathed, my chest constricting. I hadn't been taken to another city.

I had been taken to another *kingdom.*

The Ivrode River roared as I sat alone on a bench. The setting sun painted the horizon a bold shade of orange and washed the distant shores of Chess in shadows. My vision glazed as my mind drifted to Rudane.

Soon, stars would fill the sky, and the villagers would make their way to the lake to give a final farewell to those killed in the shade's attack. The dead would be sent off with honor: laid to rest in boats, their bodies clothed in white and framed with chrysanthemum blossoms. Their swords would lie on their chests, beneath their crossed arms, because they were warriors, and warriors died with a weapon in hand. An archer would fire a flaming arrow into their boat, and the flames would take them away to the afterlife, where their souls would be forever honored for their courage and sacrifice. And for the dead, there was nothing more important than honor.

I pulled my legs to my chest, wrapping my arms around them tightly, as the memories flowed as free and rapid as the river.

We used torch-lit pyres in Avonshere. The dead were covered with a silk burial shroud—a *halias.* At least, that was what we did before Natalia took control. On the run with the Ardent Pack, I witnessed many deaths, yet none were given the honor they deserved. When battles ended, the dead were abandoned, shoved in a ditch, or crammed together on a pyre that we'd light only to flee before anyone caught sight of the smoke.

I loathed every moment of those funerals. But now I wished I were back there, lying on the pyre and burning alongside the people I had failed.

"Rose?"

I turned at the sound of Ketch's voice. He hovered a few carriage lengths away from me as though he were waiting for permission to approach.

"What do you want?" I asked, the fight draining from my voice.

"We want to help you."

I scoffed.

He took a small step forward. "I know we didn't start off on the best of terms, but we really do have good intentions. You shouldn't have to face this threat alone."

"I wasn't alone. I had friends. I had a *family*." At least, I'd fooled myself into thinking I did.

"I am truly sorry for what happened that night."

I stood slowly, his words curdling in my stomach. "*That* night?"

He froze, regret sweeping across his face.

"It's been five days since we left Rudane." It wasn't Ketch who spoke, but Animo. He'd stopped a few yards away from where I sat, probably to increase his chances of blocking any escape.

I turned away from Ketch and Animo, my eyes once again falling to the darkening shores of Chess. *Five days.* The wound of the attack had closed. Megs, Hertz, the Estmars—they knew I was gone, and if they caught the trail, they'd come after me. And if they found me…

"I'm leaving."

Animo shifted into a defensive stance, his hand hovering above the hilt of his sword, Bathril.

"Must you try to stop me?" I snapped. "If you can recall, I escaped you. Twice."

"And we caught you. Twice."

I folded my arms as the dwindling embers of my anger began to steam. "I am trying to protect the people I care about."

"You're not protecting them, you're abandoning them," Animo snapped. "Do you really think that Natalia will give up after one failed attack? She will return with more forces, and her first stop will be your family's door."

The words pierced my chest like a dagger, but I refused to let him see. "What do you expect me to do? Stand by their sides so I can watch as they die?"

"You fix it!" he shouted. He took a deep breath, glancing around and then softening his voice. "Avonshere is broken, and the damage is spreading to the rest of the Twelve Kingdoms. But you have a chance to fix it."

"Who says it has to be me?"

"Aspectu Demore."

My jaw dropped. My mother used to tell me stories of the Ancient Elf. Older than the Twelve Kingdoms, Aspectu Demore was the most powerful elf alive. Her magic granted her many abilities, most importantly that of foresight. She could see the future's paths before they formed, and guide me down the one of safety.

A hint of triumph slipped into Animo's gaze. "Come with us to Medea. Let Aspectu say her piece. Then, if you are still unconvinced, you can walk away and never look back."

I narrowed my eyes. "You'll let me go?"

"I swear it."

I looked between the elf and the dwarf. The last thing I wanted was to spend more time with the duo, but Aspectu was an incomparable ally. Finding her would be worth much more than a few days of irritating company.

Raising my chin, I replied, "We have a deal."

VOICES IN THE SWAMP

Mud squished beneath my boots, splattering onto my pants as I hopped down from the wagon. I let out a huff, scraping a particularly large clump off with my heel. I wasn't usually bothered by a bit of muck, but after a full day of traveling with the sun beating down on me and my former kidnappers as my traveling companions, my rope was far past frayed. I wanted nothing more than to lie down in the shade of an evergreen as the harvest breeze whisked away my troubles. But we were in Lucia now.

Here, cypress trees grew on the edge of stagnant waters, buzzing with mosquitos. Hot, muggy air hugged the soggy ground. This wasn't a forest; it was a swamp.

I slapped a mosquito off my neck. *Rack you, Animo Terrot.* My glare found him on the opposite side of the cart, unloading supplies. He tossed the bags to the ground, careless of the mud.

"You know looks can't actually kill, right?" Ketch climbed down from the wagon, using the spokes of the wheel as a ladder. With both feet on the ground, he barely matched the wheel's height, even with his spiky mohawk adding a couple of inches.

"Just wait until I get *this* taken off." I held up my wrist, still shackled with the restrictor cuff.

Ketch raised his eyebrows. "You're not helping your case."

"Ketch, set up the campsite," Animo called, unhitching the horses. "I'll take care of these two."

Ketch nodded. Looking back at me, he said, "Come with me."

While Animo led the horses to nearby waters, Ketch and I carried the supplies to a relatively dry patch of swamp. I laid out my bedding, patting it flat, only to feel the damp ground seeping through the blanket's layers.

"Rack," I muttered, laying my second blanket atop the first. Kingdoms knew I wouldn't need it for warmth, but I had hoped to cover myself fully to avoid the mosquitos draining my blood while I slept. I sat down on my makeshift bed, cringing as mud squished beneath me. *This is going to be a long night.*

Across from me, Ketch sat cross-legged on a blanket. He rooted through a bag, extracting a series of mismatched candles draped with wax drips and sporting blackened wicks.

"What are you doing?" I asked.

"Helping us get a good night's sleep." Ketch struck a match and lit the candles, amassing a field of flickering flames before him. He picked up a candle and took a deep breath of its scent before passing it to me.

"Citronella," he explained. "It helps keep the mosquitos away."

I sniffed the candle—citrusy and sweet. Setting it next to my bed, I lay down, looking up at the trees. Golden rays of sunlight glowed against the green foliage as a hot breeze sent ripples through the canopy. I closed my eyes, letting the rustling leaves carry me back to Chess. Hunting with Megs and Hertz in Holfetine. Late nights talking with Lili. Laughing and dancing with my family at the Harvest Festival. Bloody Olstaff. Bloody Derek. More bodies I didn't get to see.

"Hungry?" Ketch's voice cut through my thoughts. He offered me an apple as though it were an olive branch.

"Thanks." Sitting up, I took the fruit though I was too anxious to eat. My mind galloped in circles—what if Natalia sent more shades to Rudane? I should have done more to protect the Estmars. But staying would have sealed their fate…

"You seem…"—Ketch's voice trailed off as he searched for the right word—"distracted."

"I'm thinking about my family back in Rudane," I admitted. Perhaps I was a fool for trusting him twice, but something about him seemed genuine. I truly believed he meant to help me.

"You don't have to worry about them," he replied. He took a bite out of his own apple before adding, "Animo has a plan."

I scoffed. "Animo's last plan ended with a kidnapping."

"Again, I apologize for that."

A slight smile crossed my lips. My eyes fell to the apple as I slid it absent-mindedly between my hands.

"I know it's hard, but you can trust us, Rose," Ketch said. "I've known Animo for a long time. He won't let anything happen to your friends."

Though I replied with a smile and a nod, I didn't believe either. Whatever horrible fate Natalia had planned would occur, and it would be my fault.

Night in the swamp was anything but peaceful. Unfamiliar creatures buzzed about while the ground continued to dampen beneath me. Clouds blocked my view of the stars, leaving the sky dark. My fitful sleep only lasted a few short hours before I was awoken by the squawk of a heron.

Groaning, I sat up, my fingers sinking into the muddy ground beside me. Animo stood across the campsite, his dark hair shining in the morning sunlight as he bridled the horses. Both he and Ketch had cleared their bedding though the latter was nowhere to be seen.

"Good morning, Rosara," Animo said, glancing over his shoulder at me.

I bristled at the name. "Don't call me that."

He paused, turning away from the horses to give me his full attention. "Why not?"

"I don't like what it reminds me of."

His eyes flicked away for a moment, and when they returned, his gaze was soft. "What would you rather I call you?"

Surprise mingled with confusion as I replied, "Rose. Rose Bennai, if you need a surname."

"Very well." He returned to the horses, guiding the chestnut mare toward the cart.

"That's it?" I blurted. "You aren't going to demand answers?"

He hitched the mare to the wagon. "You wouldn't give them to me. Besides, I'm not the enemy you think I am." His gaze met mine, simultaneously sending chills and warmth through my body. "And as someone reminded me, we have something in common."

"What's that?"

"Secrets."

My heartbeat spiked. I turned away, busying myself with gathering my dirty bedding.

Is my face flushed? It feels as though it is. I shouldn't *be* flushed when I spoke to him. Not unless the cause was anger. Yes, I had been attracted to him when we first met, but things had changed. He wasn't a mysterious stranger anymore; he was a kidnapper. A danger. If he had it his way, he would drag me kicking and screaming all the way to Avonshere. He was *not* allowed to make me blush.

Securing the straps of my bedroll, I asked, "Where's Ketch?"

"Doubling back to ensure we aren't being tracked."

My attention shot back to Animo. "Do you think we are?"

"Not really. Natalia is far more likely to cut us off from the west. But if I'm wrong, I'd rather find out before we reach the bridges."

"Bridges?"

"The swamp deepens ahead," he explained. "The only way to cross is by a series of bridges. We'll be on a fixed route for the next five days."

"So if something does come after us, we'll be trapped."

"More or less."

Unease gnawed at me as I tossed my dirty bedding in the back of the cart. The journey from Avonshere to Lucia took weeks, but Natalia's army never slept. If she sent reinforcements directly after the attack on Rudane, we wouldn't have to worry about them tracking us—not when they could be waiting at the other end of the road.

"Fetch Arthur, will you?"

It took me a moment to realize Animo was referring to the dapple-gray stallion secured to a nearby tree. "Did you name them?" I asked, untying Arthur's lead.

"Someone had to."

I led Arthur to the cart and passed the reins to Animo. While he strapped the stallion into the harness, I stroked the white stripe along the chestnut mare's nose.

"What's her name?" I asked.

"'Minette.'"

Minette snorted, jerking her head away from me, only to lean back down and nibble at my braid. I pulled my hair out of her mouth with a laugh. Out of the corner of my eye, I caught Animo smiling.

"She likes you," he said.

"She likes my *hair*."

Animo's smile faded, his gaze focused on something behind me. I turned to find Ketch in a dead sprint through the swamp. He was remarkably fast considering his short stride and came to a sliding stop within seconds.

"Followed." He gasped, doubling over and panting.

"How many?" Animo demanded, reaching for his sword.

"Two."

"Armed?"

Ketch nodded, straightening. "One had daggers, the other, an axe."

Animo nodded. "We'll have to ambush them before they reach the camp-site." He turned to me. "Rose, stay here and stay hidden."

Part of me wanted to protest and remind him that I could fight, but the more intelligent side of me knew better than to engage with unknown assailants. I slipped behind a tree, positioning myself to be hidden from the main path, but still allowing me to keep an eye on Ketch and Animo.

Animo boosted Ketch into a tree. The dwarf wrapped his limbs around a low-hanging branch, then scurried up the trunk, concealing himself in a thick patch of leaves. Animo glanced around, then took cover behind a tree on the opposite side of the path.

Time seemed to slow as we waited. The swamp's inhuman noises fueled my imagination as images of bloody mercenaries and soulless monsters filled my mind.

"Look!" a woman hissed. "Horses. That has to be them."

A gasp slipped out. *I know that voice.*

"I don't see anyone," a man replied, his deep voice equally familiar.

Oh no.

"Wait!" I leaped out from behind the tree, but not before Animo and Ketch had sprung into action. Animo took Megs down in a flash, twisting her arms behind her and holding his sword to her throat. At the same time, Ketch jumped out of the tree and landed on Hertz's back. The dwarf wrapped his arms around the larger man's throat, squeezing tight. Hertz gasped, scrabbling at Ketch's arms to no avail.

"No!" I cried. "Let them go!"

Animo's gaze snapped to me, then back to Megs. Recognition swept over him. "Let him go," he said to Ketch, lowering his blade. "They're her friends."

Ketch loosened his grip, sliding down Hertz's back and landing in the mud. Hertz stumbled away, clearly struggling to decide whether or not to draw his axe. Megs had no such qualms. Pushing Animo away, she unsheathed her daggers.

"Let our friend go."

"Megs, stand down," I ordered.

Her wide eyes landed on me. "Are you out of your mind? They kidnapped you!"

"We protected her," Animo said. "The attack on your village was no accident. Those creatures were sent to kill Rose."

"What?" Megs's confidence wavered. "Why?"

My heart pounded as Animo opened his mouth to reply. He wouldn't actually tell the truth, would he?

"Rose is heir to the throne of Avonshere."

I stumbled backward, steadying myself on a tree. *He really told them.* A thousand words spun in my mind, like a cyclone screaming for release.

"But Rose—what—I—" Megs's face twisted in confusion as her mangled sentences faded into gibberish.

Hertz lay a hand on her shoulder. "What Megs means to say is, it is impossible."

"It's true." My voice came out as a whisper, just loud enough for him to hear.

His firm expression dropped, his jaw sliding open and his dark brow furrowing. He blinked rapidly. "That… if you… why wouldn't you tell us?"

"I couldn't," I replied, tears welling behind my eyes. "The kingdoms needed to believe that I was dead. I had to bury who I was forever, or else—"

"The attack." Megs stared at me with the clarity I'd always feared. "The Queen of Avonshere—the one who took over—she sent those things after you."

I nodded. "I faked my death to escape Natalia. Now she knows I'm alive, and she will hunt me until my body lies at the foot of her throne."

Megs's expression grew distant as the gears in her head turned.

"I need the two of you to return to Rudane," I said, shifting my focus to Hertz. "Natalia knows that you're connected to me. You need to gather your families, the Estmars, and the Crowbornes, and leave. Don't tell anyone where you're going."

"Is that really necessary?" he asked.

"Yes. Natalia will do whatever it takes to find me."

He stepped back, shoulders slumping as the weight of the situation settled over him.

"I am so sorry, Hertz," I said. "I should never have put you in this position."

He didn't reply, his gaze falling to the ground.

I wrapped my arms around myself. "You'll want to change your names. And stay away from anyone who might recognize you. At least until I find a way to escape Natalia."

He nodded slowly.

"Now, I think it's best if you leave."

"No."

All eyes fell to Megs.

She folded her arms, raising her chin in defiance. "We're not leaving. We're coming with you."

"No, you're not," I said.

"Yes, we are," she replied. "You can't honestly think I'd allow some queen to hunt you down and force us into hiding. We're going to fight her."

"You don't know what you're talking about," I began. "Natalia is a powerful witch. She toppled a thousand-year-old regime in a matter of months. If we so much as step across Avonshere's border, she'll have us taken captive, tortured, and killed."

Megs let out a huff. "We're not idiots. Obviously it will be difficult, but isn't fighting better than running away?"

"She's not wrong," Animo admitted.

I shot him a glare.

"I agree with them," Hertz said. "Rose, you are my friend, and I cannot allow some queen to destroy your life. We're going to follow you as far as you go, and we will fight with you until the very end."

The words sent ice down my spine. I stepped back, unable to form words until, finally, I managed, "Who told you that?"

"What?"

"Those words. Who said them to you?"

"No one," he replied, his brow furrowed. "I only meant that I would stand by you until—"

"Don't!" I held up a hand, my breaths shortening.

"Rose, are you all right?" Megs reached out, but I drew away.

"I'm fine. I need a moment, that's all."

I turned my back on them, wandering aimlessly into the swamp. My boots sank, deeper and deeper. At last, I stopped, the wet earth settling just below my knees.

Why did he say that? Did he really not know that it was the mantra of the Ardent Pack? That it would remind me of everyone who had fought and died for my family?

"Until the very end," he had said. But he didn't know what the end looked like. I had seen it for what felt like a thousand times. The promises to return. The smiles on their lips as they told you not to worry, they would be fine. The screams. The blood. I couldn't allow that to happen again. Not to them.

"Rose."

I clenched my jaw at the sound of Animo's voice. "I think I'd rather Ketch have followed me."

"Ketch would probably drown if he walked this far out."

A slight smile raised my lips as Animo joined me. "They won't leave you," he said. "I know loyalty when I see it, and those two—"

"Are wonderful." I looked up at him, biting my lip to keep it from trembling. "They are my best friends, and I cannot lose them."

"You *won't*," he insisted. "Aspectu can see the future—she'll find a path that keeps them both safe. I'll make certain of it."

I blinked, the hot sting of tears pricking the back of my eyes. "You would protect them?"

He nodded. "I told you, Rose. I'm not your enemy."

I stared into his eyes. Deep, blue, and starlit. In that moment, he wasn't my kidnapper or leading me down the path of destruction. He was there, and he *cared*. Maybe with him, I could make it through this.

I took a soothing breath, letting it wash away my fear. "They can come with us."

CHAPTER TEN

TALES OF LOSS

If the mud was irritating, the bridges were misery incarnate. They might have been constructed to guide travelers over the swamps, but time had taken its toll on the wood boards, rotting away their structure. Moss and vines consumed the bridges, winding around the railing as if to meld it with the trees. The bridge itself was barely wide enough to fit our cart, and time and time again, our wheels caught on a vine or a snake slithered into our path, spooking the horses and sending them barrelling backward toward Megs and me. It was slow and painful travel, worsened heavily by my friends' questions.

"So, you've fought Queen Natalia before, right?" Megs asked as we walked along the rickety bridge. The boards dipped down with every step, sending waves of water across our shoes.

"For nearly two years," I replied. "My mother led the people of Avonshere

84

in a revolt against her. They called themselves the *Ardent Pack*."

"Can they help us?"

I shook my head. "They're all dead."

"Oh."

The wagon came to a sharp halt as a flurry of cursing erupted.

"What happened?" I called.

Standing on the driver's seat, Ketch replied, "The bridge broke. We'll have to stop and make repairs."

"Great." With a sigh, I leaned against the mossy railing. Craning my neck, I managed a glimpse of broken boards and a large gap in the bridge. Animo and Ketch stood at the edge, surveying the damage while Hertz hung back awkwardly.

Megs took a seat on the back of the cart. "I know that Natalia wants you dead, but I don't really understand why."

I hesitated before responding. "Natalia was a duchess, betrothed to my father for years. Eventually, my grandparents invited her to our castle in Del Hera, hoping she and my father would get better acquainted before the wedding. Only, the wedding never happened. My father met my mother and broke off his loveless engagement. Natalia kept her resentment buried for years. She ignored her duties as duchess and remained in Del Hera like a ghost, hiding away in her quarters. Eventually, my father learned why."

"Why?" Megs echoed, her wide, green eyes drinking in my every word.

"She was experimenting with dark magic," I explained. "She created creatures called *shades*—those things that attacked us in Rudane."

"Wait, she *created* those things?"

I nodded. "From humans. She found a way to split a person's soul from their body, then warp the remains into a living but unfeeling monster that obeys her every command."

Megs's jaw hung open.

"When my father realized what Natalia had done, he cast her out of Del Hera and stripped her of her title as Duchess of Elatire. She was furious. The guards were forced to physically *drag* her from the castle. She disappeared for a few weeks, and we thought we were rid of her. Then, at my parents' coronation, she returned."

"And?" Her eager gaze urged me to continue.

"She won," I said simply. Megs didn't need to know the details of how that day ended. "My mother and I were the only ones to escape. After that, Natalia tracked down every member of the Wolfe bloodline, killing them to solidify her claim to the throne."

"I'm so sorry." She reached out to touch my arm. "But why is she after you now? Isn't she already queen?"

"Natalia fears that if I return as heir, I will be able to take the throne back from her. The only way to ensure her place as queen is to kill me."

"But you were in hiding. Isn't that enough assurance?"

I shook my head bitterly. "Not for Natalia. She's a madwoman. She stole the throne and massacred a bloodline to win a kingdom that she rules like a prison." My anger swelled with every word. "I don't understand her motives, and I don't have to—she's a tyrant, and I can't do a thing to stop her."

Megs bit her lip, her arms tight against her sides. "Tell me about your parents," she said. "Your father was betrothed, so… how did that work?"

My anger subsided as I thought back to my mother telling a younger, innocent version of me their story.

"A griffin was attacking villages in Eastern Avonshere," I began. "My father needed magical aid, so he journeyed to Daria to meet with Aspectu. It took a few days to prepare the spell, and during that time my father spent time with Aspectu's assistant, Emry Avron." I smiled, the memory warming my mind. "Duty called him back to Avonshere, but once he'd defeated the griffin, my father returned to Daria, this time to ask for my mother's hand."

A dopey grin spread across Megs's face. "Aww. That is so sweet." Her smile shifted to one of confusion. "Wait, isn't Aspectu an elf?"

"Yes, she is."

"And your *mother* was her assistant."

I nodded as she put the pieces together.

"Rose."

"Yes?"

"Are you an elf?"

"*Half*-elf, actually."

"Rose!" She slapped my arm a bit harder than necessary. "How could you not tell us? How did we not know?" Before I could answer either question, she shouted, "Hertz! Get over here! Rose is an elf!"

"What?"

Within seconds, Hertz was jumping down from the cart, his shocked expression matching Megs's.

"You're an elf," he repeated.

"I am."

"Does that make you immortal?"

"Yes."

"And magical!" Megs exclaimed. "*That's* how you healed Derek. None of us understood it and then you disappeared before we could ask you about it, leaving us to wonder until our concern for you overtook our curiosity completely"—she sucked in a deep breath—"but now I know. You have magic. And—wait, since you're an elf, doesn't that mean you were born with it?"

"Yes," I replied. "All elves are ekeiders."

Her nose scrunched. "I've never understood the difference between ekeiders and other spellcasters."

I laughed slightly. Sometimes I forgot how little places like Rudane knew about magic.

"There are three types of magic-wielders. Ekeiders are born with magic. We have a natural connection with it that we can enhance through training. Sorcerers are not born with magic. They must learn to gain a connection through years of study. Finally, there are witches, who skip studying and make deals with divine beings or some kind of powerful magic-wielder to gain their abilities."

"Which one is Natalia?" Megs asked.

"She is a witch, plain and simple."

"So *anyone* can gain magic by reading a book or making a deal?"

"Not exactly. Magic exists everywhere, but you need a connection to use it. Ekeiders are born with that connection, but sorcerers and witches must forge their own. For sorcerers, this usually involves staffs or wands made of magical wood, while witches tend to rely on totems to give them control over magic."

"But you don't need a totem," Hertz said.

"No, because I have my own, natural magic. It flows through my veins and exists in every hair on my head. I could use a totem to enhance my control, but I don't have to. I rarely even need to use spoken spells." I shrugged. "My power simply… obeys."

"That is incredible," Megs breathed while Hertz nodded in agreement. "*Magic*. But why do you never use it?"

"Because Rose Bennai is human. I couldn't allow anything to jeopardize my new identity. That's why I never told you any of this."

"But we'd have found out eventually, wouldn't we?" Hertz asked. "If you're immortal, you won't age."

Megs's wide eyes grew, practically bulging out of her head. "Rose Bennai, are you telling me that you'll be forever seventeen while Hertz and I get old and wrinkly?"

Animo jumped down from the cart. "That's not how it works. Elves stop aging somewhere between the ages of twenty-five and thirty, when our bodies have reached their prime." He paused before adding, "But the second part is true."

"Is the bridge fixed?" I asked before Megs could drive us deeper down another tangent.

He scoffed lightly. "Not even close. We'll have to make camp and gather supplies."

I groaned. The last thing I wanted to do was spend the night on a rotting bridge, but we had no choice. These bridges were a straight shot to Medea. The only other option would be to spend a day backtracking, then six more days traveling around the swamp. We didn't have a week to waste—not with Natalia on our tail.

After the difficult process of reversing the horses and cart, we made camp by the broken edge. Even with wet boards, a fire was out of the question. We scattered our meager bedding across the least rotten planks, then worked on fixing the bridge until the setting sun and our growling stomachs called us to stop.

Hot and sweaty, we settled on our beds, passing out the night's rations while a single, stocky candle burned in the middle of our camp, providing light and warding off insects. I nibbled on a bit of bread and cheese, my legs crossed and my elbows propped on the edge of my knees.

"I have a question," Megs began, dusting crumbs off her hands. She lounged on her side, her head tilted toward Animo. "Why did you wait until now to find Rose?"

"It wasn't patience," he assured her. "I've spent the last two years scouring the Twelve Kingdoms for any trace of her, but every lead ran astray. In fact, I was beginning to think I would never find her. Then Aspectu had a vision of Rose at the Harvest Festival. Once we had the right kingdom, it was merely a matter of elimination."

"Wow," Megs said.

Though she was clearly impressed, beside her, Hertz wore a worried expression. "If you needed Rose's help two years ago, then all of this—Natalia and those shade creatures—it must have worsened since then."

Animo nodded grimly. "Avonshere has been in a state of decline for years. Natalia has become a paranoid tyrant. The slightest sniff of rebellion ends in execution. Losing the past two years will force plans forward faster than we'd hoped."

I pursed my lips but didn't interject. Animo knew our deal only went as far as Apsectu. I had to trust he was honorable enough to keep his word.

He set aside his bread. "We had hoped Rose could train with Aspectu. But with her coming of age in four months, our timeline is a bit shorter."

"What do you mean?" Megs asked.

"If Rose returns to Avonshere when she is eighteen, it will only strengthen her image," he said. "Underage, Natalia could contest her becoming queen, claiming she should remain as a regent to guide Rose. But as an adult, Rose will have every right to the throne."

"But Rose *is* of age," Megs argued. "You come of age at sixteen."

"Actually, in Avonshere, we come of age at eighteen," I told her.

Hertz burst out laughing, pointing at the slack-jawed Megs. "You're still a child!"

"Don't start, Baldwick!"

I smiled, leaning back against the bridge railing. Only a few months ago, we had celebrated Megs's joyous ascension into adulthood. Seeing all of that ripped away from her brought a pleasure that only a best friend could enjoy.

"That's ridiculous," she snapped. "Absolutely ridiculous. You don't have to be eighteen to be of age."

"Please." Ketch laughed. "You think that's bad? Dwarves don't come of age until we're thirty-five. And then we can't get married until we're forty."

"Forty?" Hertz gawked. "That seems excessive."

Ketch shrugged. "Many would agree with you. It's not uncommon for underage dwarves to elope in another kingdom."

"What about elves?" Megs asked, turning the conversation back to Animo. "When do they come of age?"

"We don't really come of age. But the older an elf gets, the more respect they gain." He looked between her and Hertz. "You know that there was a time when the land was one kingdom instead of twelve, don't you?"

Megs nodded. "It was… En… En-something."

"Enia," Animo said. "During the Reign of Enia, elves lived for thousands of years. They were both keepers of knowledge and powerful warriors. Then the Dark War began, the monarchy fell, and evil took control. The oldest, most powerful elves attempted to fight, but they were no match for the enemy. Only one Ancient Elf survived: Aspectu Demore."

"The woman we're to see," Hertz said.

Animo nodded. "She is the oldest elf in the Twelve Kingdoms and the only one left who remembers the Reign of Enia."

"Wait, they were *all* killed in the Dark War?" Megs asked. "Not one other elf survived? How is that possible?"

"Others survived the Dark War. But over the past thousand years… There have been more battles for elves to fight. Not all of them end in victory." He tilted his head, an awkward sort of smile crossing his face. "I realize this began with a question about when elves come of age, and to answer that I would say a century. Maybe two."

"Oh, okay," Megs said. "Um, what about your weddings? Are they… nice?"

"They tend to be lovely. The ceremonies are generally quite small. It's not about show, nor is it about the age of those involved. For elves, it's about two people swearing to be together for eternity." His expression shifted, turning somber. "It's the same vow humans make—until death parts us. Only, for elves, it means everything. There's no breaking that vow, no matter how many ages may pass." There was beauty in his words, yet his tone held regret I couldn't explain.

"That sounds nice," Hertz said.

Animo nodded but didn't respond.

"I imagine I'd get sick of him." Megs rolled over so her chin was propped on her hands and her legs were stuck in the air.

"Good thing you aren't an elf," Ketch said. "If you get married you'll only have to deal with your husband for, what, fifty years?" He let out a laugh, shaking his head. "You humans and your short lifespans."

She shot to her knees—practically eye level with the dwarf. "Who says I'll die at sixty-six?!"

"Who says you're getting married at sixteen?" Ketch countered.

The conversation quickly divulged into an argument over average lifespans and potential causes of death, led by Megs and Ketch with occasional contributions from Hertz. The three were so wrapped up in their bickering that they didn't notice Animo slip away from the campsite. He wandered to the horses still hitched to the cart a little ways from our camp.

Something about his posture seemed… different. Vulnerable, almost. His strange look of sadness gnawed at my mind. It was none of my business, and I doubted he wanted to talk about it—least of all with me—but my curiosity wouldn't let go.

Against my better judgment, I joined him by the horses. He looked up, and I realized that I hadn't the slightest idea what to say.

"Why do weddings bother you?" I blurted. *Kingdoms, why is that the question you chose?*

He sighed, gaze falling as he stroked Minette's nose.

"You seemed bothered," I said as if my continued speaking would make things less uncomfortable. "As though the topic… Were you…?" My voice trailed off. I had no right prying into his personal life.

"No, Rose." He lifted his eyes to mine. "I have never been married, attempted to be married, nor had my love stolen away."

"I wasn't—I mean, it's fine if you were—I'm not—" My cheeks flushed as I babbled.

"Well, I haven't. But I know someone who is." He paused before continuing. "There's an Aesin word spoken during an elven wedding. It means *lover, soulmate, mine for eternity*, and a thousand other things that Common words can't describe. Elves swear to be with one another for all the days of their endless lives. It's not a vow to be taken lightly."

"So your friend made that vow, but it was what? A mistake?"

"That's what I'm afraid of." He clenched his fist, letting it rest against Minette's withers. "People think that Daria is a hidden paradise of magic and wonder, but they're wrong. It's a prison masquerading as beauty. The more you give yourself to the lies, the tighter they bind you. Your mother was lucky to escape it when she did."

"Did you know her?" The question slipped out before I could think it through. My mother rarely spoke about Daria, and she almost never discussed those she had known.

"She was a friend of someone close to me."

My heart leaped. "Who?"

"My friend." He sighed, the sadness settling in his eyes. "But now my friend is married, and she will never leave Daria."

"That's why you're upset? She's trapped?"

He nodded.

"At least she's trapped in love," I offered.

He scoffed. "If love is a trap, it isn't love."

"At least she's happy."

"A happy prisoner is still a prisoner."

"And a lonely free man is still lonely," I shot back.

He raised an eyebrow. "I take it you're lacking where love is concerned."

I folded my arms. "It's difficult to find someone when your entire identity is a lie." Not to mention the issue of my immortality.

"Then stop lying."

I laughed sharply. "You're certainly one to talk. Do you expect me to believe that you don't have piles of secrets and lies?"

"I have enough to bury us both. And I have my reasons for keeping them. But you have a chance to come clean of all that. You can save a *kingdom*. Then you can find someone and live out your happy little fantasies together."

"If my hypothetical man knew the truth, he'd leave."

Animo ran his fingers through Minette's mane. "If I've learned one thing, it's that people love lies. They're like a drug that makes you forget about the knives in your back. But eventually, the guise fades—believe me, it always fades—and you're left bleeding out on the ground, alone because you never trusted anyone with the truth."

The darkness of his words sent a chill down my spine.

"Some will run when the truth comes out. But they don't matter. They were never really yours—just another person addicted to the lies." He nodded to where our companions sat laughing, their faces lit by candlelight. "It's the people who stay despite all the nightmares of the truth. They're the ones that truly matter."

My gaze locked on Megs and Hertz. I had lied to them for years, yet they were here with me, ready to fight for a cause they knew nothing about. All because of me.

"Don't waste them," Animo said.

"I won't," I vowed. "I'll protect them with my life."

He studied me. I could sense a question on the tip of his tongue, but it never came.

The chirping of crickets filled the silence between us. Suddenly uncomfortable meeting Animo's eyes, I shifted my attention to the restrictor cuff, now speckled with dried mud.

"You know," I began, holding out my wrist so Animo could see, "if you were to unlock this, I could fix the bridge in no time."

A smile flicked across his lips. "That's staying on until you meet Aspectu."

"I agreed to go with you to Medea."

"You've also tried to kill me. Thrice."

"Twice."

"I distinctly remember three times."

I huffed lightly. *So much for the moment.* "Weren't you just talking about trust?"

"I said *you* should be more trusting. I've already dug my grave. There's nothing I can do to change that now."

"Fine," I said, turning away. "I'm going to get some sleep. We'll need an early start if we're relying on mere hands to get us back on the road."

A REIGN DESTROYED

A thousand eyes watched me, scrutinizing my every movement. The desire to hide rose within me, but I forced my back to straighten as I continued down the carpeted aisle. They could stare all they liked. This was my family's throne room—I belonged there.

At the end of the aisle stood a dias, boasting a pair of silver thrones. My grandfather, King James Wolfe, stood before his throne, a crown of sapphires and diamonds anointing his head and a white wolf by his side.

My eyes locked on the crown. In a few moments, it would pass to my father, and he would become the King of Avonshere.

Reaching the carpet's end, I stepped aside, standing opposite the wolf, Zevre. My grandfather met my gaze for a moment, a smile gracing his lips before he faced the crowd once more.

All eyes turned as the double doors creaked open, revealing my father. A cloak of blue velvet fell over his shoulders like a moonlit waterfall. His hand rested on the cracked griffin claw that protruded from the hilt of his sword, Inbane. Despite his regal attire, his golden curls were bare as they awaited the coming coronation.

The court bowed as my father passed, his cloak dragging behind him. My mother followed, draped in the same shade of Avonsheran blue. Her lips held a smile as she walked, watching my father go before her. Pride filled her gaze—this was the day my father had spent his entire life preparing for.

Reaching the dais, he knelt before my grandfather while my mother stepped to the side. The people sat and my grandfather removed the crown from his own head, holding it above my father's.

He spoke, his voice resonating throughout the throne room. "Prince Leon Wolfe of Avonshere, you kneel before your people to take the oath of a king. Is this a vow you are willing to make?"

"It is," my father replied.

"Do you vow to be the protector of your kingdom, willing to sacrifice your life for those you serve?"

"I vow it."

"And do you vow to be a leader and to forge only paths that will reward your people?"

"I vow it."

"Do you, Leon Wolfe, vow to uphold the principles of your ancestors and the ways of our divine guardian, Cisin?"

"I vow it."

"Then, with my power as king, I pass the crown to you and relinquish my claim to the throne." My grandfather placed the crown on my father's head. "Rise, Leon Wolfe, King of Avonshere."

Applause broke out as my father rose, turning to face the sea of smiling faces that looked up at their new leader. My grandfather stepped aside, providing space for my mother to join my father before the thrones.

My father took her hand. "Kneel, my love." She knelt before him as a page stepped forward with the queen's crown. My father took the sparkling circlet of diamonds and held them above her head. "Emry Wolfe, you kneel before your people—"

The doors burst open. Shocked cries rippled throughout the court, shifting to rumorous whispers as they took in the woman responsible. Her dark hair was tangled and her black dress torn and smeared with blood and dirt. Scratches marred her fair skin, and her brown eyes flickered with dark fury. Behind her lay the bodies of guards, their armor shattered and stained red.

The ring of steel echoed throughout the room, as knights drew their swords, rushing to create a barrier between Natalia and the dias. Zevre growled, her ears flattened.

"Happy day for the Wolfes." Natalia's voice dripped with loathing as she strode down the aisle. Despite her rabid appearance, she carried herself with regality, her shoulders straight and chin held high.

"Natalia," my father warned, his fingers wrapped around Inbane's hilt. "You are not welcome in Del Hera. As your king—"

A sharp laugh drowned out his words. "My king," Natalia hissed. "You stripped me of my title and threw me to the rats. You are no king of mine."

"You abandoned your duty!"

I flinched at the anger in my father's voice. Beside him, my mother tensed, her fingers poised to conjure a spell. I gripped the dagger hanging around my waist.

Natalia shook her head. "No. I traded it for something better." She raised her hands, calling tendrils of pure dark magic to her palms. "Power."

My mother stepped forward, summoning her own magic in turn. Golden threads formed in her palm, winding themselves into a ball. The power she held was for healing and creating, whereas the power Natalia wielded was meant for one thing only: destruction.

Natalia flicked her hand, and the energy morphed, shooting from her fingertips like a barrage of arrows. The magic flew—straight through my grandfather's heart. Screams erupted as he fell to his knees, blood bubbling from his mouth. Zevre howled, bounding to his side. He leaned against her, a hand pressed to her back.

Chaos descended. People fought to reach the doors, while my father drew his sword, his eyes darting between Natalia and his dying father.

My mother threw a sphere of magical energy at Natalia, who deflected it with a flick of her wrist, sending it crashing into the ceiling. Stone crumbled, falling in heavy chunks and smashing into the fleeing crowd.

The aisle ran crimson, and the screams rose. Survivors pushed their way through the wreckage, only to find the doors blocked by rubble.

Knights swarmed Natalia, keeping her at bay, but only for a moment. Her magical attacks tore through their armor as if it were parchment. One by one they fell into the mosaic of bodies.

Zevre charged at Natalia, teeth bared. The witch threw a spell at the ceiling, sending more chunks raining down. One struck Zevre, and she fell with a yelp.

My mother threw herself over me, protecting my body with her own. I hugged her tight, bits of rubble peppering my skin as the remainder of the ceiling collapsed.

Finally, the barrage stopped. My mother rose, simultaneously pulling me to my feet and pushing me behind her.

"Don't look, darling." Her words were too late.

My gaze ran over the throne room, now a wasteland of dust and blood. Only a few civilians still moved, weakly wading through the rubble that blocked the doors. Zevre whined, her leg trapped beneath stone and a scarlet handprint marring her snowy coat. She scrabbled at the rubble, fighting to reach a large slab slick with—My grandfather, I realized. He'd been crushed. *In the center of it all stood Natalia, hunched over with her back to us.*

My father raced to our side, grabbing my mother's arms.

"Take Rose and flee," he commanded, blood dripping from his temple.

Pain flooded my mother's eyes. She gripped his bicep, but didn't protest.

He drew away, embracing me for a single moment and whispering in my ear, "Don't look back."

I gripped him tighter. Don't leave me.

He pushed me away, brushing his thumb over my mother's cheek. Not a word was spoken, yet everything was said.

Wiping away her tears, my mother took my hand, and we ran to a tapestry on the back wall. She pushed the hanging aside to open a trapdoor.

Don't look back. *But I did.*

There stood my father, alone against Natalia. All the knights were dead, and Zevre lay, unmoving on the ground. Still, my father faced her, cloak tattered, blood caked against his skin, and sword in hand.

Natalia hurled a bolt of magic. It exploded against my father's chest, sending him flying backward, landing with the sharp crack of breaking bones. The crown fell from his head, rolling down the hill of rubble.

I screamed, surging forward.

"Rose!" My mother caught my arm, and I stumbled.

I sobbed, reaching out to my father's smoking body. His chest rose in labored breaths as blood seeped from his wounds. I fell to my knees, my outstretched hand closing around the only thing it could reach—his crown.

Natalia's eyes met mine for a split second before my mother pulled me into the tunnel, sealing the door behind us.

"Cover your ears," she whispered, lifting me into her arms.

I clamped my hands over my ears, letting the crown's points jab my cheek as tears rolled. Screams rose then fell, growing fainter and fainter as my mother ran through the tunnel.

My grandfather, my father, my people—all dead. I closed my eyes, and the screams shifted into a howl.

It took a few seconds for me to realize the wolf's howls weren't in my dream. Opening my eyes, I found Megs sitting up and clutching her blanket, her wide eyes darting about the dark swamp.

"It's a red wolf."

She flinched at my voice. "Kingdoms," she breathed. "I thought you were asleep."

"It woke me as well." I paused, listening to the howls. "You don't need to be afraid. That wolf isn't here to hurt us."

She laughed shakily. "What? Do elves speak wolf now?"

"No, but my family raised wolves. I don't speak their language, but I learned to understand some of their tones."

"You had pet wolves?" Realization dawned in her eyes. "Is that why you've never shot one?"

I nodded. "During the Dark War, my ancestors were protected by a pack of wolves led by the first divine guardian, the shapeshifter Cisin. They became part of the pack, and after Cisin helped end the war, the wolves joined my family in Avonshere. Our bloodlines have been bound together ever since. They weren't our pets—they were friends and companions." The image of Zevre covered in blood flashed through my mind. "When Del Hera fell, they were lost."

Megs's silence urged me on.

"My grandparents were fair and just rulers. When my father came to them asking to marry for love, they agreed. Natalia should have been happy with that. She had been freed from a loveless engagement, but she didn't care about freedom. She wanted *power*. She could have killed the king and been done with it, but that wasn't enough to satisfy her darkness. She killed my grandfather, who had abdicated and my cousins with hardly any Wolfe blood in their veins"—I laughed, more in pain than humor—"She even went after my grandmother, who was on death's door in a healing monastery. But did it end there? No.

"War ensued. My mother assembled the Ardent Pack to fight Natalia. *Thousands* of men and women joined, fighting for *two years*, only to die one by one because Natalia is too powerful. She was stronger than us then, and she is stronger than us now. It's hopeless."

My eyes met Megs's, only to find her gaze filled with terror. Guilt rushed over me.

"Megs, I'm—"

"I'm fine. I think I should go back to sleep now. Good night, Rose." She lay down, turning her back to me.

For a while, I sat there letting the noise of night replace the memory of screams. The hum of the swamp and gentle laps of water harmonized with the restful breathing of my companions—but one wasn't asleep. Despite her steady breaths, I knew Megs's eyes were wide open. She wouldn't sleep a wink tonight, and neither would I.

CITY OF SHOW

Medea appeared like a mirage in the desert. We stood at the edge of the swamp, looking out at a massive stone island surrounded by a wall. The tops of gothic buildings peeked over the wall, reflecting sunlight like a beacon. A single bridge led to the city gates, arching above deep, green waters.

"It's more beautiful than I imagined," Megs gushed.

Ketch and Animo exchanged a knowing look as they unloaded our bags from the cart.

"What?" I asked, more than happy to divert my eyes from the gleaming city.

"Medea knows how to put on a show," Animo said carefully. "You see what they want you to see."

"And what *don't* they want us to see?"

"What we're looking for." He handed me a knapsack before shoving the empty cart through a patch of broken railing and into the swamp. It landed with a splash, slowly sinking between two trees rooted in muck.

"Care to explain to me why this is productive?" Hertz asked.

"We're covering our tracks," Animo replied, removing Arthur's and Minette's bridles.

Hertz's brows rose skeptically. "Do you really think Natalia will be able to track us because of our *cart?*"

"Better to be safe than dead," Ketch pitched in.

With one last pet of each, Animo released Arthur and Minette. As they trotted back down the bridged path, we turned our attention to Medea. The wooden planks we walked on quickly shifted into a bridge of pure, white stone sprinkled with gemstones. Though they shimmered in the sunlight, their shine was nothing compared to the steady glow of the mortar. *No, not mortar,* I realized. The paving stones were held together with *gold.*

"What kind of city is this?" I muttered.

We passed through the open gates of Medea and into a throng of men and women decked out in finery. Colorful feathers were woven into their hair and masks were strapped to their faces. They watched us like jungle cats on the prowl, their lips and eyelids coated in glitter.

"Why does everyone look like they ran off and joined the circus?" Hertz asked under his breath, his eyes pinned on a man in a suit trimmed with what I could only assume were dragon scales.

I bit back a laugh as we passed a woman whose low-cut gown had been constructed entirely with peacock feathers.

"This is the fashion capital of the Twelve Kingdoms!" Megs hissed.

I snorted. There were at least seven other so-called *fashion capitals* in the Twelve Kingdoms. Medea was simply the closest to Chess—and probably the most gaudy.

"This is meant to be fashion?" Hertz choked, a little too loud, earning himself a glare from a nearby woman, whose ruffled gown dripped with glass baubles.

Megs huffed, quickening her pace to walk alongside Animo and Ketch.

"I'm right, aren't I?" Hertz asked.

I looked around. I'd always heard of Medea's wealth; people paraded about from various parties, draped in fine fabrics, while the night sky exploded with grand displays of fireworks. Captured in a painting, it was a beautiful scene. In reality, it was a blinding mess strangled in silk.

"You're absolutely right," I replied.

Ahead, Animo beckoned for us to join him. Once we were within earshot, he said, "Aspectu was to leave me a message when she arrived. It will tell us the location of her safe house. In the meantime, you three should go with Ketch and find us a place to stay for the night." His attention shifted to the dwarf. "Try the Seventh Moon."

"Sounds nice," Megs said, a smile lifting her lips.

Ketch laughed. "It's not. But the locks work, and they have good ale."

"I'll meet you there in an hour," Animo said before disappearing into the crowd.

"This way." Ketch gestured for us to follow him.

Shops ran down one side of the city's main street while the other side bordered a green canal. Gondolas floated down, pushed along by men in crow-like masks, their eyes obscured by darkened glass plates. Understandable, considering the gold grout continued through the city roads and served as mortar for the buildings, giving the shadeless city an excruciatingly bright shine.

Medea's crowds quickly became a hassle, especially with Ketch in the lead. He soon turned to elbowing people in the knees to create a path, earning us several sharp glares and providing a thorough introduction to Lucian swears.

Eventually, the road sloped downward, and the crowd began to thin. Lights dimmed as the gold mortar dulled. A rotten stench tickled my nose. Was it coming from the canal? I glanced over at the water—not a single gondolier rowed by.

It's all a show.

"How much farther?" Megs glanced over her shoulder, the spark in her eye gone. The bright city had faded, leaving us a bland and empty part of Medea with a smattering of holes in the ground where gemstones used to sit.

"We're almost there," Ketch said.

I fell into step beside him. "I'm not sure I like this city."

"Only those in the first circle do," he replied.

"Circle?"

"Medea is broken into three circles," he explained. "Like this—" He formed a circle with his hands. "This is the third circle." He tightened it, letting his top fingers overlap but keeping his thumbs in the same place. "Then the second." He made the circle even smaller. "And finally, the first and innermost circle. The point we entered is a convergence point of sorts. We were in the first circle, but directly behind those shops was the second."

"What's the difference between them all?"

"The first circle is where the rich indulge in festivities and shopping until their wallets give out. The second is where we are now." Ketch waved his hands at the increasingly depressing buildings. "This is where most of the workers live—servants, apprentices, and just about anyone whose dowry is smaller than their ego. It may not be pretty here, but it could be a lot worse. Stomachs stay full of food and usually free of knives."

"And the third circle?"

He cocked his head, an eyebrow raised. "That's a different story. The third circle is run by thieves who feed off of the rich and loot the corpses disposed of in the canal. But don't worry," he added before I could question his reference to *corpses in the canal*. "If we keep our heads down, we won't have to worry about any of that."

He led us on for another minute before stopping at a run-down building, with dark and grimy windows. Its faded sign swung in the hot breeze and read *Seventh Moon Inn & Tavern*.

"I'll handle the talking," he said, pulling on the lowest of three door handles. It swung open, washing us in the stench of old ale. Darkness hung over the tavern despite the afternoon hour. Timid flames flickered on the half-melted candles scattered across the tables, providing the room's only light.

Two categories divided the pub's few patrons: those who sat alone, drinking away their morning sorrows, and those in clusters, half awake and fully drunk, their feathered headpieces hanging by a thread. Neither group was one I hoped to spend time with.

"This is the place you chose?" Hertz muttered angrily, pulling Megs closer to his side.

"It's better than the competition," Ketch replied. "Wait here, and don't talk to anyone."

We hovered by the door while Ketch approached the bar. After a quick exchange, he returned carrying three brass keys.

"Rose and Megs, room 204,"—he handed me the key—"Hertz, room 205,"—Hertz took a similar key—"and Animo and I are in room 207." The final key, he tucked into his vest. "Try not to lose them."

I nodded, sliding the key into my pocket.

We made our way to the second floor, separating into our assigned rooms. After a short struggle with the rusty lock, the door to room 204 creaked open. Inside sat two beds with a dresser crammed between them. Above the dresser loomed an open window, the canal's stench streaming in.

I tossed a bag of supplies onto the bed. "Well, I despise everything about this."

"It's not… so bad."

I stared at Megs. "Name one thing good about this place."

"We each have our own bed."

Rolling my eyes, I slammed the window shut.

"All right, fine, it's not a *nice* inn," she admitted, drawing a fresh change of clothes from her bag. "But we only have to sleep here. During the day, we can go back to the city." Her eyes lit up. "We could go shopping!"

"I'm sorry?"

"You don't want to stay here, and I want to see the city." She shrugged. "Besides, you could use a new outfit."

I looked down at my muddy and oversized attire. "I can't believe I'm saying this, but you're right. We can shop, but only if we convince Hertz and Ketch to come along."

Megs beamed.

My attempt to freshen up fell short, as there was only so much a wet cloth could do against days of dried mud and sweat. While Megs changed into a clean black dress with a sloping skirt, I was left with a dirt-flecked tunic and soggy boots.

After a bit of wheedling from Megs, both Ketch and Hertz agreed to shop with us.

Our first stop was a pawnshop on the edge of the second circle. While Megs tried on an array of masks, I assembled a practical outfit reminiscent of my hunting garb: an olive green shirt with short sleeves to accommodate the Lucian heat, a brown, lace-up bodice, simple pants, and a pair of gloves connected to leather arm bracers. It was a tight fit over the restrictor cuff, but worth it to have that ugly piece of steel out of my sight.

Ketch paid the tab while I changed, and then we were off to the heart of Medea, where the sights and smells were far more elite. Megs pulled us through shop after shop of glittering jewelry and voluminous gowns, gasping and squealing at the extravagant displays. It wasn't until Hertz reminded her of the size of her coin purse that she agreed to move past the finery. Stepping away from the spectacle, we found our way to a little shop on the edge of the first circle, perfectly balanced between glamor and affordability.

"I'll wait out here in case Animo comes looking for us," Ketch said, planting himself in a small alcove next to the door. "We're in a decent part of town, but I'd still keep an eye on your wallets."

Hertz instinctively touched the pouch on his belt.

Ketch grimaced. "Don't do that. Just—don't."

"Let's go." Megs pulled me and a confused Hertz into the shop.

Two women browsed in the back. One of them, a blonde in a surprisingly practical pair of pants, tried on a jade-and-pearl necklace, while the other, a slim girl with dark hair, watched.

"Rose, look at this." Megs drew me over to a case of rings, pointing to one set with an emerald. "Wouldn't that look amazing on me?"

"It would. But please keep in mind that it would take every coin you have to buy it."

"Might I recommend our glass jewels?" the shopkeeper suggested, swooping into our conversation. He guided us to a nearby display with necklaces, bracelets, and rings as grand and glittering as the rest. "Each piece is crafted with glass to replicate a rare gemstone. However, if you wish to have a real stone, we do have some more common options." He waved a hand at a small case of rings and necklaces. "Amethyst and agate are our bestsellers. They carry the beauty of a diamond but at the price of glass."

Hertz stepped forward, examining the display of common stones although Megs had long since stopped paying attention. Her eyes were locked on a lookalike emerald set in a golden band.

The shopkeeper smiled, opening the case so she could try the ring on.

I stepped backward, only to collide with a small figure. "Oh!" I turned awkwardly, finding the dark-haired girl at my elbow. "I'm so sorry, I didn't see you there."

"Don't worry about it," she said, her voice soft like a newborn kitten. She stepped aside, her bangs nearly obscuring her dark eyes as she watched Megs wiggle her ringed finger in the light.

"Belinda!" the blond woman snapped, her glare fixed on the girl.

Belinda retreated to the blond woman's side, muttering, "I'm sorry, Ali."

Ali said something I couldn't hear although her cross expression provided a few clues.

The shop door opened, and a man with brown hair and a faint beard stepped in. Ali's eyes lit up. "Ruger," she crooned, extending an arm.

He stepped into her embrace, pulling her close. Ali's hand slipped around his waist, then into his coat pocket, along with a flash of pearls.

My jaw dropped. *Thieves.*

I turned to alert the shopkeeper, but a hand landed on my arm.

"Don't worry about them," Animo murmured. "Jewelry's a petty theft. It will be forgotten by tomorrow morning."

"So we just ignore it?" I hissed, watching as Ali adjusted Ruger's coat. How many precious gems was she tucking away with each movement?

"Yes. We ignore it because it is none of our business. We have more important matters to attend to. For example, your listening abilities."

"What of them?"

"I told you to stay at the inn."

I rolled my eyes, facing him with a huff. "That place was a death trap disguised as a tavern."

"Decrepit and death trap are two different things," he replied. "The Seventh Moon is in the second ring, which makes it one of the safest places around. We'd be robbed in the first ring and murdered in the third. No one really cares about the second."

I'd never admit it, but his logic was sound. Why rob average travelers when there were mansions two blocks over?

"Look!" Megs thrust her hand between Animo and me, showing off the sparkling ring on her finger. "It looks like a real emerald, doesn't it?"

"Indeed it does." I nodded as Hertz joined us, casting one last look at the display cases.

"You'll want to take that off where we're headed," Animo told Megs. His gaze flicked to me. "Aspectu's safe house is in the third ring."

THE THIRD RING

The crowded beauty of Medea faded as passed through the second ring. Color slipped from the world, and the stench swelled, pressing against us like a rancid fog.

"So, this Aspectu," Megs began as we passed the Seventh Moon, "just how old is she?"

"Megs," Hertz chided.

"What?" She shrugged. "I think it's a reasonable question."

"Aspectu is one of the oldest beings in the Twelve Kingdoms," Animo replied. "That's all you need to know."

"What about you, elf man?" She jumped up onto the stone railing that bordered the canal and took long swinging steps. "How old are you?"

"Is that relevant?" he asked.

"Is that a proper answer?" she countered, brows arched.

Animo smiled, avoiding eye contact with her. With his gaze diverted, I let my attention settle on his face. He appeared to be in his early twenties, not quite old enough for his elvish nature to stall aging. Then again, elves' bodies stopped aging when they reached their physical peak…

I averted my eyes. *Oh, no. I will not explore that path.*

Ketch chuckled. "You won't get anything out of him. His past is like the canal below." He wrinkled his nose. "Better not to dive into it."

"Thank you, Ketch, for that vivid illustration," Animo said dryly.

"It certainly didn't plant any ideas in Megs's head," I added, my tone laced with sarcasm.

She smirked, her eyes twinkling with scheming glory. She lifted herself onto her toes, practically leaping along the wall.

Ketch shrugged innocently. "Oh well."

"What about your scar?"

I cringed as Megs turned, walking backward as she pointed at the tear-like mark beneath Animo's left eye.

"Where'd you get that?" she asked.

All traces of humor disappeared from Animo's face as he replied, "The foulest beast to ever walk the Twelve Kingdoms."

Megs's eyes widened "A dragon?"

"Dragons are not foul!" Ketch exclaimed. "They are highly intelligent and loyal creatures."

"Didn't mean to strike a nerve." She hopped off the rail, allowing me to release the anxious breath I'd been holding.

"Ketch is fond of anything that can fly and shoot flames at the same time," Animo said. "This way."

He took a sharp turn, leading us down a dank alley. Water dripped from clogged gutters into the flooded pathway. Places like this should be avoided like the plague.

Welcome to the third ring.

Garbage floated around our ankles as we sloshed past rows of dark windows and barred doors. The water climbed higher with every step, lapping around our knees as we reached our destination—a small house with boarded-up windows and rotting walls.

Grasping a broken piece of railing, Animo hauled himself onto the porch, splashing us with droplets of rank water. He rapped on the door. "Aspectu?"

I joined him on the porch, pulling Ketch up as Animo knocked again.

"Aspectu! Where are you?" he muttered, peering through the grimy window.

"Maybe she's out," Hertz offered.

"She wouldn't," Animo said firmly. "She knew that we were coming."

"Well, she's doing a poor job of answering the door," I said.

Animo glared, pulling a thin pouch from his pocket. "Keep watch."

"What are you doing?" I asked.

He selected a thin, metal rod with a hook at the end and a flat piece bent in an L shape. "I'm getting us inside," he replied, slipping the tools into the lock. After a moment of fiddling, the lock clicked open.

"That was fast," Megs said.

Ketch scoffed. "Please. I know half a dozen pirates that could put his time to shame."

Animo shoved the door open. "Everyone, inside."

We filed in, Animo taking the rear. He closed the door behind him, plunging us into darkness. With a scrape and a hiss, he lit a match, casting his face in an eerie, yellow glow and providing us a meager look at Aspectu's lodgings.

A skeleton of a house sat before us, with a plain wood table, overturned chairs, and a cold hearth. Cabinet doors hung open and shattered pieces of dishes lay scattered on the floor.

"What happened here?" Ketch nudged a broken plate with the toe of his boot, his expression dark.

"Nothing good." Animo strode across the room and tore down the curtains, launching a cloud of dust into the air. I winced, raising my hand against the rush of sunlight.

"A little warning next time," Ketch requested, rubbing his eyes.

Animo swore.

"I know," Ketch said, blinking heavily. "I, too, remember a time when I could see."

"Ketch," Animo growled through gritted teeth. "Look."

We followed his gaze to the wall behind us. Splinters jutted from the claw marks that tore across the wall, ending before a knife wedged in the wood, its blade stained black.

"What did that?" Megs breathed.

Animo ripped the knife from the wall. "Shade blood." He threw the blade aside, and it landed with a clatter.

"Oh no." I pushed past Animo to where the knife lay before a dull, copper stain.

"Is that—?" Hertz began.

"Blood," I finished. The blood of Aspectu Demore.

CHANGING PATHS

We returned to the Seventh Moon with more questions than answers. There was no sign of forced entry into Aspectu's house, yet there had clearly been a struggle. Shades had been injured, as well as someone who bled red, and I wasn't optimistic enough to believe it was a captain.

Animo had searched every part of Aspectu's house with an obsessive passion, but all he found was a small stack of journals hidden under the mattress. There was no note and no body, which meant that Aspectu was either captured or too injured to leave behind a clue. Either way left us with an obscured path.

As soon as we stepped through the Seventh Moon's door, Animo broke away, disappearing up the stairs and leaving Megs, Hertz, Ketch, and me in the tavern.

Ketch glanced at the stairs, then back at us. "Let's get some drinks."

A few minutes later, we were settled around a stained table with full tankards of ale. A handful of other tables were occupied, but no one was drunk enough to cause a ruckus. Yet.

"What should we do now?" Hertz directed the question at Ketch. "Without Aspectu, there's no reason to stay in Medea, is there? We could leave tonight."

Ketch laughed. "Only a fool would leave now. The way out leads us through the third ring, and believe me when I say, you don't want to be there after the sun sets."

"What about the way we came in?" Hertz asked.

"That would take us back to the bridges and force us to go toward Chess."

Hertz looked down at the table. "Right. That's not where we want to go."

"Don't worry," Ketch said, his upbeat mood remarkably undamaged. "Give Animo some time to process everything, and by morning, he'll have a plan."

I took a sip of ale, letting my gaze linger on the wooden cup. Whatever plan Animo made was bound to point us in the direction of Avonshere. Coming to Medea was meant to free me of all this, but now I was stuck in a tavern with two people trying to drag me toward death, and two more willingly running into its arms.

"If we're staying the night, we might as well enjoy ourselves." Megs flashed a smile. "Who's up for a game of bravit?"

A wide grin spread across Ketch's face. "You are going to regret that idea."

"Big words from such a small man," Megs said, retrieving a deck of cards from her boot pocket.

"Says the girl who needs help reaching the top shelf of a base cabinet." Hertz said, punctuating his sentence with a sip of ale.

Ketch burst out laughing as Megs's jaw dropped. She pointed a finger at Hertz. "You're dead, Baldwick."

He leaned forward. "Deal the cards, and we'll find out."

Without breaking eye contact with him, Megs shuffled the worn deck, then dealt five cards to each of us. We played hand after hand. Insults flew across the table as an ever-growing pile of coins passed between us. The stream of patrons in the tavern ebbed and flowed, each group getting drunker than the last. We kept a low profile at our table in the corner, leaving us mostly undisturbed and free to gamble for as long as we liked.

"I challenge your bet of three mynet and will raise you five," Ketch said, dropping his coins on the tabletop. Resting his chin on his laced fingers, he stared down Megs. "What do you say to that?"

She narrowed her eyes, keeping her cards close. "I say we break." She spread her cards on the table. "Knight's call, blades."

Ketch stared at the cards, his mouth ajar and brow furrowed. "Oh, rack. That's horrible… Oh, wait—" He smacked down four cards in the same suit and in a row. "Dragon's Bane, three through six."

"No!"

"Yes!" He clapped his hands together, grinning as he scraped the coins over to him. "Time to pay up, Mohler."

"Not so fast." Hertz laid down his cards. "Dragon's bane, shields, one through four."

"Ha!" Megs barked, pointing a finger at Ketch. "You lose!"

"So do you," I pointed out. I'd called out in the first round, having been dealt a useless array of face cards. *Stupid fae.* Bravit was the only card game in the Twelve Kingdoms where the lower cards won, and it was all due to ego.

Twelve heroes won the Dark War and were rewarded with their own kingdoms to rule. But that wasn't enough. They needed their faces immortalized on playing cards, which led to a *council* meeting to negotiate which eight rulers would be assigned the king and queen face cards and which four would be demoted to knaves. In a show of *humility*, the original fae queen, along with other cunning rulers, offered to take the knave cards, only to reinvent the already popular game of bravit so that the lowest cards won the hand.

Thanks to the pride and pettiness of rulers a thousand years ago, I was left with an empty coin purse. At least it was Hertz who won the game. Since I was abducted, I'd had to borrow my buy-in from him, so this would count as repayment.

"Let's play again," Megs said, gathering the cards.

Hertz shook his head, filling his coin purse. "I'm calling out."

"Oh, come on!" She pouted. "Quitting after a win is such craven behavior."

"It's smart," he replied, unbothered by her insult.

"Don't worry, Megs, you can still lose to me." Ketch grinned, his dilated pupils glittering like his black diamond earring in the low candlelight.

"You think you can beat me?" She gave the cards a shuffle, quickly running them back across her fingers to prevent bending. "Game on. Buy-in is two mynet."

"Get ready to lose, Mohler," he taunted, tossing his coins on the table. Megs dealt the cards, but before the game could begin, Animo barreled down the stairs.

"Drop what you're doing," he said, pulling up a chair.

"That's not the way to play bravit," Ketch replied. He held his cards up to his nose, peering over their brims. "You keep the cards hidden until it's time to win."

"Right, well, we're not leaving." Animo dropped a notebook onto the table.

I halted the cup halfway to my lips. "I beg your pardon?"

"We're not leaving Lucia." Animo's eyes glittered with excitement. "Not yet."

"Why in Kingdoms' names not?" I demanded, setting the mug down.

"Aren't we being hunted?" Hertz asked, voicing my thoughts.

Ignoring him, Animo said, "I found something in Aspectu's notes. Look at this."

We leaned in as he flipped open the notebook. He pointed at a sketch of an elegant staff with a twisting body and prongs that formed a sort of cage around a large jewel.

Animo grinned like a child who'd just opened a gift. "It's the Staff of Realms."

"I've heard of that." I pulled the notebook closer, examining it with new-found interest. "Isn't it an old fae relic?"

"Yes," he said, taking a seat. "It was lost hundreds of years ago. Rumors said it was destroyed, but according to Aspectu's notes, it was recovered nearly a year ago by Count Dorru Triani. Care to guess where he lives?"

"Don't say it," I said.

"Two blocks over." Animo slapped the book. "This is it. This is how we win."

Megs set her cards on the table. "I don't follow. How is a glorified walking stick going to help us?"

"The Staff of Realms gives the wielder power to go anywhere in the Twelve Kingdoms," Animo explained. "With something like that, we could defeat Natalia in the blink of an eye."

I straightened. This *was* it. I could be in and out of Malecare, and no one would have the slightest idea. I wouldn't have to become a queen or hero—I could be an assassin.

"Keep talking," I urged.

A smile tugged at Animo's lips. "We'll have to find a way to get the staff. Collectors never like to part with their prize jewel." He lowered his voice despite the nearly empty tavern. "Although, if a royal were to ask, the Count might be willing to make a deal."

"No," I said, my eyes darting to the idle bartender. "We do this without bringing my name into it."

The door opened and a pair of laughing men entered. Animo leaned in, his voice barely above a whisper. "The Staff of Realms may be our best chance. We have to be willing to do whatever it takes to get it."

The memory of him in Rudane, walking past corpses as though they were patches of grass, surfaced in my mind. "How far are you willing to go?'

"Do you want to win this war?"

"I don't want a war!" I exclaimed. The bartender looked up, and the pair of men began to stare. I shook my head, pushing back my seat. "I'm done."

"Rose—"

"No, Animo," I snapped. "If you have a way to get the staff without bringing my past into it, I'm willing to do it. But I will not start down a path that will end in anyone's death but Natalia's."

"Fine," he said, his posture stiff. "Tomorrow at breakfast, I will have a plan."

"I hope you do." Without another word, I retreated up the stairs and into my room.

I didn't bother to lock the door before falling face-first onto my bed. *I should leave. Leave without a goodbye, and run.* Megs and Hertz would chase me, but eventually, they'd have no choice but to give up and return to Rudane. And now that they knew what was at stake, they could protect the Estmars. It would work, but it wouldn't get me the staff.

I rolled onto my back, staring at the ceiling. *We could defeat Natalia in the blink of an eye.* I'd tried to free Avonshere the noble way, and I had failed. Maybe it was time I embraced the ghost I'd become.

Only, you can't get the staff yourself. You need Animo's help. Would he still be willing to help me if I didn't become queen?

The door opened, and Megs entered. "Rose?"

I closed my eyes, feigning sleep. Fabric rustled as she changed and climbed into bed, the waxy scent of smoke floating through the air as she blew out the candle. Her soft snores soon filled the room, but I remained awake, a million thoughts running through my mind, all of which reached the same conclusion. Natalia must die.

SILK GOWNS AND SECRET PLANS

Morning sunlight bled through a peeling corner of a blackout curtain as I descended the stairs into the quiet tavern. Animo sat, drinking alone at the bar, cuts on his face, and his shirtsleeves rolled up to his elbows, displaying the fresh bandage on his left forearm.

"What happened?" I asked, taking a seat next to him.

"Barfight," he replied simply, setting his drink down. My gaze trailed from the bandage to a dwarvish rune tattooed on his wrist. *I've never noticed that before.*

"You make friends everywhere, don't you?" I waved a hand, signaling to the bartender that I wanted a drink.

"That's why I've broken out of three prisons," Animo replied. "And into one."

"*Into* a prison?"

He took a sip of ale, dismissing the topic completely. "After you left last night, our fortune changed for the better." He passed me a letter, its wax seal already broken.

I opened the envelope, withdrawing a gilded invitation with swooping letters.

By invitation of Countess Josiane Maria Triani, the bearer of this invitation is cordially invited to attend the homecoming gala of Count Dorru Triani on the fifteenth day of Primnen. Don your finest masks and join us for a night of dancing and splendor.

Setting it aside, I pulled a second, smaller piece of parchment from the envelope.

My dear Lashier, I look forward to our business. Let us meet in the fifth-floor study at the twenty-third hour—one of my attendants shall fetch you. Bring diamonds to the sum of 90,000 mynet, and the Staff of Realms will be yours.

Cordially,
Josiane Maria Triani

My jaw dropped. "She's selling the Staff of Realms."

Animo nodded as the bartender passed me my drink. Once he was out of earshot, Animo continued. "Tomorrow night, the staff will go to Lashier. Or whoever holds his invitation."

"You want to impersonate him and buy the staff?" I shook my head. "That will never work. The Countess is bound to know who she's selling to. Not to mention the fact that sooner or later, the real Lashier will notice that his invitation is missing." The image of a faceless nobleman arriving with a brigade of lawmen flashed through my mind. Ale soured in my stomach.

"I'll take care of keeping Lashier away from the gala. And as for being recognized, Lashier himself confirmed that he has never met the Countess. He's never even been to Medea before."

"You spoke with him?" I gawked. "You let the man you intend to impersonate see you?"

"Don't worry. He was too drunk to find his own face in a mirror, much less remember mine."

"Then this is a blind deal between two people with no knowledge of one another's appearances, and the only identification we need is in these letters." I paused thoughtfully. "This might be possible. But we're missing the payment."

"Handled. Ketch is already in contact with a counterfeiter here in the city."

"It shouldn't surprise me that you know a counterfeiter."

"I'm good friends with at least seven, and three more want to rip me apart limb from limb." Animo took the letters, tucking them into his pocket. "It's your choice, Rose. What do you say?"

I hesitated. Ordinarily, I wouldn't condone criminal behavior. But without the Staff of Realms, our crusade was doomed. *The Trianis will survive the loss. Natalia won't.* The thought was all I needed to decide.

I set my shoulders. "Yes."

"Good. I've spoken with Megs, who is more than happy to help with wardrobe—"

"Wardrobe?"

"The meeting is at a gala," he reminded me. "A masquerade, to be exact."

"Why would Countess Triani choose to do business during a party?" I mused.

Animo shrugged. "She's rich in Medea. Chances are she has parties every night. At least this way our faces will be hidden."

"All that means is that there will be feathers drawn on our wanted posters."

"We're only wanted if we're caught having used counterfeit diamonds, which we won't be."

"What if she has a jeweler to inspect them?"

"I've already taken care of that. Last night, I asked around and learned who Countess Triani's favorite jeweler is, and this morning, I sent him a very urgent summons from the King of Lucia. As for the gala, the jeweler will be sending an apprentice in his stead. She's young, redheaded, and willing to lie for you."

"Megs." Unease slithered through me.

"She'll be safe. This plan may be fast, but it's not foolish. I've done this before and can do it again. Now, if you'll excuse me, I need to meet with Ketch and our counterfeiter." He drained his drink and strode out of the tavern.

I remained at the bar, swirling my cup absentmindedly. This plan was as mad as stealing sheep in midday beneath the watchful gaze of the shepherd. But if it worked, my troubles would vanish with a snap of my fingers. It was a risk I had to take.

"Kill me here and now, and I'll die happy." Megs ran her fingers over sheaths of brightly colored silk that hung on the wall of the dressmaker's shop. She held each color up to her face, looking in the full-length mirror to see if the shade complemented her skin and hair.

"Kill me here and now, and I'll die happy that it's over," Hertz muttered.

I scoffed despite sharing his sentiment. As a little girl, I loved new gowns. Standing still for dress fittings was a trial for everyone involved, but the moment it was on me, I'd spin about my quarters, tiara atop my head. Soft silk had brought a smile to my young face, and voluminous petticoats were sure to bring giggles. But now, such luxuries seemed so…*royal*.

"Be grateful," I said, pushing aside thoughts of my younger self. "With her enthusiasm, you won't have to bother choosing your own outfit."

"If that's the case, I can leave now."

I laughed, then realized he was being serious. "You're not leaving." I pulled him to a plush couch, forcing him to sit. "The last thing we need is to lose each other in this city."

Hertz sighed, settling down.

"Rose, look at this," Megs called, holding up a fabric that shimmered like a scarlet ocean. "This would look gorgeous on you."

"Stay here," I ordered, pointing a finger at Hertz before joining Megs at the display. She draped the fabric over my shoulder, holding it across the base of my neck.

"This color is perfect for you! It complements your dark hair, and gold jewelry would bring out your eyes."

"It's a little…" *Bright. Angry. Bloodlike.* Plenty of words came to mind, but I settled on "…bold."

"Ugh, fine." She pulled the fabric away. "I suppose we wouldn't have time for custom dresses, anyway. But let it be known that if you had chosen this color, you would have turned every head in the ballroom."

"Which is exactly why I won't be wearing red. We need to blend in tomorrow, not stand out."

Megs grumbled under her breath but abandoned the red fabric, moving toward a collection of elegant gowns. After a bit of searching, we found the perfect dress for her: green silk and sleeveless, with a gold, cage-like corset rising into a halter top. A pair of winglike flaps hung off the skirt, connecting it to a pair of gold bracelets.

"Oh," she breathed, her eyes wide. "It's beautiful."

"It's not enough to have the gown alone." The thickly accented shopkeeper appeared as if conjured by Megs's interest. She held up a mask decorated with golden pearls. "This gown is best paired with this mask. And may I suggest a pair of sandals? They are comfortable and fashionable and will keep the outfit airy."

"We'll take it!" Megs exclaimed, her cheeks flushed with excitement. "All of it. The gown, the mask, and the sandals."

"Wait." Hertz jumped up from the couch. "What is the price of the dress?"

"Give us one moment, please." Megs smiled at the shopkeeper then dragged Hertz to a corner while I trailed behind.

"Megs, we don't have a lot of money," he began.

"Then what's this?" She held up a hefty coin purse, giving it a shake.

Hertz's eyes widened. "Where did you get that money?"

"Ketch gave it to me."

His expression shifted to one of apprehension. "Is it…"—he lowered his voice—"*real?*"

Megs grinned, then mouthed *no*.

"Megs," Hertz hissed. "We can't rip off innocent shopkeepers."

"No, no, no, the word is *shouldn't*."

"Megs—"

"I agree with her," I said. "If we're going to pull this off, we need to appear as though we have wealth." I wasn't fond of Ketch handing my friend counterfeit money, but I could rationalize the necessity.

Hertz hesitated.

"We'll make things right later," I assured him.

He sighed heavily. "Very well."

Megs squealed, turning to face the shopkeeper. "We'll take it!"

"Excellent!" the woman replied, already packaging the gown.

"Now, we find a dress for you," Megs said, turning back to me.

I eventually settled on a gold dress with a tiered skirt. Despite the ruffles, its light fabric allowed me to run easily. And if the rest of Medea was any indication, the Trianis' manor would have so much gold in it that this dress would practically melt into the walls.

By the time we left the shop—laden with boxes of clothing—dusk had fallen, painting the sky with hues of orange. I had found a mask that matched my dress, and Megs had selected masks and outfits for Animo, Ketch, and Hertz, who, despite being in the shop, had paid no attention to what was bought for him.

"That took longer than I expected," I said as we walked back through the first circle. Already, the Lucian evening had doubled in humidity.

"It was worth it," Megs replied as we strolled through the thinning crowd. "These gowns will make us irresistible."

"You realize attraction is the least of our concerns, don't you?"

"It's called a *benefit*."

"Right." I glanced over my shoulder to find that Hertz had stopped in the middle of the road. "Is everything all right?"

"Fine," he replied. "But you two should continue without me."

"Are you going somewhere?"

"Yes. There's… something I need to do."

"Something you need to do?" Megs's copper brow arched. "You don't know anyone or any*thing* in this city. What could you possibly have to do here?"

"I…" His voice trailed off. "I'll see you at the inn."

Megs spun to face me. "Where is he going?"

I shook my head, watching Hertz disappear into the crowd. "I have no idea."

CHAPTER SIXTEEN

SEVERED

I sat at the table in Animo and Ketch's room, anxiously bouncing my knee. Three hours had passed, and Hertz still hadn't returned. As much as I wanted to look for him, I had nowhere to begin, which left me stuck inside, struggling to listen as Animo outlined tomorrow's plan.

"The Trianis' gala begins at the twenty-second hour," he began. "Medean culture does not value tardiness, so we'll want to arrive at the clock's strike, so we can blend in with the crowd. Now, let's discuss aliases."

He set three invitations on the table.

"Who's Clarissa DeVoe?" Megs asked, her head tilted as she read.

"You are." He slid the gilded invitation toward her. "The real Clarissa is the apprentice of renowned jeweler Damien Wile."

"And this is her actual invitation?" Her eyes skimmed the letter. "How did you get it?"

Ketch stuck his hand in the air. "That was all me. I kept watch at the jeweler's until the postman came and then took the letter as soon as he left."

Animo drew Megs's attention as he spoke, "Now, remember, Megs, as far as the Countess knows, you haven't met any of us. You're there to inspect the diamonds…"

Animo's words faded into a bee-like buzz as my focus settled on Ketch. Just like Animo, the dwarf bore the wounds of a fight. And judging by the amount of bandages wrapped around his arm, the confrontation was vicious. *Strange… if they fought last night, shouldn't there have been evidence in the tavern? Broken windows, overturned tables, fresh stains of liquor or blood—*

"Rose." Animo's voice snapped me back to the present. "Are you listening?"

"Yes, of course."

He raised his eyebrows. "You and I will enter together using Lashier's invitation. Megs will bring Hertz as her guest, and Ketch will use the second invitation he stole."

Ketch straightened. "That one was even easier. I went through the mansions' post boxes until I found one with an invitation. Judging by the amount of mail, Sir Antony Havasaar hasn't been home for some time." He paused. "I hope he isn't dead."

"As long as his name allows you through the doors, we'll be fine," Animo said. "Once you're inside you'll become our treasurer. You'll be watching the diamonds, so keep an eye out for pickpockets."

"Will do."

"All right." Animo stepped back from the table. "Any questions?"

Megs's hand shot up. "Do we bring weapons?"

"Yes. But make certain that they're concealed. We don't want to draw any unnecessary attention to ourselves. During the gala, we will dance, and we will mingle. If anyone asks for your name, you will use your alias. If they ask about your business, you will reply as vaguely as possible while highlighting that it was Countess Triani who sent for you. Is that understood?"

We all nodded.

"Good. You should sleep, and if you see Hertz, send him to me."

Megs and I stood, but Animo held up his hand, keeping me in place. "Rose, will you stay behind for a moment?"

Megs caught my eye, giving me a barely suppressed smile, before slipping out the door, followed by Ketch.

"What is it?" I asked, folding my arms.

"I wanted to discuss your choice of weapon for the gala," Animo began, strolling toward the trunk, laden with travel supplies. "I know you're skilled with a bow, but that's fairly conspicuous for our purposes."

"What did you have in mind?"

Finding his pack, he withdrew a small, linen-wrapped bundle and set it on the table. "This."

I pulled apart the wrapping to reveal a silver dagger with a twisting handle and sapphire pommel. My heart dropped.

"This is my dagger," I breathed, holding it as though it might shatter at any moment. "I left this in Rudane. How could you possibly have…?"

I'd knelt before my bed, dagger in hand. A scream cut the night, and the blade fell from my hands, landing on the mattress.

Anger pulsed through me as my glare met Animo's stony gaze. "You broke into my home?"

He didn't deny it.

"How could you?" I exploded.

"I sent Ketch looking for you to ensure you were safe," he explained, his tone controlled. "He saw the dagger next to your chest—"

"My *chest*?" I crossed the room to stand before him. "Animo, that chest contains the last image of my parents."

He held up a hand. "And it's safe. Ketch saw your family crest and thought it would be useful."

"Give it to me."

He obeyed, pulling the chest from his bag. I snatched it from him, cradling it in my arms like a child.

"You had no right to take these."

"They belong to the heir to the throne of Avonshere, do they not? And by your own admission, you are not her."

"This is all I have left!"

"You have your kingdom!" he snapped. "A dying land that is waiting for you to return."

"I can't!"

A neighboring guest banged on the wall and shouted for us to be quiet. I clutched the chest against me, staring at Animo. The silence hovered around us like an unreleased breath.

"I can't do this," I whispered.

"Rose," he began, but I wasn't going to listen. I turned my back and retreated to my room, wiping the tears from my eyes before pushing open the door.

Rain drummed against the window. Megs sat on the bed, her starry-eyed gaze drinking in every inch of our dresses as they hung from the wardrobe's small door.

"Is everything all right?" she asked without taking her eyes off the gowns.

"Fine," I replied, tucking the chest and dagger under my pillow. "I'm simply irritated."

"About the dagger Animo gave you?"

I huffed. "You eavesdropped."

"Of course I eavesdropped. When I catch the scent of secrecy, I hunt it to the source. It was actually quite easy with all the yelling."

I collapsed onto my bed. The stiff mattress didn't sink an inch, leaving me achy and uncomfortable as if I'd landed flat on the floor.

Megs fiddled with the bronze medallion she wore. "You know… you sounded awfully tense about the dagger and… everything." She kept her tone light, but that didn't disguise her motive.

I turned my head away from her. "I'd rather not discuss it."

"Rose?"

"Yes?"

"Hertz and I, we're here for you. Whatever it is that you have to do—steal a staff, save a kingdom, or kill a queen, we'll be there."

Words clogged my throat like rising bile.

"The story you told me in the swamp scared me a little," she admitted. "But it also showed me why you're doing this, and it's another reason to stay with you until the very end." Her voice lifted on the final four words, almost teasing.

Until the very end. I shot to my feet.

"I'm going to go take a walk." I avoided Megs's gaze, fighting to keep my hand from shaking as I pulled open the door.

I didn't make it past the hallway before sinking against the wall, my breaths short and my heart pounding. Behind my closed eyes, flames burned. The heat flared against my palms as everything—every vow, every sacrifice, every shred of hope Avonshere had, burned.

"Rose?"

I opened my eyes, forcing my breaths to calm as Hertz walked down the narrow hallway.

"Where have you been?" I asked. "We were worried about you."

"Oh." He touched his pocket. "I had to find something."

"Something as in…"

He glanced away, rubbing the back of his neck.

"Hertz, I'm your best friend. You can tell me."

"All right." He bobbed his head, a shy smile teasing his lips. "Remember the jewelry shop we visited yesterday?"

I nodded.

"They sold rings with real stones, like topaz and quartz and amethyst." He reached into his pocket, withdrawing a golden ring, set with a purple stone.

My breath caught in my throat. "Is that what I think it is?"

He nodded. "I'm going to propose to Donna."

"Hertz… this is incredible." I pulled him into a hug. "Oh—When?"

"As soon as we return to Rudane."

Return to Rudane. To his *life.* But he couldn't go back, not until Natalia was dead. And if the past was any indication, he and Megs would demand to come with me to finish the job, which meant dragging them through a wilderness of shades and death,

Kingdoms, what have I done?

"This is… good." I conjured a strained smile. "If you'll excuse me I need to speak with Animo. Good night."

"Good night," he echoed, stepping into his room.

At the click of the lock, I spun, throwing myself at Animo's door. I pounded on the wood, nearly falling into him as it opened.

He caught my arm, holding me upright. "Come to yell at me again?"

"No." I pushed past him into the room. "I want Megs and Hertz gone."

"What?"

I froze at the sight of Ketch filling small, glass bottles with black powder. "Are you making explosives?"

"They aren't lethal," Ketch assured me. "I cut the black powder with a handful of elements—I can't pronounce their names, but that's beside the point—it creates a heatless blast that uses light to disorient attackers."

"Bombs aside, why do you want to send your friends home?" Animo asked, shutting the door.

I folded my arms, planting myself by the wardrobe. "This doesn't end tomorrow. Once I have the Staff of Realms, I will use it to kill Natalia. This quest of ours will escalate from fraud to murder very quickly, and my friends deserve better than to be involved in that."

"I agree."

Relief swept over me, only to be dashed when he said, "But if you want them gone, you'll have to do it yourself. They chose to follow you. I won't deny that choice."

I threw up my arms. "They won't listen to me! And if they're harmed—" My voice broke, cutting off my words.

Animo's gaze softened. "Your fear is justified. They were supposed to be protected by Aspectu, but..." His jaw clenched. "They have me. And I promise you, I will keep them safe."

My gaze fell to the ground. I wanted to trust him, but... *what is that?*

A dark stain ran along the floor, ending before the wardrobe. I narrowed my eyes, reaching for the door's handle.

"Rose, no!" Animo shouted at the same time I pulled it open.

A body lay, slumped in the wardrobe, dried blood cascading from his sliced throat. I screamed, stumbling back.

Animo's arms clamped around me, one hand over my mouth, the other pulling me away as Ketch raced to close the door. I wormed out of Animo's grasp, wrenching his hand from my mouth.

"You *killed* someone?"

"It wasn't my intention—"

I let out an angry cry, shoving him away from me. "I cannot believe you," I snarled before turning on my heel and storming out.

His footsteps followed me to my room, where Megs sat on her bed, tinkering with small pieces of metal.

"Hertz went to get some food. I thought we could have a nice…" Her voice trailed off as she caught sight of our faces. "What happened now?"

"I did what I had to do," Animo said, ignoring her.

I spun, planting my hands on my hips. "Get out."

"No."

I clenched my jaw, holding his gaze for a moment before grabbing my satchel and packing it with whatever belongings were in arm's reach—be they Megs's or mine.

"So you're running away," Animo said, his tone laced with spite. "Is that your solution to everything?"

"Do *not* start with me," I snapped, rage boiling beneath my skin. "I agreed to theft, not *murder*."

"Should I leave?" Megs asked, glancing between us.

"Yes," Animo said in unison with my sharp "No."

"All right…" Looking thoroughly uncomfortable, Megs skirted out of the room.

I threw down the satchel, forcing myself to meet Animo's gaze. "Who was he?"

"Lashier."

I gave a strangled laugh. "Of course. The man you *took care* of. Tell me, did Ketch really steal those other invitations from post boxes, or did you pluck them off of corpses?"

"Rose—"

"Was that your *barfight*? Did Lashier resist as you slit his throat?"

"What is the matter with you?" Animo exclaimed. "How can my killing one man make me your enemy, yet Natalia's years of slaughtering your own people can't bring you out of hiding?"

"You dare justify your actions because Natalia's are worse?"

"Face reality, Rose. People die. And sometimes, to win wars, you need to be the killer."

I stepped forward, my fists clenched. "You don't think I've seen the realities of war? When I was twelve years old, I watched a village full of people be consumed by flames. I heard their screams. Smelled their flesh burning. That is my reality, and I can't walk away from it."

"But you did, didn't you? For five years, you turned your back while the people of Avonshere suffered and *burned*—"

"Natalia's actions are *not* my fault."

He stepped back, studying me as if his gaze could reveal the secrets buried beneath my words. "I know. Rose… none of this is your fault."

That isn't true.

"You didn't ask for this—you didn't cause any of it. It was forced upon you, and for that, I am sorry. But you have to act."

That isn't true, either. I could lay, unmoving for a century and Avonshere would be unaffected.

"Rose," Animo began, his voice soft and restrained. "You're angry with me. That's fine. But don't allow this to ruin our chance to get the staff."

His starlit eyes begged me to believe him, but all I could see were his lies. But what if the roles were reversed? What if he were the one staring at me with hatred, picturing bloody hands and a blackened heart? Would he forgive me? *Should* he?

"Rose?"

I let out a breath, breaking off the eye contact that had lasted far too long. "Our plans are unchanged. Tomorrow, we will steal the Staff of Realms. But after that, I will continue alone."

"Alone? Natalia will kill you."

"Not if I kill her first."

Animo shook his head. "Assassination won't fix anything. An empty throne will plunge Avonshere into an era of chaos and anarchy."

"Then find them a leader," I said. "Someone with a reasonable claim to the throne, who will let Rosara Wolfe stay dead."

"Fine." Animo started toward the door, then paused. "For what it's worth, I hope you succeed. And not just in killing Natalia."

"I—"

Guilt joined my simmering anger. I picked at the shackle clamped around my wrist. *I should say something. What he did was wrong, but I don't want him to be my enemy.* An apology might have been warranted, but the words refused to form, leaving me to blurt, "I still need something from you." I held up my wrist, bearing the restrictor cuff. "If I'm going to fight a witch, I should probably have my own magic."

"Right." He withdrew a key made of connected metal circles from his pocket. It fit seamlessly into one of the runes and the cuff snapped open.

"Finally." I rubbed my wrist, brushing bits of dried mud from my skin.

Animo set the cuff and key onto the nightstand. He retreated to the door before looking over his shoulder. "One last thing. In the future, when you find a body, it may prove beneficial to ask *why* they were killed."

Why they were killed…? His words circled in my mind, but when I finally opened my mouth to speak, he was gone.

MASQUERADE

The streets of Medea swelled with a rainbow of men and women winding their way through the city like a bejeweled serpent feeding off of the energy of the crowd. Eyes glittered behind their masks, sending signals from one elegantly dressed stranger to another. Silk, jewelry, feathers—it blended together to create a single wave of gilded glory.

"It's blazing out here," Hertz grumbled, stopping beneath a lightpost. His lack of attention in the shop had cost him dearly: the ensemble Megs had selected for him consisted of a velvet suit studded with amethyst, a decorative, one-shoulder cape trimmed in gold, and a matching feathered hat and mask, all of which were bright purple.

He struggled with his twisted cape while the thick line of attendees streamed past us, crossing the bridge to the manor's arched doorway. The golden glow of the lightposts' flickering candles turned night into day, making the sweat shimmer on the exposed skin of passing guests.

I smoothed the golden fabric of my skirt, oddly self-conscious amid the prowling Lucians. My fingers itched to readjust the dagger strapped to my bare thigh. The rough leather of the sheath rubbed against my skin with every step as though I were an assassin. An *itchy* assassin.

Megs had added a false pocket, hidden amid the dress's ruffles, allowing me easy access to the weapon. Still, with so many eyes watching, I restrained myself from touching it, settling for flexing my fingers against my skirt.

Animo's hand fell on my forearm. "Stop fidgeting."

"Easy for you to say," I muttered. "You likely—" My sentence died in my throat. There were too many people around to admit we were imposters.

A slight smile tugged on Animo's lips.

"What?"

He shrugged. "Nothing."

I pursed my lips, turning my attention back to Megs as she adjusted Hertz's cape. With his steely glare and abundance of purple feathers, Hertz bore a strong resemblance to a hexed owl. The thought brought a smile to my face, which, in turn, deepened his glare.

"Oh, lighten up," Ketch said, raising his dragon mask. "Your frown is going to spoil the night for the rest of us."

"Of course you're happy," Hertz grumbled. "You don't look like a purple chicken."

Ketch grinned, lowering his mask. It had been paired with a faux dragon scale vest, and Ketch's mohawk imitated the spikes that ran along a dragon's head and neck, giving him an intimidating air despite his short build.

"I think you all look fantastic." Megs's words drew my thoughts back to the member of our party I least wanted to think about: Animo. She had dressed him in a royal blue coat with silver embroidery running along the cuffs and collar. It set off his eyes, making him even more handsome than usual.

How infuriating.

We'd barely spoken since our fight. I knew I was the one in the wrong, but a mixture of pride, guilt, and fear kept me from admitting it.

"All done." After a final smoothing of Hertz's cape, Megs raised her mask, and we rejoined the satin wave slipping across the bridge like grains of sand in an hourglass.

Through the grand doorway stood a hall lined with golden statues of kings, queens, and warriors. A few guests dawdled to admire them, but most ignored them entirely. We didn't linger, continuing until we arrived at a choke point of guests awaiting introduction.

Animo drew Lashier's invitation from his pocket and offered me his arm. "We're introduced *together*," he reminded me.

Avoiding his eyes, I slipped my arm over his. Part of me longed to fix things between us, but the rest of me doubted it was even possible. That night in Rudane lived in my mind as a happy memory, but it wasn't real. Tonight, we wore masks of silver and gold, but that night was the real masquerade. The versions of ourselves we offered were lies, and what I had felt… maybe that had been a lie as well.

Eventually, the slow-moving line brought us to the landing of a grand staircase, where a herald stood announcing guests. Animo handed him our invitation, and we faced forward, gazing out at the lavish ballroom.

The herald cleared his throat. "My apologies, sir, but I am afraid your name is not on the invitation. How shall I introduce you?"

"Sir and Lady Lashier," Animo replied smoothly.

The herald nodded, then called, "Presenting Sir and Lady Lashier!"

Animo and I descended the grand staircase into the ballroom. A crystal chandelier sparkled above, and a gold-laced dance floor lay, unused below. Plucked notes wafted from an overhead balcony, where a tuning orchestra sat.

At the bottom of the staircase, Animo led me to the ring of guests socializing and indulging in golden drinks. Past the group, he dropped my arm.

"The Trianis should make their entrance in fifteen minutes," he said. "Then it's another thirty before the meeting begins. Until then, we need to act like we belong."

"Meaning?"

"We drink, dance, and laugh like no lives depend on our success."

I glanced at the empty dance floor. "I think you can remove one of those activities."

"You don't dance until the hosts do."

"Hm." I folded my arms, looking around at the crowd of unfamiliar masks. "I'm going to find Megs and Hertz."

"Be sure to find me when the dancing begins."

I raised a brow. "You're asking me to dance." Last night, I had accused him of murder, and now he wanted us to *dance?*

He shrugged. "Everyone dances in Medea. We might as well do it together."

"I'll keep that in mind. And I'll see you at the twenty-third hour," I said before slipping away into the crowd.

My dress choice seemed to work—I walked through the ring of guests unnoticed. Everyone was so wrapped up in flaunting their glamorous attire that they paid no mind to who passed by.

Conversation buzzed around me, like a swarm of bees. Most everyone had gathered around the dance floor, but a few had slipped away to one of the open galleries. Young women clustered about glass display cases, using the faint reflections as they helped one another with last-minute primping. I smiled slightly. *At least some things stay the same.*

The brassy fanfare of trumpets called my attention to the top of the grand staircase. A couple stood, covered neck to toe in seafoam green. Bows dotted their cuffs and ran along the woman's skirt, outlining a slightly darker strip of fabric. Gloves covered their hands, and white masks with painted features obscured all but their eyes.

"Presenting Count and Countess Triani," the herald's voice boomed.

"Good evening, honored guests," the Countess said. "I thank you all for being here to celebrate my husband's safe return." She turned to the Count, and while I hoped love filled her gaze, the words seemed lifeless, hidden behind her expressionless mask. "For eighteen months, I have longed for his company. At last, he has come home, bringing with him glorious treasures to join our collection. Tonight, let us celebrate my husband's homecoming and the opening of our southwest gallery!" The Countess held out a gloved hand, and a pair of footmen opened a door.

Applause rang out, and guests craned their necks to catch a glimpse of the treasures that lay within.

"Now, let the dancing commence!" The Countess waved her hand, and the orchestra began to play. The Count escorted his wife down the grand staircase to the center of the open floor. He pulled her close, leading her in a classic waltz.

All eyes were on them as they spun about, a wave of lace and bows. The Count dipped his wife so low that her red coiffure grazed the ground, earning him applause.

After the first stanza, the couple held out their arms, inviting their guests to join them. Couples swarmed the floor, among them a feathered purple hat and a bright-green dress.

At least one person will have a good time tonight.

I allowed myself to melt into the crowd of young women clinging to the wall like dying ivy. Their hopeful eyes lifted every time a potential partner passed by while mine fell to the floor. *No attention, no dancing. Until the bells chime the hour, I am an extension of the wall.*

"Pardon me."

Biaht. I forced myself to meet the gaze of the young man who stood before me, his silver mask ending at his nose.

"May I help you?" I asked.

He gave me a confused smile. "You are not dancing."

"No, I am not."

"We are at a dance, dear lady. And it would be a shame for someone as beautiful as you to remain aside all night." He offered his hand. "May I have the honor?"

"Thank you, but no."

The man blinked, then scoffed, walking away. Nearby women stared, some gawking while others shot glares in my direction.

"You made the right choice sending him away."

I turned to find another man standing beside me, confidence dripping from his smile.

"It was nothing personal. I am simply not in the mood for dancing."

"Perhaps the right partner would change your mind." The new man extended a gloved hand.

"I'm flattered, really—"

"But the lady is spoken for." Animo appeared by my side, twining his arm with mine.

"Ah, I see. In that case, I will take my leave." The man gave a short bow, then moved along toward a group of beckoning wallflowers.

"I tried to warn you," Animo said, leading me to the dance floor. "Everyone dances in Medea."

"I didn't think they'd be so persistent."

"You're a beautiful stranger—of course they'd pursue you."

I froze, so focused on his flippant use of the word *beautiful* that I scarcely registered him bowing to me. Hastily, I dropped into a curtsey, rising as the first notes floated from the violinist's bow.

Animo pulled me close, his hand on my waist. Our eyes locked, gazes caged behind our masks. He took my hand, and the dance began.

I followed his steps with ease. My ruffled skirt fanned out like a blooming flower as Animo spun me, then guided me back to his arms.

"These balls are a game," he whispered, his cheek against mine. "Players compete to be the most powerful. Those women you were with—the ones by the wall—they have no power. They're desperate to be chosen, which is why they won't be. But women like those,"—he nodded to a group of women sipping champagne, seemingly unaware of the men watching them from afar—"they are the desired ones. Their self-assurance is like a narcotic. Men want the power of choice, but these women don't *need* to be chosen. That makes them all the more desirable."

"Perhaps you should be dancing with one of them instead of wasting your time with me."

Animo smiled, his eyes glittering behind the silver mask covering the left side of his face. He spun me out once more. When I returned to him, he held me close, my back pressed against his chest. "This dance isn't for pleasure, Rose. It's my final chance to get through to you."

He pulled me through a quick twirl so our eyes could meet. "Every time I try to make my case for why you should return to Avonshere, you find a reason to shout or storm off. But tonight we are surrounded by a thousand ears, eager for a drop of gossip. If we dance like proper guests, no one will pay us any mind. But if you cause a scene, people will turn… *persistent.*"

I tensed. Every word rolled off his tongue like a threat.

I moved closer to him, slipping my arm around his neck as an excuse to lean up and whisper, "Choose your next words wisely."

A smile flicked across his lips. He lifted a hand to my chin and leaned in close. "You're a hypocrite."

My jaw dropped, fury flashing through my veins. The music soared, and Animo spun me out. When I returned, I latched onto his arm, digging my nails into the fabric of his coat.

"I am a killer," he whispered, his warm breath tickling my ear. "That, I won't deny. But you are wrong if you think I am a man who murders in cold blood. I killed Lashier to protect Ketch, which you would know had you bothered to ask."

Guilt blossomed inside of me but was stifled by the anxiety that preceded Animo's every word.

"That night I made a choice between two lives, which is *exactly* what you are doing right now. You are choosing your own life over the innocent lives of thousands."

"I'm not the one they need."

"They need a queen. And you're the only one with a legitimate claim to the throne. That's why it has to be you. There is no rebel army in Avonshere, only terrified and desperate civilians. If you want to defeat Natalia—truly defeat her—you will need help. If we resurrect Rosara Wolfe, we can use her claim to forge alliances with other kingdoms and, with their help, free Avonshere."

"You speak of *war.* Not simply finishing a fight, but *magnifying* it. Animo, thousands more people will die if this escalates."

"It's the only way."

I shook my head, fixing my gaze on the embroidery running along his lapel. "I don't believe that."

"Look me in the eye, and say that again."

I raised my gaze, cursing the way my lip trembled as I did so.

"Rose," Animo began gently. "You must understand that in Natalia's regime, the wicked thrive and the good suffer. If you enact your plan and kill Natalia, you will leave the kingdom vulnerable, and a new tyrant will seize control."

"You don't know that."

"Aspectu does." His words sent a dull knife through me, sawing slowly at my hope.

"She… What did she see?"

"A thousand futures where Avonshere falls into ruin and only one where it rises to glory. That future is with *you.*"

My lips fell apart. "What… why…"

"Why wait until now to tell you?"

I nodded.

"I thought it should come from Aspectu. It was her vision, only she knows the path you must take. And if I'm being honest, I wasn't sure you would believe me."

My gaze fell. *I believe you now.* I slipped my arms around Animo, hiding my face against his chest as tears threatened my eyes. He held me close, guiding me in the dance's numbing rhythm.

Why had I ever thought finding Aspectu meant freedom? Even if she had been able to save Megs and Hertz, she would still have forced me to return. And without her… without her, the choice fell to me.

We cannot trust that child to lead us.

I tightened my grip. Animo tensed, drawing back and slowing our dancing as the music tapered out.

"Rose? Are you all right?"

I pulled away, shaking my head as unseen smoke wrapped around my throat, pulling it tight. "No, I'm not. You're sticking your nose into matters that don't concern you. You know nothing of what I've endured. All you are doing is running me in circles and assigning blame that I can't carry. You and I are not the same."

"Rose—"

"No." I raised a shaking hand. "The dance is over and so is this conversation."

Lifting my skirts, I pushed through the crowd of dancers applauding as the conductor gave a humble bow. Anger, pain, guilt, terror all swelled inside of me, pressing against my chest and attempting to break the seams of my soul. I slipped through the first door I could find and into a gallery.

I dropped to my knees behind a display. Pressing my hands over my mouth, I set my feelings free. Choked, strangled sobs fought to escape as my chest heaved with drowning breaths. I closed my eyes, leaning against the marble case.

A memory surfaced: bark scratching against my back, dulled by my wool cloak. Head against my knees, I'd trembled, unable to go but terrified to stay as I listened to the screams.

My eyes snapped open. I shot to my feet, my body begging to run. Maybe if I never stopped moving, my past wouldn't catch up to me.

"A masterpiece."

I flinched at the voice, spinning to find a man in a black-and-gold mask standing in the doorway.

"My apologies. I did not mean to startle you." He closed the door, cutting off the hum of party guests.

I forced a smile to my face. "That's all right. I was going to leave anyway."

"Leave? Why would you abandon the company of art such as this?" He held out a hand, crossing to stand before the portrait of a young woman. "Look at her."

His passion pulled me to the painting. Pale, purple flowers were woven into the woman's hair, matching her gown and beautifully contrasting with her dark skin. Her lips lay in a flat line, and her gaze seemed to look past me to something unreachable.

"She seems sad," I said.

"She was cursed to die," the man replied, unbothered by the notion. "Her parents thought they could fight prophecy by hiding her away." He pointed at the painting. "This is the only portrait ever painted of her. A few days later, she disappeared. It's likely she died, but legends say her disappearance allowed her to escape her curse. Of course, that was hundreds of years ago. By now she has most certainly faced her fate."

"You seem to know a lot about this painting."

"I know every piece in Count Triani's collection." The man scratched his cheek, where the edge of his mask rubbed against his short beard. "It is one of the most acclaimed in all the Twelve Kingdoms."

"Indeed it is." My mind strayed to the Staff of Realms and the approaching hour. "If you will excuse me, I must return to my companions."

"Of course." He gave me a bow, and I replied with a curtsey before returning to the ballroom.

I hovered along the edge of the dance floor, scanning the room for my companions. Skirts flared and masks glittered, yet none belonged to my friends.

I slipped through the crowd, my eyes darting about until they landed on a dwarf leaning against the dessert table.

"You seem to be enjoying the evening," I said, joining Ketch as he finished off a sugary bun filled with cream.

"Tavern food is one level above scavenging through garbage like a raccoon." His pupils eclipsed his gold irises as he gazed upon the array of pastries. "This is suitable for a palace. You should try some."

"I'm not sure I can eat tonight."

Ketch bit into a tart, taking his time to chew and swallow before speaking. "I spoke with Animo."

I made a noise between a sigh and a scoff.

"He was protecting me, Rose," Ketch insisted. "His plan was to drug Lashier, but the man was too drunk to keep anything down. We took him into the alley, and he put the pieces together. Intoxicated and enraged, he attacked me. He got his hands on a broken bottle and was ready to end my life when Animo..." He made a slicing gesture before his throat.

"I *know*. I know and I'm not angry. But he... he said—" I pressed my lips together as tears formed behind my eyes.

Setting aside his pastry, Ketch took my hand. "Talk to him. Even if you can't tell him what is hurting you, explain that it isn't him. If you don't, he will honor your wishes and leave." His wide eyes implored me to understand.

"Do you really want that?"

I shook my head. "I don't know."

BEHIND THE MASK

I stayed with Ketch at the dessert table until Animo came to fetch us. "It's time," he said, refusing to meet my eyes.

"I need to speak with you first," I said.

"No time. The bell strike is in five minutes."

"Animo—"

He walked off before I could say another word.

I huffed quietly. *So this is what it's like arguing with me.*

I followed him up the grand staircase and into the dark, empty upstairs. Moonlight fell through the windows in a checkered pattern, illuminating the hall just enough for us to find our way. Animo strode ahead while Ketch's shorter legs slowed him down. I hovered in the middle struggling to maintain my composure. It could all end tonight. I would have the Staff of Realms and, in a matter of minutes, be at Malecare, slitting Natalia's throat.

You assume. I hadn't any idea how many guards Natalia had lining the halls. And how did I even use the staff? Did I simply picture where I wanted to go? If that was the case, the closest I could get would be the bridge at the foot of Devil's Canyon.

What if I can't do this? I had it in me to take a life, that, I was certain of. But if my assassination attempt turned into an actual fight, I was done for. *Of course, when I finally realize I need Animo's help, his back is turned and exuding the explicit message of* stay away from me.

Ketch's words surfaced in my mind. *Talk to him… or else he will leave.*

I couldn't be queen. But if I could convince Animo to change his plan and agree to help me on *my* path, maybe we had a chance of defeating Natalia. If he ever forgave me, that was.

I lifted my skirts, running to pace him. "I need to speak with you."

"Later."

"No, not later." I grabbed his arm, forcing him to a stop. "I—"

My words fell into a huff. How was I meant to begin? *I'm sorry I've been awful and still won't tell you everything, but I need you to blindly agree to help me.*

"And that's why we aren't talking," Animo said. "Because you *can't* talk."

He started to pull away, sending a lightning strike of panic through me.

I tightened my grip. "No. Ketch, you continue to the meeting. We'll be right behind you."

"Rose, we can't—"

"We have to." I pushed open the nearest door and shoved him inside.

"What—"

I shut the door, plunging the room into darkness. Moonlight filtered in through a single window, providing enough light for our elf eyes to adjust. Animo's silhouette stood, clear before me, but black shrouded his face. He may be furious with me, but my pent-up emotions refused to be held back any longer.

"I'm sorry. I'm in the wrong. I've been in the wrong this entire time, and I've been a hypocrite. I lash out because I am afraid. Terrified, really. And that fear made me push you away, but now I can see that I need your help." The words tumbled out, until none were left. "So… help. Please."

Animo stepped forward, lifting his hands. They slid past my face, grazing my hair before landing on my mask's tie. With a gentle tug, the ribbon unraveled, and the mask dropped into his hand.

"Why did you do that?" I whispered.

He removed his own mask before replying. "I don't want your honesty to be hidden behind a mask." A moment of silence passed between us. "Why did you run all those years ago?"

"Because I was afraid and because my hope was gone." I took a breath before forcing out the words "And because I knew I couldn't be the queen my people needed."

"Why are you running now?"

"Because everything I am is a lie."

"Is this a lie?"

"No," I said quickly. *But it isn't the whole truth.* The words pounded against my mind. I knew I should say them and let the cards fall where they might, but my lips refused to move.

Animo studied me in the dark before saying, "I will help you."

"Even if I don't become queen?"

"One matter at a time."

Tears of relief pressed against my eyes. "Thank you."

"Now, let's get the Staff of Realms."

I nodded, quickly wiping my eyes, then followed Animo to the door. He opened it for a split second, then pushed it shut again, leaving the tiniest gap. I waited in silence until he drew back.

"It's the girl from the shop," he murmured. "The one with the thieves—she's carrying the Staff of Realms."

"What?" Why would that girl be here? What did she want with the staff?

"Stay close." Animo stepped out into the hall, gesturing for me to follow. I slipped off my shoes and tiptoed along behind him.

We turned the corner just in time to see the small, dark-haired girl disappear up a spiral staircase, a golden staff strapped to her back. I gripped my shoes tighter. If she escaped with the staff…

No. If she were leaving, she would have already used it. She's not done here.

Animo and I crept up the winding staircase, careful not to be seen. The stairs fed into a long hallway, an open door spilling golden light across the dark floor. Voices floated from the room, too faint to discern.

Animo's eyes narrowed as the girl stepped through the door. We crept closer as a male voice exclaimed,

"Ah, Belinda! Thank you, dear girl. As promised, the Staff of Realms. Ah, ah, ah!" I envisioned the man pulling the staff away from eager hands. "It is not yours yet. Not until you bring your buyer."

"He's on his way."

My heart dropped at the sound of Ketch's voice. Why was he in a meeting with thieves? Unless…

I met Animo's gaze and the harshness in his eyes all but confirmed my suspicions: every part of this deal was a con.

"Be ready for anything," he warned.

I shoved my feet back into my slippers, then followed him inside.

Megs sat in a plush chair, her hands clasped in her lap and Hertz hovering over her shoulder. Ketch stood in the middle of a stare-off with the man I'd met in the gallery, only this time, I saw through his disguise—he was the thief from the jewelry shop. It explained the dark-haired Belinda who stood by his side, holding the Staff of Realms. Behind her stood a man I didn't recognize, and surprisingly, Countess Triani herself.

Wait. I narrowed my eyes, examining the woman. The pale-green gown and full-face mask were perfect replicas, but the hair exposed the woman's lie: wisps of blond peeked out from her red hairline, just above her ear.

"And who might you be?" the thief asked, his narrowed eyes studying Animo and me.

"I go by the name of Lashier," Animo replied. "I am here to deal with Countess Triani."

The thief glanced over his shoulder. The man behind him shook his head and the thief sighed. "You may go by that name, but you are not him." He nodded at the door. The unfamiliar man closed it, sliding the deadbolt into place.

Animo tensed, but his gaze remained firm. "And you are no broker to the Countess. Whom am I really addressing?

The thief's lips curved in a vile grin, and he bowed. "Ruger Cunningham, at your service."

"I doubt that."

Ruger's smile flattened. "Am I not to know the true name of whom I am dealing with? Or is that a secret you'd prefer to take to your graves?"

Megs let out a squeak, and Hertz placed his hand on her shoulder.

"And what purpose would that serve?" Somehow, Animo's voice remained steady in the face of Ruger's threats. "If you wanted to kill us and walk off with the diamonds, you would have done so already."

"When you kill the messenger, the sender remains a threat," Ruger said. "I suspected you were imposters, but I couldn't know for certain until I saw you, *Sir Lashier.*"

"And now that you know?"

"I have no use for you."

"We have diamonds," Hertz exclaimed, stepping forward. "Take them and let us go."

"Stay out of this," Animo snapped.

Ruger laughed. "A negotiator." He stepped closer to Hertz, his hands clasped behind his back. "Do you not realize that we can just as easily pluck the diamonds off your twitching corpse?"

My hand shot to my dagger as Megs grabbed Hertz's arm.

"Of course, I have a feeling that won't be necessary." Ruger backed away, his gaze flicking to Animo. "Dwalrin or Hokfiend?"

With no response, he held out his hands. "Lies are meaningless, and there are only two counterfeiters in Medea capable of a short-notice job like this one."

"Dwalrin," Animo said.

"A good choice." Ruger flopped into the chair beside the fake countess and tossed a leg over his knee. "Hokfiend has always been a greedy fellow."

Ketch snorted. "Says the con man."

Animo held up a hand to silence the dwarf. "What exactly is your plan? Steal the Staff of Realms and sell it out from under the Countess's nose?"

"Yes," Ruger replied simply. He leaned forward, elbows planted on his knees. "And it was a perfect plan. My beloved poses as Countess Triani, and we sell to the unwitting Lashier."

"And we leave by *fifteen past*," the fake countess chimed in pointedly.

Ruger glanced at the clock. "Right you are, my dear." He stood. "Belinda, tell Dante to come in and handle these three. And take the staff with you."

Belinda moved toward the door, but I blocked her. "You're not taking that anywhere."

A hand fell on my shoulder, only to be jerked away—Animo slammed his fist against the man's jaw. Taking the second of distraction, Belinda sprinted past me, into the hall.

Megs yelped as Animo landed a kick, knocking the man to the ground. Steel rang out as Ruger and the "Countess" drew blades.

"Animo!" Ketch held up a small vial, then smashed it against the ground.

A loud bang rang out as white light flared, encompassing my vision. An arm wrapped around my waist, dragging me into the hallway. I pulled away as my eyesight slowly returned.

"Rose, it's me," Animo said, his hand on my arm. "We need to leave."

Ketch pulled Megs and Hertz out of the room. "Let's go, follow my voice." The two blinked, stumbling after the dwarf.

I shook my head. "Belinda. Which way did she go?"

"We don't have time—"

"I need the staff!" I looked up and down the hall. The door to the staircase was closed, but I clearly remembered leaving it open. My gaze met Animo's. "I'm sorry."

"Rose!"

I broke free of his grasp, running down the hall. Armor clanked behind me. I spared a glance back—guards thundered into the hallway. Animo and Ketch readied their weapons as Ruger and his companions tumbled out of the room.

I hesitated at the stairwell. *Animo can handle them. It's up to you to find the staff.*

I tore down the stairs, my skirt hiked up to my knees. In the fourth floor hallway, I spotted Belinda. Pushing myself harder, I closed the distance between us before throwing myself against her. The breath flew from my lungs as we slammed against the stone floor.

Belinda squirmed out of my grip. Gasping for air, I reached out, wrapping my fingers around the Staff of Realms. It slid off her back as she ran away.

A breathless laugh bubbled up. Climbing to my knees, I caressed the twisting gold. *I did it. I have the Staff of Realms.* I closed my eyes, pressing my forehead against one of the prongs that protected the azure jewel. *I did it.*

Strong hands jerked me to my feet, wrenching the Staff of Realms from me. I screamed, thrashing about as guards swarmed me, forming an inescapable ring.

Countess Triani—the real Countess Triani—strode forward, taking the Staff of Realms from the guard. Anger radiated from every feature of her unmasked face.

"Take her to the study."

The guards obeyed, leading me down the stairs and into a bookshelf-lined study on the third floor. The Countess followed me in, then ordered, "Leave us."

The guards bowed, exiting with an abundance of clanking. The Countess shut the door, turning the lock sharply.

"You foolish girl," she snapped in a low tone. "We had a deal. What were you still doing up there? Did Cunningham's greed overtake his sense?"

"Cunningham?" The truth struck me, though I didn't quite understand it. "You hired thieves to steal the Staff of Realms."

The Countess's eyes widened. She stepped back, gripping the staff like a weapon. "Who are you?"

"An associate of a man called Lashier. We were summoned here under the pretense that you were selling the Staff of Realms."

"*Selling?*" The Countess laughed numbly. "Oh, that greedy, despicable man." She shook her head and began pacing before the door.

"Ruger Cunningham thought he could get two payouts for a single job," I said, more for my own benefit than the Countess's. "He was already here to steal the Staff of Realms, so why not sell it and have the buyer on hand as a scapegoat? The only question is why a Countess would want her prized possession stolen."

The Countess stopped pacing. "If you were a wise girl, you would rescind that question."

I folded my arms and stared at her, unblinking. Her grip on the staff… it wasn't threatening. It was *fearful.* My mind dissected the moment I'd first touched the staff. Smooth metal, warm from Belinda's body, and completely ordinary.

My jaw fell slack. "It's not real," I murmured. "It never was, was it?"

"You do not know what you speak of," the Countess hissed.

"I rather think I do. I think you lied about having a priceless relic. But with so many collectors running about, you realized you couldn't maintain your ruse, so you decided to fake a theft in order to save face."

"No!" Countess Triani flinched at her own shout. "It was *real.* My husband would never lie about this find." She took a deep breath, running a hand down the bodice of her dress. "No matter. If I can make my own messes, I can clean up after them as well." She crossed to the desk, exchanging the Staff of Realms for a letter opener. I backed away, slipping my hand into the false pocket where my dagger waited.

"I do apologize," she said. "It was never my intention to have others involved in this mess. But as you have already realized, I have a reputation to uphold."

Before I could draw my dagger, the doors burst open. In strode Ruger Cunningham, the fake countess by his side and a pile of unconscious guards behind him. The fake countess had removed her mask, revealing her as the blond woman from the shop: Ali.

Countess Triani's face blazed as red as Ali's wig. "You—"

Ruger grabbed her wrist and twisted, driving the letter opener into her stomach. The Countess released a strangled cry that quickly faded into breathless, agonized moans. She fell to her knees, a hand pressed against the blade lodged in her abdomen.

"Take the staff," Ruger told Ali. He advanced toward me, drawing a curved knife from his coat pocket.

I gripped the dagger strapped to my thigh, ready to draw. "You won't have much luck. It isn't real."

"Oh, I heard," Ruger said. "But it was the Countess's dying wish to protect her reputation. And it is my living wish for that secret to die with her." He pointed his blade at me. "And you."

I drew my dagger. "Good luck."

Ruger advanced, driving his knife toward my stomach. I moved aside. The sharp blade skimmed off my corset's boning, slashing the fabric but missing my skin. I sliced downward, cutting Ruger's arm, before whirling away to prepare for another attack.

Ruger growled, pressing a hand to his bleeding arm and smearing his own blood on the hilt of his knife. "You'll regret that."

"Rose!" Megs shouted from the doorway.

Ruger's gaze darted to her, giving me a window to attack. I charged, slashing again. He threw his blade forward, but I caught his wrist, tearing the knife from his hand. I shoved him toward the window, summoning my magic as I planted a sharp kick against his chest. Glass shattered as he was propelled through the window.

Exhaustion washed over me. I gripped my head against a sharp, pulsating pain.

Megs yelped. She wielded the Staff of Realms, using it to ward off Ali's blade. Megs knocked Ali back with a shove, then spun the staff, slamming it into the other woman's head. The fake staff snapped in two as Ali dropped to the ground.

Megs gawked at the halves, her eyes wide. "Rose, I am so, so sorry—"

I rubbed my forehead. "It's fine. It's not real."

"What—?"

"You shouldn't be here. Where are the others?"

"Upstairs fighting the guards. I came to help you."

"I don't need help from you, all right? I need you to be safe." Why couldn't I get through to her? Why couldn't she understand that her staying by my side made things worse?

A moan drew Megs's attention from me to the Countess. "Oh, Kingdoms." She dropped to her knees, ready to help. "There's so much blood… Rose, you have to use your magic."

On the woman who tried to kill me? Bitterness swept over me, laced with guilt.

"Rose." Megs's pleading gaze bore into me, and I caved.

Sweeping my skirts back, I knelt on the other side of the Countess. Her eyelids fluttered, her lips moving silently. Both hands were pressed around the letter opener still lodged in her abdomen, staining her gloves red.

I placed my hands over hers. Magic flowed through my fingers and into her body, but something about it was distorted. It spread like cracking ice, losing focus and drifting away. In my mind, I could see the Countess' severed veins and open lung. The ghostlike imprint of my fingers touched them, meaning to mend, but my magic flickered out.

I pulled my hands away, dread settling in my chest. "I can't heal her."

"What do you mean? You healed Derek. His wound couldn't have been any worse—"

"I said I can't," I snapped.

Megs recoiled and my guilt flared.

I looked down at the Countess. "I'm sorry, but you're dying."

She let out a sharp sob. "You think I don't know that?" She waved her hands at the dagger, then winced.

"I'm so sorry." Tears welled in Megs's eyes.

"It's my fault," the Countess said. "I never should have let her touch it."

"*Her?*" I repeated as the points connected in my mind. "You let someone hold the Staff of Realms."

She nodded.

"Who was she?"

The Countess sobbed, her tears streaming down her neck and pooling on her collarbone. "My death."

I clenched my fists in my skirt. "I need her name."

"What does it matter? I'm dead. Let me take my secrets with me."

A wave of dark anger washed over me. "You're dying because of what you did. Death will not release you from your lies, and if you die before telling me this name, you will drag a thousand more down with you."

"Who are you to speak to me like this?"

Like a cracking whip, my darkness sharpened. I grabbed the Countess by her shoulders, digging my nails into her flesh. Her cry fell upon my deaf ears. "I am the woman with the power to make your final moment full of pain or peace," I hissed. "So I will ask you again. Who. Was. She?"

"Rose!" Megs exclaimed.

The Countess's lips trembled as she fought to form words. "A—a historian. At least, she claimed to be."

"And her name?"

"'Elizabeth Sconcewood.'"

"And she *is* the one who took the staff?"

The Countess nodded fervently. "Yes. I let her see it and touch it, and she disappeared." She drew in a shaking breath as another tear rolled down her cheek. "That's all I know, I swear it. Now let me be."

I released her, and she fell against the wall with a rough thump. I pushed myself to my feet, and my gaze met Megs's. Confusion twisted her features, laced with... my heart sank. Betrayal.

My lips flattened into a firm line. "Let's go."

She stood. "Why would you do that?"

"I needed answers."

"She was in *pain*."

"I am well aware."

"Rose." Megs grabbed my arm, forcing me to face her. "You threatened a dying woman. You *hurt* her. Why couldn't you just heal her?"

"Why couldn't you stay upstairs?" I shot back.

She dropped my arm.

I picked up the pieces of the broken staff, though at this point, I didn't think Megs would care about fulfilling the Countess's wish for secrecy.

"Rose!" Megs pointed behind me.

I spun. A bloody hand clutched the windowsill, shards of glass lodged in its knuckles. An enraged groan resonated, and the head of Ruger Cunningham appeared.

"Run!" I shoved Megs, but she didn't need the encouragement. We sprinted past the fallen forms of guards and back to the staircase. Up the spiral stairs we went, only to slam into Animo.

His gaze landed on the broken staff.

I raised my hand. "It's a decoy, and we need to go."

Animo pressed his back against the wall, gesturing for me and Megs to pass. He fell in line behind us as we raced up the stairs and back to the fifth floor corridor.

Darkness loomed before us. Splatters of blood and small blades littered the stone tiles along with faint scorch marks.

"Where are Hertz and Ketch?" I asked, looking about the hall.

Animo moved to the front of the group. "I sent them to find us a boat. Guards have blocked every entrance to the manor, so we'll have to use the roof." He pushed open a small door leading to a servant's stairwell and gestured for us to follow.

Up we went, then down another dark hallway as faint shouts followed us. The guards were searching the manor bottom to top, giving us the tiniest window of escape.

I raced up a final staircase and onto the roof. A hot wind blew, rippling the fabric of my skirt. Candles shone in the windows opposite us, dull compared to the stars glittering in the endless sky above. I took in a deep breath, brushing loose hairs from my face.

Animo slammed the door behind us, barring it with a dagger before marching over to me. "What happened back there? And don't say *nothing*. You're covered in blood." He wiped a droplet off my shoulder, revealing unbroken skin. "And it isn't all yours."

"Countess Triani is dead, Ruger Cunningham is chasing us, the real staff is in the hands of a thief, and if we don't leave quickly, we might be on the hook for murder."

"Then we ought to run faster." Animo strode to the rooftop railing.

"How do we get down?" Megs asked, her arms wrapped tight around herself.

"We'll have to jump," Animo replied.

"We're seven stories up," I said, peering over the railing. Vertigo swept over me like the rocking current of the canal. I drew back. "I am not jumping into that."

A bang tore through the air, and the roof door shook.

"Would you rather stay and face whatever comes out of that?" Animo asked.

I laughed sharply. "I am not jumping into a river of decomposing bodies."

"Oh, rack you, Ketch," Animo muttered.

"I'm sorry, what?" Megs squeaked.

Another bang rattled the door. Megs yelped, Animo swore, and I drew my dagger.

"We're out of time," Animo snapped. "The neighboring rooftops are too far, we'll be smashed bugs on the cobblestone. The canal is our only option."

"Rose, listen to him." Megs's voice shook, her eyes flooded with terror. "I am not dying on a rooftop."

I took a steadying breath. "All right. Animo, take Megs. Bring her and Hertz back to Rudane." I nodded to the door. "I'll deal with them."

"I'm not leaving you here," Megs argued.

"That's not your choice," I replied.

She clenched her fists. "You're not in control of me."

"Animo, take her to safety," I said, ignoring the anger flaring on Megs's face.

"I'm on her side," Animo replied. "We should *all* leave. Now."

"Go," I snapped.

"Why? So you can run away again?"

"So I can keep myself from drowning in the blood of people whose deaths I'm responsible for!"

The door flew off with a final bang. Megs screamed, stumbling back as the heavy plank of wood tumbled past her.

The Cunningham gang filed out onto the rooftop. First came Ruger with his curved dagger and bloody face, then Ali and the second man from our meeting whose cheek now bore a dark bruise, followed by Belinda and a muscular man I didn't recognize.

"I've been robbed before," Ruger began, striding forward. "But never by the same person twice. There's a reason for that."

Instinctively, I pushed Megs behind me.

"Your protection won't help," Ruger said. "None of you will survive. I'd like to kill you personally,"—he pointed his dagger at me—"Dante, you can handle him,"—Ruger gestured to Animo, and the muscular man nodded—"and, Ali, dear, if you would be so kind as to dispose of the little one, I'd greatly appreciate it."

I raised my hand. "If you take a single step forward, I will send all of you flying so far that you'll cross into Elwrite."

"You're awfully confident for a girl who couldn't even heal a knife wound."

My facade of strength wavered.

Ruger smirked. "As I thought." He tossed a glance over his shoulder. "Kill them."

Animo drew a blade. "Off the roof!"

I snatched Megs's arm, dragging her to the edge. "Jump."

"Not before you."

"Megs—"

"I'm not letting you stay behind!"

Ali's right hook collided with my face, knocking me down. White spots burst across my vision as my head smacked against stone.

I blinked slowly as my eyesight returned. Above me, Megs grappled with Ali, their arms locked together. Animo's blade met Ruger's while Dante lay, moaning on the ground beside them.

"Deal with that one, Elias!" Ruger shouted, nodding in my direction before slashing at Animo. I struggled to my feet as the bruised Elias advanced.

Megs elbowed Ali, giving herself just enough of a window to draw a small knife. She sent it spinning toward Elias, lodging firmly in his arm. He shouted, doubling over. I sprang forward, slamming his head into my knee before throwing him to the ground.

Megs knocked Ali down. Stumbling away, her gaze landed on the blood wetting Elias's sleeve. Her eyes widened.

I ran to her, offering my hand. "Come on. We'll jump together."

She slipped her hand into mine, her gaze transfixed on Elias.

"Guards!" Belinda shouted from the door.

Animo and Ruger broke apart, a silent truce flashing in their eyes. Megs and

I ran to the window as the Cunningham gang regrouped. *They're the guards' problem now.* Holding onto Megs's shoulder for balance, I stepped onto the roof's edge. The image of a net formed in my mind. My magic flowed through the ropes, tying them into unbreakable knots. Though it was unseen, I knew it was there.

I jumped.

Megs shouted. Wind kicked my dress up around my thighs as I fell. My spell caught me, holding me aloft like a bird riding the breeze.

"I love that you have magic!" Megs shouted, practically hanging over the edge.

"It's your turn," I called back. "Jump."

She didn't hesitate, swinging her legs over the side of the roof and slipping into the air with a scream. I extended ends of my spell to catch her as she fell.

Her fear melted into a whoop of delight. She moved her limbs as though she was swimming. "This is amazing!"

I grinned. "Where's Animo?"

"Holding off the guards."

"What?"

Pain shot through my arm. I screamed—a short arrow was lodged in my bicep. My magic wavered, and Megs and I plummeted toward the canal.

Squeezing my eyes shut, I threw the ends of my invisible net out. The spell caught us, rougher than it had before. I gripped my arm as blood dripped down my skin. On the rooftop, one of the Triani's guards reloaded a crossbow.

"What are you doing up there?" Ketch called from below. He stood in the bow of a gondola, rowed by a wide-eyed Hertz still wearing his feathered hat.

I clenched my teeth, unable to reply without losing all control of my magic. My head throbbed from the strength of my spell, and every movement sent fresh pain through my arm.

With a few muttered curses, Ketch drew a slingshot and sent a stone flying. A shout rang out from above followed by a crossbow splashing into the canal.

"Get down here, now!" Ketch shouted.

I took deep, rattling breaths. The threads of my spell were tight and ready to snap. I squeezed my eyes shut, my hands shaking as I lowered us toward the gondola.

Something hard slammed into my shoulder. I yelped, opening my eyes just in time to see a dagger splash into the canal.

"Animo!" I cried. My head spun, my vision blurring. Somewhere on the rooftop, Animo shouted.

With an invisible shove, I sent Megs careening to the other side of the canal, landing on the stone street. A heavy weight lifted from me as I released the spell keeping her aloft. I turned my attention to Animo, who stood on the edge of the balcony, locked in combat with two of the Trianis' guards.

I threw my magic at the guards, knocking them back. "Jump!" I called to Animo.

He threw himself over the edge without hesitation.

I cast my net out as he plummeted, the threads of my magic pulling taut. The moment Animo hit the net, it snapped.

We hurtled toward the canal like a pair of rocks. I screamed as I fell, a sharp sting racing across my skin as I smacked into the water. I surfaced as Animo splashed down beside me.

"Are you all right?" he asked, looking worse than I felt. His breaths came heavily, and blood and exhaustion covered his face.

"Yes." I choked, gagging on the rotten water. "Are you?"

"I am."

I took a deep breath that I regretted immediately. The rank stench flooded my nostrils, leaving a burning sensation in its wake.

The gondola floated over to us, now bearing Megs. Ketch hung over the bow, holding out a hand.

"Get in," he said. He and Megs hauled us on board while Hertz continued rowing. Once inside the boat, Animo grabbed an extra oar, propelling us away from the manor. We didn't stop until the lights of the first ring had faded.

I exhaled slowly, for once grateful for the thick stench of the second ring.

"So," Ketch asked, looking between me and Animo, "what did we miss?"

CHAPTER NINETEEN

LOST FOREVER

I spent an hour in the bathtub, scrubbing the canal's filth from my skin until the water turned cold and pink from blood. I climbed out, wrapping myself in a towel as fresh blood trickled, running across my skin like external veins. Dabbing it away, I called upon my magic. Power flickered within me, reaching toward the arrow wound in my arm. It wound itself around the hole like the strings of a purse. When I tried to pull it closed, the strings broke. My heart plummeted. When had my magic become so weak?

"Sinet caelai san esede," I recited, letting the Aesin words strengthen my ekeider powers. This time the wound scabbed, but left me with an aching head.

A foul taste filled my mouth. Years ago, I had mastered healing spells. I was the one who had kept the Ardent Pack alive during the months of brutal battles.

I'd healed everything from small scratches to tattered organs. How could that power fail me now?

A knock sounded on the door. "Animo wants us in his room," Megs called.

"I'll be there in a moment." I shivered as I pulled on my clothes. Part of me wanted to warm myself with a spell, but most of me knew that it would be a waste of what little energy I had. And a tiny part in the shadows of my mind wondered if I would even be able to cast it.

I drew my damp hair over my shoulder, taking in the scent of the honey soap Megs had brought from Rudane. *Smells like home.* I tossed my dress onto a chair, then picked up the pieces of the broken staff before joining my companions in Ketch and Animo's room.

Each one of them bore the marks of a harsh night. Scratches climbed up and down Megs's arms from where I had dropped her on the street, while Ketch sported an inexplicable bruise on his forehead. Only Hertz seemed fine, simply bearing a small cut on his chin.

Animo, on the other hand, was far from fine. He'd cleaned the blood from his skin, donning one of his few shirts—if not his only shirt—free of stains. Bruises marred his knuckles while the cuts on his neck and forehead continued beading with blood despite being shallow.

I tossed the broken staff onto the table and pulled out a chair across from Hertz.

"Dragon in the room," Megs began, joining us at the table, still dressed in her green gown. "The staff isn't real."

"This one isn't," I clarified. "The Countess *had* the real staff, but it was stolen by a woman named Elizabeth Sconcewood."

Animo and Ketch exchanged a speculative glance.

"It could be her," Ketch said.

"Who?" Megs asked.

"Aspectu."

I straightened. If Aspectu had the Staff of Realms, then everything we were looking for would be in one place.

Hertz held up his hands. "Wait, stop. Last I saw, we were being tricked by thieves, then chased by guards. When did all of this happen?"

"I can explain," I said. "The meeting was a trick. Because Countess Triani lost the real Staff of Realms, she hired Ruger Cunningham to steal the fake before her recently returned husband could uncover the truth. Ruger sent the girl, Belinda, to steal the fake staff just before the twenty-third hour. She was to bring it upstairs so he could resell it to Lashier, who would then become a scapegoat."

Megs chimed in. "Only, Ruger realized that we were also frauds. Though, I'm not exactly sure how."

"Elias Cunningham," Animo said. "He was at the bar the night we stole Lashier's invitation."

"Cunningham," I repeated. "Ruger's brother?"

"Most likely." Animo sighed. "He spent the night drinking with Lashier. I thought he was a friend, not the errand boy of a forged countess."

Ketch groaned. "Rack. I remember him."

"All right, then Elias was able to identify that Animo was *not* Lashier," I said.

"Which put us in a standoff with Ruger," Animo added. "Between that and Rose's and my delay, we wasted enough time that the Countess's guards had already discovered the staff's disappearance."

"Then came the guards, who took me to the Countess's study, which is where she revealed that the real staff had been stolen," I finished. "And after that came fighting and running and then more fighting." I looked at Hertz. "Does that clear things up?"

He nodded, though his blank stare suggested he hadn't comprehended a word.

"There were five total thieves," Animo said, his arms folded and his fingers tapping lightly against his bicep. "Three men and two women."

"Ruger, Ali, Elias, Dante, and Belinda," I recited, counting on my fingers.

"Do you think that was all of them?" Megs asked.

"Absolutely," Ketch said. "A gang of five fills all the positions needed for a heist. Ruger's the leader. He plans and oversees all the heists. Then you have the muscle."

"Dante!" Megs exclaimed, perking up. "He was huge compared to the others."

"He'd have to be. It's the muscle's job to beat the way out when things go wrong."

Megs leaned forward. "What about the women?"

"Two. One pretty, one small…" An odd smile twisted Ketch's lips. "The first is a grifter. Her face alone will open locks, and her ability to lie will empty the vault entirely. As for the little one, she's a thief, plain and simple. Likely some kind of orphan or stray. Small enough to fit into tight spaces and disposable enough that it won't matter if she's caught."

"And Ruger's brother?" Megs pressed. "What's his job?"

Ketch let out a snorting laugh. "A family member who drinks on the job? He's the throwaway, no doubt. He likely plays the lookout most of the time. Too bad tonight he was given the role of the Countess's butler."

"How do you know all of this?" Megs practically lay on the table, her chin in her hands and her attention transfixed on Ketch's every word.

He pushed up both his brows. "Life."

"Wow." She picked up the broken shards of the fake staff, twirling them around. "Why didn't we think to steal the staff?"

"Because it's a crime," Hertz exclaimed. "Crime never works."

"I know. You have to work to make crime." She tapped the staff against her forehead.

Hertz rolled his eyes, exhausted. "Is fraud and impersonation not enough for you?"

She waved the notion away. "I've done that before. But I've never experienced a real heist. Not as the heister, at least."

Hertz sighed as though he were one sentence away from a headache. "Why does any of this matter? What we need now is to find the real staff."

"What *I* need to do," I said. "This is where it ends for you two."

Megs dropped the shards. "Are you serious? You would have died on that rooftop if it weren't for me." She pointed at Ketch and Animo. "And if you want to find Aspectu, you'll need the help of the two people who have actually met her."

"I'm aware of that. Animo has already agreed to help me." I met his gaze, momentarily afraid that he had changed his mind. To my relief, he nodded.

"Ketch and I will help Rose find Aspectu and the Staff of Realms, and then we will defeat Natalia."

"Why can't we help too?" Megs demanded.

"Because you are not warriors," I said. "Or thieves. But if you stay with me, that is exactly what you will become." *That, or worse.*

"You're right, Rose," Hertz said. "We're not warriors. But we're your friends, and if you tell us to leave, Megs will hunt you down, and I will not stop her. I'll be by her side until we find you."

I clenched my jaw. "I don't want your blood on my hands."

"And I don't want to spend the rest of my life waiting and wondering if you'll ever come home."

Tears pressed against my eyes. "I can't get rid of you, can I?"

He shook his head. "Not a chance."

Megs stood, planting herself by his side. "We will follow you to the ends of the Twelve Kingdoms, whether you like it or not. *And,*" she added before I could object, "we'll be in far more danger if you don't bring us with you. Think about it: Hertz and me, alone against an army of shades. We wouldn't stand a chance. But with you, Animo, and Ketch, we'll be just fine."

I gripped the arms of my chair, forcing myself to think of anything *but* Megs and Hertz fighting shades.

Ketch clicked his tongue. "Sorry, Rose, but I think you've lost this battle."

"I agree," Animo said. "At this point, Natalia's forces could be anywhere. If we let them go off on their own, there's no telling what they'll encounter."

I sighed. "Fine. But you have to promise me that when we find Aspectu, you will do *whatever* she tells you to do."

Megs nodded. "We promise."

"I promise," Hertz echoed.

"Very well then," I said. "If Animo's hunch is correct, Aspectu has the Staff of Realms, which means the next logical step is to find her."

Ketch grimaced. "It's not that easy. Aspectu spoke to Animo just a few days before we arrived, and she still intended to meet us here. That drastic of a change is not a good sign. Especially considering the state of her house."

"But if she had the staff, she could go anywhere," Megs pointed out. "She could have escaped the shades, then come back for Rose."

"Then why didn't she?" Hertz asked.

"We need to track Aspectu," Animo said, ignoring him. "Ketch and I will create a list of her most likely destinations, and we can go from there."

"Maybe she went to a hideout," Megs offered.

Ketch tilted his head. "She could have gone to Daria."

Animo shot him a deadly glare. "She wouldn't have."

"Daria," Hertz repeated. "As in the city of elves?"

"Is there another Daria?" Ketch asked.

"She won't be there," Animo insisted, his words directed at Ketch. "It's been months since she left. To go back now would be suicide."

"Why?" I asked.

He sighed, a tight smile pulling on his lips. "The elven king and Aspectu don't see eye to eye."

I folded my arms. "Is it safe to assume that your association with her puts you in the king's poor graces?"

His expression darkened. "Something like that. And he wouldn't be too fond of finding the resurrected Crown Princess of Avonshere wandering about his kingdom, either."

"The elf king wants me dead?"

"The elf king is weak," he said sharply. "He's sided with Natalia before, and he'll do it again. Going to Daria will only end in pain."

"Will Aspectu be there?" I asked.

"No."

"Ketch?"

Ketch hesitated, glancing between me and Animo. "It would be dangerous for her to return... But not impossible."

"Ketch!" Animo exclaimed.

"She has supplies there," Ketch said defensively. "Maybe Natalia's attack was more than simply the shades. Maybe Apsectu needed something powerful to heal herself or fight back. If so, Daria is the best place to look for her."

"That settles it," I said. "We're going to Daria."

"Rose—"

"No," I said before Animo could finish. "It's clear that everywhere I turn, there will be someone eager to kill me. I'm running toward the point of Natalia's sword, and the Staff of Realms is the only chance I have to evade it. If there's any chance we can find it in Daria, we have to take it."

"You don't know what you're walking into," he warned.

"You keep telling me to be a leader. A *queen*. If that's true, then you should be glad to see me taking the lead."

His eyes hardened. "Fine. We'll leave in the morning."

"Good." I clasped my hands together and turned to face my friends. "Get plenty of rest tonight. Tomorrow the real journey begins."

"In that case, let's celebrate our last night of reliable food," Ketch said. "Drinks are on me!"

One by one they filed out of the room, leaving me and Animo alone.

I folded my arms. "Are you going to tell me why you're fighting against us going to Daria?" His courage bordered on suicidal—it couldn't have been the threat of death holding him back.

"We all have our pasts," he said, stoking the crackling fire. "Mine has shown me the darker side of the world."

Had our alliance been stronger, I would have pressed. But the ice below us was thin, and I doubted that adding to my hypocrisies would improve matters, leaving me to watch him in silence.

He stared into the fire. His eyes reflected the glow of the flames, but the warmth died within. Something else burned, a dull, cold blaze in his hollow gaze. *Pain.*

I opened my mouth to speak, but Megs burst into the room.

"We've been robbed."

Animo and I raced past her and into my room. Nothing appeared to have been moved. My gown remained, draped over the chair back, all the drawers were all in place, and the nightstand—*no.*

I rushed forward. "They took the restrictor cuff."

"And my ring." Megs shook her head, tossing her purse onto the bed. Lifting her skirts, she hurried toward the door. "I need to find Hertz."

"They left the gowns," Animo said, eyeing my gala dress. "They weren't here for riches."

"You think the thieves were after something in particular?"

"Perhaps. What did you have other than the restrictor cuff?"

"Not much." *I had some clothes and travel supplies, but nothing*—it struck me like bells at the final hour. "Oh, Kingdoms…" I threw the pillow off my bed, tearing off the sheets and then searching the floor underneath. "No, no, no! They took my chest."

Animo's eyes widened. "That had the Wolfe family crest on it."

"I know."

"If they trace it back to you—"

"You don't have to tell me," I snapped. I let out a curse, flinging the pillow across the room. Whoever took the chest was one step closer to exposing my secret.

"We're a long way from Avonshere," Animo began, his voice calm but his fists clenched. "Maybe I'm wrong. Maybe they don't know what it means, and when they find they can't open it, they'll abandon it."

"Is the thought of my family heirloom thrown in the gutters meant to comfort me?"

"Better forgotten than traced back to you."

I shook my head. "We can't leave anything behind. Natalia can't know what we're after."

Megs raced into the room, followed by Hertz. "It doesn't seem like anyone else was robbed," she said. "Ketch is downstairs asking around."

"What was stolen?" Hertz asked.

"The restrictor cuff and my chest, containing the only portraits of my family that weren't destroyed," I said with a light huff.

"As well as the ring I wore to the Gala," Megs added. "But they didn't take any of our money. At first, I thought I'd lost the ring on the roof. Then I saw the window."

Animo examined the open window. "The lock is broken."

"So thieves broke into your room and stole three things of unknown value." Hertz furrowed his brow. "Why?"

"Either they're fools, or they knew who we were." I left my friends, crossing to Animo's room. The broken staff lay on the table, now dull and battered. *Like me.*

Animo followed me, closing the door behind him. "What are you going to do with it?"

"Get rid of it." I pushed open the window, overlooking the canal. With as much distance as I could manage, I threw the shards out. They splashed down, one after the other. I pulled the window shut, then pointed at the closed wardrobe.

"We can't be tied to anyone's murder. You need to get rid of Lashier and make certain no one sees you."

He nodded. "I'll take care of it."

I released a shaky breath. The chest was the only loose end left. It hurt to admit it, but my best hope now was for the chest and its memories to be lost forever.

PART THREE

CHAPTER TWENTY

FAR FROM HOME

A light breeze blew strands of hair into my face. I tucked them behind my ear, taking in a deep breath of forest air. Our journey had taken us far from Lucia's swamps and into the open meadows of Southern Elwrite. From there, we traveled north until the cool shadows of trees fell over us once more, wrapping me in their comforting embrace.

My thoughts strayed to our last morning in Medea when Animo had handed me a letter that smelled strangely of salt and rum. It read:

The Estmars have left for the safe house. I will send a second confirmation when they arrive, but I doubt Natalia will chase them. It is clear that they know nothing of value. Before they left, I had them instruct anyone who might be at risk to leave town.

We'll port in Shab in two weeks' time. Awaiting further instructions.

- CH

They're safe. The Estmars are safe. I'd held the letter against my chest as gratitude swelled within me. I'd looked up at Animo as the final shreds of my resentment dissipated. "Thank you."

Later, I asked about the mysterious *C.H.*, but he replied simply, "She's an ally."

The conversation ended, and C.H. faded to the back of my mind. Her identity didn't matter, not if she protected my family. Besides, I had more pressing matters to worry about. The closer we came to Vaera's border, the darker Animo's mood became. He refused to explain why and grew more reserved when one of us asked a question—especially if the question had to do with the king.

"If we're going to be attacked the moment we cross the border, I should know," I said, sitting on a stump. Twilight had fallen, forcing us to make camp less than a day's walk from Vaera. While Megs, Hertz, and Ketch dealt with the bedding and rations, Animo built a campfire on a bare patch of dirt.

"Do you really think I would allow us to walk into a trap?" He arranged logs in a teepee formation atop a pile of kindling.

"I think you're being a hypocrite."

His eyes snapped to mine, flashing with irritation, before settling into amusement as a faint smile traced his lips. "Perhaps I am."

I leaned forward, resting my elbows on my knees. "That doesn't bother you?"

"Not in this case." He returned to fiddling with the sticks. "We both have things we'd rather keep to ourselves. You have been denying me answers for over a month now—it only seems fair I do the same."

"I suppose you're right. And if you refrain from asking about my past, I'll refrain from asking about yours."

"Good." For a moment, he seemed satisfied. Then he sat back. "I have a better idea. I ask you a question about your past, and if you answer it, you get to ask me a question about mine."

My eyes narrowed. "You want to trade truths." If his past inquiries were any indication, he would dig at my worst memories and drag my darkest secrets to light.

But if we're to be allies, I need to know things about him. And, more importantly, about what awaits us in Daria.

I held out my hand. "Deal."

We shook on it, and then Animo returned to assembling the fire. "Why do you think killing Natalia is all it will take to save Avonshere?"

That's surprisingly non-invasive. "Because there is still good in that kingdom, and once Natalia is dead, it will finally have a chance to grow."

"And who will lead them?"

I raised a finger. "Ah, ah! That's a second question."

"Fair enough. You ask."

I paused thoughtfully. Chances were he had intentionally started off with a light question. Eventually, he would pull on the wrong thread of my tapestry of lies, and I'd have to stop our game before the whole thing unraveled. I needed to choose my questions carefully.

"Why did you leave Daria?" I asked.

"I saw the truth. The city I called home was a place of blissful ignorance—a cage masquerading as a haven." He drew a piece of flint from his bag and began raking a knife across it, sending sparks skipping toward the kindling. "Now, I want to know whom you'd have lead Avonshere."

"Someone… capable. Someone who will care for the people and help rebuild what was destroyed." *Someone who won't hurt them like I did.* "My turn. What—?"

"I am not going to accept *someone capable* as an answer," Animo said, halting his blade at the top of the flint. "That is an assumed part of leadership, not a specific quality the next queen needs. You can either give me a better answer, or I get to ask another question."

I huffed, folding my arms. "Fine. Ask again."

While he thought, he gave the flint a sharp scrape. Sparks flew, catching the kindling and Animo's brow twitched. "What really happened that night in Darvyn?"

I stiffened. Dead leaves twisted, urging the flames to grow, licking the logs. In my mind, the wood turned to flesh. Charred limbs draped haphazardly atop one another. People screamed. I ran.

Animo's features fell, his curiosity shifting into concern. "I'm sorry. I didn't mean to awaken anything."

"It's fine." I spoke the words harsher than I'd intended. "Just… warn me before anything in Daria kills us."

I stood before he could ask another question, crossing the clearing to where Megs sat, her back against a fallen log and a strange, bronze object in her lap. Hertz slept a little ways away, using his cloak as a blanket and his arm as a pillow. I dropped onto the log with a huff, expelling my pent-up emotions.

"Is Elf-Man nettling your head?" Megs asked, smirking as she twirled a small brass tool between her fingers.

"Something like that."

She raised her eyebrows, clearly drawing the wrong conclusion. Using the slanted tool, she pried a lidlike panel off the bronze sphere.

I furrowed my brow. "What is that thing?"

"My invention!"

"*That's* the message sphere?"

"I'm not calling it that. But yes."

I leaned forward as she poked around with her tool. Runes—likely dwarvish—had been carved into the metal, and inside sat an array of gears streaked with soot and speckled with sparkling, orange powder.

My lips twitched. "The crystals didn't work, did they?"

"Not… exactly. I mean, they *ignited*, but they didn't set off the message."

"I told you not to fool around with magic."

"Maybe you're right. Maybe I should let someone more *experienced* handle it." She offered me the sphere with a smile. "Care to take a look, Madame Ekeider?"

"I can heal a stab wound and knock you across the clearing, but I don't know any spells for message spheres."

"Again. I'm not calling it that."

"Fine, portable time saver for people with poor handwriting."

"I do not have poor handwriting!"

"I've seen chickens with better penmanship," Hertz grumbled, his eyes still closed.

Megs kicked him playfully. "Go back to sleep." He rolled away, tugging his cloak higher.

"I can't help," I repeated.

"Fine." Megs scrunched her nose as she struggled with something inside the device. "If only I could figure out what's stopping it… Ah!" Something snapped. "Biaht."

"I take it that wasn't supposed to happen."

"No. Although it might work…" a yawn drowned her words. Rubbing her eyes, she set aside the device. "That's tomorrow's problem. I'm going to get some sleep. Good night, Rose."

"Good night."

She pulled her blanket up to her chin, curling her limbs into a tight ball. As the season progressed, so did the chill of night, though it still wasn't cold enough to make me miss Lucia.

I drew my knees against my chest and stared into the crackling fire. Within a day, we'd be at Vaera's border. In all my worrying about not finding Aspectu, I hadn't even considered what would happen when we did find her and the Staff of Realms. Once I had my hands on the staff, there would be no more running. But could I actually manage it?

It wasn't the act of killing I was afraid of. No, what scared me was the chance of being caught. If something went wrong, if I were seen in Avonshere, I would end up trapped behind palace walls for the rest of my life. And as an immortal halfling, the rest of my life was a terribly long time.

"You know, these quests often go smoother if you refrain from worrying so much." Ketch took a seat on the log beside me, letting his feet dangle above the grass.

"Is that what you do?" I asked. "Run into danger without a thought?"

"I find it best not to wallow in fears of the future or in the misery of the past. Sure, that makes life dangerous, but it makes it exciting, too." He rubbed the place where his ear used to be and grimaced. "Although that type of living does have its downsides."

"I'll stick with my way of living," I said, stretching out my legs.

He wrinkled his nose. "Farm life and hunting? That's the way you want to live?"

"I want to live in safety. If that means farming, then so be it."

"Is it really safety you're after, or an escape?"

I scoffed. "Now you sound like Animo."

"'I'll take that as a compliment."

The chirps of crickets filled our silence before I spoke. "May I ask you something?"

Ketch nodded.

"I'm on this quest because of my duty to Avonshere. Megs and Hertz are here because of their love for me, and Animo is here because of his loyalty to Aspectu. But what about you? Why are you putting your life on the line for something that shouldn't concern you?"

"Because I have nowhere else to be." He paused, rubbing his hands together. "A few years ago, I was in Vargo due to questionable, alcohol-influenced decisions. One thing led to another, and before I knew it, I was trapped in the Salt Mines of Sheildore."

"I've heard of that—It was a prison work camp, but it was shut down decades ago, wasn't it?"

Ketch laughed bitterly. "That was a treaty-inducing lie. Sheildore kept its gates open for the worst lawbreakers of them all. No one who entered was ever seen again."

"Sults," I muttered. Vargo was no stranger to skirting beneath the rules. Of all the Twelve Kingdoms, it had the most treachery written into its monarchy. They were the first kingdom whose founding family died out, and it wasn't due to natural causes.

"Don't worry," Ketch assured me. "Sheildore's no longer an issue."

"Am I to assume that you had something to do with that?"

"I had everything to do with it. Well, me and an elf who knows his way around black powder."

I didn't need any prompting to imagine what came next. "Animo destroyed the mine."

Ketch nodded. "He saved me from Sheildore. I owe him my life."

I glanced across the campsite at Animo, his back against a tree as he sharpened his sword. "So that's why you stay with him."

"I stay with him because he has a *purpose,*" Ketch explained. "A long time ago, I lost my way. And when I received a second chance, I realized that I could return to Pikbrie and try to salvage what I had left behind, or I could use my life to do something that matters."

"Wait, why was Animo in Shieldore?"

Ketch bit back a grin. "There were rumors of a lost princess in Vargo. He thought it was you."

Of course he did.

"I'm going to get some sleep. I'd suggest you do the same." He slid off the log, then flopped down onto his blanket, tucking his arm beneath his head.

"In a minute."

I sat on the log far longer than a minute, staring aimlessly at the ground until soft footsteps approached.

"I truly am sorry," Animo said.

I kept my gaze low, avoiding his. "Does it happen to you when you think of Daria? Do the memories take over?"

"Sometimes," he admitted. "But mostly, they cause anger."

"You were hurt there?"

"I was."

I bit my lip. "I'm sorry… I don't mean to hurt you or be a hypocrite. But I need to find the staff."

"I understand. And it's not you that hurts me. It's going back when I can't do anything to help."

I raised my eyes. We were the same, he and I. Scarred hearts beat in our chests while broken lands watched us. The only difference was our role. Animo was the hero, willing to sacrifice everything to save his home. But me? Was I meant to be my story's queen, or was I destined for something much worse?

"You should sleep," he said. "I'll keep watch."

He returned to the fire, and I settled on the ground, blades of grass tickling my bare arms. The forest hummed with life, but the noise no longer brought me peace. When the sun rose, I put on a refreshed smile, letting the smoke in my mind dissipate.

Time to face Animo's ghosts.

CHAPTER TWENTY-ONE

THE TUNNEL

"How much longer til we reach the border?" Megs asked for the third time in fifteen minutes.

"Not long," Animo replied, also for the third time in fifteen minutes.

I stifled a groan at the repeated exchange. We'd been walking for five hours, and my steps had grown sluggish against a path of never-ending Elwritian ground.

"Let's take a break," Ketch suggested, already sliding the bag from his back.

"Good idea." Animo tossed his pack onto the ground. Shading his eyes, he surveyed a looming tree. "Think I could climb that?"

Ketch shrugged. "You could probably make it."

"Why would you climb?" Hertz asked.

"To see the border," Megs said before Animo could even attempt a response.

"How is he meant to see a border in a *forest?*"

"Trust me, he will," Ketch said as Animo began his climb. The elf scaled the tree with ease, disappearing into the green foliage.

"Here." Hertz handed me one of our flasks.

"Thank you." Tilting my head back, I drained the last few gulps of water. "How many do we have left?"

He rummaged through his pack. "Two full, one half full."

"And rations?"

"Two, maybe three days. Either way, it's scarce." He heaved the bag onto his shoulder with a clank of tin pots. "Maybe we should stop and hunt before continuing to Daria."

I shook my head. "We can't stop. Once Natalia realizes we're after Aspectu, she'll have no trouble predicting where we're going. Even a short delay could cost us."

"About that." Megs joined us, a weathered scroll in her hand. "I've been looking over the map, and Avonshere is about the same distance to Vaera as Lucia is. If Natalia expects us to go to Daria, is it possible that she's already there?"

"Yes." Animo dropped from the tree, landing on the balls of his feet. "And if Natalia goes to Daria, she'll receive a much warmer welcome than we will."

We all looked at Ketch, but instead of contradicting Animo, he nodded.

Rack.

"So we could be walking right into a trap?" Hertz asked angrily.

Ketch held up a hand. "Now hold on. We *do* have an advantage. There are only two safe ways in and out of Daria. One is the king's private road—a direct path from the palace to the sea, which is guarded at all times. The only way through it is with signed approval. The other option is a secret tunnel known to a select few."

"How are there only two ways?" Megs asked. "Is the city surrounded by a wall or something?"

"Something," Animo muttered.

"The king's road," I began, refocusing the conversation. "How long would it take Natalia to gain access?"

"If she wrote to the king and asked for permission, it could take weeks," Animo replied. "But the elven guard isn't as equipped as they used to be. Natalia could easily fight her way to the king, who will fold the moment he realizes he's in danger."

"Are you telling us that everyone in the city would turn us over to Natalia?" Hertz asked.

Animo held his gaze with one of stone. "It wasn't my idea to come here."

Doubt slithered into Hertz's eyes. He gripped his pack tighter.

Animo snatched his bag from the ground. "Let's keep moving. I caught a glimpse of the border, and we're close."

We quickly gathered our belongings, then set off with Animo in the lead. Ketch lagged behind, his eyes locked on his friend's back.

"Is everything all right with him?" I asked in a low voice.

"Normal," Ketch replied.

"If the elf king is the enemy, how are we supposed to stay safe in Daria?" Hertz asked, either oblivious to or ignoring my and Ketch's conversation.

"Aspectu has been an outcast among the elves for twenty years," Animo called from ahead. "Her home sits on the outskirts of Daria, and she and the king have an agreement to keep their noses out of one another's business. He doesn't bother her, she won't bother him."

"So the king is, what, afraid of her?" Hertz asked.

"Aspectu is the last of the elven elders. She survived the Dark War and knows more about magic than he ever will." Animo glanced over his shoulder. "He's terrified of her."

We maintained a steady pace through the forest. Though we were weeks into the harvest season, green leaves rustled above me, shaken by a refreshing, morning breeze. It was one of Elwrite's many charms: no matter how cold or snowy the climate grew, the grass stayed green and flowers bloomed in a pastel rainbow.

I plucked a plump, pink flower from a nearby bush. One by one, I picked the petals, dropping them into the lush grass and leaving a pale trail in my wake. I watched the next float to the ground, landing on a blade of gray grass.

The flower fell from my hand as I raised my eyes. "Kingdoms!"

All color had drained from the world. A river of skeletal grass split the forest in two. Across it loomed great trees cloaked in shadows, their ashen bark dripping sinister tidings like sap.

"That's it, isn't it?" Megs said. "That's the border."

"On this side, we're in Elwrite," Animo said, his hollow tone directed at himself rather than us. "Once you step across, you're in Vaera."

Hertz set his shoulders, his fingers brushing the axe strapped to his back. "No time to waste, then."

"Not so fast." Ketch stopped Hertz mid-step, then gestured at the forest. "We're not going in there."

"Why not?" Hertz asked.

Ketch stared at him like he was a child asking to play in hot coals. "That's the *Silver Forest*."

"Sounds pretty," Megs said, earning herself Ketch's hot coal stare.

"What's the Silver Forest?" I asked.

"Its true name is *Silvaris Mortane*," Animo said. "Travelers misunderstood. Believing the name referred to the trees' color, they began calling it the Silver Forest. They had no idea that its Aesin name meant *trees of death*."

My eyebrows shot up. "I beg your pardon?"

He smiled humorlessly. "Remember how I told you there were only two ways out of Daria? The forest is why. Centuries of dark magic have cursed it and every being who sets foot inside. Many travelers ignore the legends, but out of every hundred who enter, only one will make it out alive."

"But won't our tunnel take us through the forest?" Megs asked, her voice unusually high.

"The tunnel is protected by magic," Ketch assured her. "The curse won't be able to reach us."

I gazed at the lifeless treeline. It stood still as though something blocked the wind from entering. Like the walls of a tomb.

"Rethinking the Daria plan?" Animo asked.

I shook my head. "No. We have to find Aspectu."

"Then we should be going—we're only at the border." He led us along the edge of the dead path, careful to avoid the colorless grass.

"There's a cave a little way down," Ketch explained as we walked. "It will take us straight into Daria and keep us away from all *that*." He gestured at the dark tree line.

"What exactly is in the Silver Forest?" I asked.

"Ooh." He took a deep breath. "To start with, everything in the Silver Forest is eager to kill you. The worst of them all are the goblins—they practically rule the forest. Well, them and the witches."

"Witches live in there?"

"They love the dark magic."

"What do you—?" I stopped myself. "On second thought, I don't want to know."

"Probably best. Stories lead to curiosity, and curiosity leads to actions."

"Finally, something we can agree on," Hertz muttered.

I glanced over at him. I hadn't even realized he was listening.

"You know," Ketch began. "Actions are what drove the Lost Prince of Daria to his fate."

"The Lost Prince of Daria?"

"The grandson of Salvator Regiis. He was born the same day the Goblin–Elf Wars ended and grew up hearing stories of the heroism and sacrifice that led to peace. But when he grew older, he learned the truth behind the tales. He went into the Silver Forest to confront the goblins and set things right. That was the last time Daria saw him."

"Did he die in the forest?" I asked. "And what was the truth? Did the war not end as he believed?"

Ketch's eyes twinkled victoriously. "You see—"

"We found the cave!" Animo called.

The spark in Ketch's eye faded. "Until next time," he said, hurrying ahead.

"He's an odd fellow, isn't he?" Hertz commented.

"Maybe… but I like him." I nudged Hertz with my elbow. "Let's go."

We joined the others at what appeared to be a long boulder protruding from the Silver Forest, narrowly reaching Elwritian soil. A thick crack split the stone face, barely wide enough to fit a person.

I gawked. "*That's* the entrance?"

"It gets bigger." Animo drew a bottle and linen-wrapped torch from his bag, pulling the cork out with his teeth.

I sniffed. "Is that rum?"

He nodded, dousing the torch with the brown liquid.

I glanced at Ketch. "And you're all right with him burning it?"

The dwarf grimaced. "He can burn all the rum he likes. It's long been ruined for me."

"Shieldore?"

He shook his head, his disgusted frown deepening.

"Don't run out of conversation so soon," Animo said, balancing the torch between his knees as he lit it. "It's a long journey from here."

"How long?" Hertz asked.

"Three days, maybe four. No time to waste." Animo passed the torch to Ketch, then squeezed through the crack, disappearing into darkness.

I had to trust Animo's word as we made our way through the tunnel. Our flickering torchlight cut the darkness, illuminating the stalactites that hung like dragon's teeth. Ghostly shadows danced along the wall in unnervingly shade-like shapes.

The constant gurgle of water filled the hours, joined by the rustle of bats' wings overhead. My steps became that of a corpse, mindless and heavy as Animo's every warning haunted the cavern's echoes.

Am I doing the right thing, or am I leading us to our doom?

Darkness answered my unspoken question. I continued down the slick and uneven path, allowing my doubts to bury themselves in my mind. Not gone, not forgotten, only buried.

A woman's voice called to me.

I sat up. My companions slept in a circle around the burning torch—none had spoken. I pushed myself to my feet, looking about.

A woman stepped from the shadows, the hem of her dark-green dress brushing against the cavern floor. Dark-brown hair fell over her shoulders in gentle waves, and her eyes—her eyes matched the blue of the sky, laced with veins of gold.

"Mother?"

She smiled. "Rose, I've missed you."

"Mother!" I ran into her open arms.

"Oh, darling," she crooned, stroking my hair.

"I need your help," I cried. "I'm not like you. I can't lead armies or inspire the people to fight. I don't know what to do anymore. Everyone wants me to return to Avonshere, but I don't know if I can."

"You should return," she said.

"But what if I cause more harm than good?"

"Darling... I know you will."

I pulled away as a dark glint slipped into my mother's eye.

"You left Avonshere in such a hurry. You didn't have time to kill all who were loyal to you."

"I never meant for anyone to die."

"Didn't you?" She shook her head, her gaze filled with disappointment. "If only they could see you now."

"I can bring about a better future. I can kill Natalia—"

Her sharp laugh cut me off. "No daughter of mine would ever believe such childish fantasies. Returning to Avonshere would be your demise."

"No." I pointed a trembling finger at her. "No, because you aren't really here. You're dead. You're just in my imagination."

A hint of sadness entered her eyes as she gazed at her hands. "You're right. I am dead."

Her skin ripped open. Blood trickled from her eyes, wrists, lips, and neck until every inch of her spilled scarlet. I watched, horror-struck, as the blood dripped against the cave floor.

"No." I backed away. "Stop... please."

My mother shook her head, splattering blood across my face. I tried to scream, but her hand closed around my neck. Black spots blurred my vision as she forced me to the ground.

"You can't escape this," she hissed. "Death is coming."

A pale figure caught my gaze—a woman clad in white, her ice-blue eyes fixed on me. I opened my mouth to call to the Woman in White, but my mother's grip tightened, cutting off my breath. I drew my dagger and stabbed—

I shot up, thrashing about, my grip tight on an invisible blade.

"You're alright." Animo caught my wrists, stopping my wild, weaponless stabs.

"Where—where is she?" My eyes jumped about nervously, but all I found were shadows.

He pulled me close. Without thinking, I curled into the embrace, allowing his warmth to envelope me. "You were dreaming," he said, his fingers buried in my hair. "Whoever you saw, she wasn't real."

I released a shaky breath, nestling my head atop his shoulder. Silence hung, broken only by the steady drip of water.

"Water hitting stone sounds the same as blood." I slipped out of Animo's arms.

"It was your mother, wasn't it?" he asked as I settled on my blankets.

"How did you know?"

"Consider it a lucky guess."

Our silence returned. The memory of my mother's blood lingered on my skin—and not only from tonight.

"You hear her screams every night, don't you?" Animo asked.

"More or less." I stretched my hand toward the torch. Heat lapped at my palm but didn't reach my heart.

Maybe if it touched my skin… I drew back, clenching my fist. *Feeling what they felt won't make things right.*

Animo's gaze followed me, a deep pool of concern. I pulled my legs against my chest, resting my head on my knees.

"You know the feeling, don't you?" I asked.

A sad, half-smile curved his lips. "More or less."

"Whose screams haunt you?"

His eyes found the flame. "No one's. My mother died when I was an infant, so I have no real memory of her, alive or dead."

"Then what do you hear?"

He lifted his gaze, bearing every drop of pain he held. "A laugh."

GONE ONCE MORE

I was going mad. My steps floated and dragged simultaneously, borne of instinct rather than choice. The shadows grew as the torch's flame dwindled, twisting into nightmarish mirages against the cave walls. Every blink conjured an image of my mother or the Woman in White, leaving me to wonder if I'd seen them before or after my eyes shut.

The seconds slunk by like hours, until the flickering light landed on an arch of stone stacked against the solid wall. My heart lifted its heavy head. Could this be it?

"Is…" Megs's voice wavered on the word. After so long, reality was indistinguishable from the tunnel's shadowy facades.

"It is." Animo slid the torch into a waiting sconce and drew a tarnished key from his pocket. He dusted off a small crevice in the rock face.

A keyhole, I realized with a start. Cleverly concealed in the cavern wall, the keyhole was nearly invisible to the untrained eye.

Animo slipped the key into the lock and gave it a slow turn. The wall slid back with the rough grating of stone. Blue light spilled from within as if the doorway was a portal to lands unknown.

I followed Animo through the arch and into a gaping cavern. Luminescent crystals wound their way through the walls, their pale-blue light reflected on the shallow pool carved into the stone floor. The rippling light danced across the walls, casting a ghostly aura. Desks and cabinets encircled the room, all strewn with books, parchment, and other clutter. Jars and bottles littered the shelves, packed with herbs, and a cauldron hung over a cold hearth.

"Aspectu?" Animo called, looking about the room. "Aspectu!"

Oh no.

Animo swore before disappearing down the hallway, his footsteps followed by slamming doors.

"He's happy," Megs muttered.

"Aspectu's gone." Animo stalked back into the cavern. "From the look of this dust, she's been gone for months."

"Is there anything here that can help us?" I asked. *We've come all this way… it can't be for nothing.*

"There are some things. Spells, herbs, artifacts." Ketch gestured at the shelves.

"Nothing like the Staff of Realms." Animo's glare found me. "I told you this would be a waste of time."

"Well, now we know," Ketch said.

Animo's glare deepened, shifting to the dwarf.

Mostly, my memories cause anger, he'd said. Why had I insisted on coming to Daria? I should have trusted Animo's instinct instead of wasting days and dragging him toward the monsters lurking in his mind.

"Where do we go from here?" Megs asked, looking to me for answers.

"I don't know." I wrapped my arms around myself. Surely, there was *something* here that could help us. "We should search. There's a chance Aspectu left a clue behind that could lead us to her next location."

"Maybe she's somewhere in the city," Megs suggested. "We could at least take a look."

"No," Animo said firmly. "She's not welcome in Daria. If she's not here, then she's somewhere else in the Twelve Kingdoms."

"How about this?" Ketch began diplomatically. "There's nothing we can do tonight, and I think all our ropes are frayed"—he cast Animo a pointed look—"so we should wait until tomorrow to look for clues."

"I agree with Ketch," I said.

"Great!" he said, keeping his tone light. "Luckily for us, Aspectu has a very large home. Let's go find some rooms, knock off a bit of the dust, and get some rest."

"It's midday," Animo said sourly.

"Then we can start the search early," I replied, my tone snippier than intended.

He scoffed. "Enjoy your pixie chase."

I sighed as he stalked out of the grotto. *This has to be worth it.*

Ketch clapped his hands together. "All right, we're currently in Aspectu's workshop. This is where all of her books and herbs and whatnot are kept. Deeper into the caves are her vaults and storerooms for the particularly dangerous items."

"Let's start there," Megs exclaimed, shimmying the pack off her shoulders.

"*Or*"—Hertz redirected Megs to a cluttered desk—"You and I can search this room, and Rose can go with Ketch."

"Good idea," I said as her mouth opened in protest. "Ketch, lead the way."

We ducked into a new tunnel, leaving Hertz with a pouting Megs. The glowing crystals continued down the passage like unmined metal, casting their blue light across the rough stone.

"What are these?" I asked, running my fingers along one of the veins. Magic coursed through it, igniting my own power.

"Layvas crystals," Ketch replied.

"What do they do?"

"Other than glow? I have no idea. Probably nothing."

Even if they were only for show, the layvas crystals' magic swelled like a warm memory. *Or a healing spell.* My fingers fell, tracing the cold wall as thoughts of my last healing attempt filled my head. The moment the connection broke, the crystals' power faded from me. My magic slipped into dormancy as though I'd stepped out of the sunlight and into the shadows.

Weak, helpless shadows.

Ketch led me through the serpentine tunnel, ending at the vault. What was left of it, that is. The thick, stone door lay on the ground, split in two. An army of boot prints marred the dust its destruction had left, leading into a cryptlike room of empty shelves.

Ketch swore violently, picking his way over the rubble.

"What happened?" I asked, cautiously following him into the vault.

"They took everything! Artifacts, weapons, grimoires, even…" He shook his head. "I can't believe it. Aspectu had hundreds of spells protecting this place. Breaking through would take an immense amount of power."

"Natalia?"

"She's not the one I'm thinking of."

"All right—Aspectu was attacked in Medea, then managed to steal the Staff of Realms, and *then* was robbed by someone with powerful magical resources." I rubbed my temples. "None of this makes sense."

Ketch shrugged, his shoulders settling into a dejected slump. "We need to find Animo."

"You're sure he'll know what to do?"

"No. But he deserves to know who we're up against." He shook his head. "I hate to do this to him."

Do what to him? My mind itched to know, but I restrained myself. Animo had opened the door to his past twice now, revealing small yet intimate details. I couldn't break that trust, no matter how much my curiosity tempted me.

"Racking sult." Animo stormed into the vault, the smashed stone grating beneath his feet. He reached into a nook, extracting a small, metal stand. "This is where she kept it."

"Kept what?" I asked.

"The seeking crystal—it's how she found you in Rudane. We could have used it to track her down, but now it's in the hands of that—" his sentence turned into a garbled string of curses. He hurled the stand at the wall, the metal resonating sharply against the stone. "It's Regium, I know it is."

"The king of Vaera," Ketch said, clarifying for my benefit.

"Are you sure?" I asked. "It could be Natalia."

"If it is, it means that she has him under her thumb," Animo said darkly.

"We shouldn't waste any more time here," Ketch said. "We should regroup and make a new plan."

Animo huffed. "Fine."

Ketch climbed over the broken doors, then offered me his hand. I accepted, crossing gingerly as the slabs growled and grated with every shift of weight. I hopped down, glancing back just in time to see Animo rise from a crouch and slip something into his pocket.

Aspectu's guest bed might have been soft as a newborn rabbit, but that didn't stop me from tossing and turning for hours. Between the ever-glowing layvas crystals and my own doom-riddled thoughts, sleep remained a laughable fantasy. My open eyes latched onto the ceiling, letting the lights blur together in dull hypnosis.

We had spent hours discussing our options. Animo and Hertz insisted we leave immediately while Megs and I fought to stay, leaving Ketch as the tiebreaker. He had asked for the night to mull it over, but I suspected his decision had already been made; he would side with Animo, and we would leave Daria without a single lead.

And then? What are we to do with no clues and an army of shades after our heads? Aspectu could be anywhere in the Twelve Kingdoms. If we failed here in Daria, we might lose her for good.

I threw the sheets off of me. This would *not* be the end. My life in Rudane had been reduced to ashes. All I had left was the staff.

I pulled a light robe over my borrowed nightgown and tiptoed outside. First, I returned to Aspectu's workshop, scouring it once more. Then I searched the tunnels, unoccupied bedrooms, and additional vaults, but they were either useless, empty, or vandalized.

Hours slipped by and I found myself wandering aimlessly until the sound of rushing water drew my steps. The tunnel curved, opening into a mouth curtained by a massive waterfall. A shadowed figure stood at the cave's edge, his back to me.

"Animo?" I asked.

He flinched at the sound of my voice, tucking something into his pocket as he turned to me. "Rose, you're awake."

"I couldn't sleep. The crystals are too bright."

"They can be rather irritating."

I joined him at the tunnel's mouth, following his gaze past the waterfall. Blue lights dotted a hill, atop which sat a pale palace with pale, twisting spires.

"What is that?" I asked.

"That's the Evishal Palace," he said dully.

"So that's where the royal family lives." My mother had mentioned it in passing, describing it as a magnificent citadel. But in Animo's eyes there was no majesty, only cell bars and waking nightmares. "Have you ever been inside?"

"A few times."

"Is it one of the places you broke into?"

He shook his head. "Never in, always out. It has secret passageways running throughout the walls. Queen Viria had them installed in secret when the palace was built. She may have loved the king, but she never trusted him. And she was right not to."

"How do you know all this?"

"The secret was revealed after Viria's death. Many members of court were told, or they stumbled upon them by accident. The entire court lives there, you know. Everyone else lives in the lower town." He pointed at the specks of pale-blue light running along the hillside.

"Except for Aspectu?"

"She's always been an exception."

Drawing my robe tighter, I leaned against the wall opposite him. The waterfall's cool spray misted my skin, raising goosebumps. "I searched the cavern again."

"Did you find anything?"

"Nothing." I paused before asking, "What do you think happened to her?"

"I don't know," he admitted. "I truly don't know."

"Animo—"

"I know what you're going to ask. You want to know why I left." He gazed into my eyes, allowing me a glimpse of the pain that festered in them. "I don't want to talk about it."

"How do you know Aspectu so well?" I asked instead.

He relaxed slightly, his shoulders dropping comfortably. "She raised me. Everything I know, everything I am, I owe to her."

"How old is she?"

His brow furrowed. "Where did that come from?"

"Well, you said she raised you, and you must be three hundred or so, making her, what, a thousand?"

Animo laughed, and for a moment, the pain disappeared from his eyes, replaced by a flash of weightless mirth. "I'm not three hundred years old, Rose."

"My apologies… four hundred?"

He shook his head, the faintest hint of a smile lingering on his lips.

"Five hundred?"

"You're not even close."

"Then how old are you?"

"I'm not telling. Not after you guessed three hundred."

"You really will tell me nothing, will you?" I kept my tone light, but Animo's smile fell.

"Some things are better left as secrets."

"I know."

Our eyes met, unlocking every secret we had and bearing the scars hidden in the darkest crevices of our hearts.

"Isn't it lonely keeping all your secrets?" I asked quietly.

"Sometimes. I have Ketch, but…" He sighed. "I trust him with my life, yet I still can't bring myself to tell him everything. I suppose that leaves me with Bathril." He tapped his sheathed blade.

"You can't talk to a sword."

"You can if you don't mind looking like a fool."

I laughed. "Tell me, what sort of conversations do you have with a weapon?"

"I can't—they're quite intimate, and I would never betray its privacy."

I rolled my eyes.

"You mock me, yet your family possessed Anasir, a blade blessed by the divine guardian Cisin. Surely someone in your line has spoken to it."

"Please. That sword was used to end the Dark War—my ancestors have probably prayed to it."

He laughed, sending a wave of warmth rippling through me. I turned my head, letting my hair cover my smile as I brushed my fingers against a vein of layvas crystals.

"Why don't they dim at night?" I asked.

"Elves don't need much sleep, so Aspectu didn't bother covering them."

"Elves are strange."

"*You're* an elf."

"Halfling." I yawned, rubbing my eyes. "Can't you use magic to dim them?"

"I don't use magic."

"Never?"

He shook his head.

"Why?"

"It's not my way." He turned away, his gaze returning to the distant palace. In the pale light, his scar looked like a tear caressing his cheek—a single crack in his otherwise hard exterior. "Good night, Rose."

"Good night," I echoed. With a final look at Animo, leaning wistfully in the cavern's mouth, I slipped away.

BEFORE THE ELF KING

My dreams were free of the Woman in White. Maybe it was the magic of Daria, or perhaps my mind was simply too exhausted to create any nightmares, but for a while, I slept soundly. Then a strange force took my hand, pulling sharply. I jerked awake, struggling against the touch.

"It's me," Animo hissed, shoving my dagger into my hand. "We've been found."

"We what?" I blinked groggily, my grip slack around the hilt.

"Elves are at the door. Ketch took Megs and Hertz into the tunnels. They're safe, but we need to hurry."

An explosion shook the cavern, sending loose rocks raining onto our heads. Animo froze, dread settling in his eyes as they locked on the door.

"You need to leave," he whispered. "Go to the tunnel and follow Ketch back to Elwrite."

"But—"

"He's here for me, Rose, not you."

I clutched my dagger to my chest. "What did you do to him?"

His gaze met mine, drowning in silent pain. "I lived."

"Animo—"

Heavy footsteps cut me off. Animo wrapped a hand around my waist, pulling me behind the door as it opened. Boots stomped into the room. Fabric shuffled and drawers slammed. Animo held me close, his arms tight with tension.

A voice shouted something in Aesin, and Animo relaxed slightly. Then the elf came into view, his eyes widening as they landed on us.

Animo threw the door closed, flying past me to land a punch against the elf's jaw. He drew Bathril, raising the blade above his opponent. One strike was all it would take—but he hesitated.

The door banged open, knocking me against the wall. Pain burst through my temple as my skull slammed against stone. I slumped, sliding to the ground and clutching my throbbing head.

Rough hands dragged me upright, pulling the dagger from my grasp. Animo surrendered Bathril, his movements dazed.

The elven guards marched us through the tunnels and into the blazing sunlight. I blinked hard, clearing the tears and waterfall spray from my eyes. Daria rose against the horizon, the cream-colored spires of the Evishal Palace splitting the blue sky. Every step took us closer to its doors. Closer to the king who was behind it, craving Animo's blood.

My heart pounded. Was this how it would end? All those years I spent hiding from Natalia and her shades, only for me to die at the blade of the elf king's sword? Or would the king save me for Natalia?

My stomach twisted, tying itself into a thick knot. Natalia had years of vengeance pent up inside of her. And after what she did to my mother… mercy would be my last, unanswered plea.

I glanced over my shoulder for one last look at freedom. Misty rainbows danced along the raging waterfall that obscured the cave's entrance. Orange flashed as a head peeked out. My eyes widened, and I snapped my gaze back toward Daria.

Megs. She was supposed to be in the tunnel with Ketch and Hertz. Why had she moved?

Oh, Kingdoms, please don't try anything stupid.

The guards led us up a smooth stone path into town. Elegant marble homes lined the road while elves lounged about clothed in long gowns and robes. An odd stillness hovered around us. No one worked and few spoke, almost as if the city existed for the sole purpose of beauty.

The path rose into a staircase as we reached the foot of the palace. I risked a quick look over my shoulder. No sign of Megs. Relief and dismay battled inside me as the guards marched us through the palace's ivory maw.

Boots clicked on the polished marble floors as we were marched down the airy, column-lined hallway. Gathered elves draped in delicate robes of pastel silks whispered behind their hands as we passed, their eyes pinned on Animo. They closed around us as we were brought to a halt before a set of double doors.

Someone shouted a command in Aesin, and the crowd parted, revealing a freshly bruised Ketch dangling between two guards.

"You were supposed to run," Animo muttered as the guards deposited Ketch between us.

"Well, I didn't."

"Were—?" I glanced at the guards. "Where did they find you?" I widened my eyes, attempting to transmit my true message to Ketch.

He nodded slightly. "I was in the workshop. I'd tossed out our luggage, then came back to find you two. I suppose the *bread* and *fire* will have to handle the tunnel alone."

Beside me, Animo grimaced.

Well, that's the last time I attempt to communicate with Ketch using codes. At least I'd understood his meaning: Hertz and Megs were safe in the tunnel. For now, anyway.

The doors swung open with a great creak. The guards dragged us forward, shoving us unceremoniously to our knees before a dias on which sat four thrones of varying heights, intricately carved of opal and jade. On the tallest throne sat a man clad in rich, purple robes, a thick, silver circlet resting on his long, brown hair—the very king who wanted us dead.

An empty throne stood on one side of him. On the other sat a woman with light-brown skin and golden hair. The skirt of her silk gown pooled at the foot of her throne like a lavender lake. Like the king, the queen boasted an elegant circlet, though hers was far more decorative.

The fourth and final throne carried a young girl, fifteen or so, and a perfect replica of the queen, down to the lavish dress and silver circlet. Between her throne and the queens hung an awkward gap as though a fifth throne had once stood there.

The Lost Prince of Daria was last seen walking into the forest. Ketch's words echoed in my head.

"*Oex* Regium, *Oei* Sapientiae, *Eian* Pura." The guard inclined his head to each of the royals as he spoke their Aesin titles. He continued speaking in Aesin, most of which fell deaf on my ears, but I caught Aspectu's name in the jumble along with the words for *traitor*, *girl*, and *dwarf*.

After a few moments of the guard monologuing—all while pacing before us with a self-righteous air—the king stood. "Animo Terrot." King Regium's voice slithered across each Common syllable. "After all these years, you have returned. Why?"

"Perhaps I was homesick." Animo's words dripped with contempt.

"You are a traitor," Regium snapped. "You broke the most sacred laws of Vaera!"

"Laws?" Animo laughed. "Your laws are meaningless without the morals to back them, *marcix*."

The word drew gasps from the gathered elves. Regium glared down at Animo, venom coating his gaze as cold, Aesin words left his lips. Animo flinched, breaking eye contact for the first time.

My stomach twisted. I could have slit open every vein in his body and allowed the blood to pour out, and he'd be in less anguish than he was now, forced to his knees before the king.

"I caused nothing." Animo's voice shook as he switched back to Common.

"I am the reaper, combing through the fields which you have sown. They are the fields of a coward."

Regium rushed from the dias, bringing his hand down hard against Animo's cheek. The slap rang out, echoing throughout the room.

"Do not dare speak to me in such fashion," Regium snarled.

Animo glared up at him as the imprint of the king's rings flared on his cheek. "Then don't deserve it."

Fury burned in Regium's eyes, assuring me that the slap was just the beginning of the punishment he had in store for Animo. "You…" Regium's voice shook with scarcely bottled fury. "You think I deserve this? After all the sacrifices that I made to protect Daria, you think that I deserve this torment?"

"You never sacrificed a thing," Animo snapped, rising to his feet despite the guards that attempted to shove him down. "You have sat back and watched others lay their lives down for you and for your kingdom. Then you use their bones to build your city of cowards."

"That is not true," Regium snapped. "I have sacrificed the things most dear to me to ensure our race would endure. I lost my love—"

Animo laughed sharply, his breaths coming in ragged spurts. "*Lost* is not the word I would choose. You threw away the very reason you should have fought."

"I provide peace. And I lost my wife because of it. Her loss cut through my very soul." Regium looked at the empty space between thrones. "Unlike my son's."

"He would kill you where you stand," Animo said, matching the king's stone-cold gaze.

"He would fail."

Animo's eyes blazed with murderous rage as he threw himself against the guards' grasp. Two more joined the struggle to contain him, their faces reddening from the strain. On the other side of Animo, Ketch struggled, kicking the guards who held him. They lifted him higher, binding his trashing limbs and gagging him to silence the spew of profanity.

Sweeping his robes behind him, Regium returned to his throne, shouting an order in Aesin.

Animo's eyes widened. "No! She has nothing to do with this."

"Or does she have everything to do with it?" Regium settled on his throne, slipping into Aesin. The words sent a fresh wave of fight through Animo.

"If you lay a single hand on her, I'll—"

A guard slammed his fist against Animo's stomach, knocking the breath out of him. I yelped, my gaze skipping between him and the king.

The double doors swung open. An elf woman, clad in a white gown, rushed in, her mouth agape and her violet eyes wide.

"*Qi fectie?*" she exclaimed, striding toward the dias.

Regium waved his hand dismissively. "*Accipeum.*"

The guards dragged Animo and Ketch from the throne room. The elf woman's gaze followed until the door shut. With a toss of dark waves, her attention returned to the king. She spoke in Aesin, emphasizing her words with angry gestures.

The king's sharp reply doused her fire. He pointed at me and asked a question.

I shrank back as the woman's studying eyes fell on me. She replied in a flat tone, her words satisfying the king.

"*Ospetie,*" he said. I knew that word: *you may.* She had permission, but what for?

The woman bowed before the king, then strode toward me, a placid smile lifting her lips. "I am Bellatora Regiis. I understand this must be confusing for you, but I believe I can help." She extended a hand. "Will you join me?"

Violent king or smiling princess? The choice was easy. I took her hand, and the guards stepped away.

The elf queen rose from her throne, speaking for the first time. "We shall accompany you."

"Excellent," Bellatora said, shifting so my arm was locked with hers.

Queen Sapientiae strode down the dias, followed by her daughter. "Do not worry, dear girl," Sapientiae said, taking my other arm. "You are safe now."

SECRETS OF ELVES

Like the rest of the palace, the guest quarters were a sea of creamy marble accented with jade. A massive four-poster bed stood on one end of the room, its rose-gold curtains rippling in the cross breeze from an open window. On the other end sat a settee and a pair of chairs laden with golden pillows. Above them hung a chandelier of dangling layvas crystals, their glow dull in the afternoon sunlight.

Bellatora took a seat, smoothing her pale pink skirts. "I do hope you will forgive my father's behavior. The man you were traveling with is, regrettably, an enemy of Daria."

"Oh?" I feigned surprise. A game was at play among these elves and until I knew the stakes, I would act the fool and keep my mouth *shut.*

"He is more than *an* enemy of Daria," Sapientiae said, shutting the window sharply. "He is *the* enemy."

"You are lucky we found you," Bellatora added as the queen joined her on the settee. "Otherwise, there is no telling what he may have done to you."

I forced myself to smile. "Indeed. I am very lucky."

Sapientiae pointed at the floor beside her chair, and Pura dropped to her knees, obeying like a pet. Revulsion grew inside of me like a weed. Uncomfortably, I ran a finger through my hair, wincing as it snagged on a tangle.

"Perhaps there is a place for me to freshen up?" I asked, itching to be free of the queen's scrutinizing presence.

"Yes, of course." Bellatora rose, directing me to the washroom. A clawfoot tub stood against the wall, a small chandelier sparkling above it. Water ran by magic instead of the rudimentary system of pipes I had grown accustomed to in Chess, and a quick examination of the tub revealed it was enchanted to remain warm. I almost regretted having bathed the night before.

After relieving myself, I selected an ornate hairbrush, running it through my tangles. My hair relaxed the moment the bristles touched, falling into soft, silky waves.

Kingdoms, where has this been all my life?

I brushed the visible dirt off my feet, then returned to the sitting room. Queen Sapientiae looked up as I entered and gestured to the couch. "Come, join us."

I glanced about as I sat. "Where is Bellatora?"

"She had matters to attend to," Sapientaie said airily. "The crown princess's schedule is always full, you know."

"Yes, of course. I can only imagine what kind of responsibilities she has."

An elf maiden joined us, carrying a tray of tea. The queen looked past the newcomer, her piercing eyes tracking my every move.

I shifted uncomfortably. Somewhere in the palace, Animo and Ketch were prisoners, but instead of rescuing them, I was trapped at teatime.

The elf handed me a filled cup. I set it in my lap without taking a sip, asking, "What will happen to those men who kidnapped me?"

Sapientaie sipped her tea. "What would you like to happen?"

"If they have committed crimes against Daria, then they should be punished accordingly." I carefully selected each word to satiate the queen without encouraging violence.

Her smile dropped. "And how should they be punished for the crimes they committed against *you*? The traitor claims you are innocent, yet he was desperate for your freedom. Having witnessed his behavior, it is difficult not to draw conclusions."

I gripped the handle of my teacup as the servant exited, leaving me alone with the queen and her daughter. "Why am I here?"

"You are here because Daria is a civilized place." Sapientaie nodded at my cup. "Please, drink."

I forced myself to take a sip although my anxious stomach protested it.

"I apologize," she said, her light smile returning. "My stepdaughter would chastise me for being a poor host, accusing you like this. Perhaps we should begin again. Why don't you tell me your name?"

"Ro—" *Rosara Wolfe.* I caught the name on my lips. "Rose. My name is Rose." My stomach turned nauseously.

Something isn't right.

"Rose," she repeated. "Tell me, who are you?"

"I—"

—am the Crown Princess of Avonshere. I am the only one who can save my kingdom. Yet I am the reason it suffers.

I swallowed hard, fighting the truths that swarmed my mind.

"The truth, please," she said. "Otherwise, we'll have quite a mess on our hands."

I didn't have a chance for honesty. I threw myself over the side of the couch, expelling the scant liquid souring in my stomach.

Sapientaie scoffed with disgust. "I did warn you."

Wiping my mouth with the back of my hand, I dragged myself upright. Sweat laced my brow as hot and cold tingles ran across my skin.

"I had your tea laced with a potion that compels you to tell the truth. Should you fight against it, well…" She waved a hand at the mess I'd left on the floor.

"Why?"

"Surely you know."

"Not the potion—*this!*" I threw my hands out. "Why did you bother acting kind if you never believed me?"

"Bellatora insisted that until your identity was assured, we were to treat you with the same respect as any other guest," she explained, rising to her feet. "Sometimes I worry that she has grown too soft and trusting."

I scoffed. "That's why she left. You sent her away so you could drug me."

"My husband desires results, and she hindered them." Sapientaie took her daughter's hand, pulling the princess to her feet.

"And now that you have the truth?"

"We shall contact Queen Natalia and ensure that Vaera's alliance with Avonshere remains strong."

No. I clenched my fist. *She can not leave this room.*

I shot to my feet, flinging myself at the elf queen. With a wave of her hand, I crumpled, sharp pain flashing through my legs.

"Do not bother trying to escape. This room is enchanted with blood magic, which means your powers are nothing here."

"My powers are nothing anywhere." I winced as the words slipped out.

"Then Queen Natalia's job will be all the easier."

I pressed my forehead against the cold floor as Sapientiae's footsteps retreated. The door shut, the lock clicking into place.

I'm trapped. I'm dead.

A tear slid down my cheek. It was my fault. I had insisted we come to Daria. I had fought to stay the night. I alone held the blame for our deaths.

I'm so sorry, Animo. He didn't deserve this—neither did Ketch. The image of the two of them marching to an execution block hung in my mind.

I can't let them die… but I can't save them… But I have to.

I pushed myself up. *I will save them.*

But first, I needed to escape. I forced myself to vomit—voiding my stomach of all truth potion—then examined the room. The queen's claims were unfortunately true. Not only was my magic inhibited, but the windows were sealed tight.

There has to be something I'm missing. I scanned the room. A strip of white fabric caught my eye, dangling from… the *wall?*

There are tunnels running all throughout the Evishal Palace. I rushed to the wall, running my hand along the seamless marble. If not for the fabric, the door would be invisible.

I felt about, pushing and prodding every inch until, with a tug of a layvas crystal sconce, the doorway peeled open. A squeak of joy bubbled up as I gazed at the dark, cobwebbed tunnel looming before me.

"I'm coming," I whispered. "I'm coming, and I will save you."

FORBIDDEN KNOWLEDGE

Darkness pressed around me, black as pitch. I ran my hand along the wall, letting the connection guide me through the tunnel's turns. Minutes crawled by as my weak sense of direction faded—my hope draining with it.

Am I going to die in this tunnel? My steps slowed as hypnotic images spun in the darkness. *I despise the dark.* I pushed forward—

Pain burst through me as my face smacked into stone. I stumbled back with a yelp.

What in biaht did I hit?

Reaching out blindly, I found a wall before me. But was it a dead end or a door? I felt around until my fingers latched onto a handle. With a sharp tug, the wall shifted forward. Light sliced through the endless black as the door swung open and I stumbled out, blinking hard as I regained my bearings.

Bookshelves loomed above me like ancient trees, each one brimming with leather-bound volumes. *The Great Library of Daria.* A labyrinth of literature with works dated back to the Reign of Enia.

I covered my gaping mouth. Never, in a thousand lifetimes, had I expected to see this.

The door I'd come through had been cleverly disguised as a shelf. I pushed it shut, taking careful note of which book served as the lever.

I set off down the row of shelves, glancing about to ensure I wasn't seen. Books alone watched me. They called to me, singing their ancient songs as I passed, my gaze skimming their spines. *If only I had time…*

A carefree laugh broke my spell. I ducked into an alcove, pressing my back against the wall as the voice neared. She spoke in Aesin, nudging my memory.

Rack. It's Bellatora.

A male voice responded, doubling my regret—King Regium walked by his daughter's side.

If they find me, I'm as good as dead. I pulled my robe tight around me, keeping its hem away from the alcove's edge.

Footsteps grew close. Light. Feminine. I tensed. Should I run? Could I make it back to the tunnel's door before she caught me?

"*Tempe unar.*" Bellatora appeared beside me. Her eyes locked on mine, widening. She stepped back, running her fingers along the books' spines before turning away.

"It is not here, Father," she called. "Someone must have borrowed it."

"*Borrowed…* Bellatora, why are we speaking in Common?"

"Why not?" She returned to her father's side, leaving me frozen, too frightened to breathe.

"We can ask Desmin who has the book—"

"It is no matter. I will read it some other time. Come, let us return to Sapientiae."

Their footsteps departed. I exhaled, slumping against the wall. *She covered for me… the Crown Princess of Vaera covered for me.* Why would she do that? Did she honestly believe I was innocent?

I risked a glance around the corner. Bellatora strolled along, her arm laced with her father's. At the end of the aisle they stopped. A new voice spoke, shifting the conversation into Aesin.

I narrowed my eyes. Regium maintained composure, but his smile tightened as he said goodbye to Bellatora. *Something is happening.*

The crown princess left, and the discussion dipped to hushed whispers. They soon faded, and I slipped out from the alcove. I kept a keen eye on the aisle entrance as I crept backward.

They're gone. All I need to do is reach the door—

I collided with another being, knocking us both to the ground. My fists clenched as I scrambled to my feet, prepared to fight.

"*Rumif aella!*" An elf in deep maroon robes exclaimed as he collected fallen books from the floor.

"Oh. Forgive me. I did not see you there." I knelt to help him.

The elf stared at me, his brow furrowed. He opened his mouth to speak, only for a laugh to overcome him. "Is this some game you and Bellatora are playing? Are you attempting to see who can speak Common the longest? Or perhaps you wish to see whose Common is better."

"Um… yes." I stood, passing the books back to him. "We have long debated who is more fluent."

He laughed again. "That is no debate. Your Common far exceeds the crown princess', Emry."

Emry. He thought I was my mother. How could he think I was my mother? Surely a kingdom allied with Natalia would be well aware of her bloody plights.

"What brings you to the library today?" The cheery smile on the elf's face sent a pang through my chest. *He has no idea he's speaking to a ghost.*

"I'm merely browsing."

"Any subject in particular?"

That depends. Do any of these books provide a map of the palace's secret tunnels with a special addendum dedicated to breaking out of the dungeon? I shook my head, keeping my borderline lunacy to myself.

"In that case, might I suggest this one?" The elf shifted his stack of books, balancing it against his hip as he pulled a green volume from the shelf. "It is a history from Elwrite that explores the origin of the unicorn's choice."

I accepted the book, thumbing through its ornate pages. The unicorn's choice had always intrigued me. While most kingdoms allowed the order of birth to dictate which heir assumed the throne, Elwrite left the decision in the hands of a unicorn, a creature naturally drawn to goodness. My wishful thoughts had often imagined a world where Avonshere did the same. Perhaps the unicorn would have chosen someone else as heir.

"It's a fascinating story, but not what I'm looking for today." I handed the book back to the elf. "Are you aware of a grimoire that focuses on illumination spells?"

"Why, of course!" The elf added the green book to the stack in his arms, then guided me through the shelves to a section of grimoires with cracked and peeling spines. He retrieved a thick, white volume, presenting it to me with a flourish. "*The Book of Light.*"

I cracked open the cover. Sharp light blazed to life on the page, scorching my gaze like the sun's rays. I shut it with a snap, quenching the glow. With this in hand, I wouldn't even need a spell to find my way through the tunnels.

"Oh!" The elf exclaimed. "Before I forget…" He flicked his fingers, gesturing for me to follow. He made his way out of the shelves' shadows and into the thick hall that cut down the library's center. Tables filled the space and pedestals stood in a row along the shelves' edges, featuring ancient artifacts, including an original copy of *The Epic of Twelve.*

Rainbow fragments fell on the floor as the sunlight shone through the massive stained glass window on the back wall. It depicted the first King of Vaera, Salvator Regiis, his arms extended wide as though welcoming us into the Great Library. Two, long displays stood beneath him. One held an elegant rose-gold sword, but the other sat empty.

"Here we are." The elf pressed a small leather notebook into my hands. "I found it on one of the tables a long time ago. Ever since, I have been waiting for the chance to return it to you."

"Thank you, but… what is it?"

His smile twitched into confusion. "Your diary."

"My diary?" I ran my fingers over the leather cover. My diary. My *mother's* diary. She had held it in her hands and poured her heart and soul into it. I hugged it against my chest. "Thank you. This means more to me than you can possibly imagine."

He beamed. "I am happy to see you again, Emry."

A scream cut the air.

"Kingdoms!" I exclaimed, nearly dropping the diary.

"What is it?"

"The scream."

"What scream?"

"Just now. Didn't you hear it?"

He shook his head. "I did not hear a thing."

Dread swept over me. I shoved the diary into my robe pocket. "I have to go."

"Come back soon!" he called after me.

I sprinted through the aisles, skidding to a stop before the tunnel door. With a quick glance to ensure I was alone, I pulled the concealed lever. The shelf slid open, and I flipped open *The Book of Light*. Its pages glowed golden, illuminating the passageway and sending spiders fleeing.

As I pulled the door shut, writing caught my eye. *Iblitha*. Library. Someone had marked the doorway. I started down the tunnel, watching the corners for more cues. They waited, carved in the stone with arrows directing my path.

The scream sliced through the tunnel, echoing with fury and pain. Shivers crawled down my spine. Though my mind fought against the idea of the voice belonging to Animo, I knew better than to hope.

I pushed forward, following the arrows to an exit marked, *oesin los solrae*. Throne room balcony. I closed *The Book of Light*, plunging the tunnel into darkness. With a shove, the door opened, and I slipped onto the vacant balcony.

I crept to the railing, concealing myself behind the thick marble balusters. Below, King Regium sat on his throne, looking on as guards restrained a man with black hair: Animo.

"*Itrae*," Regium commanded, his icy voice slicing the air like a frozen blade.

A guard advanced, wielding a violet crystal like a blade. He pressed it against

Animo's neck. Animo crumpled to the floor, convulsing and screaming. I gripped *The Book of Light* tighter, forcing my gaze away from the scene.

Regium waved his hand. "*Saete.*"

The guard pulled the crystal away. Animo remained on the ground, his chest heaving and his skin shimmering with sweat.

"I found that in Aspectu's vault," Regium said, without a hint of sympathy for his prisoner. "It is a pretty little thing, is it not? The pain it causes is… impressive."

"*O cis Viria. O cis ei, tes sotip ei.*" Animo trembled with rage.

Regium sat up straight, his expression darkening. "Do not utter the language of elves, you insolent boy!"

"The only one you have to blame for these words is yourself," Animo snapped. He switched back to Aesin, his flow of words turning the king's face purple.

"Enough!" Regium flew across the room. He snatched the crystal from the guard's hand, driving it into Animo's neck.

I squeezed my eyes shut but couldn't block out Animo's screams. He thrashed about in my mind, one slip away from the pit that held my parents' memories.

The screaming stopped. I looked up as the king shoved the crystal into the guard's gloved hand. Animo slumped between his captors' grips, his strength weaker than smoldering coals.

Regium shook his head. "This is your fault. None of this would happen if you behaved."

Animo raised his chin. "You mean if I would give up my mind? Let myself die slowly through ignorance and weakness?" He shook his head, his shoulders sinking. "Do you miss them?"

Regium stiffened. "Leave us." The guards dropped Animo, bowing to their king before filing out.

Animo pushed himself up on shaky legs. "Afraid they'll hear the truth? We both know they only obey you because they have no choice."

Regium paced before the dias. "I do not command the will of my people."

"But you twist it. You manipulate their minds to make them obedient."

"I give them peace."

"That's pointless without free will!" Animo shouted. "You gave yourself peace and your people a life so hollow it may as well be a grave!"

"You miss the way the world used to be, but you were never there," Regium spat. "You did not live through the bloodshed to see my sunrise. I changed our world for the better."

"Your world is mindless and cruel."

"Crueler than the old world?" Regium's robe swished as he spun to face Animo. "Is my world of peace crueler than the world that took your mother's life?"

"Better to die a warrior's death than to live on as a coward."

"Watch your tone," Regium snarled.

"Or else what? Have you finally found the mettle to finish the job? Make this night my last, and let tomorrow be the day you're finally rid of me." White-hot loathing dripped from Animo's every word. "Will you be king enough to swing the sword, or will you pass it off, letting the bloody sins fall to another? All the while you hide behind closed doors—a coward."

Regium retreated to his throne. "I will not give you the honor of dying by my hand. Your end will have no luxury, no honor. You will be taken into the Silver Forest and chained to a tree, where death will be imminent and painful without a drop of sunlight to comfort you. Yes… you will die in that forest as you should have all those years ago."

Animo scoffed lightly. "You're still a coward, after all."

"And you never learned respect."

"I respect those deserving. My mother taught me that."

"She passed along her courage, it is true," Regium agreed. "As well as her foolishness."

"You killed her."

"I loved her."

A sinister feeling wrapped around me. What I heard was forbidden, yet I was incapable of turning away.

"I loved you, too," Regium admitted, his expression softening. "My son."

The words dug into my chest. *Son.* How could the king who tortured

Animo call him *son*?

"Blood is the only thing you gave me," Animo said. "I owe you nothing. Not love nor respect. Everything I am is in rebellion of you."

All traces of humanity vanished from Regium's face. "I offered you mercy. Remember that. *Ustos!*"

The guards marched back into the throne room, restraining Animo once more. Regium raised his chin in a kingly fashion. "Your courage and arrogance will die within the Silver Forest. Once and for all, I will be rid of you."

"*Navu.*"

A sick crack split the air as the hilt of a guard's sword collided with Animo's skull. Blood poured down his temple. He dropped to his knees but was on his feet before another hand touched a blade.

Animo broke free of their grasps, throwing punches like a madman. He knocked one guard to the ground then grappled another, snapping his leg. The guard howled in pain, crawling away from Animo.

The final guard ignored his sheathed sword, raising his fists in a challenge. With a single kick from Animo, he flopped to the ground like a rag doll.

Animo faced Regium, weaponless and drenched in blood and sweat. His gaze pinned the king to his throne, like a fox stalking a rabbit.

"You would not kill your father," Regium said, though he could not restrain the fear seeping into his voice.

"Are you certain?"

Regium rose slowly. "You foolishly believe that you are better than me. But all of your defiance runs you in a circle, back to me."

"I'm not like you."

"You are," the king replied. "It is why you blame me for all of your failings. Strange, you seem to forget which of us has taken the most lives."

Animo tore across the throne room in a violent rage. Silver flashed. A dagger clattered against marble. And Animo collapsed on the ground.

CHAPTER TWENTY-SIX

THE LOST PRINCE

T he world fell away. Only Animo existed—hands pressed to his abdomen, blood seeping through his fingers. All I knew was him. And all I could do was scream.

Regium's gaze snapped to me. "*Emea tu!*" he roared, pointing. The guards spun, their wide eyes latching on their prey. Shouting back and forth in Aesin, they raced from the throne room.

Fighting down the horror and fury boiling inside of me, I turned to the tunnel. But the door had closed, leaving a pristine wall behind.

No, no, no...

Footsteps pounded on the stairs. I cast one last look at Regium, meeting his callous gaze with one of my own. My anger flared scarlet. *I will watch you bleed.*

I tore my eyes away from Regium and Animo's limp form, sprinting down the hallway. My bare feet slapped against the floor, knocking off dirt as I ran, *The Book of Light* clamped under my arm. Deserted halls loomed as I took turn after turn. Finally, I ducked into a dark corridor far from the throne room.

I collapsed against the wall, my heart pounding as I sucked in heavy breaths. *Animo is dead.* The words echoed in my mind. *He's dead.*

Shaking, I pushed my hair out of my eyes. What was I meant to do now? An army of guards was hunting me, and my only allies were either locked up in the dungeon or stranded in a cave.

You're all alone.

I closed my eyes, letting my head rest against the wall as legends played out in my mind. The greatest stories always ended in death. Usually, the villain's. But sometimes, it was the hero who fell in tragic glory—like harvest leaves, burning so bright as they fell, only to wither and decay.

That could have been me.

Flames licked the edges of my memory. *It should have been me.*

A hand fell on my shoulder. I bit back a scream, spinning around. Bellatora Regiis stood before me, the tunnel door open behind her.

She raised a finger to her lips, her narrowed eyes ominous below her hood while her layvas-crystal lantern cast a ghostly sheen upon her fair skin.

"Follow me," she whispered, retreating into the passageway.

I hesitated as the blue light faded down the hall. It could be a trap. Though she had protected me once before, there was no guarantee Bellatora wouldn't sell me out to Regium.

The light paused, and her voice echoed back at me. "I have no intention of hurting you. I will keep you safe until we free my brother."

Brother. An ache swelled in my chest. I opened my mouth, but the words refused to form.

"What is it?" she asked, joining me at the tunnel door. "What is wrong?"

I swallowed hard. "He's dead."

Her brow furrowed, more in confusion than sadness. "Can you be sure of this?"

"The—the king stabbed him," I stammered, taken aback by her lack of emotion. "His blood was everywhere."

"Did he have a pulse?"

"I couldn't check."

"Good." Bellatora set off at a brisk pace.

"*Good?*" I scampered to catch up. "I saw him on the ground, bleeding out."

"I believe you did," she replied, guiding me through the tunnel's turns. "But I also know my brother, and he is not a man to die easily. I have been told a thousand futures, and none of them show Animo dying at the hands of our father."

She paused at an intersection and passed me the lantern. "Follow the arrows to my quarters. I will find my brother and free the dwarf."

"Wait." I caught her arm. "Animo—is he really the king's son?"

Her gaze fell to her feet. "Yes."

"And his mother—"

"The truth is often complicated." She interjected, her voice sharp. "A single side can never tell the entire story."

I nodded, drawing back. "One last thing… I need you to bring him back alive. Ketch, too." My voice wavered, revealing more than I knew was hidden.

"I will." She raised her chin as composure slid across her face like a mask. With her cloak billowing behind her, she disappeared into the darkness.

I stumbled out of the tunnel and into Bellatora's lavish quarters. Thrice the size of the Estmar's house, they stood as a staple of elvish architecture, with a wide balcony lined with ornate columns. Plush couches furnished the sitting room along with an elegant table and desk.

Setting down the lantern and *The Book of Light*, I followed a short staircase into the sleeping chamber. Wardrobes lined the wall across from a four-poster bed, draped in silk sheets.

I glanced down at my robe now laced with dust and cobwebs. Bellatora wouldn't mind if I borrowed something, would she?

I thumbed through her collection of dresses, withdrawing a pale-blue gown with airy sleeves that fell at my wrists. The soft fabric tugged on my heavy eyelids. I sighed. If only I could curl up in it and sleep for a thousand years. Alas, my dreams would have to wait until the day's nightmare ended.

I slipped out of my nightgown and into the dress, using the mirror to lace up the back. Taking my mother's diary from the robe's pocket, I hid the old clothes in the wardrobe's back corner.

I returned to the sitting room, my skirts sweeping the floor. The sun hung low in the sky, its golden rays swiftly fading beneath the treeline. I settled down in a plush armchair, tucking the diary behind a pillow. Pulling my knees against my chest, I watched the last memories of sunlight burn away.

The doors burst open. Bellatora and Ketch rushed in, carrying Animo's limp body. I shot to my feet, trailing behind as they deposited him on the couch, careless of the blood soaking Animo's abdomen.

"Is he alive?" I asked, my eyes overwhelmed by the sight.

"For now." Ketch used the back of his hand to wipe droplets of blood off his forehead, only to smear it deeper into his skin.

Bellatora wiped her hands on her skirt, stepping away. "I can brew a potion to heal him."

"No." Ketch interjected sharply. "Rose can do it. You ought to clean our trail."

Bellatora nodded in agreement. Hand pressed to her stomach, she slipped out of the room.

"Ketch…" My gaze fell. A week ago, I had failed to heal a simple arrow wound. Could I trust my magic to save Animo's life?

"You aren't going to perform any spell."

My gaze snapped to his. "What? Why would you send Bellatora away if you knew I couldn't heal him?"

His jaw clenched. "Animo made me swear that no matter what happened, I would never use any form of magic to heal him."

I stared at him, aghast. "You'd let him die to keep that vow?"

"I'm not the one who insisted we come here!" he snapped.

I jerked back as if slapped.

Ketch winced, raising a hand, regret filling his gaze. "I'm sorry, Rose. This isn't your fault. He's my best friend, and…" he stared at Animo's body.

"I understand."

He turned away. "I can't watch this."

"I'll stay with him."

Ketch gave me a grateful look before retreating to the balcony. I settled on a footstool beside the couch.

Animo lay motionless and as pale as the moon. His features had settled into a relaxed state I hadn't seen since the night we met. The memory brought a smile to my lips. For a single happy moment, we had danced without the threat of shades or looming criminal deals. Now he was dying, and I was powerless to stop it.

That's not entirely true. Ketch promised to never use magic on him, but I didn't. Animo had saved me in Rudane. He'd risked his life for me time and time again, even upon our arrival at the palace. I'd forced him to return, and he had still fought to keep me free of Regium.

His wishes could rot.

"Hate me if you will," I whispered, grasping his blood-slicked hand. "But I will not let you die."

I exhaled slowly, drawing on my power. It lifted its head sleepily—I pulled harder.

I don't care if it takes every drop of magic in my veins. I will save him.

A bead of blood slid down my wrist. Eyes narrowed, I opened Animo's palm. Thick gobs clung to its center, dark compared to the scarlet staining the rest of his skin. I brushed my thumb against the clump, wiping it away. A fresh wave of blood flowed from—from a *cut*. A deep cut straight through the center of his palm.

"Ketch," I called. "Come here. *Now.*"

The dwarf rushed inside, his eyes wide. "Is he—?"

"Not even close." I dropped Animo's hand, marching to a vase on Bellatora's table and plucking the flowers from it. Without hesitation, I threw the water onto Animo's face.

He jerked awake with a shout before falling back, grimacing.

"What in the name of murderous trolls do you think you're doing?" Ketch shouted at me.

"He's not dying," I snapped, setting down the vase with a thunk. "He was pretending the entire time."

Ketch's jaw went slack. "Oh, you little…"

"How am I the one in the wrong?" Animo moaned, his uninjured hand pressed against his temples, and his eyes squeezed shut.

I glared at him. "You pretended to be dead."

"To fool Regium," he shot back. He pulled himself upright, cradling his bleeding hand in his lap. "He would never dirty his hands enough to examine a body."

"I despise you," Ketch growled, his arms crossed and a scowl twisting his face.

"My ruse was good enough for Regium and the rest of these pathetic sults. I assumed they would drop my body somewhere, and I could escape. I didn't expect I would lose consciousness."

"How did that happen?" Ketch asked.

"It doesn't matter."

"Why didn't you tell me your plan?"

Animo shrugged limply. "It wasn't much of a plan. He tried to stab me. I blocked, and the blade went through my hand." He gestured to the bloodstains on his shirt. "I turned away and pulled the dagger out so he wouldn't see."

"Huh." Ketch's glower clung to his face as though it would never lift. "How did you avoid bleeding to death?"

"I lay on my arm to slow the blood flow to my hand."

"Sounds awful."

"Better than dying."

"I can second that," I added. "I saw you in the throne room."

Animo's gaze flicked to me. "How much did you see?"

"Enough," I replied. "You writhing on the floor as the king planned your execution."

The door swung open. We all jumped as Bellatora swooped in. Relief flooded her eyes at the sight of Animo. "You're alive."

Animo met her gaze with one of resignation. "Bella."

"You are truly a fool," she said, delight turning to anger as she twisted a bloodstained cloth in her hands.

"Nothing is new, then," he replied dryly.

Bellatora marched over and slapped the back of his head. "You could have been killed!"

"I'm used to it."

She shook her head. "You should be ashamed of yourself… running about as though your life doesn't matter. Sooner or later, you will face the consequences of your recklessness."

"I know what I'm doing." He slouched, glaring up at her.

"Hmph." Bellatora rolled her eyes. She pulled a key from her pocket, crossing the room to unlock a cabinet.

Animo's wary gaze followed her. "Whatever spell or potion you have for me, save it. I'll be fine." He wrapped his bleeding hand with one of her silk handkerchiefs, though it wouldn't last long; the flow of blood remained concerningly steady.

She pulled open the cabinet door. "I am not making a potion. If you wish to reject someone's healing, you can reject Rose's. Mind you, this is the last time I help you in this way." She turned, holding my dagger in one hand and Bathril in the other.

I laughed with relief. "Our weapons."

"Your gratitude is appreciated," she said, handing me my dagger. "Animo had never seemed bothered by me walking through spider-infested tunnels and stealing from our father."

Animo rolled his eyes as she passed him his blade. "While you're rooting through your stash, pull out some sleeping willow leaves."

"Last time you were here, I gave you enough to put a dragon to sleep for a hundred years! How in kingdoms' names have you been through it all?"

"They drugged me for a week," I said.

Bellatora turned on Animo. "You *drugged* her?"

"And kidnapped me."

"I had my reasons." Animo shot me a glare.

I offered him an innocent look in reply. *That's what you deserve for pretending to be dead.*

He stood, securing his sword belt around his waist. "And for your information, sleeping willow leaves have mainly medicinal purposes."

"That makes no difference," Bellatora exclaimed, fetching Ketch's slingshot from the cabinet. "Why Aspectu thought it was a good idea to send you out on your own is beyond me."

Ketch snatched the slingshot from her and flopped onto the second couch. "He's not alone. He's got me."

"Ah, yes." She sank beside him, slinging an arm around his shoulder. "That does not make me feel better."

Ketch pouted, drawing a laugh from the crown princess.

Animo's expression darkened. "I suppose I should be congratulating you," he said, his attention keen on his bandage's knot. "A wedding is a reason to celebrate."

Her face fell. "You know."

"I'm happy for you," he said, though his flat tone suggested otherwise.

"You don't understand—"

"If you want to place your head beneath Regium's boot, be my guest," he said, his voice sharp. "You always have been a devoted lackey."

"That's not fair," she snapped.

Animo's nostrils flared as he shot to his feet. "I'm going to clean off some of this blood."

Bellatora closed her eyes, waiting until the washroom door had closed to meet Ketch's eyes. "How did he find out?"

"Aspectu told him a month ago."

She moaned, slumping against the couch. "He was not meant to know… not now. Not when it makes him think I've given in to Father."

"Is he wrong?" Ketch asked.

"*Yes.* I did not marry Talos because of my father." Bellatora looked at me and sighed. "Talos is my husband. For over a decade, my father wanted me to marry him, yet I had no interest… When Animo left, that is what he saw."

"What changed?" I asked.

"I did." She turned back to Ketch. "I love Talos. I married him because I love him. My father's wishes had nothing to do with it."

"That's not how Animo sees it."

"Tell him," she urged. "Help him see that I am not my father's mindless pet."

"I'll tell him why you married Talos. But that is it." He walked toward the washroom, leaving me alone with Bellatora.

"I'm sorry we had to meet this way," she said, conjuring up a smile. The mask she wore was so pristine, I could barely see the heartache lingering in her eyes. "How are you?"

"Alright," I replied. As all right as one could be after thinking their—*someone* was dying before their eyes.

I took a seat beside Bellatora. "Should we be concerned about your husband coming home to find us?"

She shook her head. "Talos is in the Great Library. He was granted access to study some of the most ancient and dangerous grimoires. It will be at least a week before I see him again."

"He sounds dedicated."

She smiled, and any doubts I had about her marriage washed away. "He is."

I leaned forward, a new subject nibbling at my brain. "What exactly happened between Animo and Regium?"

Her shoulders tensed. "That is not my story to tell. All I can say is that their disagreement ended with Animo leaving Daria."

"And that is why Regium wants Animo dead? Or is it because of Aspectu?"

"Regium blames Animo for the past," she said somberly. "Just as Animo blames Regium. Both of them have truth to their claims, as well as falsehoods. As for Aspectu, she is persecuted for her own actions. While their association did not help Animo, she is not the reason he suffers."

I nodded, my curiosity nudging me forward. "Did the king really kill Animo's mother?"

"That is complicated." Bellatora's tone indicated that the conversation was over.

"I have no idea how you are going to escape," she said, striding to stand before the balcony. "My father knows that you and Ketch are fugitives, and it will not be long before he finds out that Animo survived."

"What about the passageways? Can we use them to escape?"

"Perhaps. My father knows that they exist, but… It's the strangest thing. Every time he finds one, he forgets how to open it." A smile quirked her lips.

I grinned. Maybe she wasn't her father's lackey after all.

"You may stay the night," she said, returning to my side. "But I'm afraid that is all I can offer you. Our father may be a coward, but it is those with the most fear who fight the hardest to destroy that which threatens them. And in this case, the threat is you."

WHISPERS IN THE NIGHT

"Why wouldn't she tell me?" Bellatora's hushed voice drew me from my sleep. I opened my eyes, lifting my head slightly. The ghost-like curtains floated about in the midnight breeze. From my vantage point on the couch, I had a clear view of Animo and Bellatora standing on the balcony, their backs to me.

"Maybe she thought you would parrot it back to the Regium," he said.

"Animo," she warned.

"I don't know." Irritation slipped into his tone. "Now she's gone, and there's nothing we can do to change it."

"But she's certain about what she saw?"

"Yes."

"Poor Rosara."

I stiffened at the sound of my name. Had Aspectu seen my future? If so, why wouldn't Animo have said anything? I eased my head back down, watching the pair through my lashes.

"Do you believe she is capable of it?" Bellatora asked.

"Defeating Natalia? I do."

"You know that is not what I am referring to."

Unease trickled into my stomach.

"Aspectu saw Rose as the victor," he said.

"*Potential* victor. Her success is not guaranteed. The only certainty Aspectu saw was Rosara at the center of the darkness. For all we know—"

"Bella, stop." Animo's tone sharpened. "Rose isn't here to destroy the Twelve Kingdoms."

I stifled a gasp. *Destroy the Twelve Kingdoms?* No. That wasn't possible. I couldn't be the end of the kingdoms… could I?

"Things can change," she said.

"You would know about change."

She released a slow sigh as she folded her arms.

"I'm sorry, Bella. I just…" he shook his head. "I can't believe you doubt her. She is Emry's daughter. Your *best friend's* daughter is here, and you question her intentions."

"That is not fair," Bellatora said sharply. "Emry was a sister to me when I had none. But that does not mean her daughter will share her loyalty. You should know better than anyone that bloodlines do not dictate motives."

He scoffed, tilting his head away from his sister. "You must be proud to use that one."

"Pride is not the emotion I feel. It is worry." She took his hand. "You are embarking on a quest that you cannot turn back from."

"You think I can turn back *now*?" Disbelief filled his words. "I chose my path years ago, and the point of retreat is far behind me."

"And if you fail? I know why you chose this path. I know what you think you will gain, and I worry about what will happen if your plans do not come to fruition."

"My future is clear. Aspectu told me so."

"Aspectu told me futures as well. Futures of loss and death."

"You fear for me, Bella, but you have no reason. Whatever future she warned you of is a fleeting option. The future she saw for me is certain."

"I only want your safety."

"And I will be safe," Animo said. "But only when this is finished."

"Very well… I will aid you—and Rosara—in whatever ways I can."

"Thank you."

"Now, please rest." Bellatora hugged her brother, then slipped away to her bedchamber.

Animo remained with his back to me, silhouetted in the moonlight, the vast and starry sky before him. How could he be so sure of my goodness? In the time we had known one another, I had lied to him, fought him, and rejected my kingdom more times than I could count. Yet for some reason, he chose to trust me. Had Aspectu shown him more than he'd admitted, or—

Animo turned. I shut my eyes, steadying my breaths as his footsteps neared. A light weight landed on my shoulders as he draped a soft blanket over me.

"I won't let that future happen," he whispered. "I swear it."

His footsteps faded, leaving me tense and far from slumber. *That future.* The future in which I destroy the Twelve Kingdoms. Aspectu had seen it; it was *real.* And in that dream I'd had of my mother, she had said that returning to Avonshere would mean the death of all those still loyal to me. Could her words be more than a nightmare? Could they be a warning?

Could I let the Twelve Kingdoms burn?

My mind drifted to five years ago. Power had surged within me, stronger than my control. I'd fought to contain it, but it broke free and—

I shot up.

"How long have you been awake?"

My gaze snapped to Animo. He sat in the shadows, his legs resting on the desk and a book in his hand.

"I just woke up." I pulled the blanket off of me, hoping he would believe my lie.

"It's nearly the first hour. You should rest longer."

I shrugged. "I'm not really tired."

I stood, wandering onto the balcony. Below spanned the city of Daria where layvas crystals glowed from every house's window like a swarm of blue fireflies. I rested my elbows on the railing, closing my eyes. The night's cool breeze brushed my skin as Animo's steps followed me outside.

"Go ahead," he said.

I opened my eyes. "What?"

"You know that Regium is my father. And I know that you must be angry that I withheld that, especially considering where it's led us."

"It was because of *me* we came to Daria. Regium would have taken us captive whether or not you shared his blood. Besides, if you had no connections here, we would both be dead by now."

"I suppose that's true." He leaned against the railing, gazing down at the city. Did he see its beauty, or were crystals' glow the flickering forms of ghosts?

Or perhaps, the ghost is asleep in the bedroom.

"She's your *friend*, isn't she?" I asked. "The one who married into a cage."

He nodded. "She insists she did it for love, but my father will do anything to have his way. He wanted Bella to marry Talos, and the idea that he would use magic to alter her emotions is far too real for me to dismiss."

"Has he done that?"

He nodded again. "I've seen it."

I should say something, but what was left? Words of hope would be a lie, and to ask if he was all right was useless. We both knew the answer.

Well, what would he ask you?

"Would you… care to talk about it?" I regretted the words the moment they left my lips, but to my surprise, Animo nodded, straightening.

"After the Dark War ended, the elves were tasked with protecting a number of powerful grimoires. That's why they built the Great Library. Of course, the first library wasn't like the one here in Daria. It was a fortress. And for a time, the elves of old were able to protect it. But eventually, a rumor spread that one grimoire could give mortal beings the power of an ekeider. It wouldn't turn them into a witch or sorcerer but imbue magic into their blood."

"Is that true?"

"The spell exists, but not in any of Daria's grimoires. It was lost long before the rumor. But that didn't stop campaigns of goblins rushing to Vaera. They formed an army and attacked the Great Library, slaughtering thousands of elf warriors, Salvator Regiis included."

"Then how does the library still stand?"

"Because before the goblins arrived, Salvator's sole heir had evacuated the grimoires. The retreat was a tactical decision meant to protect the spells from falling into goblin hands. But once the heir… my *father* learned of the library's loss, he fled to Daria. The city became Vaera's new capital, and when the goblins arrived, he welcomed them with open arms, proposing a peace treaty. They would stop their attacks and in return, Regium would give them their pick of grimoires." He clenched his fists. "When a loved one is killed, you don't offer their murderer your coin purse. But that is exactly how my father thought he could end the Goblin-Elf Wars."

"Thought," I repeated. "The fighting continued after the goblins' wishes were granted?"

"Not at first. My father's cowardice earned over a hundred years of peace. It was during that time that your mother lived here."

My spirits lifted. "Was her life here… happy?"

"According to my sister's stories, yes. It wasn't until a few months after Emry left that the goblins returned. None of the spells had succeeded, and they were convinced Regium had tricked them with false grimoires."

"But he didn't, did he?"

Animo shook his head. "For a manipulative coward, Regium's cunning is poor. The grimoires he gave were real, and he would have given them more if not for my mother."

Sapientiae flashed through my mind. She bore no resemblance to either Animo or Bellatora, providing a foreboding preface for the next part of Animo's story.

"Her name was Viria, and she was everything Regium isn't. She knew better than to give in to the enemy and she would *never* in a thousand lifetimes retreat. She sent an army to meet the goblins before they reached the city, but after so many years of peace, the soldiers were ill-prepared. My mother… she could have rallied them, had she been at the front. But she was with child, and

Regium insisted she remain in the palace."

"With child? You?"

"Me. It's funny to think of all the trouble Regium might have saved if he'd let her go."

"Don't say that." I spoke the words harsher than I'd intended. "It's just…" *Just what, Rose?* He was right. But that didn't mean I was fond of the idea of his death.

Animo cleared his throat. "The elf army retreated almost immediately. Upon their return, Aspectu looked into the future and saw the goblins attacking the Great Library within the week. My mother wanted to gather every elf capable of holding a blade—they'd defend the library or die trying. But my father objected. Bella claims they fought so loud, the whole city heard. Regium refused to let his soldiers fight. He said that if she wanted to die, she could do it on her own."

My jaw dropped. "No… there was an army. She couldn't stand against them by herself."

"But she did. The day after I was born, the goblins arrived and my mother was the only one to face them. Needless to say, victory did not lean in her favor."

"I'm so sorry, Animo."

"I never knew her." His voice wavered. "All I have are memories preserved by Aspectu. And what is there to show for her sacrifice? *Nothing.* The goblins walked out with every grimoire they could get their claws on, and my father did *nothing.* My mother's death should have given him a reason to fight, but instead it deepened his fear. It was Salvator's death all over again. Regium fled, building a paradise to escape his pain instead of embracing it and letting it fuel his fury. He should have slaughtered every goblin that crossed the threshold, not used his pathetic fright as a pillow, smothering the free will out of his people."

"By altering memories?"

"Altering memories, casting complacency spells, mood enhancers embedded in doorways—anything that would numb the minds of his people."

I gasped softly. "The elf in the library… I heard you screaming, but he didn't. Was that Regium's doing?"

"Most certainly," Animo replied. "The spells he's cast are strong. They leave behind powerful magical residue that, over time, can become dangerous, especially to the young. Older elves have fully developed minds, they can handle the power. But infants and unborn elves can't.

"When Sapientiae was pregnant, she interacted with so many of Regium's spells that the magic affected Pura. It was too strong for an unborn child and altered her development, softening her mind while she was still in the womb. Now, she can't think for herself. Every action is at the beck and call of her mother—she's a shell of a being, and it's all because of him."

"I'm so sorry."

"It's not my loss."

"She's your sister."

"No, she isn't," Animo said. "My sister was destroyed before she breathed her first breath. The girl who walks these halls is a prisoner with a mind dominated by her mother and a life led by Regium."

"Can she be saved?"

"I don't know." His fists clenched against the railing. "I want to make him pay for everything he's done."

"Why don't you?"

"It's not time," he said bitterly. "Aspectu says I need to wait until everything is in place. So that's what I do. I sit and I wait, and I don't do a racking thing."

The urge to take his hand and tell him everything would be all right washed over me. I fought it, wrapping my arms around myself. He didn't need my empty words of comfort. He needed blood.

"Are you cold?" he asked.

"Oh, I suppose a little." I stumbled over the words.

He reached out, rubbing my arms. The warmth of his palms traveled through the thin fabric of my sleeves, sending goosebumps racing across my skin. He pulled his hands away.

"Maybe I should grab you a blanket," he suggested.

I nodded, and he returned to the living room. As he pulled the blanket off the couch, it knocked over a pillow, revealing my mother's diary. He picked it up inquisitively.

"Oh, that's mine."

He looked up. "Yours?"

"My mother's. The elf I mentioned earlier—the one from the library—he mistook me for my mother and gave it to me. Apparently, she lost it before she left."

Animo handed me the diary, then wrapped the blanket around my shoulders. "What does it say?"

"I'm not sure. I haven't even opened it yet."

"Shall we?"

I nodded. Holding the diary between us, I unwound the cord and lifted the cover. Notes and sketches filled the old parchment. My eyes raked over it, soaking up every stroke of my mother's pen.

"Wait." He pointed at a note in the page's margin. "That's not Emry's hand."

"What?"

"It's Aspectu's." He took the book, holding it so the moonlight illuminated the writing as he flipped through the pages. Each one had a body of text written by my mother, while smaller notes littered the edges, scrawled in an unfamiliar dialect.

"What language is that?" I asked.

"Ancient Elarian," Animo replied. "It hasn't been spoken since the Reign of Enia."

"Can you read it?"

He shook his head. "I only know a handful of words."

"Why did Aspectu have my mother's diary…?" A thought struck me. "Did she give it to the library elf so he could give it to me?"

"I have no idea," he admitted, handing the book back to me. "But if Aspectu was writing in Ancient Elarian, it must have been to keep her words away from prying eyes."

"It might have been helpful if she had written in a language we knew as well," I said, wrapping the cord around the cover.

"Chances are she expected to be with you when you found it." He sombered, gazing at the distant waterfall.

All I had were memories preserved by Aspectu. Animo knew his mother through fragments of the past, and his sister on the arm of his abusive father. Of course, he would gravitate to Aspectu, the one woman who stood her ground through Regium's reign.

And now she's gone.

I placed my hand atop Animo's. He twitched but didn't pull away.

"We'll find her," I said.

His gaze held mine, his walls wavering. "I hope so."

Silence engulfed us as we stood there, eye contact unbroken. At a certain point, someone should look away or risk the implications growing… *deeper.* But with the moonlight reflected in Animo's already starlit eyes, I was helpless to move. Not that I wanted to.

"What about your friends?" he asked.

"Hm? Oh! Oh, kingdoms, I'd forgotten about them." I looked back at the waterfall, though there was nothing to see.

"Do you think they'll try storming the palace?"

I laughed, more in worry than amusement. "It is only a matter of time."

CHAPTER TWENTY-EIGHT

THE QUEEN'S HUNTER

I lounged on the couch, enjoying the morning sunshine while Animo and Ketch poured over a hastily sketched map of the palace. The tunnels were our obvious escape route, perhaps *too* obvious.

"The enchantments keep Regium from opening the doors, but they won't stop him from planting guards at the exit." Animo circled a point on the map. "This is the most direct route out of the castle, which also makes it the most dangerous."

"Is there a door near the stables?" Ketch asked. "If we're on horseback, we'll have better chances of making it through the city."

"I believe so…" Animo turned the map, lightly running his quill down a path.

The door opened and Bellatora slipped in, cheeks flushed and fear radiating from her eyes.

Animo's grip closed on Bathril's hilt. "What's happened?"

"A visitor has arrived from Avonshere," she began, her hand clenched against her stomach. "The Queen's Hunter."

"Who?" I asked.

"He's Natalia's number one weapon," Animo explained, his shoulders tense. "Invulnerable and skilled in hand combat, archery, and swordplay. No one knows his identity, only that he's more than capable of destroying his enemies."

"Have you fought him?"

"Not yet. Natalia keeps him close, except for special assignments."

"Like killing me," I said dryly.

"Not today." He rolled up the map, shoving it into his pocket. "We won't let him."

"Animo's right," Ketch said, tossing an explosive vial between his hands. "I'll blow him to smithereens before he touches you."

"All that will do is bring the entire guard running," Bellatora snapped. She pulled a layvas crystal sconce, opening the tunnel door. "You will hide in the passageway until he finishes searching my quarters. When he fails to find you, he will assume you fled Daria, forcing him to chase phantom trails."

"If he finds the tunnels, we'll be ruined," Animo said.

"He *won't*," she replied. "I will keep him away, I swear. But you must hurry and gather your things before he arrives."

We obeyed, quickly gathering our belongings. I tied my dagger around my waist while Animo and Ketch scrambled to strike every trace of our presence from the room.

A knock rapped on the door.

"One moment!" Bellatora waved her hands wildly, directing us to the tunnel. I grabbed *The Book of Light* while Animo threw a fuming Ketch over his shoulder. We ran inside, and Bellatora closed the panel behind us.

"Hello, Father!" her voice floated through the wall.

Stone scraped softly, and a tiny sliver of light cut the dark as Animo opened a peephole. I leaned forward, watching as Bellatora took a seat, a porcelain-doll smile painted on her lips. "I have been waiting for your arrival since the moment I learned of our guest's presence."

"I wish it was not necessary," Regium said, joining her on the couch.

Heavy footsteps followed, and a man stepped into view. A black cloak covered him, its hood drawn low over his masked face. Silver flashed off the daggers strapped crisscross to his chest.

A gasp slipped from my lips. "I know him."

"What?" Animo whispered.

I shook my head. My heart pounded as my eyes followed the cloaked figure's steps.

Bellatora took Regium's hand, her eyes as wide and innocent as a fawn's. "Father, what has happened?"

"We are faced with an unfortunate dilemma," he explained. "The prisoners that the Queen's Hunter came to collect have... escaped."

Her hand flew to her chest. "How can this be?"

"Their method is still unclear."

"Well, you must find them." Her attention turned to the Hunter. "And you must hurry. If they manage to leave the city, it will be all but impossible to catch them."

Regium forced a laugh. "My daughter exaggerates. We have no reason to fear losing them. Mark my words—they will be found before the sun sets."

The Hunter folded his arms. Though his eyes were concealed by his mask, I had no doubt he glared at the elf king.

"If I may ask, what are your intentions with these prisoners?" Bellatora asked. "Are they to be taken to Avonshere?"

"Only their heads," the Hunter said, his deep voice muffled by his mask.

Animo tensed beside me like a spring wound too tight. I brushed my fingers against the back of his hand. He flinched at the touch, his sharp gaze snapping to me. It softened, and he gave my hand a slight squeeze before returning his attention to the peephole.

"Good." Flecks of worry flickered behind Bellatora's pristine smile. "Traitors and liars should meet such an end."

Regium clapped his hands together. "There you have it. It is clear that my daughter played no part in the escape. Surely our time is better spent overseeing the shades."

"Shades are here?" she asked.

"They are clearing the lower town and Aspectu's old cavern."

"You believe that Aspectu is involved?"

"Undoubtedly." The king shook his head somberly. "And I truly thought we were done with that wretch."

"I'm sure she won't bother you after this," she assured him.

"As always, you are correct." he graced her with a golden smile before turning to the Hunter. "Are we finished here?"

The Hunter's head turned slowly, scanning the room. I held my breath as his gaze passed over our peephole. Finally, he said, "We're finished."

Bellatora held her smile as they exited, but the moment the door shut, her guise fell. She crossed the room, opening the panel. "They're gone."

We tumbled out of the wall, pulling cobwebs off our arms.

"We need to get you packed," she said, fetching satchels from the cupboard. "The tunnels are the safest location, but in the event someone lets the secret slip, you need to be ready to run."

While Bellatora gathered supplies, Animo motioned for me to follow him into her bedroom.

"You said you'd seen the Queen's Hunter before," he said.

"Once… In Darvyn." My chest tightened, but Animo's gaze urged me to continue. "The town was destroyed. I thought I was the only soul alive when I saw a man in a cloak. I didn't know if he was friend or foe, so I watched from a distance. He went to the ruins of my home, and he *cried* before them. For a moment, I believed he could be an ally. I was about to go toward him when he… changed."

"Changed how?"

I shook my head. "I don't understand it. There was something about his posture that shifted, and every part of me screamed to run. So I hid in the shadows and watched him leave."

"Is that all?"

I nodded. "That's all."

"Strange."

"Indeed." Strange to think that if I'd stepped out from the shadows, I, too, would have died in Darvyn.

Animo and I returned to the living quarters and immediately had fully packed satchels thrust at us by Bellatora. "Take them," she urged.

I pulled the strap over my head, shifting the bag's weight to my back. "Thank you for everything, Bellatora."

She might doubt me, but that didn't change the fact that I'd be dead without her help. I reached for *The Book of Light*.

"Oh, no… I am afraid I can't let you take that." She eased the book out of my grasp. "It is an ancient volume and a part of the Great Library of Daria. You understand, of course."

"Of course," I said, despite my disappointment.

"You can, however, take these." She handed me a small sheet of spells written with flourishing letters. "I took the liberty of transcribing a few of them for you. I thought you may benefit from a little extra light."

I gave her a smile, tucking the parchment into my satchel. "Thank you."

A knock sounded at the door, and we all froze. "Bellatora," Regium called. "May I come in?"

Her eyes bulged. "Um… one moment."

She waved her arms and we dove into action: Ketch leaped into the open passageway as Bellatora stashed *The Book of Light* behind a pillow.

"I'm afraid this can not wait." The knob turned.

Animo grabbed me by the waist, dragging me onto the balcony. I caught one last glimpse of Ketch, pulling the panel shut, his pupils dilated with fear.

Regium's voice floated from the living quarters. "Darling, I am so sorry to bother you, but the Queen's Hunter has a few additional questions."

"Your father mentioned a passageway," the Hunter said. "He claimed there was an entry in your room."

"Passageways… yes, I do remember there being passageways…" Bellatora kept her tone innocent as she led the Hunter down a senseless tangent of faulty memories.

Animo touched my arm then gestured to the vines growing along the palace wall. "We have to climb," he whispered.

Protests swirled in my mind, but the Hunter's looming presence pushed me forward. I gripped the vines with one hand and held my skirt in the other, easing myself onto a thin ledge. The vines shifted, pulling away from the wall. Clenching my jaw, I forced my gaze forward.

Do not look down.

I shuffled along the ledge, my shaking fingers tight on the vines. Animo followed, his back to the wall. He nodded to a balcony on the floor above us.

Climb there.

I tucked my hem into my waistband, then gripped the vines with both hands. Mustering all the courage I had, I began to climb.

Inside, Bellatora laughed. "I have proven myself a fool. The doors were in the *ceiling* not the *floors*! Or was it the other way around?"

"I tire of your lies," the Hunter growled.

"How dare you?" she exclaimed. "I am the Crown Princess of Vaera."

"And I am Queen Natalia's Hunter. Do not forget your place." The Hunter's bootsteps neared the balcony. I quickened my pace, ignoring the peeling vines.

"Wait!" I froze at Bellatora's shout, hanging off the palace wall. "I remember how to open it."

The Hunter's footsteps retreated. I climbed the final lengths to the other balcony, rolling over the railing. Animo followed and together we slipped inside an empty bedchamber.

He cursed. My heart leaped as I spun around, fully expecting to see the Hunter behind us. Instead, I found Animo glowering as his right hand dripped blood onto the floor.

"Let me see that," I said, reaching out.

He pulled his hand back. "It's fine."

"Blood is spilling out of your palm. If we want to survive this, I'll need your sword hand working."

"That's not my sword hand," he said, drawing Bathril with his uninjured hand. "This is." He slashed through the drapes, tearing off a strip of fabric, which he proceeded to wrap around his bleeding hand.

"We can't stay here. It's only a matter of time until we're found." He pulled the knot tight with his teeth. "Now that the Hunter knows about the passageways, we'll have to find another route."

"What about Ketch?"

"He'll be fine."

"All right, then what about us? If we can't use the passageways, how are we to escape?"

"I'm working on that." Animo paced the floor, glancing about as he muttered under his breath. His eyes landed on the wardrobe, and a smile tugged at the corner of his lips. "I have an idea."

"This is a ridiculous idea," I muttered.

Animo and I walked down the hallway, draped in elegant, white cloaks, hoods drawn low over our faces. We'd yet to encounter any elves, but should we cross paths, the hoods would conceal our identities. At least, that's what Animo claimed.

"We look like monks," I said. "Even the most brainless elf would question us."

"They're not the ones we're evading," Animo replied, his eyes flicking over adjacent doorways. "The Hunter will expect us to hide in the shadows, not blend into the crowd. So long as he doesn't see our faces, we'll be fine."

A door flew open before us. Animo's hand shot out in front of me as an elf ran out.

"He's angry," the elf said, darting off.

"Who is *he*?" I asked.

A shout answered my question: "Your own daughter!" Fury rang in the voice of the Queen's Hunter. "Her Majesty will be most displeased."

Hide.

Animo and I grasped at doorknobs, only to find them locked. Regium's pleading voice grew closer every second. Animo grabbed my arm, dragging me behind a thick column.

The door banged open.

"She is not responsible," Regium argued. "Those criminals must have threatened her."

"This is not the first time she has been an inconvenience to Queen Natalia," the Hunter warned. "Should this behavior continue, we will have to take drastic measures."

Regium's voice trembled as he replied. "I will handle it."

"Be sure that you do."

Their footsteps faded. After a few moments, Animo and I stepped out from behind the column.

"What will happen to Bellatora?" I asked.

"She'll be fine," he assured me, though the tightness of his voice revealed his concern. "Let's move."

I followed in silence. Animo led me through the palace's turns without hesitation until we reached a set of double doors.

"This way to the courtyard," he said, giving the doors a push. "From there, we can…"

His voice trailed off as our sights landed on the swarm of elves packed into the courtyard. Angry conversation swelled, and several elves bore deep scratches on their arms.

Animo touched my wrist, whispering, "Walk slow. Don't draw any attention to yourself."

I nodded stiffly, stepping into the crowd. Head low, I wove my way through the sea of elves.

Walk slow. Don't draw any attention… none of this is King Regium's fault. I froze at the thought. Where had that come from? Why did it tug at my mind?

Animo's hand settled on my back, nudging me forward. "Don't listen," he said through clenched teeth. "It's a spell."

Of course. Regium gathered everyone here for the sake of control. But judging by the elves' glares, he was stretching his magic too far.

An elf maiden gasped, pointing at Animo. "You're bleeding!" My stomach plummeted at the scarlet splotches of blood blooming on his cloak. "Did the shades attack you as well?" she asked.

"No, it's just a scratch." Animo turned away, accidentally catching the eye of another elf. The elf's eyes widened.

"They're here!" he bellowed.

Animo drew Bathril, knocking the elf maiden in the face in the process. With the flat of the blade, he struck the shouting elf, sending him crumpling to the ground. The crowd broke apart, screaming and fleeing the courtyard.

Animo flung off his cloak. "Run."

We sprinted toward the exit. A dark shape dropped before us—a shade. It unleashed a horrid scream, swiping at us with its sharp claws.

"Go back!" Animo shouted, swinging Bathril.

I ran into the palace, the unmistakable sound of steel slicing flesh ringing behind me. My dainty shoes slipped on the pristine floor. I flailed about for support, falling to my knees as I rounded the corner.

With a sharp clang, the Hunter's sword collided with the wall, exactly where my head had been a second ago.

I rolled away fluidly, flinging off my cloak. Dagger in hand, I dodged the Hunter's first blow, preparing to drive my blade into his leg. He met my blade with his own, the force pushing me back. With his free hand, he clamped a rune-engraved cuff around my wrist.

I swore as the magic drained from my body. *Why do so many people have restrictor cuffs?* I swept my foot under his leg, knocking him down. With my skirt balled up around my knees, I dashed deeper into the palace.

"Rose!"

I spun at the shout. Megs and Hertz stood, smiling and waving at the end of an adjacent hall. Their excitement shifted to warning as they pointed at the ground. A gossamer line reached across the corridor, like a strand of spider's silk.

It's a trap. I glanced over my shoulder, ensuring the Hunter had seen my turn before sprinting forward and leaping over the wire. The crossbow twanged behind me as the Hunter tripped the trap.

"Yes!" Megs cheered as she and Hertz fell into step beside me.

I spared a look behind us. The Hunter gripped the short arrow protruding from his knee.

"How did you find me?" I panted.

"Ketch," Hertz replied. "He told us where to go—he'll bring Animo."

An inhuman scream echoed from outside. My stomach plunged. Shades swarmed the palace grounds, their numbers rapidly bleeding inside.

"Keep going!" Animo sprinted past us, dragging Ketch along. Both were drenched with shade blood and scarlet soaked through Ketch's mangled sleeve.

Animo led us down a wide corridor lined with elegant pieces of stained glass. My heart pounded in time with our feet as the screams drew closer.

We took a sharp turn, only to find ourselves face-to-face with another shade. My stomach twisted at the sight of its claws slick with scarlet blood. Animo drew his sword, sending the hilt smashing through a stained-glass scene.

"Jump!" he ordered.

I needed no further urging to fling myself onto the ground. A jolt of pain shot up my legs as I landed, rolling to avoid additional injury.

Megs grunted, stumbling upright. "Come on!"

She hauled me to my feet as Hertz dropped behind us. In the corner of my eye, I caught Animo's jump, his ink-stained blade flashing in the sunlight. Ketch followed, accompanied by a screamed curse.

An arrow grazed my thigh. I yelped, glancing up to find the Hunter knocking his bow. We took off for the tree line, more arrows nipping at our heels. Hertz shouted, clamping his hand over the shaft that protruded from his bicep.

My muscles ached, and warm blood dripped down my leg as an army of screaming shades joined the arrows flocking behind us.

Gasping for breath, I sprinted into the trees. My foot caught on a root sending me tumbling to the ground. In a flash, my dagger was in my hand, prepared for a fight. Only, none came. The ghoulish legion stood, frozen on the forest's edge.

Dread washed over me. I pulled myself up on a tree, its bark cracked and gray. "Why did they stop?"

Animo gripped Bathril with white knuckles. "They cannot enter the woods. All those who do are cursed."

"Cursed?" Megs asked, tucking a stray curl behind her ear. "What do you mean *cursed?*"

No sooner had the words left her mouth did a brown mass lunge at us with a shrill yowl. Animo swung Bathril, slicing it in two. The halves smacked into the dirt, limbs twitching as its acidic, golden blood sizzled.

I gaped at the creature. Rows upon rows of spikes covered its back, and two great horns protruded from its round head that bore a short nose and large ears like saucers. Never in my life had I seen a thing like it.

Animo sheathed his sword, his lips flattening into a grim line. "Welcome to the Silver Forest."

PART FOUR

ENTER THE FOREST

The forest was dead. Not a wisp of wind blew, leaving the leaves hanging like victims of the noose. The thick canopy blocked almost all rays of light from reaching us. We stumbled through the shadows, our nervous eyes scanning the woods. Beasts of every shape and size lurked amid the brush and stalked us from above. Even the trees seemed to watch us, waiting. The forest was the predator, and we were the prey. What could prey do but run?

After hours of walking, we made camp near the riverbank. According to Animo, it was as good a spot as any, although he warned us to stay clear of the water—there was no telling what lingered beneath the surface.

As my companions lit a fire, I found myself staring at the river, shimmering like spilled ink. Something unseen moved below, sending a hypnotic ripple across the water's surface and a chill down my spine.

"Wondering what's down there?"

I jumped at Ketch's voice. He stood on the riverbank beside me, a thick bandage peeking out from his shirt.

"I'd rather not know." I turned away, sending pain shooting through my thigh. The arrow wound wasn't too deep—a light bandage had been enough to staunch the bleeding—but it still throbbed every time I took a step. Thanks to the restrictor cuff the Hunter had used on me, I couldn't even attempt a healing spell.

"*Creatures of darkness are meant for the shadows*," Ketch recited. "It's from a poem—"

"*Ocit el Saira*," I finished. "*The Epic of Twelve*. I'm familiar."

My parents read it to me every night when I was little. The *Epic* told the story of my ancestor, Tybalt Wolfe. While the Dark War raged and a wicked and powerful ruler sat on the throne, Tybalt sought out the divine beings who lived in hiding. With the help of the divine guardian Cisin, he urged them to take action. Including Cisin, twelve divine beings agreed. They each blessed a blade and bestowed it upon twelve heroes—the High Twelve. Armed with their blessed blades, they vanquished the ruler, ending the Dark War. To honor the High Twelve, Enia was divided equally, forming the Twelve Kingdoms.

As a child, the story delighted me, filling me with hope. It proved that no enemy could stand against good. Then Natalia massacred my home, marring my thoughts of goodness with red.

"I've always liked the *Epic*," Ketch said. "The High Twelve were ordinary beings who saw a chance to do something great. Most would shrink back at such a calling. But they answered with the force of an army."

I resisted rolling my eyes. "Is this really the time? We're trapped in a forest brimming with monsters. We could be torn to pieces at any moment."

"Terrible things can always happen," he replied. "Even immortal beings such as elves can be struck down in battle, drowned in the river, or trampled by their horse. It's no excuse to avoid your destiny."

I glanced at the campsite, where Megs, Hertz, and Animo sat around the crackling fire—a dangerous but necessary source of heat. "I'm not interested in making peace with my destiny."

"It's not just about you, Rose," Ketch said, unusually somber as we wandered to the camp. "Think about it."

"Think about what?" Animo asked. He stacked another log in the fire, sending a wave of sparks flying. Far from the flame sat a small pile of unlit torches crafted with strips of the blue gown I'd borrowed from Bellatora. Fortunately, Megs had packed the green and brown hunting clothes I'd bought in Medea. If not for her forethought, I'd be trudging through brambles with a tattered skirt.

"Nothing," I replied, taking a seat. "What now?"

"I have a rough idea of where we are," Animo said. "If we can keep ourselves alive, I should be able to guide us to the border."

Hertz's brows raised. "*If?*"

"If," Animo replied.

Hertz gripped his axe tighter.

"What about the Hunter?" I asked. "Can we be certain that he won't follow us?"

"It's a safe assumption," Animo said. "The border stopped the shades, which are as disposable as bread crumbs to Natalia. If she won't allow them to enter, it's highly unlikely she'll have her prized warrior put his soul on the line."

"*Soul?*" Hertz asked, as if repeating the word would result in a reassuring explanation.

"The Silver Forest is full of curses," Animo explained. "Touch the wrong plant or step into the wrong territory, and you'll suffer the consequences."

"Are we cursed now?" Megs asked, shifting uncomfortably.

He nodded. "Until we escape the forest's borders."

"And if we don't?" I asked.

He held my gaze. "We will."

Silence closed, like a fist, around us. The fire crackled and popped, emitting the occasional burst of sparks.

Ketch cleared his throat. "I'll take the first watch. My eyesight is better than all of yours." His inhumanly dilated pupils confirmed his statement. He settled down on a tree stump, slingshot in one hand, explosive in the other.

The rest of us settled in our respective sleeping spaces. Hertz lay on his side, letting his wounded shoulder breathe while Megs opted for her back, crossing her scratched-up arms atop her chest.

I leaned against a thick tree trunk, my gaze falling to the restrictor cuff clamped around my wrist. *If only I could heal them.*

Animo sat beside me. "Their wounds aren't too serious. They'll heal quickly."

"That doesn't erase it," I said quietly. "I care about my friends, and I don't want to see them hurting like this."

"It's not your fault they're in pain."

I snorted in disbelief.

"I mean it, Rose," he said. "They chose—no, *insisted* on following you. Their injuries are the fault of Natalia and her Hunter. The fact that you are unable to heal them now is the Hunter's fault as well."

Is it? Was it really because of the Hunter and his cuff that I was helpless to heal my friends, or was it the fault of my magic? *Or is it simply* my *fault?*

Like everything, magic required energy. Spellcasters were unable to create magic—only manipulate it. The act pulled from an internal well of energy. With training, wells could deepen, allowing the caster to perform more powerful spells. There had been a time when my well was deep enough to heal a battlefield of dying soldiers. But after so many years of dormancy, my well had dried. Had I continued practicing, I could have an ocean of power at my command. But I chose to hide, leaving me with a pitiful puddle of magical potential.

"May I see it?" Animo indicated the restrictor cuff. I offered him my wrist, which he took gently, turning it over to examine the restraint. His brow furrowed.

"Is something wrong?"

He tapped a finger against a small marking on the cuff. "This rune isn't magical—it's a signature from the dwarf who forged it."

"Meaning?"

"The restrictor cuff I had bore the same mark."

"That doesn't mean anything. The same smith could make hundreds of these, thousands even."

"Except, the cuff I had was the first and only time that smith had ever forged something like this." He met my gaze with resignation. "This is the same cuff."

I swallowed against my tightening throat. "It was stolen along with my chest."

He nodded. "Which means whoever stole from us in Medea is in league with the Queen's Hunter."

Tears pressed against my eyes. The Hunter had my chest. *Natalia* had my chest. Generations of Wolfe women had placed their futures inside a box that now lay in the hand of my enemy.

"She can't open it," Animo reminded me.

"I don't care. I don't even care that it's lost to me. I care that it's with *her*. Natalia has taken everything from me, and now she has the only remaining images of my parents." My shoulders slumped. "How could everything that belonged to me fall to *her*?"

"It didn't *fall* to Natalia. She *took* it." Anger emphasized his words. "Natalia has no right to your throne and no right to your memories. Yet you let her take them."

My jaw dropped. "*Let*? I had no choice in the matter."

"But you do now." He took my hand. "If you return to Avonshere the right way, you will have an army waiting for you, ready to restore everything you lost."

"We had a deal, Animo. No throne."

"I won't stop trying to convince you."

I pursed my lips. "I had an army. The Ardent Pack were the most loyal fighters you'd ever seen. Note the *were*."

"Things have changed."

I shook my head. "Not enough. No one in their right mind would fight for me now. Not after what happened."

"Then what do you call me?"

"An absolute fool."

He scoffed, releasing my hand.

"She's right, you know," Ketch said from across the clearing. "You are a fool."

Animo rolled his eyes. "Whatever you say, Goosehandler."

Ketch froze, his pupils constricting to mere slits. "What. Did. You. Say?"

Animo's eyes widened, his lips trembling as he fought back a smile. "I forgot they didn't know."

"Oh… you forgot? The one thing I made you swear never to speak of again? You *forgot?*" Ketch's voice rose to a screech, scaring winged creatures from the branches above.

"I'm sorry," Animo said, now fully laughing.

"Yeah." Megs grinned, propping herself up on her elbows. "Take a breath, Goosehandler."

She nudged Hertz, who smiled slightly, craning his neck to better see the dwarf's beet-red face.

Ketch yowled like a feral cat cornered in a barn. "How could you?"

Animo raised his hands in defense. "It slipped out."

"*Slipped out?*"

"I always heard that dwarves had two surnames," I began. "A family name and then another name that is earned through actions." I broke into a smile. "Tell the story, Goosehandler."

"No," he snapped, pointing a finger at me. "You will never know. None of you will ever know."

"I've been trying to get that story for years with no success," Animo said. "But I've done plenty of speculating."

Ketch chose a different finger for Animo.

"You will suffer, Terrot," the dwarf growled, stalking away.

"Where is he going?" Megs asked, her voice garbled with laughter.

"To either collect firewood or light himself on fire," Animo replied. "Or collect firewood to light *us* on fire."

"Then he can be Ketch Goosehandlerarsonist!" Megs collapsed into another round of laughter.

"Who started a forest fire," Hertz added.

She cheered. "Yes, Hertz! Bring the heat!"

"Won't that be Ketch when he burns us alive?" I asked.

"In all fairness, Ketch will probably burn himself alive before he gets around to us," Animo said. "He has the scars to prove it."

"Shieldore?" I asked.

"No, that's the three-inch scar on his leg. The burns were from a completely different prison."

"How many prisons have you been locked up in?" Megs asked, laying back.

"Eight," he replied.

Ketch stalked back into the camp. "All right, you rotten elf. It's your turn to collect firewood."

"I thought that was what you were doing."

"It was." Ketch held up a handful of twigs, spite simmering in his eyes. He dropped them into the flames one by one, each landing without a single spark. "Alas, I am but a dwarf and can only carry so much."

"How long will this grudge last?" Animo asked.

"Guess." The word carried enough venom to fell a giant.

Animo climbed to his feet. "Very well, I'll go. But I'd like you to join me, Rose. We'll be safer in numbers."

"Of course," I replied, although I was not fooled in the slightest. His concern had nothing to do with safety—the two of us alone was the perfect excuse to continue our conversation.

Try your best, Terrot, I thought as we ventured from the fire's comforting glow. *I will not be swayed.*

CRAVING BLOOD

Dead leaves crunched beneath my and Animo's feet. I kept a hand on the hilt of my dagger as we wandered through the dark forest—I might as well have been back in the cavern's tunnel, the way the shifting shadows mimicked all kinds of beasts.

"Relax." Animo's voice cut through the tense ambiance. "This place can kill you no matter how tight you hold on."

I clenched my jaw. "You're nothing but comfort."

"You'll learn to live with the constant fear. It used to keep me awake at night, but now it's like a lullaby."

"I take back what I said earlier. You're not a fool—you're a madman."

"I've been called worse," he said, kneeling beside a fallen branch, wide as my bicep. He slipped a piece of rough wire beneath it and planted a foot atop, bracing the branch as he drew the wire back and forth, sawing through the wood.

I hung back, my eyes skipping from tree to tree, watching for movement. The sawing stopped.

"I don't think it's mad to fight," Animo said.

"It's mad to love war."

"So when everything with Natalia is finished, you'll give it all up? Run away to some far-off corner of the Twelve Kingdoms?"

"I'm going to live like I did in Rudane," I replied, setting my chin as I met his gaze.

"You were a huntress in Rudane. Your livelihood depended on killing."

"I searched for food to keep the people I cared about alive," I snapped. "That's not war."

"*Life* is war." He tossed the wire aside, stomping on the branch and splitting it in two. "Everyone has an enemy. Either we destroy it, or it destroys us."

"You really are bloodthirsty," I said, my heartbeat quickening. His words should have sparked terror, but instead, they were like a magnet, imploring me to draw near him.

He gazed at me, his eyes clear and certain as he spoke. "If living makes me bloodthirsty, I'll drain the world dry."

"You can live without fighting."

"Not if your life is to be worth anything. Life is full of struggles. It's up to you to make the choice to run or to stand your ground."

"What if you're running toward the point of a blade?"

"Then make sure that yours is at the ready," he replied, his voice as cold and hard as steel. "And take that sult down with you." He picked up his wire saw. "You collect some kindling while I finish with this branch."

Flustered, I knelt to gather sticks. *I'm not like that. I don't want to fight… do I?*

"I got under your skin, didn't I?" Animo asked. I could only imagine the satisfied smirk on his lips.

"No," I said stiffly.

The saw grated as he asked, "What happened?"

"What are you talking about?"

"You're afraid of yourself. That doesn't happen without a reason."

"I thought you knew everything about me." Though my tone teased, my heart pounded with dread. "Surely a thousand years on this earth gives you such insight."

"I'm twenty years old, Rose."

I glanced up at him. "Really?"

He nodded, yanking the saw through the wood. "You're half elf. Surely you know how we age."

"My mother always said that elves' bodies develop at the same rate as a human's, but our minds grow at twice the speed."

"Many consider that to be a myth." Animo repositioned the saw beneath the branch. "They say elven mothers tell that to their children so they'll behave. How insufferable of a child were you?"

"Ha, ha." I laughed humorlessly, topping off my armful of sticks. "Do we have enough?"

He split another log off the branch, then gathered the small stack. "I think so—"

A twig snapped amid the trees. We froze. My eyes fixed on Animo as he scanned for danger.

He threw down his load, shoving me behind a tree. I stifled a cry, gripping the sticks against my chest. He raised a finger to his lips, peering around the tree's trunk. Calming my breathing, I followed suit.

A human-like figure crouched in the leaves. Long, greasy hair covered her face, and a dress woven of grass and vines hung from her thin body. She dug at the ground with her spindly fingers, pulling up roots and stuffing them in her pocket. Once it was full, she rose, back still hunched as she darted into the brush.

Animo waited a moment before stepping out from behind the tree, gesturing for me to follow.

"What was that?" I whispered.

"A tree elf." He gathered the fallen logs, his gaze still fixed on the bushes.

"That was an *elf*?"

"*Tree* elf. Part elf, part goblin. Their race was born here, and they're cursed because of it." Anger tightened his voice. "The dark magic soaked into their brains, making them violent and erratic. While goblins seek magic more than anything, tree elves are set on having one thing only—the flesh of their parent races."

"As in—"

"Us."

"Oh."

Animo sighed, shaking his head. "This place… tree elves are intelligent. They learned how to speak the language of the trees and defend themselves against campaigns. Yet everything they could have been was ruined. Cursed."

"Maybe some can escape."

"It wouldn't do them any good. They're highly susceptible to light. Even if they made it out of the forest, they'd be burned by the sun's rays. They're trapped, fated to die as prisoners. Everything in Vaera is fated to die." He stared aimlessly at the ground, then closed his eyes. "We need to get out of here," he said, more to himself than to me.

We gathered the dropped firewood in silence before returning to camp. Not that it offered us any more protection. The Silver Forest sought our deaths, and if we weren't careful, our fate would be worse than anything a tree elf's twisted mind could conceive.

THE RUINS OF VALINTROS

Morning came, yet there was no relief from the crushing darkness of the forest. We hiked for hours, picking our way through the thorny brush that grew chaotically, snagging our clothes and scratching any exposed skin.

The terrain arched upward as we walked, and the sharp branches morphed into a leafy grove. Vines snaked across the ground, now littered with chunks of rubble. A new chill laced the air, haunting in a beautiful, ancient way.

The forest deepened as we walked, the grass shifting into a carpet of moss. Stone arches towered above us, chipped and overgrown, held together by sheer might—the abandoned skeleton of something once great.

"What is this place?" I breathed.

"Long ago, it was the Hall of Valintros." Animo ran his hands across a broken stone pillar. "Before Daria, Valintros was the heart of the elven kingdom. Now it's a graveyard."

"Is it safe?" Megs asked, rubbing goosebumps from her arms.

"As safe as one can be in this place," he replied, leading us through the archway.

A view of the leafy canopy replaced the ceiling. Moss and vines encroached on the ruins, winding around broken tables and climbing the cracked walls. In thick, stone chairs sat pale skeletons with arrows and knives protruding from their bones.

"What happened?" Hertz asked.

"Goblins," Animo said darkly.

My brows lifted. *Is this the place he told me about? The old fortress where the goblins had defeated Salvator Regiis.*

Animo's finger grazed an arrow embedded in an elf's bone. Scraps of frayed fabric were still pinned between the wooden shaft and the skeleton's ribcage.

"Is there anything here we could use?" I asked.

He shook his head. "Whatever the elves left is sure to have been picked clean. But it will give us shelter for the night."

Though the sun was hours from setting, we made camp in the remains of a dining hall. Skeletons stared through gaps in the crumbling walls, yet their sightless gaze gave me no trepidation. For the first time since entering the Silver Forest, I almost felt comfortable.

An owl hooted, gliding above us as Animo lit the fire. The dry wood caught quickly, crackling as the flames devoured the kindling.

Megs began to hum, swaying back and forth. Her humming shifted into vocalizing a jaunty tune I knew well.

Da, da, da, da,
Da, da, da, di-ah!

I grimaced. "I'm not sure singing is a wise idea."

"Our fire is one of the few lights that burn within this domain," Animo said. "We have already drawn attention to ourselves."

Megs grinned, bursting into song.

He spins her round and round and round,
Tomorrow, though, he won't be found,
Gone away to fight the war,
Like the other men before.

"Enough singing," Hertz said through clenched teeth.

"No, thank you!" She climbed onto a broken table, dancing in circles. Ketch hopped up beside her, and together they belted.

He'll leave the girl without the lies,
One 'I love you' then he flies.
Hold him close, say goodbye,
Tell him quick before he dies.

Yellow eyes gazed from the brush. The ring of steel sliced the forest as Animo and I drew our blades.

Da, da, da, da,
Da, da, da, di-ahhh!

The verse ended in a scream as Megs's gaze locked with the creature's. She stumbled off the table, followed by Ketch. The dwarf pushed her behind him as he loaded an explosive into his slingshot.

"Why don't they attack?" Hertz asked, his knuckles tight on the handle of his axe.

"Why does a spider wait to devour the fly?" Animo replied, his eyes jumping between us. "They're waiting until the moment is right—when we're defenseless, caught in their web. That's when they'll strike."

A chill slithered down my spine.

Hertz glared at him. "Disturbing anecdotes aside, we need to find a way out of here."

"Funny, I've been hoping we'll get even more lost," Megs quipped, unable to keep the shake from her voice.

"Our path is straight," Animo said. "So long as we follow it, we will find our way out."

"All we need to do is keep walking," I added, taking a seat. The eyes had vanished, but the hair-raising sense of being watched remained.

"We can make it," I said, mostly to myself. We hadn't come all the way to Daria to die in some forest, no matter how cursed it might be.

We will survive.

Animo settled beside me. "You're afraid," he said quietly.

"Of course I am. This forest won't be satisfied until it has our lives within its jaws." I shook my head, rubbing my eyes. "And now I'm talking about it as though it were a being."

"In many ways, it is."

"What?"

"Magic cannot be created, nor can it be destroyed. Spells channel the magical energy into an object or target. Once the spell is finished, the magic has to go somewhere. More often than not, it sinks back into the world around it."

He nudged a dark sprout, peeking up through a crack at our feet. "This forest is riddled with magic. It's why the goblins came here in the first place. Between the elves of old and the witches who have come, masses of magical energy have been released and found their place in the ground, water, air, and trees."

I gazed at the canopy above. Branches creaked in the wind, but now it sounded like the creaking of aged bones. Instinctively, I slid closer to Animo.

"What did it do to them?" I asked softly.

"It gave them life. The trees, or *viti*, as we call them, are living, breathing creatures with minds of their own and even the ability to move. They're docile for the most part, but when angered, they are practically unstoppable."

"Perhaps we shouldn't anger them," I suggested shakily.

He smiled slightly. "That would be ideal."

I leaned back against the wall, tilting my head to meet Animo's eyes. "How do you know so much?"

"I may not have favored my time in Daria, but it taught me much about magic, even though I don't use it."

"You said that before… Why not?"

His gaze dropped. "Regium abused the powers he was given. I don't want to be like him."

Like him? How could Animo think that was possible? Regium was a selfish coward manipulating the masses for his own benefit, while Animo was risking his life for the sake of a kingdom that wasn't even his. He was the hero.

If only I was the princess he was here to save. We could dance as we did in Rudane and live a happy life away from bloodshed. Alas, my destiny lay behind the helmet, charging toward the enemy as I attempted to be something I was not.

When will Fate realize she chose the wrong girl?

FUTURES WRITTEN IN FLAME

Sleep evaded me. The frozen silence of the Silver Forest was louder than a scream in the night, leaving my mind to wander, picturing clawed and scaly creatures slinking through the shadows.

Grass tickled my bare arms. Only it wasn't the gray grass of the Silver Forest; it was green, shadowed by night and dried by rime's cold air. My heart pounded as I huddled in the bushes, listening to my people dying.

I turned over sharply, forcing a gasp from my tight chest. The memory faded as I sat up, wiping my eyes before tears could form.

"Are you all right?" Animo watched me from across the campsite, Bathril in his lap and a whetstone in hand.

"Fine," I replied sharply. "I… I was thinking about something that happened a long time ago."

"This place brings out the worst in people. It's best to keep your mind busy." He dug a second whetstone from his bag, holding it out to me.

I joined him by the vine-covered wall, examining the stone. "What is this, an enchanted elven sharpening stone?"

"I told you, I don't use magic."

"Not even to cut a few corners?" I raked the whetstone across the blade of my dagger with a satisfying scrape.

He paused, his stone poised below Bathril's hilt. His gaze drifted to the rune tattooed on his wrist. "I made my choices. And they've kept me from becoming like him."

"You don't regret them?"

"I didn't say that." His eyes met mine, vulnerability twining with inquisition. "Do you regret yours?"

Yes. And if I had the choice, I would change them all.

I couldn't bring myself to say the words, instead asking, "What do you think?"

"I think that you have regrets, and you wish a lot of things were different. I also think you spend more time wishing instead of doing."

I bit the inside of my lip, scraping again with the whetstone. Old thoughts plagued my mind—worst of all, the realization that they were exactly that: thoughts. What had I done to change things? To amend my wrongs? Nothing.

A groan rose from the lump of brown cloth and spiky hair that was Ketch. He rolled over, glaring at us. "Must you make so much noise?"

"Would you prefer to face goblins with dull blades?" Animo asked.

The dwarf stretched his limbs. "I'd prefer to be well rested."

"Then shut up." Megs dragged herself upright, eyes still closed as she pushed her hair away from her face. "I had finally fallen asleep, then you started talking. How do you people live like this?"

"It's usually easy for Ketch," Animo said. "He once slept through an earthquake."

"Really?" I asked.

"I wish I could say no."

Megs slid into a cross-legged position as she attempted to wrangle her unruly curls into a ponytail. "What were you doing while Ketch was napping?"

"Evacuating the village," Animo replied, sheathing Bathril.

"Always the hero," she mused. Satisfied with her hair, she pulled the message sphere out of her bag and began tinkering. Only Hertz remained asleep, barely visible beneath the long, drooping branches of a snow-white willow tree.

"It's an annoying habit of his," Ketch said, yawning.

Animo leaned back, arms crossed. "If we're going to talk about annoying habits, let's talk about you sharing a rather elaborate version of your life's story to everyone you meet."

"I only do that when I'm drunk."

"As I said, everyone you meet."

Ketch replied with a rude hand gesture.

"I like Ketch's stories," Megs said thoughtfully. "It's like reading a book, only you don't have to sit around for hours staring at pieces of paper."

I rolled my eyes. "You're hopeless."

"Why? Because I'd rather go out and do something—"

"Oh, please." I scoffed. "You don't have the patience to read a shopping list."

"Ladies, ladies." Ketch held up his hands, cutting off Megs's retort. "There is a simple way to solve this. I'll tell a story, and Rose can read a book."

"What does that solve?" I asked in time with Megs's, "Where is she going to get a book in the woods?"

"Here." Animo pulled a small leather volume from his satchel—my mother's diary.

My jaw dropped as I took it. With all the chaos in Daria, I must have forgotten to pack it. I held it close, the old leather comforting against my fingertips. "Thank you."

He smiled, settling back as he said to Ketch, "Well, get on with your story."

Ketch cleared his throat. "Ages ago, the dwarf lands of Pikbrie were held hostage to an endless purge of dragon fire. Mines were attacked as the great dragons searched for gold to add to their hoards. Streets ran red with the blood of dwarves, and ash fell like rime snow. It seemed the land would forever be darkened by smoke."

I swallowed hard.

He continued. "It appeared nothing more could be lost, yet the dragons found something to take. They killed King Colomnus Fotressbuilder of Family Marrs, leaving Pikbrie leaderless. The people went into a panic. How were they to go on? Could a new ruler rise from the ashes of their kingdom?"

The longer Ketch spoke, the more targeted his words seemed.

"The crown fell to King Colomnus's firstborn, Rona. The moment she took the throne, she was thrust into a rope tug between fighting and retreating, but she chose neither. Against the judgment of her advisors, Rona herself faced the dragons and did what no one before her had done. She spoke to them.

"Now, dragons cannot speak our tongue. Until that moment, it was believed impossible for any other race to communicate with them. But when the dragon leader, Theydran, gazed into her eyes, he knew she was not there to bring harm. He used his magic to open his mind and join his thoughts with Rona's. Only it was more than their thoughts, Theydran merged their *souls*. He created an unbreakable bond that brought forth treaties and a peace that has lasted nearly a thousand years."

Ketch leaned back, a soft smile on his lips. "What Rona did that day was remarkable. She earned the name *Peacemaker* for ending the Dragon War and became the first of the dragonriders."

Animo leaned over, whispering in my ear, "Now you get to hear the life story."

I grinned as Ketch shot us a glare.

"It's not a life story if it hasn't happened."

"Fine." Animo amended. "Your hopes and ambitions."

"You want to be a dragonrider?" I asked.

"I was training to be one." Ketch's smile turned wistful as a shine slipped into his eye. "I was going to be the greatest dragonrider the Twelve Kingdoms had ever seen."

"What happened?" Megs asked.

His face fell. "I made a poor choice. And then another and another. I ran away from home and fell in with the wrong sort. I didn't even make it to the choosing—that's when the dragonriders meet with the hatchlings, hoping that they'll be chosen for a bond."

"What happens if you aren't chosen?" I asked.

"You don't become a dragonrider. See, dragons are temperamental creatures. If they don't like you and you try to ride them, they will do one of two things: eat you alive or burn you alive."

"Ah."

"Can anyone be chosen?" Megs asked, propping her chin on her palm. "Or do you have to be a dwarf?"

"I suppose anyone can," Ketch said thoughtfully. "But bonding with a dragon is a tricky thing. In order to be a dragonrider, you have to do what Rona and Theydran did—merge your minds in an irreversible ritual. You hear each other's thoughts and feel each other's emotions. Joy, pain—everything. Even when you retire from Pikbrie's ranks, you will be connected. And when one of you dies, it will be like the other lost half of themselves."

"Biaht," Megs said in awe. "How do you get a dragon to choose you?"

"It's easiest when the dragons are young. Full-grown dragons tend to be set in their ways and, frankly, moody. Dwarves spend time with hatchlings during their first year. Then, if things go well, they can go through with bonding. Dwarves are best suited because we're small. We can ride hatchlings once they're seven months old, whereas humans would have to wait until the dragon is well over a year."

"Still…" Gears turned behind Megs's eyes.

"No," I said.

"Spoilsport."

"You'd fall off!"

"Actually, the saddles have very strong belts that keep you on," Ketch offered unhelpfully.

"Still, no." Megs with a crossbow made me nervous, and that *didn't* shoot fire.

Ketch patted her on the shoulder. "She can say no to you, but not to me." He smiled as if the thought would make her feel better. "Someday, you'll be able to say that you knew Ketchnoori of Family Runix before he was famous."

"You're already famous in Vargo," Animo said. "Fourteen failed escape attempts, was it? I heard it's a record."

"Rose," Ketch began, ignoring him. "May I have the book?"

I tossed my mother's diary to him. With a final glare at Animo, he thrust it before his face, methodically turning each page.

Biting back a smile, I leaned against the stone wall, tilting my head. If I stared hard enough at the canopy, I could almost imagine hints of sunlight seeping in between the leaves.

Something snapped. I drew my dagger, rocking onto my heels.

"Sorry, that was me," Megs said sheepishly, her tool shoved inside the message sphere.

I lowered my blade. "Aren't you done with that?"

"Nope! But Ketch and I talked that night in Aspectu's cavern, and I think I finally know what's wrong with it. It needs a stronger ignition. Something that burns like dragon fire."

"How do you expect to shove dragon fire into that thing?"

"Not *actual* dragon fire. Something that burns *like* dragon fire," Megs corrected. "Dragon saliva, for example."

"I am not helping you get that."

She raised a brow. "So that's the limit to our friendship? Harvesting saliva from a dragon's mouth?"

"Yes, certain incineration is where I draw the line."

Rolling her eyes, she returned to the device. With another snap, her smile vanished.

"That *wasn't* me," she whispered.

Animo shot to his feet. "Strike the campsite."

Without question, we gathered our belongings, shoving them beneath a stone table. Animo stamped out the fire, trapping the smoke under a piece of rubble. We took cover behind Valintros's crumbling walls. In the corner of my eye, I glimpsed Megs on the ground, clutching the message sphere against her chest. Weaponless. Afraid.

That was you once. I closed my eyes, cutting off whatever dark thought wanted to follow.

Voices rose from the other side of the wall, joined by sharp cackles. Carefully, and with dread-soaked regret, I peeked over the wall.

A train of small beings marched through the forest: humanlike in form, with rough, grayish-green skin and pointed ears that extended straight out from their bony heads. A cluster of them carried a long, squirming sack above their heads.

I ducked down, waiting until the scuffling of the campaign was too distant to be heard. Finally, Animo stood, gesturing for us to do the same.

Megs's voice trembled. "What in biaht was that?"

"Goblins," Animo replied.

"How were those goblins?" I asked. "I've met goblins and they're... not that." The ones I'd met had warmth and intelligence, but the ones marching through the woods radiated madness like how a fire radiates heat.

"These are Silver Forest goblins," Animo explained. "They've been corrupted by their pursuit of dark magic. This infernal forest destroyed their minds, filling them with a lust for something forever out of their reach."

A menacing thought wormed through my head. "If it destroyed their minds, could it destroy ours?"

He sighed heavily. "Yes—but we'll be fine if we leave soon. The magic of the forest is slow working. It would take a long time for it to fully penetrate our minds."

"How long?" I demanded.

"Depending on your strength of mind, a few months to a year."

"Well, that's not terrible," Megs said uncertainly.

Beside her, Ketch fidgeted, shifting his weight while his fingers toyed with the cord on my mother's diary.

I folded my arms. "Is there something you would like to add, Ketch?"

He shook his head, his eyes fixed on the dirt. "Nope."

"Are you certain?"

He glanced up, meeting Animo's threatening gaze. "This is what locked me up in Sheildore!" he exclaimed. "I fold under questioning!"

"Ketch," I warned, stepping forward.

"It would take months for us to become completely bewitched, but the curse is already eating at our minds," he blurted. "It started the moment we entered the forest and won't end until we leave."

Megs whirled on Animo. "Why did you say a *year?*"

"Because the magic preys on vulnerable minds," he retorted. "Ergo, fearful minds."

"I'm not scared," she squeaked. She cleared her throat. "I'm not scared."

"Lying can also weaken your mind," he said.

She shrank back, her arms wrapped tightly around herself.

"In other words, we have weakened minds that are slowly being corrupted by this dark-magic-infused death trap of a forest?" I asked, my voice rising with every word. "How could you not think to mention this?"

"I never wanted to come here!" he snarled. "I told you to stay away from Daria."

"So this is my fault?"

"More or less."

Rage flashed through me. "You were the one who lost Aspectu!"

"Because I was tracking *you* down! Saving *you* from being ripped apart by shades!"

"Stop arguing!" Megs shouted, her trembling hands pressed over her ears.

I wrapped my arm around her shoulders, forcing down my anger. "She's right. And I have a feeling fighting is on the list of things that will weaken our minds."

"It will be slow," Animo replied, anger lacing his voice. "It's already working. That's why we're turning on one another. And it will only worsen. We won't realize how far we've fallen until it's too late."

Ketch shook his head somberly. "We're lobsters in a pot."

"Frogs," Megs said.

"What?"

"The saying is *frogs in a pot.*"

He frowned. "You eat frogs?"

"We farm a lot of things in Chess, but lobsters are not one of them."

Ketch wrinkled his nose. "But why would you eat frogs? Lobsters don't have souls—anyone who looks in their eyes can tell. But frogs? Frogs see everything, and they hold grudges."

"Is this really important?" I couldn't help the bite in my voice, as irritation ate at my mind.

"It's distracting us from our impending doom, so I'd say it's at least a little helpful," Ketch pointed out.

"Then keep talking while we pack up camp." I cast a pointed glance at Animo. "We're not staying here a second longer than we have to."

We retrieved our belongings from under the table. A voice nagged at my mind as I plucked brittle leaves off my satchel's strap. Like an unscratchable itch beneath my skin, the unformed thought irked me.

"How can we be sure we aren't lost?" Megs asked, squeezing her balled-up cloak into her bag.

"We're going west," Animo replied.

Megs's eyes darted between us. "Isn't that deeper into the forest?"

"Don't worry," he said. "We have someone waiting at the end."

"Oh, good, you have a plan," I said dryly.

He huffed sharply, tossing his bag to the ground. Beside him, Ketch groaned, unwinding the cord of my mother's diary. "I sense an argument brewing. When you two are finished and ready to leave, let me know. In the meantime, I'll be reading."

Animo folded his arms, his narrowed eyes locked on me. "Has anyone ever told you that you're a pessimist?"

"Has anyone ever told you that your plans include a one-way ticket to Biaht?"

"People—"

"I don't remember your plan being much better," Animo replied, cutting off Ketch.

"Listen—"

"My plan was hijacked by an evil king, a shade army, and a forest that wants to kill us!" I snapped.

"All of which would have been avoided if you had just listened to me!"

"Everyone!" Ketch shouted, planting himself on the broken table. "We need to leave! Now!"

Animo drew Bathril. "Goblins?"

"Worse." Ketch held up the book. "The Curse of Valintros."

"What?" Animo demanded.

"There's another curse?" Megs cried.

Ketch read aloud, "*Those who enter the sacred hall must make themselves worthy to the spirits that haunt it or else remain their spoils forevermore.*"

Animo swore. "Why didn't you tell us this sooner?"

"It's your book!"

"It's Rose's!" he snatched the diary from Ketch.

"I haven't quite had the time for reading lately! And technically speaking, it's my mother's."

That was unnecessary. Your anger is unnecessary. But how did I stop it?

"What does this mean?" Megs demanded.

"We may be in trouble." Animo flipped through the pages, his lips moving silently as he read.

"Does that mean we have a slim chance being fine or that we are certainly doomed, and you're trying not to scare us so that our minds don't get possessed by evil magic?" Megs asked.

Animo swore again.

"Certainly doomed." I snatched the book from his hands, shoving it into my satchel.

He slung his bag over his shoulder. "We need to go. The curse is said to lure travelers in, trapping them forever with the spirits of those who died."

"We're trapped here?" Megs exclaimed.

"Not yet. But I would recommend running."

Megs grabbed my hand and took off. Our boots pounded on the cracked remains, kicking rocks and scattered bones as we ran. An odd sort of fog clouded my mind, like a pull telling me to go back.

I've forgotten something . . . but what?

Animo's stride surpassed me and Megs. He led us through the crumbling ruins, out an arch, and down a stone bridge before skidding to a stop, throwing out his arms. A deep ravine cut through the forest, spanning nearly ten feet across.

"Of course," Megs said, her voice high. "There's a broken bridge overlooking an abyss."

Ketch squatted at the edge. "I doubt that it's an abyss—the bottom is likely littered with sharp rocks eager to impale us."

"Not helpful," Animo snapped, surveying the chasm. Despite the nauseatingly long drop, the gap appeared to be jumpable.

"I'll go first," he said, dropping to his knee. "Ketch, hop on."

Ketch climbed onto Animo's back, keeping a tight grip on his shirt. Megs and I stood back, giving them space. Animo sprinted down the path, launching himself over the ravine. The two sailed across, landing in a roll that sent Ketch flying through the air and crashing into the bushes.

The dwarf scrambled to his feet, swearing and coughing as he plucked twigs out of his clothes.

Animo pushed himself up, breathing heavily. "It's your turn! Get a running start, and jump to us."

I nodded, readying myself. "It's just a jump. We can do this." I rubbed the restrictor cuff's lump beneath my arm bracer. *If only I could use my magic.*

Drawing in a deep breath, I prepared to move and—

"Wait!" Megs yelped, grabbing my arm. "We forgot Hertz!"

"Don't be—" I froze. "Rack, we forgot Hertz!"

"We have to go back and get him," she said, tugging me back toward the arch.

"Wait!" Animo shouted. "It's dangerous in there!"

"We don't have much of a choice, do we?" I called back. "Stay there. We'll be back shortly."

"Rose!" Animo's eyes locked on me, clouded with warning. "Don't let them take you."

The words didn't have a chance to settle before Megs pulled me beneath the arch and back into the Ruins of Valintros.

LOST IN THE FOG

"**H**ertz!" Megs called, fog lapping at her ankles as she scrambled up an incline. "Hertz!"

"Shh!" I hissed, my gaze darting about the empty forest. I wasn't clear on the details of Valintros' curse, but I had enough intelligence to *not* announce my presence to whatever spirits haunted it.

The air had shifted—I'd known it the moment we'd passed under the arch. Fog rolled along the ground, while the sensation of spying eyes lingered on my spine. Whatever comfort I had felt before had evaporated the moment Animo crossed the chasm, leaving me with an internal bramble patch of creeping dread and guilt for leaving one of my best friends behind.

"We have to find him somehow." Megs rubbed her neck, then cursed, dropping to her knees and patting the ground. "My medallion fell off."

"We don't have time for this," I said. We were far too vulnerable to waste even a second searching for jewelry.

Megs ignored me, crawling along the forest floor. "Ah, ha! I found it!" She held up her medallion triumphantly. Her eyes widened, and a grin spread across her face. "Rose, look."

Climbing to her feet, she showed me the medallion. Strange, dark slivers stuck to the metal.

"Lodestone," she explained. "It's attracted to metal." Her gaze grew distant, the gears in her head turning. "If we had a bowl… Oh!"

She dropped back to her knees, pulling the message sphere from her bag and prying the top panel off. "Give me your flask."

I passed it over, still blind to her plan.

She poured water into the curved panel before adding a fallen leaf to the odd compilation. Then came a sliver of lodestone atop the leaf. It floated, spinning slowly.

My brow furrowed. "Are you going to explain what you're doing?"

Megs grinned up at me. "It's a compass. Animo said we were going west. That means the campsite is east." She eased the makeshift compass into her palm, following its gentle spin. "This way is north, which means… That's east." She pointed into the forest. "I know where we're going."

"Megs… that was brilliant."

She offered me a shrug of faux modesty. "I know. And, I know that despite your constant complaints, you are incredibly grateful for my presence."

"I am. Truly."

Her smile lifted, warming her gaze. "Let's find our friend so we can get as far as *racking* possible from here."

We followed the compass, hiking east until the outline of Valintros's dining hall materialized amid the rising fog. A windless chill cut through my clothes, biting my skin.

"Hertz?" Megs's voice wavered. "Are you here?"

I gestured for her to stay back as I advanced cautiously, my eyes scanning our surroundings. Beneath the hanging limbs of a white blossomed tree lay a dark shape covered in a worn, green cloak.

"Hertz!"

I rushed forward, Megs on my heels. We dropped beside him, and I pressed my fingers to his neck. A sigh of relief slipped free as the steady thrum of his heartbeat pulsed against my fingertips.

"He's alive."

"Good." Megs covered her mouth, stifling a yawn. "I don't blame him for falling asleep. I'm exhausted."

I echoed the motion. After catching mere minutes of sleep last night, the ground called to me, enticing as a warm blanket during rime.

"Maybe we should take a nap…" she muttered, her eyelids drooping

No, we can't do that… but it would feel so wonderful to rest.

I lowered myself, twisting to lie on my back. My eyelids fluttered. Drooping, white leaves hung above me.

Willow leaves.

I forced my eyes open, throwing myself out from under the willow's canopy. "Megs!" Alertness doused me like ice as I caught her arm, dragging her to safety.

She blinked rapidly, shaking away the drowsiness. "Wha-what happened?"

"It's a sleeping willow tree." I pushed myself up as my own head finished clearing. "Animo used the powdered leaves to put me to sleep for a week. I imagine they're even more potent while on the branch."

"Can we move him?"

I reached out, gently touching the soft leaves. Sleep teased my mind but was not strong enough for me to succumb. With a sharp tug, I broke a short length off the hanging foliage. I shoved it into my satchel.

"We should be able to get him out, but we'll need to be careful," I said.

With the aid of fallen limbs, Megs and I managed to pull Hertz's leg out from the willow's radius. Gripping his ankle, we hauled him to freedom.

"Hertz," she said, shaking him gently. "Wake up."

"Is it time to leave?" he mumbled, blinking slowly.

She smirked. "Only if you want to avoid being trapped in the cursed ruins."

His eyes snapped open. "I've missed something, haven't I?"

"Just our company splitting up after Animo and Ketch jumped over the abyss," she said, hauling him to his feet.

Hertz closed his eyes, rubbing his temples. "I'm never going to sleep again. Where do we need to go to reach this…"—he winced—"abyss?"

"Technically, it's a chasm with rocks at the bottom." Megs's face fell into a grimace the moment the words left her lips.

"That's not important," I said. "What matters is that we found you, and it's time for us all to go."

Megs took the lead, guiding us with her compass. The fog thickened as we ventured through the ruins, rising above our heads and clouding our vision.

"Is this the right way?" she asked, nervously tilting the compass.

"Of course it is," I replied, though the uncertainty in my voice betrayed me.

Hertz extended his arm. The fog closed around it, obscuring everything below his elbow. "Is the curse the cause of this?"

"I'm… I'm not sure. Wait!" I dug through my satchel, retrieving my mother's diary. I flipped through the pages, landing on a handwritten entry marked *Valintros, ninth of Marsai, 1168, RT.*

Today, Bella and I visited the Ruins of Valintros. It is the most incredible place I have ever seen. As I walked through the arches, I could feel the presence of the elf warriors of old. Their longing is etched upon each weathered stone. It is why the ruins have chosen to turn on all who cross the threshold. Those who enter the sacred hall must make themselves worthy to the spirits that haunt it or else remain their spoils forevermore.

They are cursed. Fated to exist in death and thus, fated to bring forth death to all who enter. Now, Valintros is a prison for those who gave their lives to protect it—it has been since the hall fell and will be until Daria is no longer ringed in darkness.

I was safe because Bella accompanied me, providing her protection. For those of Salvator's descent may enter without fear of harm.

Salvator's descent. We needed someone of Salvator Regiis's bloodline to escape Valintros. Someone like Animo.

My throat tightened. "Run."

Megs and Hertz stared at me with wide eyes. "What?"

"Run," I repeated. "We have no protection against the curse. We have to run."

We raced into the fog blindly, our feet slipping and sliding on snakelike vines and loose rubble.

You will become their spoils forevermore.

Ghosts watched us. I felt their gaze, a chill radiating through my bones. No matter how fast or how far we ran, we could never escape them.

Fated to bring forth death.

A woman screamed behind me.

"Megs!" I spun, scouring the fog for a glimpse of red hair. "Megs?"

"Rose!" Hertz shouted somewhere at my side.

"Hertz!"

Silence pressed around me.

"Hertz?" I took a step back, unsheathing my blade.

Silence met my words.

"Rosara Wolfe," a voice as sharp as knives hissed in my ear. "You should not be here."

I spun again, only to be met with more fog.

"Who are you?" I asked, flexing my fingers around my dagger's hilt.

"We are the Lost. The ones who fell and the ones who may never leave."

"Why not?"

"We are cursed."

The breathless voice ticked the back of my neck. I twirled, slashing through the fog. My blade passed through the air, sending wisps swirling.

"Your mortal weapons will not harm us." With an invisible hand, he knocked the dagger from my grasp.

I jerked away. "What do you want with me?"

"To see."

Fog shifted, curling into fingers and brushing against my cheek. I tensed, frozen in place.

"I could not show myself while the Regiis-born watched over you. So I lured you back."

Realization struck me. "You made me forget Hertz."

"Yes."

"Why? Why am I the one you want?"

The opaque hand closed around my throat, lifting me off the ground. I gasped for air, thrashing about to no avail. My vision swam as voices sang inside my head. Every memory I'd ever held flashed through in unison, as well as those I had not yet lived. Life and death merged together in an ataxic tapestry.

The ghost's grip slackened, dropping me to the ground. I fell to my knees, drawing in breaths as though I were drowning.

"Are you going to kill me?" I asked.

"Not today."

"Then what do you want?" I snarled, pushing myself to my feet.

"We want you to see the light of day."

The fog lifted. Faceless shapes materialized, their translucent skin formed of shimmering mist. Long elven blades extended from their hands, as though carved of crystal.

A figure stepped forward, the outline of a crown hovering atop his brow. "I have seen your future, Rosara Wolfe, and it is great. It has become the future of the Twelve Kingdoms themselves. You are a catalyst capable of unimaginable destruction and indescribable hope." He offered me my dagger. "Do not fail us."

I took the blade, my fingers phasing through the spirit's. My grip tightened, and the ghosts faded, leaving me alone in the clear forest.

What was that?

"Rose!" Hertz called, Megs's voice echoing with his. "Rose!"

I sheathed my dagger, sprinting toward the sound. Jumping over a fallen wall, I landed in a small clearing at the ruins' edge, where my friends waited.

Megs squealed, engulfing me in a hug. "What happened? We were together, then we weren't."

"It was the spirits that haunt Valintros," I explained. "They revealed themselves to me but let me go."

"Why?" Hertz asked.

I shrugged, pulling away from Megs's embrace. "They must have realized we weren't a threat."

You are a catalyst capable of unimaginable destruction. The words etched themselves in my mind. The spirits weren't fooled. They knew *exactly* the kind of threat I was.

"Oh! We found something." Megs ushered me to a crumbling stone wall, pushing aside vines to reveal a stone hatch. "We're not sure what it is, but while we're here…"

The slightest smile teased my lips. "Let's see what's inside."

Together, we pulled open the heavy hatch. A staircase loomed behind, plunging into darkness. One by one, we descended the steps. A curtain blocked the bottom. I swept it aside, letting blue light spill over us.

"Woah," I breathed.

An armory lay before us, lit by shards of layvas crystals. Weapons lined the walls, their steel shining and their points free of cobwebs. Swords, bows, spears—each one was forged with the elegant strength of elven warriors.

"It's from before the Goblin-Elf Wars," I realized, reaching out to touch one of the swords. Ornate carvings ran down the blade, reminding me of Bathril.

"It's incredible." Megs gazed at a display of spears. "Especially with all the wicked things running about."

A chill seeped into the armory, like the first breeze of harvest. In the faint light, I caught a glimpse of a crowned silhouette.

"They protected it," I murmured.

The spirit raised a hand, pointing at a bow. *Take it.*

I picked it up, examining the carvings that wrapped about the wooden limbs, meeting in a leather-wrapped grip. Resting the bow against my leg, I picked up a quiver of arrows and slung it across my back.

"You should arm yourselves too," I told my friends, my gaze fixed on the spirit. It nodded slowly. *Thank you,* I mouthed.

Megs and Hertz studied the armory walls carefully before selecting their weapons. Megs took a few small daggers and a sheath that wrapped around her bicep, while Hertz settled on a wooden shield.

Freshly armed, we ascended the stairs, careful to reseal the entrance behind us. With the fog lifted, our path was clear. For the first time since we entered, the Silver Forest almost seemed to exist during the day.

We followed the path below the looming arch and onto the broken bridge. The treeline stared at us from across the chasm, still and empty.

"Rose," Megs began nervously. "Where did they go?"

"They're a little ways down. I'm sure of it," I said. *Animo, please… you have to be here. You can't abandon me now.*

One by one, we jumped across the ravine, collecting fresh bruises with our landings. Dusting ourselves off, we spread out, searching for our companions.

Five minutes passed, then ten. Animo and Ketch were nowhere to be found.

VISIONS OF DARKNESS

My muscles ached with every step I took. I pushed forward mechanically, ignoring the blood drying in the crook of my elbow—a scarlet mark courtesy of the thorny brambles that lined our path, their points reaching for our skin.

Megs, Hertz, and I hiked west in a close group. We'd searched for Animo and Ketch for as long as we could afford, but eventually we had no choice but to move on. They were surely dead—or on the brink of death at least—while we still had a chance of survival.

The temperature dropped, indicating the falling night, but I kept walking. Someone waited at the forest's end. If we could reach it, we would be free.

"Rose." At Hertz's voice, I turned. He stood beside Megs who slumped against a tree, her eyelids fluttering. "We need to make camp."

I shook my head. "Not here. We're too exposed."

"Rose!" he snapped. "She needs sleep."

"She can make it." I forced a smile for Megs. "Just a bit farther. I promise."

She nodded while Hertz held my gaze with a deadly glare. I flexed my fingers around my bow. When had he become someone who glared? Was it the forest's doing or was it my own path, once more causing irreparable damage?

I clenched my jaw as we resumed our trek. Hertz's feelings didn't matter. Survival did.

Minutes crawled by, stretching toward the hour mark when we arrived at the rotting remnants of a cottage. I pushed the door open with my shoulder. It fell to the dirt floor, cracking and sending a puff of dust into the air. I coughed, burying my nose in my elbow.

We stepped inside. Hertz struck a match, lighting a candle he'd brought, while I reset the door.

Megs looked about nervously, her arms wrapped around herself. "Are we sure no one lives here?"

Cobwebs covered the windowless stone walls, and the wooden beams were nothing but rot and twisting vines. The bare cabinets' doors either hung ajar or had a corner broken off. An overturned table lay in the center of the room, rimmed with toppled chairs. Against the back wall sat a bedframe, its mattress and sheets devoured by moths to the point of mere scraps of fabric hanging off of ropes.

"No," I replied. "No one lives here." They were long gone. Likely decomposed.

"Good," she murmured as Hertz led her to the corner. He kicked aside fallen boards before laying his cloak down. With a mumbled word of thanks, she curled herself into a ball, her eyes already closed.

"I'll keep watch," I said.

Hertz nodded, avoiding my gaze as he settled against the wall. Within minutes, they were both snoring.

I set down my bow. My legs throbbed, yearning for relief. If I was to keep watch all night, I wouldn't be standing. With a soft sigh, I reached for a fallen chair. Magic shot through me the moment my fingers touched the wood. My head snapped back as energy wormed its way through my body, smothering my senses and stealing control of my limbs.

Orange light flared to life. I sat before the table, candles flickering from the home around me. Across from me, a woman knelt by an overturned chair, wailing with her hands pressed against the side of her head.

"Calm yourself." My lips moved, and the voice of an old woman rose from my throat.

Realization settled over me. *It's a memory. I'm in the* past.

"Make it stop!" the woman begged, rocking back and forth.

"You asked for this. I warned you that there would be a price to pay, and you still asked for power."

"To save my home!" The woman's head snapped up.

Natalia. If I had control over my jaw, it would have dropped. My enemy knelt before me, no more than twenty years of age, racked with more emotion than she'd shown in the past decade.

"The Darkness cares not what your motives are," the old woman said. "It only cares what you can do for it."

Natalia stumbled to her feet. "I will not serve it."

"Then it will not serve you."

Natalia took a deep breath, brushing the tears from her cheeks.

"You chose to accept it. The only way to be rid of it now is to pass it to another."

Dark understanding flooded Natalia's eyes. "You...you *witch*."

My lips drew back in a smile. "You are the witch now, my dear."

Natalia shook her head, staggering toward the door. She wrenched it open and ran outside.

The woman followed, pulling me along within her skin.

Natalia hunched over, muttering to herself. She shook her head violently, then unleashed an awful scream, dropping to the ground as convulsions twisted her body.

My heart wrenched, as though torn in two. One side filled with sick satisfaction watching my parents' murderer in pain, while the other knew horror, dread, and… pity.

Natalia stilled. She took in a breath, rising as though she had been reborn.

She's done it. The old woman's thought echoed in my mind. *At last, I am free.*

Natalia raised her arm. Black energy slithered through her fingers, lingering around her ring.

Her ring… Ever since I'd known her, Natalia had worn the same piece of jewelry—a thin copper band and a twisted silver one, connected to form an X shape. As a girl, I couldn't understand why she was so partial to it. But now I saw; it was her totem.

"The Darkness wants me to prove myself," she said, her voice hollow as though she were in a trance, staring at the magic dancing across her pale skin. "To be the witch… I think I shall."

Her gaze met mine, and her power exploded. It tore through the old woman, ripping apart her skin and pulverizing her bones. But before her soul could move on, she cast one final spell—

I snapped back to my own body, falling backward onto the dirt.

Hertz shot to his feet, his axe raised. "What happened?"

"I… I had a vision."

"A vision?"

"Yes. And you can put the axe down—it can't harm us." I waved a hand as I climbed to my feet. "It was a memory from the woman who lived here."

His brow furrowed.

"Before she died, she locked her memories in this cottage," I explained. "When I touched the chair, I entered her final memory. It showed Natalia on the day she gained her powers."

"What does that mean?"

"I'm not sure."

He sat back down with a huff. "Then it's worthless."

"It's not worthless. I know what Natalia's totem is. If I take it from her, she'll be defenseless."

"*If.*"

I clenched my teeth, fighting back a retort. *It's the forest's magic. Arguing will only make things worse.*

"I'm sorry," I said, my voice tight. "The situation we're in is… terrible. You have every right to be angry with me, especially after I left you behind." *Even though it was the ghost king's doing.*

"You think I'm angry that you left me?"

"Aren't you?"

"I'm more concerned about what will happen next. Megs, Ketch, Animo—they're all so rash. They'll jump off a cliff without a single thought of what might be at the bottom."

"Sometimes jumping is the only option."

"And sometimes there are rocks below." Hertz shook his head. "I thought you were different, Rose. I thought you were wiser."

I folded my arms. "If I remember correctly, *you* were the one who insisted on coming along. *You* jumped, and if you're hurt before our journey's end, I won't be at fault."

"You were ready to run off alone, with two men you barely know," he shot back. "Men with *criminal* histories. Forgive me if I wanted to protect you."

"What purpose does that serve if I'm going to jump to my death?"

"What are you doing?" Megs scrambled to her feet, hastily rubbing the sleep from her eyes. "You can't fight, that's what the forest wants."

I ran a hand through my knotted hair, exhaling slowly. "You're right. And I'm sorry, Hertz. This place is working its twisted spell on all of us. I think it would be best if we disregard everything we've said. At least, until we make it out, and then we can sort everything out."

He nodded. "I agree."

"Good," Megs said. "Now, if we've finished—"

A woman's scream tore through the night. I drew my dagger as Hertz pushed Megs behind him.

"That's not one of our party," I whispered.

"But that girl… she's in pain," Megs said. "We have to help her."

"We don't know her," Hertz said. "For all we know, it's a trap set by a witch."

Or a tree elf, or goblins, or some other vile creature we've yet to encounter.

"Rose, please," Megs begged. "We're here to save lives, aren't we?"

"*Avonsheran* lives."

"So?"

I sighed, shoving my dagger into its sheath. *You know she's right… but there's no telling what's waiting at the scream's source.* Doing the "right thing" could save a life. Or, it could mean forfeiting our own.

"Rose…" Megs's green eyes implored me to agree.

"Fine," I said. "We can investigate. But that doesn't mean we'll act."

She smiled slightly, then ran to gather the cloak she'd slept on.

Hertz grabbed my arm. "This is what I was talking about," he said in a low tone. "You're jumping."

"If we don't, then someone else's blood will be on our hands. So what do you say? Are you going to protect me, or not?"

He stared down at me, exhaustion dousing his fury. "I'm with you, Rose. Until the very end."

Those words, spoken with anger buried alongside strained affection, stirred a memory. Another man had sounded like that just hours before he had found the end.

I picked up my bow, clenching my fist around the grip. *Hertz will not die tonight. I vow it.*

GOBLINS!

Blazing light flickered amid the dark trees, its source growing brighter with every step we took. An intense sense of foreboding gripped my chest. The screams had faded, replaced with… cackling?

I signaled for Megs and Hertz to stay back, then slunk forward, practically crawling to avoid being seen. Dirt rubbed against my pants and caked on my elbows. I stopped at a fallen log, peering over cautiously.

Fire raged before my eyes, the dark shapes of goblins dancing around it. They laughed and sang, their foreign words teeming with maniacal glee. One stood above the rest, clad in dull furs and exalted on a stump throne. At his side stood a smaller goblin, flipping through the pages of a leather-bound book. He passed the volume to the leader, who stood, addressing the campaign.

He hissed in the goblin tongue, earning a chorus of cheers from his clan.

"Kingdoms."

My whole body flinched at the sound of Megs's voice. She crawled to my side, and I pushed her head down.

"What are you doing?" I demanded in a whisper.

"I wanted to see what was happening." She peeked over the log, her eyes widening as the leader held up a white crystal, glowing with magic. "Do you speak goblin?"

"A few words."

The leader spoke proudly, raising the crystal high, then hurling it into the fire. Sparks flew, popping wildly.

"He said *sunlight*," I murmured. "And... *cave*, I think."

"What? What do caves and sunlight have to do with throwing things into a bonfire?"

"I'm not sure. But this appears to be a ritual."

"For what?"

I shrugged.

Something shifted on the clearing's edge. Megs gasped, pointing at a bundle of dark linen—no, not linen. A *woman* lay in the dirt, her hands bound and bloody.

"We have to help her," Megs whispered.

I grabbed her wrist. "No. I'm sorry, but there are too many of them."

"We can do this." She pulled out of my grasp. I dove at her, narrowly missing her ankle as she darted into the forest.

"Megs!" I clamped my hand over my mouth. In a stroke of fortune, the goblins remained focused on their leader. Biting back curses, I slipped into a tree's shadow, settling on my heels as I nocked an arrow.

The goblin leader raised a vial of iridescent liquid, shimmering orange before the fire's glow. He called out a word—*unicorn*—and tipped it over the flames. The droplets splattered against the burning wood, sizzling and spitting sparks.

"Where is she?" Hertz crept to my side, gripping his shield.

I pushed him back. "Stay hidden."

"Where did she go?"

"They have a hostage. Megs is trying to save her."

Anger blazed in his eyes. "How could you let her do that?"

"*Shhh!*"

I turned my attention back to the goblin camp. The leader spoke, capturing the gazes of the campaign. None of them saw Megs sneaking along the treeline. She crouched by the prisoner's side, exchanging soft words. The girl nodded, and Megs drew a blade, quickly cutting through the ropes.

"We need to get her away from them." Hertz began to rise, but I pulled him down.

"We'll only draw their attention," I hissed. "We have to let Megs do this on her own."

"But—"

The goblin leader thrust a vial of scarlet liquid into the air, shouting in his native tongue. I recognized a word: *ekeider.*

"Oh, no," I breathed, clutching Hertz's arm. "This is a ritual to gain magic."

"*What?*"

"Animo told me that ekeider blood can be used to give non-magic beings powers. That's what these goblins are after."

"*Now*, can we help Megs?"

"No—look, she's almost to safety."

Megs helped the captive stand. The girl took a wobbly step. Her ankle twisted, and she fell with a cry. The campaign's heads swiveled as one, like a green wave preparing to crash on my best friend.

"Run!" Megs shouted, shoving the girl toward the woods. She stumbled away as Megs drew a second blade.

The hoard of goblins swarmed my friend. She screamed as they clutched her arms with clawed hands, dragging her forward.

I shot to my feet, drawing back my bow and letting an arrow fly. Before my first target fell, I had another arrow nocked.

Drawing their weapons, the goblins charged toward me. Megs curled into a ball, sobbing as blood trickled down her skin.

"Get her!" I shouted at Hertz. My bowstring twanged as I let arrow after arrow fly. Each one landed soundly in my target's flesh.

The goblin leader glared at me from across the clearing, still clutching the vial of blood. He dropped from his throne, storming over to Megs. She struggled weakly as he grasped her arm, dragging her toward the fire. Hertz appeared at the treeline, his eyes widening as they locked on Megs.

My aim faltered. I shifted from the approaching goblins to the leader. *Keep her from the flames… kill him before he can hurt her… stop him from using the blood… Megs… goblin… vial of blood…* My scattered thoughts seemed to fuel the arrow's trajectory. It sailed through the air, driving itself into the leader's hand, piercing flesh and glass alike.

The goblin roared in pain as his blood flowed alongside that of an ekeider. He thrust a crimson-coated hand at me, shouting enraged words.

The campaign surged forward. I reached for an arrow, but they pressed around me, leaping to grab my arms and pin them behind my back. They dragged me to my knees, stripping me of my weapons before pulling me down into the clearing.

They shoved me to the ground beside Megs and Hertz. She hunched, still crying, while he sat, frozen and wide-eyed. The goblin leader grasped my chin, his sharp nails pricking my cheeks.

"You have destroyed the first magical blood to enter goblin hands in over a decade!" He shouted in Common. His rectangular eyes narrowed. Releasing my chin, he pushed my hair behind my ear. A smile twisted his lips, bearing his razor-sharp teeth in a wicked grin. "Garblesh."

"Yes, Ekkshu?"

"We have a new sacrifice."

Ekkshu raised his dagger, its silver blade glinting in the firelight. My heart pounded as he ran its cold tip across my cheek and down to my neck, tracing its curve before setting it against my collarbone.

"No!" Megs sobbed, straining feebly against the goblins' hold. "Please, no…"

Tears welled in my eyes. I took in a deep breath, forcing my voice to be even. "Megs, don't."

"I—" She hiccupped. "I'm sorry, Rose."

"I know. It's all right. You'll be all right."

It was a lie, and she knew it.

"The blood of an Ekeider," Ekkshu rasped. "With it, we shall obtain the magic Fate has forbidden us."

Hertz's gaze fixated on the ground, his jaw slack. Shock kept him frozen, but at least it would reduce his pain. The same could not be said for Megs. She slumped in the goblins' grasp, sobbing silently.

Ekkshu's blade pressed against my skin. I closed my eyes, preparing myself for the final strike. *Rose Wolfe… it is time to die.*

Glass shattered. My eyes flew open as goblins screamed. Ekkshu doubled over before me, shards of glass lodged by his eye and his hand limp around his dagger. I snatched it from his grasp as Animo burst into the clearing, Bathril drawn and Ketch on his heels.

I twirled, slicing the throats of two goblins. They dropped, their shrill cries fizzling into gurgles as blood bubbled from their mouths.

"Kill them!" Ekkshu snarled, his teeth bared as he backed away.

Disorientation fading, the campaign tightened their circle, jagged blades at the ready. I kicked and slashed, holding them at bay. Animo swung his sword, cutting through the ring. He dashed through the opening, plating himself behind me. We fought back to back while Ketch pulled Megs and Hertz out of immediate danger.

Small bodies fell, piling around us. Ketch rejoined the fray, firing small explosives at the attackers. A clawed hand jerked me away. Ekkshu snatched the blade from my hand and sliced down my arm. I cried out as blood rose, trickling down my skin.

"At last…" his eyes glowed with victory. He strode to the bonfire and held the dagger above it. My blood dripped from the blade's point, sparking as it hit the flames. The goblin leader cackled, extending his arms. "Magic shall be ours!"

"No!" Megs surged from the sidelines, dagger held high. Her eyes blazed like the bonfire as she sprinted toward Ekkshu.

It happened in a blink. Megs's dagger slid from her hand as Ekkshu pulled his blade free. Scarlet slicked silver, splattering onto soft, white skin. She fell to the ground, her eyes—once so bright and alive—now cold and lifeless.

I sank to my knees as tears blurred my vision. I couldn't move. The moment trapped me, forcing my gaze to follow Ekkshu as he knelt beside her still form. He drove his dagger into her chest, carving down her torso. I fell forward with a strangled cry. He plunged his hand inside, tearing out her heart.

Megs… Sobs wracked my body. *Please, no.*

Ekkshu stood, her blood dripping from his fingers. His eyes locked with mine; his teeth bared in a smile. Battle clashed dully around me. Swords cut through flesh, bodies dropped, limbs snapped. But *he* walked through the fray, untouched. The bonfire loomed before him, awaiting the ritual's final piece. I clenched my fist against the dirt.

Fight…

She's dead…

Fight…

It's my fault…

FIGHT.

I forced myself to stand, throwing myself at the nearest goblin. We toppled to the ground, and I slammed my fist into his face. Bones cracked, shifting beneath my knuckles. I rolled off him, snatching his rough blade and swinging it at another attacker. She screamed, skin splitting and blood spurting. I drove my pain into the dagger, cutting my way toward Ekkshu.

He picked up the grimoire, flicking it open. I charged, swiping with my blade. Ekkshu leaned back, dropping the grimoire. I dove, thrusting my dagger at his chest. He caught my wrist, twisting it so the blade pointed at me. He pushed, and the point sank into my flesh. I screamed as pain flared from my side, sharpening as the weapon slid free. Stumbling, I fell to the forest floor, my hand pressed against my bleeding wound. My chest heaved with shaky breaths as Ekkshu retrieved the grimoire and approached the fire once more.

A hand slid around my waist. Animo pulled me to my feet, wrapping my arm around his neck. His free hand brushed my cheek as his gaze traveled over me, taking in my wounds with wide eyes.

"Stay with me," he murmured.

"We have to stop him from completing the ritual," I said.

Animo shook his head. "He doesn't matter." He gripped me tight, turning to shout at Ketch, "Get us out of here!"

Ketch nodded. He slammed an empty capsule against a goblin's head, dropping the creature with a spray of glass. Behind him, Hertz stared numbly at Megs' body, his shield abandoned at his feet.

Ketch drew a green-tinted bottle from his pocket and sent it flying into the bonfire. Animo pushed me down, covering my body with his own. The bottle exploded, sending a rush of flames through the clearing. It faded as quickly as it came, leaving goblins rushing about, slapping the fire, scorching their clothes and hair.

Ekkshu struggled to stand. His flesh sizzled, the rank odor filling the clearing. He gripped the singed grimoire in one hand and Megs's blackened heart in the other. "*Ov eure sahl aei erden sive,*" he read in Aesin. "*Lav daes icha uthae ertas il de heliv orvu. Lav mavine erdas!*"

He hurled Megs's heart into the fire. The flames roared, piercing the black canopy. Orange rippled, racing through the trees like a blazing ocean wave. The bonfire shifted to a violent shade of purple, sparks flying every which way. Animo tightened his grip on me as gold and violet rained down, singeing our skin.

The fire lifted off the ground, the flames spiraling into a tight ball in midair. It blasted apart, searing us with a hot rush of air. The light faded, and a small, shiny object dropped into a pile of ash.

Silence stilled the clearing. Our breaths echoed, ragged and worn as we inhaled the charred air. A tiny, hushed moment that seemed to stretch an eternity.

Then, chaos erupted.

The goblins surged forward, lunging like rabid dogs for the object. I pulled out of Animo's grasp, diving into the fray. Someone shouted my name, but it fell on deaf ears as I hacked my way through the hoard of monsters.

Sharp claws dug into my leg. They yanked, pulling me to the ground. I rolled onto my back—Ekkshu leered down at me, blade raised.

I kicked, knocking him to the ground. Frantically, I twisted, scrambling through the throng on my elbows. The object glinted before me, pounding in time with my heart. I reached out, closing my fingers around the metal.

Something stirred inside of me. A dark creature emerged, breathing in the bloody air with joy. The beast within stretched its wings, slithering through my body.

At last.

Pain shot through my shoulder as Ekkshu drove his blade into my flesh. I screamed, swinging my dagger. My blade slashed through his neck, replacing his wicked grin with a shocked gawk.

I fell back as pain reverberated through my bones. The beast roared, clawing at my mind. Barriers crumbled. My blood boiled as magic thrummed through me. The restrictor cuff shattered, slicing my wrist.

I doubled over with a scream that seemed to come from leagues away. A fresh wave of agony sliced through me. Black swarmed my vision and noise blurred. The sharp burn racked my body, smothering my senses. My power flared, lashing out like a whip.

Everything stilled.

"Rose." Calloused hands fell onto my shoulders. Animo cupped my chin, my eyes refocused. "Rose, look at me."

"'nimo…" I choked, breathing heavily. "What happened?"

He didn't answer. Ketch and Hertz hovered behind him, unease lingering in their gazes.

"What?" I turned my stiff neck.

"Rose—" Animo reached to stop me, but he was too slow.

The forest *bled*. Scarlet dripped from branches, landing on the cracked and blackened bones of goblins. They lay scattered across the clearing, splattered in ash and gore. Only one body lay untouched: Megs's pale form, marred by her blood alone. The metal shards of the restrictor cuff littered the blood-specked grass.

I covered my gaping mouth.

I did that.

My eyes ran over the carnage as bile rose in my throat. I had done all of this.

ONE HAND IN THE SKY

In Chess, the dead are honored. They are laid to rest in boats and bid farewell with flames that would light their way to the afterlife. Warriors ascend to Eterios, a hallowed hall where their sacrifice and courage would be forever praised and never forgotten.

We buried Megs in the river. Her limbs, weighed down with rocks, sank to the bottom, fading into the black depths. Nothing lit her way to Eterios. No flames honored her memory. Only darkness.

I sat on the riverbank, gazing vacantly at the water's obsidian sheen. My reflection stared back at me, tainted with blood. Nausea settled in my stomach. The pain that split me before had subsided, leaving only the ache from my stab wound. But within me lingered the strange, dark beast. It prowled the shadowed corners of my mind, its cracked shackles clanking with my heart's every beat.

Animo took a seat beside me.

"Do we have to go?" I asked quietly.

He shook his head. "We have a few minutes while Ketch and Hertz make camp." He dipped a cloth into the river, sending a ripple across the inky surface. Extending a hand, he asked, "May I?"

I nodded, offering my arm. He took it gently, wiping the dried blood from my skin. My cuts stung as the cold cloth pulled away their flimsy scabs. Pink-tinted water ran down my arm, tickling my elbow.

"Why did it break?" I asked.

"When you touched the totem, it sent a surge of power through you. It was enough to shatter the cuff."

"*I* did this?"

"Don't worry. The cuff was old, shoddy craftsmanship. It was bound to break sooner or later."

Fresh blood beaded from my cuts. Animo reached into his satchel, withdrawing a bandage.

I turned my wrist as the blood spread, running across my wet skin like cracking ice. Nothing blocked my magic. But would a healing spell work?

The thought had barely formed when my skin began to knit itself back together. A soft gasp escaped my lips. The cuts on my wrist disappeared along with the ache in my side. I brushed my fingers against the rough bandage Animo had applied to the stab wound. No pain. No blood. A chill ran down my spine.

His hand closed around mine. "Are you all right?"

"I think I am." My heart pounded relentlessly, shaking the beast.

Let me out, it seemed to beg as it raked its claws against my insides.

Animo's grip tightened. "Do you know the reason for the goblins' ritual?"

"They were trying to gain magic. Somehow, it created this." I pulled the necklace from my pocket, examining it for the first time. Silver twisted in an ornate frame around a black stone that seemed to swirl, not with reflected light or color, but with pure darkness.

"What you're holding is a Reyth totem," Animo said. "It's a profoundly dark piece of magic that amplifies the power of the one who created it. Because the goblins used your blood, the totem believes that *you* are its creator."

"What?"

"It was a blood magic ritual. The goblins must have thought they could siphon an ekeider's magic, but that's not the way the spell works. This totem is tied to you and your kin. No one else can use it."

I clenched my fist around the totem. "So Megs died for nothing."

"She traded her life for another. That's not nothing."

I shook my head. The girl Megs had saved had run into the forest alone and unarmed. If she wasn't dead already, she would be soon. "Death takes who she pleases," I said bitterly.

"Do you believe that?" he asked. "That death is an unstoppable force led by divine whim?"

"In Chess, children are taught about three afterlives. Biaht, for those who lived evil lives; Idycen, for the ordinary; and Eterios, a land of glory and rest, whose doors open only for those who lived great and noble lives."

Animo tilted his head as he gazed down at me. "What do you believe in?"

"I believe in Cisin."

"And when you die?"

I shrugged. "I'll cross that bridge when I reach it."

"Hmm." He leaned back on his hands. "As a boy, I was taught that when elves die, the first elf, Duaex, takes their spirits to the Everlands. It's said to be a place of sprawling hills and blooming meadows where our eternity continues in peace."

"That sounds beautiful."

"It's a lie."

My eyebrows raised. "Are you certain?"

"Certain enough to stake my life on it."

"If you don't believe in Duaex, or Biaht, what do you believe in?"

He shrugged. "I'm not sure. I believe that there's something out there, but it's not a divine guardian."

"Now you doubt the guardians?"

"I've always doubted them. But that's a conversation for another time." He stood offering me his hand.

I let him pull me to my feet. "Thank you for giving me this moment," I said.

He withdrew Megs's medallion from his pocket, setting it gently in my palm. "Her resting place should not go unmarked."

I ran a finger over the medallion's surface. Flecks of dried blood lingered in its crevices. My heart ached itself into numbness as I hung the medallion on a nearby tree, its bronze coating dull in the lightless forest. At the tree's base, I drove one of her daggers into the dirt.

And then it was over: my final memory of Megs. A life forgotten as the water flowed.

Animo led me to camp. Ketch stoked the cracking fire while Hertz sat against a tree, holding Megs's second dagger. He cradled it in his arms as though it might shatter at too sharp a breath. Beside him lay her bag, its flap pushed back to reveal the bronze curve of the message sphere.

A creation that will forever be unfinished. I clenched my jaw, fighting to keep my sorrow at bay.

"What kept you?" Hertz asked, his voice dull.

I stared at the dirt. "We marked her grave."

His lips trembled. "It shouldn't have happened this way. She shouldn't have died, not here. Not in this place. She should—she should have—"

"She should have gone out with one hand in the sky." My tear-filled eyes met his.

He nodded.

"What does that mean?" Animo asked.

Hertz let out a pained laugh. "She always wanted to reach the unreachable. We told her that one day, she would climb too high and fall. But she said—she said 'that's the way I want to go—with one hand in the sky.'"

I hugged my knees, biting my lip to keep it still. She should have fallen from the height of glory, not been dragged down into ash.

"I want to be eaten," Ketch said. Three sets of alarmed eyes landed on him.

"You heard me," he said. "I want to be boiled alive and then eaten. But what my captors won't know is that before I was made into dwarf stew, I swallowed poison. They'll eat me and die after a week of excruciating pain."

Animo's brow creased. "It concerns me that you've thought this out."

Ketch gave a barking laugh. "And you haven't?"

"Yes, tell us, Animo," I urged, grateful for the distraction. "How do you intend to die?"

He leaned back, stretching out his legs. "I don't know the details. But I know that when it happens, I want it to be for a reason. I want to go down with my blade buried in someone else's chest."

Cold silence settled as the firelight reflected the burning passion in his eyes. I knew exactly whose chest he wanted to drive Bathril into.

I straightened, clearing my throat. "I want it to be quick. I don't care how it's done or by whom; I just want it to be over fast." My gaze met Ketch's. "There's no need to wallow in the inevitable, is there?"

He gave me a half-smile.

"What about you, Hertz?" I asked.

He gaped at us as though we had spontaneously grown multiple heads that glowed green. "I want to die in a bed surrounded by my loving family. What is wrong with all of you?"

We released a round of shaky laughs. I lay back, my heart lifting the tiniest bit at our lingering smiles.

"Are we heartless?" Hertz asked. His smile faded along with our laughter.

"No," Animo said. "You are suffering a loss that no one deserves to bear. Soon, your tears will return, along with pain, emptiness, and guilt. It will strike you like an arrow in the chest, and the scar it leaves will never truly heal. You should enjoy the denial while it lasts."

Silence fell over our company. Silence like death.

I exhaled sharply, cutting off my thoughts before they formed. "How much farther is the border?"

"A few days, perhaps," Animo said. "Our path has twisted, but we're on course."

"And your… *friend*." Hertz's nose wrinkled on the word. "The one meeting us at the end of all this. Can we trust them?"

I snorted. "That would be new."

Animo glanced at me, his brow raised. I averted my eyes, letting them fall to the ground.

"Yes," he replied. "We can trust her."

Coals simmered, their orange light dimming as the night dragged on. Ketch and Hertz slept across the clearing, torn cloaks covering their bodies. Animo leaned against a tree, his gaze fixed on the treeline like a stone sentinel.

I sat, cross-legged before the dying fire, Bellatora's list of spells resting on my knee. Holding out my hands, I recited, "*Lumaia vaccerae.*"

A sphere of pure, white light formed between my palms. I gasped, my lips curving into a smile as the light swirled. Focusing my magic, I urged the sphere to grow. Its glow flickered, brightening for a moment before burning out. I sighed, shaking my tingling fingers.

"For your first attempt, that was impressive." Animo crossed the campsite, taking a seat beside me.

"Fifteen seconds won't be particularly useful if we find ourselves stuck in another pitch-black tunnel."

"I'll bring a torch."

I rolled my eyes.

"I knew it," he said. "You don't trust me."

"What? No, I—" I huffed. "Animo, you have proven yourself trustworthy a hundred times over. My problem isn't you, it's this place. This racking forest of curses that makes me long for the nightmares of sleep. It's ruined me."

"I understand. I've been fighting my thoughts since we crossed the border. I don't always win."

"I can't blame you for that."

But you can blame him for leaving. The dark thought twisted its way up, like a flower decaying before its first bloom.

"Where did you go?" I asked, my tone edging toward confrontation. "We looked for you at the crossing point, but you weren't there."

"I know, and I am truly sorry. But leaving you was not a choice we made. Not long after you returned to Valintros, we were found by a witch. To keep the tale brief, she showed us that there was a bottom to that abyss."

"Oh."

"You sound disappointed. Were you hoping to blame me for not being there?"

I picked at my fingernail. "Maybe."

His gaze dropped. "Is that the forest speaking or you?"

"I don't even know. I don't want it to be, but… I don't know."

"I understand."

You shouldn't.

I sighed, shoving the list of spells into my satchel. My fingers brushed against the sleeping willow branch. It was a poor apology but the best I had available. I held it out to him. "I found this in Valintros. You said you had run out, so I swiped some."

"A sleeping willow tree?" His brow raised as he took the branch. "What else did I miss?"

"A lot."

I told him everything about Valintros. Hertz's encounter with the willow tree, the ghosts, the armory—every part except my vision. While I spoke, he assembled a makeshift mortar and pestle and ground the leaves into a fine powder, pausing briefly to examine my bow.

"It's enchanted," he said, his fingers caressing the ornate carvings. "One of the ancient kind that's incapable of missing."

"Incapable?"

"In a way. Its aim is drawn from thought. The arrow will fly at whatever the archer focuses on. It's a dangerous skill to learn, but once mastered, this bow is unbeatable." He passed it back to me.

"What about Hertz's shield?" I asked.

He craned his neck. "The craftsmanship matches a line of heavily enchanted shields. Whoever holds that will be hard to kill."

Pity Megs didn't have it.

I pushed the thought aside, drawing the totem from my pocket. "And what about this? What are we meant to do with a totem?"

Animo's eyes narrowed, shadow clouding his starry gaze. "This totem is dark magic, born of blood and death. And dark magic doesn't play fair. It's a disease that offers you glory and power but takes your soul as collateral." He took my hand. "I need you to promise you won't use it."

"Why would I use something evil?"

"*Promise* me."

"I promise."

He exhaled, relieved. "Good." He swept the sleeping willow powder into a small, silver vial before offering it to me. "A show of good faith."

"Thank you." I took the vial, offering him the totem in return.

He pushed my hand away. "I can't take that."

"But you can't use it. It would be safe with you."

"That's not the point. The point is for you to make the right choice."

I closed my fingers around the totem. Aspectu had seen me at the center of darkness. It was a *certainty*. Could this object be the cause? Did it contain the power to destroy the Twelve Kingdoms? Or did I?

"Why are there no answers?" I asked.

"We're all cursed." Animo reached into his satchel, withdrawing a leather volume splattered with scorch marks.

I sat up straight. "That's the goblin's grimoire."

"It's an *elf* grimoire," he said sharply. "The one stolen the night my mother died."

I touched his arm. "I'm so sorry."

His jaw tightened. He opened the grimoire, turning the browned pages. Aesin words were scrawled across them, joined by ink sketches of broken and twisted bodies, creatures of nightmares, and a thousand more images of gore.

I drew back with a grimace. "What kind of being would cast these spells?"

"Those who crave power above all else." He fingered the fragment of a torn-out page. "When I was a boy, my father told me that my mother died giving birth to me. In his version of the story, the goblins attacked while he was at her bedside, too distraught to realize Daria had been invaded. And like a fool, I believed him."

His fist clenched around the pages. "When I was nine, I learned the truth. The idea that my mother's murderer lived was unbearable—I wanted vengeance. So I marched into the Silver Forest, sword in hand, ready to kill every goblin I laid eyes on. But the campaign was stronger than I'd anticipated. They took me captive, holding me for a ransom that never came. Eventually, I managed to escape and steal this grimoire.

"When I returned to Daria, I expected a joyous welcome. I had survived a fight with our sworn enemies and retrieved an ancient relic. But when my father saw me, he told me that I should have died. He would rather preserve his precious sense of peace than see his son alive."

I had no words. There *were* no words.

"My *father* summoned the campaign to the city. He returned the grimoire and ordered my death to appease them. Do you know what it's like to beg your father to let you live? It destroys you. Because you know that no matter what you say, he will never choose you."

He turned the page. "Goblins have sought magic for centuries. That campaign would have killed every ekeider they laid eyes on without tasting a drop of success." He closed the grimoire with a sharp snap. "I'm glad they're dead."

Darkness lingered in his gaze, but I didn't fear it. It wasn't a force of evil, seeking to corrupt. It was justice. Vengeance. Love.

But me? My darkness was destruction. A catalyst.

It is certain.

THE TOUCH OF SUNLIGHT

I would have traded a life trapped in Valintros, cursed to spend eternity with the lost souls of elven warriors if it would have made Ketch stop talking. Morning till night, that dwarf talked. He told stories—both true and fictional and somewhere in between—and he sang songs, and then he just *talked*.

There was no conversation, no singular language he spoke in, just endless, *endless* words. I had half a mind to shove the vial of sleeping willow leaves down his throat and drag him all the way to the border. The longer we spent in the forest, the shorter my temper grew as the curse darkened my mind.

Animo's fuse shortened as well, leaving him with a constant scowl, while Hertz retreated to his mind entirely. He trailed behind like a shadow, scarcely speaking even when spoken to. Though I feared for him, I couldn't help but prefer his stoicism to Ketch's... Ketchness.

"But why?" Ketch asked as we picked our way down a hill. "Why did someone decide to take a piece of wood and stick four more pieces of wood on the bottom of it and then *sit* on it? It's baffling!"

"Will someone please shut him up?" I begged, rubbing my temples.

"Shut him up or stab him?" Animo asked irritably. "I'm not particular at the moment."

"Neither am I. I'll accept anything that puts an end to his noise."

"You two are despicable." Ketch turned, walking backward so he could glare at us. "I try to fill our days with frolic and fun, and you mock me? You are simply—"

"Ketch!" Animo lunged forward.

"What—?" Ketch jumped back. His leg caught on a tree root, sending him tumbling to the ground. "Ow," he moaned.

Animo held out his arms. "Don't move."

I gripped my dagger. "What is it?"

"It's the viti," he murmured. "They're awake."

"The magical trees that will kill us if we anger them?" I asked, my voice rising an octave.

"Yes."

Hertz drew his axe. "Anger them like stepping on their roots?"

"Or waving an axe in their face," Ketch hissed, edging his way off the twisted roots. Animo cringed, grabbing the dwarf's arm and yanking him to flat ground.

"Stow your axe," Animo ordered. "Viti only attack when provoked. If we move slowly and quietly, we'll be safe."

Hertz hid his axe beneath his cloak, his dark eyes trailing across the shifting canopy. Branches rustled, their leaves clacking against each other—a cryptic song passed through the windless air. Was my mind playing tricks, or were they truly conversing?

Animo waved us forward. "Follow me. *Carefully.*"

I fell in line behind Hertz. We picked our way through the forest, avoiding the roots that snaked along the ground as though we were giants navigating a mouse's maze.

My foot caught. I stumbled, catching myself above the ground. My heart pounded as I looked to the trees. Still. Silent. *Safe.*

My breath released in a slow sigh. I began to straighten, but something caught my eye. The totem lay on the forest floor; it must have fallen out of my pocket when I tripped. I could have left it, but the thought stirred a strange sense of detachment.

Who knows. There could be a use for it in the future. I slipped the chain over my head, tucking the jewel beneath my shirt.

Bushes rustled. I stiffened. Animo's head turned, his hand hovering over Bathril's hilt.

A pale shape lunged from the brush. It slammed into me, knocking us both to the ground. I threw up my arms, protecting my face as sharp nails slashed. Pain shot through my forearms.

A deep bellow rang, followed by a blur of wood as Hertz slammed his shield into my attacker. He dragged me to my feet. I stumbled behind him, finally catching a glimpse of the tree elf that writhed on the ground, my blood slicking her nails.

A guttural growl bubbled from her throat. Her narrowed eyes locked on me as her tongue flicked over pointed teeth.

Animo rushed past us, sword drawn. "Get her to the border," he told Hertz.

"We're not leaving you," I said.

"I'll be fine."

"But—"

"Go!" He swung at the tree elf, slicing through her wrist. She shrieked, blood spurting from the stump of her arm. Animo stepped back, twirling Bathril.

"Come on!" Ketch waved us toward him. Hertz obeyed, pulling me along as the dwarf pointed into the forest. "The cliff is half a league that way. We'll meet you there."

"Understood. Rose—"

The tree elf leaped onto Animo's back, sinking her teeth into his flesh.

"Animo!" I nocked an arrow.

Keep your focus, Rose. The arrow will follow your thoughts. You have to focus on the tree elf, not Animo. Not the blood wetting his shirt, or the near-misses of the tree elf's claws…

"Rack." I lowered my bow.

Bone cracked as Animo slammed Bathril's hilt into the tree elf's head. She fell off him, gripping the wound. Regaining her balance, she swiped. Her nails caught his wrist, and Bathril dropped from his grasp.

The tree elf snatched the blade, swinging wildly. Animo jumped backward, narrowly escaping a slash.

I have to do something to stop her… but what? Animo's words surfaced. *The dark of the forest makes them highly sensitive to sunlight.*

Dropping my bow, I summoned my magic, throwing every drop into the spell. "*Lumaia vaccerae!*"

Light burst from my fingertips, banishing the forest's shadows. The tree elf unleashed a horrible shriek. She fell, convulsing in the dirt, her sharp nails clawing at her eyes. My hands shook as power continued to flow. With a cry, I cut the spell short. The light faded, but warmth lingered in my bones.

The tree elf howled in agony. Blood dripped from her ruined eyes, clumping around a dark nerve that hung from her empty socket like the string used to sew on a doll's button eyes.

Animo raised a hand, drawing our attention. He touched a finger to his lips, then gestured for us to walk away.

I pointed at the tree elf, raising a brow.

Leave her, Animo mouthed. *We've fought enough.*

I nodded, picking up my bow and trailing behind Ketch and Hertz. *Mercy won't matter here. The forest will kill her soon enough.*

A twig snapped beneath my boot.

The tree elf's head swiveled. I nocked an arrow as she lunged, her bare feet pushing off the root-laiden ground.

Roots.

Trees.

Rack.

The arrow flew past her head, lodging into the trunk of a tree. The tree elf tackled me to the ground. I buried my face in my shoulder, bracing myself for the final blow—

But it never came.

The tree elf knelt above me, her sightless sockets aimed at the canopy. The trees creaked as they unfurled their branches. She joined in, mimicking the viti's language.

What have I done?

I crawled away as the branches' speed increased. They spun like a dancer's limbs, creating a harsh wind. With a frightened cry, the tree elf darted into the brush.

"Run!" Animo shouted.

We sprinted through the trees, ducking and dodging as branches whipped above our heads. A thick limb slammed into the ground beside me, spitting dirt and sending a sharp tremor racing beneath our feet.

I stumbled, struggling to stand. A vine like branch wrapped around my waist, lifting me into the air. Splinters dug under my nails as I fought to loosen its grasp.

"Rose!" Ketch skidded to a stop below. He loaded a glass bottle in his slingshot and sent it flying at the branch. It exploded, sending shards raining down and flames racing along the dry bark. With a shrill rattle of leaves, the vitus dropped me.

I landed on my legs, shock racing through my bones.

Ketch dragged me to my feet and shoved me forward. "Go! Catch up with Hertz."

I raced away as he loaded another projectile. Ahead of me, Hertz shouted, hacking at a limb. It recoiled, its leaves falling like gray blood.

"Hertz!" I slid to a stop by his side. "Are you injured?"

"No. But I can't fight these things for much longer."

"I know… I know, and I'll get us out of this?"

"How?"

Magic. The answer was so clear… how had I not thought of it before?

"Stand back," I instructed. I focused on the vitus, channeling my magic into a severing spell. Power flared within me, growing stronger, sharper. My magic slashed through the vitus's trunk. Chips of wood flew. The vitus groaned as it toppled, snapping other viti's branches as it crashed to the forest floor.

I dropped to my knees as my magic faded. *That power… where did it come from?*

Hertz tugged my arm. "Rose, get up. We need to keep going."

I followed his pull. Together we ran through the forest, dodging attacks. I shot arrows at the swinging branches, each one finding its mark.

"Rose!"

A branch slammed into my back. I hit the ground, the air rushing from my lungs. Light seemed to dance before my eyes. Pure, white daylight.

"Am I dying?" I gasped. "I see light."

"So do I," Hertz replied. He began to laugh. "It's the edge of the forest."

A sharp cry of relief slipped out as he pulled me to my feet. Hand in hand, we raced toward the light, breaking free of the Silver Forest with a joyful whoop. I dropped to my knees, my fingers sliding into soft, green grass. I gasped softly, twisting a blade as my eyes adjusted.

Blue sky stretched before us, merging with the glittering ocean. The cliff's edge hovered a hand's length from where I sat. Far below, waves rolled, crashing against the rocky base. My head spun as I peered over.

"Think we could make it?" I asked.

The corner of Hertz's lips lifted. "In this case, I'm willing to jump."

Ketch burst from the shadowy treeline, Animo trailing behind him. The dwarf raised his bloodied arms with a giddy laugh. "We made it! The end of the Silver Forest."

"Is it time to jump?" I asked.

"Not until we see her," Animo replied, sheathing Bathril.

I frowned. "How is your friend meant to reach us here?"

Before Animo could respond, a vitus reached out, shoving him into Hertz. The two tumbled to the ground.

"Get back, you lousy hunk of wood!" Ketch shot an empty vial into the tree trunk. It reared its branch then whacked him off the edge of the cliff.

"Ketch!" I shouted, throwing myself forward. He plummeted toward the waves, his scream fading into a sharp splash. Ripples expanded from where he hit, but his head did not surface. "Ketch!"

"What is that?" Hertz pushed himself up, shielding his eyes as he pointed to the horizon. A dark shape lingered. It shifted, its silhouette lengthening as it turned to the side. Reflected light blinked from a thick pole—*a mast*, I realized.

"It's a ship," I said.

"Ship?" Animo's eyes widened as he gazed at the incoming vessel. "On the ground, now!"

We flattened ourselves against the dirt as the boom of cannon fire exploded above us, tearing into the viti. Shards of wood rained down.

"Who in Biaht is shooting at us?" I yelled, covering my head.

"Don't worry," Animo shouted back at me. "She's friendly!"

"Who is *she*?" Hertz demanded.

"No time! Roll!"

Animo threw himself off the cliff's edge. With a string of mental curses, I flung myself after him, screaming as I fell. Air rushed around me, ripping apart my braid as I tumbled.

I crashed feet-first into the icy water. It closed over me, freezing my lungs. With a sharp kick, I pushed myself toward the surface. Sunlight rippled above me, cut by a shadow. Strong hands reached into the water. They closed around my shoulders, pulling me up and over the edge of a rowboat. I gasped for air as the hands dropped me on the boat's wooden floor.

"You're all right," a blond sailor with a sun-tanned complexion said, patting me on the back.

"Animo—" I choked, coughing up water. "Hertz, Ketch—"

"All fine. They're in the other boats." A woman with light-brown skin and braided hair gathered in a high ponytail spoke this time. The ocean breeze rustled her loose, white shirt as she offered me her hand. "Camilla Hawkins. Captain of *The Dragon's Bane*."

"Rose Wolfe," I replied, squinting in the sunlight. "What's *The Dragon's Bane*?"

PART FIVE

CHAPTER THIRTY-EIGHT

UNEXPECTED REUNIONS

T*he Dragon's Bane*, it turned out, was the great ship that had fired at us on the cliff. Camilla and the sailor who rescued me—whose name I learned was Sol—rowed us alongside the towering vessel while Animo, Ketch, and Hertz followed in a second boat. A rope ladder dropped from above, and my rescuers held it steady while I climbed. I reached the top and another sailor helped me over the ship's rail and onto a bustling deck. Stepping aside, I took in the scene.

Barefoot men and women spread out, sitting on barrels, playing cards, coiling ropes, or swabbing the deck with mops. Bottles filled half their hands, and patches covered their eyes.

Animo climbed over the rail with a wince.

"Animo!" I threw my arms around him. He tensed, sucking in a sharp breath.

"I'm glad you're safe."

His arms slipped around my waist. "As am I."

A dark head popped over the railing.

"Hertz!" I pulled away from Animo, greeting my friend with an embrace the moment his feet hit wood. Ketch followed, and I pulled him into the hug.

"I see the Silver Forest is wearing off already," Ketch said, patting my elbow.

I drew back, brushing damp hair from my face. "Indeed it has."

Camilla strode past us, her hand lounging on the hilt of her cutlass. Planting herself before the main mast, she turned, one hazel eye running over our soggy company while a leather patch ordained with silver tentacles obscured the other. "Please refrain from dripping blood on my deck."

Animo grimaced as he rolled back his bleeding shoulder. "Every time I see you, I'm reminded of how little you care."

"I value my ship above your life," she replied, her eye flicking over to him. "That sounds like caring to me."

"I suppose I should have specified. I'm reminded of how little you care about *people's* lives."

"Depends on the being." A grin lifted her lips.

"It's good to see you," he said, returning her smile.

"Aw…" she teased. "Was it the enraged viti or raging forest fire that softened you up?"

"How did you know the fire was connected to us?" Ketch asked.

Camilla snorted. "When Terrot tells me to patrol the coastline as a precaution, I expect it to end with explosions. What was it this time, witch troubles?"

"That's a story for later," Animo said. "Are our rooms prepared?"

She nodded. "You'll be bunking with Ketch. Her Highness"—I twitched at the title, but Camilla didn't seem to notice—"will take his old room." She nodded at Hertz. "That one can stay with the Crowborne boy."

My heart lurched. "*Crowborne?*"

"Derek Crowborne." Camilla looked back at Animo. "I didn't feel comfortable including it in our letters, but we've had a bit of a stowaway problem. We found the boy hidden in our cart along with the Estmar girl."

"Lili is here?" I exclaimed.

"She was in the galley last time I saw her. She—"

I didn't give her a chance to finish; I sprinted to a hatch, descending the ladder into the ship's dark underbelly. The steady rock of waves beneath us sent my head spinning. Black spots bloomed in my vision, and my legs wobbled on the wooden rungs before hitting the solid ground.

I blinked rapidly as my eyes adjusted, taking in the looming hallway lit by swinging lanterns. Placing a steadying hand on the wall, I called, "Lili?"

"She's further down." Camilla dropped to the ground beside me, lifting her patch to reveal a perfectly intact eyeball. "It helps me adjust to the dark," she explained, catching my stare. "The whole crew wears them."

The captain led me down the hall, her gait smooth, moving in time with the ship. She stopped, gesturing to a short door. "Here we are."

I ducked into a small dining room. A pair sat at the table, laughing with their hands clasped between them. Though her back faced me, I recognized my sister's mousy hair in a heartbeat. The boy who sat across from her looked up, his green eyes widening.

"Lili." Derek pointed at me.

"What—Rose!" Lili leaped up to hug me. "You're alive! Oh!" She drew back enough to survey my bloodstained outfit. "You're hurt."

"No. Well, yes—but I'll be fine. Not all of it is mine, anyway."

Her eyes widened. "Whose is it?"

"It's goblin blood mostly."

"*Goblins?*" She covered her mouth. "You fought goblins? But there are no goblin tribes in Chess."

"Chess?" A pang shot through my exhausted mind. "Lili, we're on the outskirts of Vaera."

"What?" Lili's jaw dropped, and Derek shot to his feet. She sank into a chair. "I knew that we had moved, but I had no idea we'd gone so far. Camilla insists we stay belowdecks anytime we pass by a port. She said that our lives would be in danger if we were seen—it's why she came to Rudane." She shook her head. "I don't understand, Rose. What is happening?"

I clenched my jaw. She deserved the truth, but how was I meant to tell her that I had spent the past three years lying to her?

Derek rounded the table to stand behind Lili, his hands resting on the back of her chair. "Are you alone? I only ask because a few days after the Harvest Festival, Megs and Hertz set off after you. I was hoping you would be together."

My throat tightened. The words pounded against my mind, but my mouth refused to open.

"Rose?" Concern flicked across Lili's face. She took my hand, her loving warmth scalding against my skin. "Is everything all right?"

Before I could respond, a knock rapped on the door. Hertz stepped inside, his wet clothes replaced with sailor's garb that fell short on his ankles and wrists.

"Hertz!" Lili's face lit up as she hugged him.

Derek smiled, looking between me and Hertz. "I knew you would find each other. But where's Megs?"

Hertz's lips flattened into a somber line. "That's… the two of you should be seated."

Lili backed away, her hand slipping into Derek's as they sat. "What happened?"

"We were attacked in Daria and forced to enter a dangerous forest," Hertz began.

I turned away, grief clogging my throat. I couldn't bear to watch as the world of the kindest boy I knew shattered.

Camilla waited in the hall, leaning against the doorframe opposite the galley. "Was the reunion all you had hoped?"

"It could have been better." I took a deep breath, swallowing my heartache. "Why is Lili here? Animo told me that the Estmars were in a safe house."

"Mr. and Mrs. Estmar are. Their daughter and her doe-eyed boy stowed away in hopes of finding you."

My insides coiled like a snake. *Lili threw away her safety for me.*

Camilla detached herself from the wall, gesturing me to follow her deeper into the ship. "Your cabin is beside your sister's. I've taken the liberty of removing all of Ketch's things and providing fresh clothing." She stopped before an arched door, looking me up and down. "It should be close enough in size."

"Thank you."

She pushed the door open. "These are your quarters. Once you've finished tidying yourself, you'll find me on deck. We have much to discuss."

Camilla lowered her patch as she returned to the ladder, leaving me alone as I stepped into the cabin. Portholes brightened the small room with afternoon sunlight. A mattress sat, tucked away in a wall hollow, and a dresser, trunk, and mirror, filled the cabin's other half.

I stood before the mirror, gazing at the mess I had become. Knotted remnants of a braid, fair skin marred with dirt and blood, and the ghost of tears lingering on my cheeks. I sighed, tugging the totem from under my shirt. I fumbled with the chain, my wet fingers slipping on the clasp. Accepting defeat, I left the totem on as I stripped off the rest of my clothes.

I dipped a cloth in the washbasin left on the dresser, wringing out clear water. Grimacing, I began to scrub, working at the fresh and dried blood that caked my skin. Every wipe darkened the rag, leaving it and the water stained pink.

I tossed aside the cloth as fresh blood beaded from my wounds. Pressing my fingers against the deepest scratch on my arm, I called upon my power. Magic sliced through me, sharp and bitter, like lightning racing through my veins. I gasped as the wound vanished, closing without a trace of a scar.

Unease bubbled inside of me. The beast within stirred, shifting and snorting, my magic swirling like tendrils of smoke from its nostrils. A month ago, I could barely cast a spell without feeling drained, but now... now something powerful lived inside of me.

With a single thought, the rest of my wounds healed. The sharp thrum of energy surged, skipping beneath my skin. Was magic meant to feel like this? I'd hidden that part of myself for so long; change was understandable, but this sensation wasn't what it used to be. It was strong. Dangerous, even. Yet there was a part of me that wanted more.

I re-braided my hair and slipped into a simple, maroon dress that fell just below my knees. Pushing the sleeves up to my elbows, I wrapped my dagger belt around my waist; I wanted to remain armed at all times, but an elven bow seemed excessive.

As I knelt to lace up my boots, the totem fell forward, swinging from my neck. I froze, my eyes locked on its black gem. *I'd had it on when I used my magic.* No… I'd had it on when I had used *its* magic.

Nausea flooded me. I dropped to my knees, planting my hands on the ship's floor.

The beast healed you. The beast saved you from the tree elf. The beast is still inside of you.

Gasping for air, I ripped the totem from around my neck. The chain snapped in two, leaving red marks on my skin. With a faint cry, I hurled it across the room. It bounced off the wall, hitting the floor with a dull thunk.

My neck throbbed. Leaning back, I touched the injured skin. A silent spell formed in my mind, but my magic remained dormant.

Every shred of hope disappeared. I curled up into a ball, tipping over sideways. My gaze landed on the totem lurking in the corner. It slid back and forth with the ship's rocking. The chain scraped against the wood, like claws scratching on a door.

On my mind.

I closed my eyes and covered my ears as the noise fell over me like a blanket of stone. *What is happening to me?*

CAPTAIN'S ORDERS

I squinted as I climbed out the hatch and onto the deck of *The Dragon's Bane*. Sailors set the sails, preparing for departure as the heavy, barnacled anchor raised. I'd thought the fresh air would clear my mind, but the scent of decay laced the salty sea breeze, reminiscent of Medea's canals.

I found my way to Camilla, who stood by the railing, peering through a spyglass. She glanced over her shoulder as I approached.

"I see the clothes fit," she said.

"They do, thank you."

"Your thank yous are adding up," she commented, turning back to the spyglass.

"What are you looking for?" I asked, following her gaze along Vaera's dark coastline.

"I want to be sure we aren't being followed. We've been going up and down the coast for the past month, never staying in one place for too long. So far, we haven't picked up a tail, but I'm not taking any chances." She collapsed the spyglass, sticking it into a pouch that hung off her belt. "Come, I'll show you around."

Camilla led me across the deck, weaving through the array of sailors with sweat dripping down their backs and their sleeves rolled up to display tattooed arms.

"*The Dragon's Bane* is the fastest ship in these waters," she said, her hands clasped behind her back. "She was built for a Lucian duke before his—shall we say—*unfortunate* fall from power." A satisfied grin slipped across her lips.

"Do I—?"

"Sol!" She called to the sun-tanned sailor who had pulled me from the ocean. "You met our sailing master, Sol," Camilla said as the sailor approached.

He inclined his head, sunlight rippling over his eyepatch embossed with a compass symbol. "Your Highness."

"You don't have to call me that," I said quickly. "Just Rose is fine. Preferred, actually."

"Hm." Camilla's uncovered eye narrowed. She turned sharply, leaving me scurrying to match her long stride. "*The Dragon's Bane* is state of the art in every way. Even equipped with eight cannons." She patted the wooden railing, a proud smile on her lips. "You won't find a better ship in the Twelve Kingdoms."

A copper-skinned sailor approached. Though light wrinkles around his eyes suggested he was in his thirties, gray flecked his long, dark hair and beard. Around his neck hung his plain, black eye patch.

"Rose, meet Dobbins," Camilla said, gesturing to the sailor. "He's our master gunner, in charge of all these cannons."

"And every other weapon aboard *The Dragon's Bane*," Dobbins added. His attention shifted to Camilla. "That's what I wanted to talk to you about. Our supply of black powder is running low."

"We'll dock in Nicia within the week," she said, unbothered. "We can restock there."

He nodded slightly and left without another word.

"What are we doing in Nicia?" I asked.

"Scheduled restock," Camilla replied. "Supplies don't last too long at sea. Produce rots, and alcohol gets drunk." She flashed me a smile.

"Ketch must like you."

She laughed. "He may be fond of me, but he's not so fond of my drink. Rum and lime keep sailors healthy but make dwarves seasick."

"I see." I paused for a moment. "How do you know Animo?"

She leaned against the ship's railing. "Two years ago, Terrot was looking for a thief to go on what most people called a suicide mission. They were right, of course, but I cheated death just like I cheated Natalia Thornsworth."

My stomach dropped. "You stole from Natalia?"

"Mhm. I snatched a ring from her vault."

My hand slipped to my vacant finger. *So that's how he found it.*

"That's when Animo told me about his grand quest to find the long-buried Princess of Avonshere." Camilla shrugged. "I found that it could be beneficial to my business."

"What is your business?"

She smiled, sweeping stray braids over her shoulder. "I'm a retrieval specialist. People hire me to obtain certain items, and I... obtain them. Whatever means necessary. Sometimes I'm not even hired—I simply go where the bounty takes me."

I raised a brow.

"That's a fancy way of saying she's a pirate." Ketch sauntered over, his limbs a patchwork of bandages. He hoisted himself onto the railing, dangling his legs overboard amid the spray of crashing waves.

Camilla reached past me to give him a playful shove. "Piracy is a business, thank you very much."

"What does Animo need with a pirate?" I asked.

"Camilla's quite skilled with thievery and smuggling," Ketch said. "Those come in handy."

Camilla shrugged. "I'm a woman of many talents." She clapped her hands together. "Now, let's get to business. The legendary princess has finally arrived, which means it's time for war."

There it was. Animo hadn't hired Camilla to protect Lili nor to rescue us from the Silver Forest; he had hired her to drag me down the path to war, a cannon pointed at my back.

"Rose is still hesitant on the war part," Ketch said.

"We don't have time for hesitancy," Camilla replied. "Terrot has had years to prepare a plan. She can get on board with it or go overboard."

"I'm right here," I snapped. "And we're going to finish Natalia without starting a war."

Camilla tossed me a bored look. "Revolutions begin by a single stroke of the sword, but it takes a hundred more deaths to win freedom."

"I disagree."

She glared down at me. "Your opinion does not define the truth."

"All right—" Ketch began.

Camilla held up a finger. "Don't interfere. As a matter of fact, get out of here. *Her Highness* and I need to have a little chat."

Ketch hopped down, his mouth set in a firm line.

I folded my arms. "I will not start a war because a pirate says so. If we follow Animo's plan, thousands of people will die. My way only kills one."

Camilla tilted her head, her eye examining me carefully. "You've lost someone. That's what your friend was doing in the galley—he was telling the stowaways. You lost someone, and you blame yourself."

I pursed my lips.

Her posture softened. "As captain of this ship, I am responsible for the lives of my crew. Sometimes plans go awry, and sometimes people I care about die. When that happens, I am faced with a choice: I can either let the pain of that loss consume me, or I can pick myself up and keep going for the rest of my crew." She glanced over her shoulder at a group of sailors rolling dice atop a barrel. "My men need a leader they can rely on in times of hardship. As do yours."

"I don't have followers."

"What do you call the five people belowdecks who've risked their lives for you?"

My jaw clenched. "I never asked for them to do that."

"But they did. Perhaps it was because they believe in you, or perhaps it was because of something greater that's at play. I know what you're going up against, and I know that it's not just about you. You may be the leader of this fight, but you're not the only one who it will affect."

"I don't want to *be* the leader."

She planted a hand on her hip. "Is there anything you do want? I've heard stories about Rosara Wolfe, the great heir who will defeat Queen Natalia and bring healing to the Twelve Kingdoms. But now that I see you, I can't say I'm impressed."

"That makes two of us."

Camilla smirked. "You can love it or hate it, but war is coming, and we're the ones at the helm."

She pushed past me, leaving me alone with my thoughts. A single unanswered question settled in my mind: why would a pirate want to start a war?

SCARS UNHEALED

The wind picked up as afternoon shifted into evening. Though the crew remained on deck, scaling swinging ropes like surefooted primates, Camilla ordered the rest of us to stay in our cabins until morning. I'd settled into my nook-like bed, my mother's diary in my lap as the ship rocked me into a state of relaxation.

Her words revealed a side of her I had never known existed. The first twenty-five years of her life were filled with adventures with Bellatora and lessons from Aspectu. My heart ached with each turned page. How had this curious and eager young woman become someone forced into a life of war and tragedy?

My gaze shifted from my mother's words to those scrawled in the margins. Animo had identified the hand as Aspectu's, but that begged the question:

why had she written in my mother's diary? And why encrypt it in a forgotten language? Could the knowledge truly be so valuable that no one but her could know of it?

A knock came at the door.

"Come in," I called, stowing the diary under my pillow.

Ketch stepped into the room, blood seeping through his bandages.

"Do you want me to take a look at that?" I asked, gesturing to his cuts.

He waved a hand dismissively. "Don't worry about it. I've got a special something stashed away for occasions such as this." He wiggled his brows as he dragged the table into the center of the room. It wobbled as he climbed on top of it.

I jumped to my feet, preparing to catch him in the more-than-likely event that he fell. "What are you doing?"

"About a year ago, Animo and I spent a few months sailing. When we left, we weren't able to take everything with us. Camilla put most of our things in storage, but there were a few items I didn't want pirates to get their paws on."

He raised himself up on his tiptoes and gave the ceiling a sharp shove. A hatch popped open. Dust rained down, settling on his mohawk as he dug about the dark compartment. Glass clinked as he withdrew a burlap sack. "Take this, will you?"

I took it, careful not to break its contents. "What's in here?"

"Booze, mostly." Ketch slid the panel into place—the wood grain blended seamlessly with the rest of the ceiling. He hopped down from the table, dusting off his hands. "But there is one thing of particular importance."

He set the bag on the ground and riffled through the collections of bottles until he found a dainty, teardrop-shaped vial. With a grin, he held it up to the porthole's fading light. "Aspectu's healing elixir."

"Healing elixir?" I exclaimed. "Why would you leave that behind?"

"We didn't. She gave us two bottles, one for me, one for Animo. Animo didn't want his, so I put it here for safekeeping." He popped the glass cork and took a swig. "Ahh…That should take care of the internal bleeding. Want some?" He offered me the bottle.

"I'm fine." I sat back down on my bed. "Why is Animo so resistant to magic?"

"I've always assumed it stemmed from his father being an *uchlet*."

"A what?"

"It's a dwarvish term. And not a polite one."

"*Uchlet*," I repeated. "I may have to use that one day."

He grinned, raising a large bottle. "Cheers."

"Cheers."

His answer didn't sit right with me. Animo never took issue with me and Aspectu having magic. The only time he fought against it was when we attempted to heal him. Was there a deeper reason for his aversion, or was it simply determination bordering on insanity? Curious as I was, I knew better than to ask. We'd spent too long arguing back and forth about whose turn it was to spill their secrets. It was time I started moving forward, even if I wasn't on the same page as everyone else.

I plucked a round bottle from the sack and started toward the door. "I'll see you later."

"Woah, woah, woah!" Ketch nearly dropped his bottle as he ran to stop me. "That isn't yours."

"It was hidden in my room."

"It was my room first," he argued. "And if Camilla sees that, she'll take my entire stash and fill it with lime. Do you know how disgusting that is?"

"Look, I'm not trying to reveal your secret, but I need a peace offering. Now, get your booze and go."

Ketch glared, muttering under his breath in dwarvish as he packed up the bottles. He selected one with a label penned in runes and offered it to me. "Take this one instead."

"Fine."

We traded bottles and set off our separate ways—Ketch to the galley and me to Animo's cabin a few doors down.

He answered the moment I knocked, his wet hair dripping onto his fresh shirt. His gaze fell to the bottle in my hand. "I see you found Ketch's stash."

"I'm not sure I would use the word *found*, but I managed to snag a bottle."

"If that bottle is the healing elixir, I'll save you some time and say no."

I rolled my eyes. "Relax. Talking you into taking care of yourself is more trouble than it's worth. If you want to bleed to death, it's entirely your choice."

A smile tugged at his lips. He stepped back. "Come in."

His cabin resembled mine—small, scant furniture, enclosed bed—although it had the addition of a dwarf-sized hammock in the corner. A mess of papers and open books lay scattered across the table, along with a pile of bandages and assorted medical supplies.

"You've been busy," I remarked.

"I had Camilla store some of our old research," he said, clearing off a chair for me. "We've got maps and letters and books on legends and lore and other things that are almost entirely useless." He sighed, running a hand through his hair. A single strand fell between his eyes, though he didn't seem to care. "So, how can I help you?"

I offered him the bottle. "I brought a peace offering."

"*Dragonflame*," he read, taking it from my hand.

"You know dwarvish?"

"I've picked up a few words from Ketch." He fetched a pair of glasses. "It just so happens that he says the words *dragon* and *flame* on a regular basis."

I laughed, toying with my tunic's hem as Animo poured the drinks.

"So, why now?" he asked. "I mean, we've had our moments, but why let this be our olive branch?"

"After the Silver Forest, I feel it's necessary. I said things that I regret, and I want to make certain that things are all right between us." I took a deep breath. "The truth is, there's too much happening and too many people at risk for me to handle this alone. You protected my family, and you have done everything in your power to protect me. I still can't agree to start a revolution or become a queen, but I need us to work together."

He handed me a glass. "I understand why you don't want to fight. Despite everything, you have a great deal at stake. I can't make any promises—"

"Then don't. I'm not looking for hopeful oaths. I want this to be over, so I won't spend the rest of my life looking over my shoulder to find a bloodthirsty queen or smoldering kingdom. Let's agree to trust each other and deal with the rest when it comes."

"I'd like that." He swirled his drink slowly. "For what it's worth, I agree that the Staff of Realms should remain our priority. Even with *The Dragon's Bane* and its crew, we're severely outmatched. We would never last in a true battle."

"I'm glad we agree." We might not have been on the same page, but at least we were in the same chapter. I raised my glass. "To new beginnings."

He smiled, tapping his drink against mine. "To new beginnings."

We threw back the liquid. Pain flared, searing my throat as I swallowed. I burst into a fit of coughs, tears springing to my eyes. "What is that made of? Actual fire?"

Animo grimaced, setting aside his drink. "It's enchanted whiskey—a specialty in Pikbrie. Rack you, Ketch," he muttered. Taking a pitcher from the dresser, he poured fresh cups of water. He passed one to me, asking, "Are you all right?"

"I think so," I replied, a hand on my burning throat. I drained the glass in a single gulp, letting the cool water soothe the sting. Animo followed suit.

"I am going to kill that dwarf," he said, turning to pour himself a second glass of water. Scarlet splotches soaked through the back of his shirt.

I stiffened, setting aside my cup. "You're bleeding."

He swore, examining his shoulder in the mirror. "It's where the tree elf bit me."

"Let me help." I stood, extending a hand, but he drew back.

"I don't need magic."

"I spent five years pretending to be human. I think I can manage rebandaging a wound." I pointed at the chair. "Sit."

His jaw tightened, but to my surprise, he followed my finger. I stood behind him, reaching for the hem of his shirt. My fingers brushed against the fabric, and I hesitated.

"We need to take your shirt off, so I can examine the wound. Try not to move your shoulder."

I helped him maneuver the bloody garment off his body, uncovering fair skin marred with scars. Thick, rough slashes. Thin, deliberate cuts. They ran across his back, a gallery of tortured memories.

My stomach twisted, my fingers hovering above a dark mark on his spine.

"Is something wrong?" he asked.

"No," I replied, forcing my attention to his bandage, now soiled with blood. I untied the knot and began to unwind the dressing.

He hissed as I peeled the last layer of fabric from his skin. "How bad is it?"

My lips fell apart as I stared at the wound. "Your stitches are broken," I said, fighting to keep my voice even. They were more than broken—they were *chaos*. Blood gathered in thick clumps around the teeth marks held together by rough, uneven stitches. Some leaned too far one way while others barely kept the skin closed. One thing was painfully clear: Animo had done them himself.

"You're judging me, aren't you?" he asked softly.

"I'm not judging," I insisted, fighting back the image of Animo sewing his own back closed with only a mirror to guide his hand. "I'm—" I sighed. "Would it have been so difficult to ask for help?"

"Help is not a luxury my life allows."

"You have Ketch."

"It's easier to do it myself."

"Easier to stitch or easier to avoid using magic?" My voice carried an unintended edge.

"Rose—"

"Relax. I have no intention of wasting my energy on you." I snatched a cloth, dipping it in a bowl of water. "If you want to be stuck by a needle, so be it."

"Thank you."

The rawness of his voice carved through my heart. I clenched my jaw as I dabbed at his wound. Blood flowed steadily despite my attempts to quell it. I placed a folded piece of cloth against the gash.

"Hold this," I instructed. Animo applied pressure as I threaded a clean needle. With a deep breath, I returned to the wound.

He clenched his fist as I slid the needle through his skin. I could have used magic to numb him, but I knew he would refuse. All I could do was stitch and do my best to ignore his pain.

"You want to ask, don't you?" he said. "About my scars."

"It's none of my business."

"It's all right. Really. Talking might actually help."

"Then tell me about them. Any of them." *Help me understand you.*

"You see the one on my lower back?" With his free hand, he tapped a thick, dark mark just above his waistband.

"I do."

"It's from Sheildore. Courtesy of my first escape attempt. I'd almost made it—all I had to do was get through one lousy portcullis."

"What stopped you?"

"I was fast, but it was faster. It dropped onto me, impaling my side and leaving me trapped in the mines for another month."

My arms twitched with the urge to embrace him, but I kept my hand steady as I pulled the suture tight. "Are all of them from escape attempts?"

"Not all. Many are from fights, mostly involving knives. Others are from plain stupidity." He raised his hand, still bandaged from his stab wound in Daria. "See this?" he showed me a scar just below his wrist. "That was from a rock."

"A rock?" I laughed, tying off the stitches.

"I was climbing a mountain, and it happened to be sharper than I had expected."

I bit my rising lip as I gathered fresh bandages. "What about the one beneath your eye?"

His shoulders tensed, a shadow falling over him. "I don't want to talk about that one."

I paused, setting aside the bandages. He avoided my gaze as I sat down, the muscle in his jaw twitching. I slid my hand beneath his chin, slowly turning his head toward me. His eyes met mine, the silver streaks now cracks in his carefully constructed wall. My thumb brushed against his scar. He flinched.

"He gave it to you, didn't he?" The question came as a whisper, but Animo's reply was silent. The pain in his eyes made everything clear.

His own father…

"I'm so sorry." They were stupid words. Meaningless, really.

He nodded, his gaze downcast. I climbed to my feet, picking up the bandages and returning to his wound. Moving his hand to secure one end against his chest, I wrapped the bandage around his shoulder.

"I had escaped the Silver Forest," he said, his voice hollow, like an echo. "I assumed he would be happy to see his son return with an ancient grimoire in hand. Instead, I was met with his fury. He dragged me to my room, shouting that I had betrayed him and Daria. My actions *upset the peace*, and nothing is more important than his peace. Amid the arguing, he snatched the sword from my hand and…" His voice trailed off. "I left that very night. I didn't say goodbye to anyone, not even Aspectu."

I knotted the bandage.

"I saw something in him that day," he said. "Before… I thought he was afraid of losing us or of his people being attacked again. But that day, I learned the truth. He's not afraid of losing anyone; he's simply a coward. He'd throw his children in front of an army if that's what it takes for him to survive. But I fight back. And he hates me because of it."

Animo shot to his feet, crossing to the porthole. He planted a hand against the wall, looking out at the darkening horizon.

I wiped my hands on a cloth, leaving it bloody. "Is that why you fight? To not be like him?"

"No. When I was thirteen, Aspectu found me. She told me that she'd had a vision of a future where Vaera was free and that I was a part of it. But in order for this future to occur, I had to find the Crown Princess of Avonshere and help her start a war."

My lips parted in a silent gasp. That was why he had found me. Why he was so insistent on war.

"It was all to save Vaera," I said.

"Regium doesn't care about his people. He lets them throw their lives away for his own security." His voice rose with passion. "Someone has to free them, and I am the only one still fighting. I—" His eyes locked on mine, and a hint of guilt slipped into his gaze. "I never meant to drag you along or trick you in any way. I truly thought you would want to return and claim your throne."

"I know." My insides had knotted themselves beyond repair. "I should want to save Avonshere. I *do* want to, I just—"

I huffed. I couldn't bring myself to finish the sentence.

Animo stepped forward. "You can tell me."

I stared into his eyes. Part of me wanted to tell him, to confess every secret I'd ever kept, but I couldn't. Not when I'd been just as cowardly as his father.

I took a step closer to him, tilting my chin forward to hold his gaze. A blade's width separated us now. My hand slid to his bicep, and our eyes followed.

"I want to know about that scar," I said quietly, my fingers settling on a small, round mark.

A smile flicked across his lips. "Years ago, Aspectu took me to Avonshere. She warned me it would be dangerous, but I expected to be attacked by shades, not shot by the crown princess."

I froze. Darvyn, a few months before my mother's death. I had been hunting when I heard a twig snap. The next thing I knew, I was helping carry a dark-haired boy back to my mother. But he hadn't been alone. A woman had been with him…

My jaw fell slack. Those ice-blue eyes stared at me from the depths of my memory.

"I know who she is," I breathed. *How could I have forgotten her? How could I have forgotten* him?

"Yes," he said slowly, his brow furrowed. "It was you… I thought that was clear."

"No. I mean, yes, I was the girl who shot you, but the woman with you was Aspectu. She's the woman I've been seeing in my dreams."

"What?"

"I've been having dreams of this woman in a white dress," I explained, pacing before the table.

"For how long?" he questioned, his eyes following my movements.

"They started the night of the Harvest Festival. Right before the shade attack. At first, I thought they were just dreams. I didn't realize it was *her*."

"What was she doing in these dreams?"

"It varies." Flashes of dreams ran through my mind. "The first time she was warning me of something, then the floor was covered in blood, and I heard Natalia's voice telling me I was going to die."

"Natalia was in your dreamscape?"

"My what?"

"Dreamscape," Animo repeated. "It's the land you travel to when you sleep. Most people live in it without any control, but ekeiders, and even some witches, are able to control what it looks like and what they do within its borders. Powerful dreamwalkers can even enter the dreamscapes of others. Did your mother never teach you this?"

I shook my head. "She raised me more as a human than an elf."

Animo's eyes widened, struck by thought. He reached into his pocket and pulled out an opalescent pendant the size of a chicken's egg. "Was Aspectu wearing a necklace like this?"

"Yes!" I snatched it from his grasp, turning it over. "What is it?"

"It's a dreamstone. It channels magical energy and helps the user dreamwalk."

"So Aspectu was dreamwalking?"

"I believe so."

I stared at the necklace in my hand. "How did you get this?"

"I found it in her vault. It must have been dropped during the raid."

"The last time I saw her was just before we reached Daria. If she needed this to dreamwalk, she must have been there." My shoulders sank. "We were just days behind."

"Hey, look at me." Animo reached out, lifting my chin. "We haven't run out of luck yet. This is merely a spare—Aspectu's dreamstone never leaves her neck."

"Then why did she stop visiting me?"

"I wish I knew," he said, watching me closely. "But if she visited you at all, it means she had a message so important that she couldn't wait to tell you in person. She is a seer, after all. Perhaps she had a warning for the future."

Thoughts of my dreams swelled in a sea of blood and death. If that was the future Aspectu foretold, then we had already lost.

A SISTER'S LOVE

"All that, yet you still can't tell us a single part of your grand plan." Camilla lounged in a chair, her feet propped on the table. Animo and I had gathered her, Ketch, Hertz, Sol, and a few other sailors in the dim galley, eager to share the news of Aspectu's dreamwalking. Although my tale elicited shock from Ketch, Camilla looked on with a flat expression.

Animo placed a hand on the back of my chair. "We know that Aspectu has a message for Rose. Once we find out *what* she is trying to say, our path will become clear."

Camilla quirked a brow. "That could take years. I'm not waiting around for some elf to use her words." She pushed her chair back, addressing the sailors. "We keep course, docking in Nicia before the week's end." Her cold gaze landed on me. "Do us all a favor and have a plan by then."

She strode from the room, her crew following in her wake.

"*Uchlet*," I muttered.

Ketch choked on his drink.

"In all fairness, you really don't have a plan." Hertz sat across the table from me, toying with an empty cup.

"Yes, we do," I said. "Kill Natalia, that's the plan."

"That's really what you want?" Hesitation bloomed in his eyes. "Murder and move on?"

"It's the only way I know to end it. But something tells me Captain Irritable won't approve."

"No, Cam's fine with murder." Ketch stood on his chair as he poured himself a fresh drink.

"*But* we'll need more information before we can act," Animo added. "Our best course is to communicate with Aspectu. Once we provide a tangible plan, Camilla will bend."

I rolled my eyes. "Is that all?"

Animo's soft laugh floated from behind me. "Camilla's rough, but she gets better."

"The word is controlling, not better," Ketch said. "Look, I love Cam, but if you say that she is friendly and cooperative, you're lying to yourself."

"At least we aren't stuck on a ship with her," I said dryly.

"I like her."

I jumped at the sound of Lili's voice. She stood in the doorway, looking in. *How long has she been there? Did she hear my plan to kill Natalia?*

"Camilla's taken care of me," Lili said. "She's even teaching me about the ship."

"Oh... well, that's wonderful." I stumbled over the words.

She ducked her head, tucking a strand of hair behind her ear. "Could we talk, Rose?"

"Now's not a good time. Later, though."

"Tomorrow?" Hope lifted her voice.

I nodded, forcing a smile onto my face as my stomach twisted with fear. "Tomorrow."

She beamed back at me before returning to the hall, her footsteps fading toward the deck.

Tomorrow. Tomorrow, I would face Lili with the truth. I could only pray it wouldn't destroy everything we had.

"Maybe you should get to know Camilla," Hertz suggested, blind to the anxiety that spiraled within me. "Like Lili did."

"The difference is that Lili doesn't stand in Camilla's way," Ketch said.

I narrowed my eyes. "What is that supposed to mean?"

His gaze darted between me and Animo. "Well, I mean—it's just that—you know… You're the one we're relying on if this quest is to go any further."

"Avonshere is your territory," Animo said, pulling my attention from the sweating dwarf. "Camilla knows that, and she isn't fond of being outranked."

I smiled bitterly. "Lovely."

I stood on the deck of *The Dragon's Bane*, watching the ebb and flow of waves against the skyline. The morning sunlight danced across the water, a kaleidoscope of white and blue. I had promised Lili a conversation, but the thought of even *looking* at her gave me the urge to fling myself over the railing.

"Rose." A voice spoke—Derek hovered behind me, his hands fiddling with his pockets. "I… I wanted to… um, talk."

"About what?" Folding my hands behind my back, I led him to an empty table beside the cabin door. I took a seat, but he remained standing, nervously tapping the hilt of the dagger that hung from his belt. With a pang, I realized it was Megs's.

I hadn't spoken about her since escaping the Silver Forest, and it wasn't something I wanted to delve into now. Maybe it made me callous, but I had no intention of ever revisiting that night. Not even for Derek.

"Sit," I said. He dropped into the chair as though his limbs were made of lead.

"I wish to discuss the, um, situation with me and Lili."

A smile slipped across my lips. *Lili's doe-eyed boy*, Camilla had called him. It seemed things had finally escalated beyond longing looks.

"I see. You and Lili are engaged in a romantic relationship."

He blanched. "I—I don't know that I'd call it a *relationship*—"

"Oh, then what is it?"

"Well, it's me…"

"Yes."

"And Lili…"

"Of course."

"And, well…" His knee bounced as though he was ready to bolt at any second.

I reached out, taking his hand. "I'm happy for you, Derek. Lili, too."

"You're all right with this?"

I bit back a laugh. "You've practically been in love with her for years. She's no different."

He flushed. "You could have said that before and saved us some time."

"I could have. But it was more fun watching you two pretend."

He laughed nervously, but his posture relaxed. "Do you think the Estmars will approve?"

"Of course they will. Firstly, they adore you, and secondly, they would never stand in the way of Lili's happiness. And you certainly make her happy."

He smiled, sliding his chair back. "Right. Well, thank you, Rose. This went much better than I anticipated." He took a step away, then hesitated. "Lili and I are meeting Sol for a lesson on the quarterdeck. You should join us. Lili… she's been worried about you. Maybe if you could talk to her—"

"I will. Soon."

"All right." He bobbed his head, then climbed the steps to the deck above the captain's cabin.

"Well, that was underwhelming."

I turned to find Camilla standing over my shoulder. She leaned against the doorframe beside a flickering, mother-of-pearl candle.

"Am I to assume if it had been your sister, there would have been death threats?" I asked.

"Actually, I despise my sister. But if it were someone else I cared for, I'd make it clear that I am more than comfortable disposing of bodies."

Well, aren't you delightful? I pointed at the first conversational shift I found—the candle. "What is that?"

"It's a Mahori light." Camilla took Derek's seat across from me. "The Madorian Monarchy is on foul terms with us landwalkers, so we have to take precautions. That candle is an offering to Mahori, the Divine Guardian of Madoria and Commander of the Storm and Seas. While it burns, we have his blessing to sail through Madoria."

"I remember the story of the Madorian fallout," I said. "When their blessed sword was lost, they blamed all the other rulers, swearing to cut all ties until the thief revealed himself. But he never did."

In a way, the fallout had improved over time. When Madoria broke into clans of warring families, many seaside cities began worshiping the divine beings that resided in the ocean, along with clan leaders, to fall into their good graces. Though it was a gray area where treaties were involved, it had allowed trade to resume through Madoria. Yet the scars of betrayal remained.

Camilla propped her feet up onto the table. "Don't be fooled. That sword was found. Whoever did must have underestimated the problems it would cause and opted to hide it away until the secret of its location died with them." She picked at a broken fingernail. "It's probably stuffed in someone's cellar, gathering dust. It's too late to mend things with the Madorians, and something like that isn't easy to sell."

"Do you really think so?"

She scoffed. "People only buy artifacts if they can use them or display them—"

"No, I mean about it being too late to fix things with Madoria."

"Oh." She paused thoughtfully. "I'm not sure. It certainly wouldn't be an easy task."

"Not easy doesn't mean impossible."

"I'd wait until after you defeat an evil queen to solve hundreds of years' worth of hostility." She rose to her feet. "Now, if you'll excuse me, I have a ship to captain."

Camilla departed toward the forecastle, leaving me alone. Well, not *alone*. A handful of sailors lingered on the main deck while twice as many scaled the ship's rigging. The sails around them snapped taut as new wind pushed us forward. Perhaps Mahori *had* blessed our voyage.

My eyes followed the sailors as they swung from the ropes. How did they have so much courage? With a single slip, they would plummet, crashing into the waves, or worse, onto the deck.

Maybe they aren't thinking of the fall but focusing on the climb. The higher you rise, the farther you have to fall, but if you *don't* take the risk, you'll never leave the ground.

Before I could unravel my own logic, I followed Derek's trail to the quarterdeck. A sailor watched the wheel in Camilla's stead, while Lili, Derek, and Sol gathered around a collection of barrels, each one holding a length of rope.

I cleared my throat, gaining their attention. "May I borrow Lili for a moment?"

Sol held out a hand. "She's all yours."

Lili set down her rope, dusting off her skirt as she followed me up to the stern deck. We came to rest at the back of the ship, overlooking *The Dragon's Bane's* substantial wake.

"I'm glad you came over," she began, brushing strands of mousy hair from her face, though the strong ocean winds made her efforts futile. "We've hardly talked since you got here, and, well… I have a lot to say."

"I know," I replied. "I know what it is you want to talk about, and I've been too afraid of what you might say—"

"What *I* might say?" She stared at me blankly. "Do you think I'll be upset with you?"

"Shouldn't you be? I lied to you for years. I put you and your parents in danger—"

"I stowed away on a pirate ship!" Lili exclaimed. She burst out laughing. "Oh, all this time, I thought you would be angry at me for trying to chase you down."

"That *was* foolish. But aren't you angry that I lied?"

She shook her head. "I'm not. Camilla told me the truth. I know that you're the crown princess, and I know that you're in danger. Yes, I'm terrified for all our safety, but I am not angry with you."

Tears welled in my eyes. Before she could say another word, I pulled her into a hug. "You really aren't angry?"

"Not at all. I'm shocked, of course, but I've had a while to process everything and…" She drew back, a shy smile on her lips. "I can see it."

"See what?"

"You as a queen."

"Oh." I turned away. "I don't think that's going to happen."

"Why not?"

"Because to the people of Avonshere, I'm dead. And it's better that way. My last time leading them ended with the deaths of those most loyal to my family. I could never allow that to happen again."

"Oh." Lili's gaze fell. "But that was years ago, wasn't it? You were a child."

"Sometimes children make unfixable mistakes. Time can't change everything."

"But it can change you. And if I know one thing about you, it's that you're a leader. You've been protecting and providing for us ever since you came to Rudane."

"That's not the same as leading a kingdom. Especially not in a war."

"It is in principle," she said. "You are a born leader. Everyone knows it."

"They can't see all of me. They don't know how many times I've failed, and neither do you."

"No, I don't. All I see is the Rose standing before me, and she is more than capable of doing this." Lili gazed at me with such wide-eyed innocence that I almost believed her. "Ask anyone. They'll say the same thing."

"I appreciate the vote of confidence, but it's not that simple."

"Yes, it is." She grabbed my hand and dragged me down to where Sol and Derek tied knots with spare rope. "Sol, is Rose fit to be Queen of Avonshere?"

"That's not fair," I said. "Sol doesn't know me."

"I would still like to hear his answer," she replied. "Sol?"

He looked between us. "Yes. Rose is certainly qualified. Under her, Avonshere will be rebuilt into the thriving kingdom it once was. It's what we're here for."

"Thank you." Lili plopped onto a barrel, clearly satisfied with his answer. But I wasn't finished—Sol's reply had picked at a different subject.

"You say that's what you're here for," I began. "But it makes no sense for Camilla to be helping out of the goodness in her heart."

Sol cracked a smile as he tied a new knot.

"What has Animo promised her?" I asked.

He chuckled, setting aside the rope. "It isn't my place to discuss it."

"I'm royalty."

"With all due respect, your family has been off the throne for seven years."

I folded my arms. "I deserve to know what I'm dealing with."

He shrugged. "Very well. If you want the truth, you can have it. Natalia rules your kingdom with an iron fist. The nobility has been massacred, and those who survived your last war are starved and terrified. But hidden beneath all the blood and muck is centuries worth of treasure."

"Treasure?" I repeated.

He nodded. "Abandoned manors are easy prey for looters, but we've kept a close eye on the black market. Nothing of real value has left Avonshere's borders. It remains there, a bounty fit for a queen."

"*Pirate* queen, you mean."

He smiled, though I failed to see the humor.

"That's your plan, isn't it?" I snapped. "Leverage a young, weak ruler to gain control of an entire kingdom. You take what you like and leave me to bear the weight of your indiscretions."

Regret filled his eyes. "No one is saying you won't be a good queen—"

"Only that you plan on stealing from me!"

"What's going on here?" Camilla demanded, striding up onto the quarter-deck.

I whirled on her. "You're going to steal from Avonshere."

"Yes."

"That's it? No defense, no explanation?"

"I don't need to explain myself to you," she said. "Your kingdom is dying.

With my help, it can be revived."

"*Help*? How is this helping anyone but yourself?"

She arched a brow. "Why don't you ask one of your starving citizens? See if they would really choose dusty items above their freedom."

I bit back a spew of curses, pacing in short strides until I could respond with something other than *rack you*. Finally, I asked: "Does Animo know about this?"

Camilla's cold glare softened slightly. "It was his idea."

CHAPTER FORTY-TWO

FACE-TO-FACE

I paced my cabin, fuming. Thieves, pirates, vigilantes—I was done with them all. Once we docked in Nicia, I would leave. I'd march right into Avonshere and—

And what?

The question stopped me dead in my tracks. Without the Staff of Realms, I'd never get close enough to kill Natalia. But how was I meant to find the staff without Animo's help?

A knock came at the door. With a muttered curse, I yanked it open.

"What?" I demanded before Animo could speak. "Come to suggest Camilla stab me in the back? Or would you prefer to do that yourself?"

He didn't even blink. "I brought something," he said, holding up the dreamstone. "I've been promising you a face-to-face with Aspectu for months and I think it's time that I deliver."

I stepped back, my anger dimming. "Has it really been months?" Though every passing moment felt like an eternity, the idea that I'd left Rudane *months* ago seemed wrong.

Taking the opening, Animo entered my cabin, pushing the door shut behind him. "I know that you're angry with me."

"And for good reason." My hands landed on my hips. "Kingdoms, Animo, how could you think letting Camilla steal from Avonshere is a good idea?"

"Look at Medea. It's the richest city in Lucia and rife with crime. I'm not saying it's ideal," he added quickly. "But Camilla is someone you want on your side. She has connections, however unethical they may be. And now she has a reason to see Avonshere restored."

"I don't like it. And I don't trust that she'll keep her word."

"You don't have to trust her. You don't even have to trust me." He raised the dreamstone. "Trust Aspectu."

"As much as I'd love to speak with her, I have no idea how to use that."

"An incantation will help." He passed me a slip of aged parchment bearing an Aesin spell written in Aspectu's hand. Slipping behind me, he brushed my hair to the side. "The dreamstone will help focus your magic and reach out to Aspectu's mind. When she feels your call, she'll meet you in your dreamscape." He fastened the clasp around my neck before drawing my hair back into place.

"Right, easy." My eyes drifted to the totem lying in the corner. If I used its power, could I strengthen the spell?

No. I wouldn't use it. I didn't *need* to use it.

Setting my shoulders, I read, "*Ambai ne omniin cu illa.*"

"Wait, no—!"

Aspectu stood before me, her eyes closed. A faded world encompassed us, shifting like smoke at twilight.

"*Aspectu.*"

Her eyelids fluttered but did not open. I took a step forward, my feet dragging as though the mist was made of wet mortar.

"Aspectu," I repeated.

This time, her eyes opened. Her pupils widened as they locked on me.

"Rosara." The name slipped from her lips as a whisper, echoing throughout the dreamscape.

"You've been visiting me for months," I said. "Why?"

Aspectu closed her eyes, pain contorting her features. She gasped slightly before reopening them. "Where are you?"

"Where—what—Aspectu, are you all right?"

"Answer me first. Quickly."

"I'm on The Dragon's Bane.*"*

She shook her head, her gaze searching the misty ground. "That's not enough. I need to know exactly where you are."

"We're sailing along the western coast of Mydor. We'll dock in Nicia in a few days."

She exhaled slowly. "Good. Good."

"We can come find you. Where are you?"

Her gaze slipped into vacancy like the night she had visited me in Rudane. "It's… it is difficult," she said softly. "You cannot simply find me."

"Why not?"

Her breath hitched, growing ragged. A moan of pain escaped her, and she doubled over.

I shrank back. "Aspectu?"

She grabbed my arm, a hot sting erupting where her skin touched mine.

"Aspectu, I need to know why you've been visiting me."

She cried out, her grip tightening.

"Aspectu, please—"

The world spun as I was ripped down into darkness. A new image came into focus: a limestone hallway stretched out before me, illuminated by the layvas crystal sconces that lined the hall.

The Evishal Palace. *But why—and* how—*was I here?*

I tried to open my mouth to call for Aspectu, but it remained shut. I couldn't move, I couldn't speak. Something held me prisoner within my body.

A cold voice resonated from below. "Aspectu Demore, come and face me."

Natalia. Though my mind urged me to run, my feet stepped forward, peering around a column.

In the courtyard below stood Natalia Thornsworth backed by a legion of soldiers clad in Avonsheran blue. A black dress clung to her frame, split down the front to reveal matching black trousers. In all my life, I'd never seen her wear anything lighter than gray.

Except that. My gaze found the totem on her finger—half silver, half copper—before lifting to her face. Stern eyes, barely touched by wrinkles and rich brown hair... she couldn't be far past thirty.

It's another memory. But whose?

Natalia's lips turned down into a scowl. "The sooner you show your face, old bat, the sooner I will leave Daria intact."

"Wait!" King Regium ran into the courtyard, his hands raised in surrender. "Before you act, you must know that Aspectu Demore is not here."

"Then where is she?"

"Gone," he replied, mustering an air of regality. "I banished her myself when she was caught consorting with traitors."

"One of those traitors is Emry Avron. She and her daughter escaped me." Natalia drew her sword, Eathraze, directing its point to the elf king. "I need them found."

"I assure you, if we had any information—"

"I assure you, that if I find anything that even hints at your involvement in this matter, I will return, and I will burn your city to the ground."

Regium stiffened, his trembling fists clenched at his side. "Whatever services you require, Vaera will aid you."

"Good."

"Animo!" A hissed whisper drew my gaze. Bellatora stood in a doorway, her hand outstretched. "You cannot be out here."

I barely had time to register it was Animo's memory before the scene shifted, swirling from a pale palace to boots, striding along a cobblestone street. A simple skirt covered the memory-holder's long legs. I pulled a hood low over my—her—face, concealing myself amid a murmuring crowd.

All around, people whispered and pointed, their eyes wide with fear and wet with *sorrow. I pushed through the crowd, making my way to the base of a bridge. The bridge. The one connecting Malecare with the city below.*

A deep ravine loomed before us, but my gaze raised to where a woman's mutilated body hung, swaying in a gentle breeze. Dried blood caked her dress, its cracked tracks lingering on her legs and toes. Deep gashes split her skin, now hollow and littered with flies. My eyes dropped to the shards of silver and diamond that lay scattered on the red-stained cobblestone. A broken crown for a broken queen.

A strangled gasp slipped free, followed by a cry in a voice that was neither mine nor Animo's. The vision twisted, pulling me away from the sight of my mother's mangled body.

Darkness surrounded me. With a quiet scrape, light split through a small hole. I moved forward, peering into Bellatora's quarters.

She paced the room's length, wringing her hands as she argued with her father. "If you had seen her—"

"It would change nothing," Regium snapped.

Bellatora stopped, her lip trembling. "She was torn to pieces. And now her daughter is left on her own. We must help her, father."

He stepped forward, resting his hands on his daughter's shoulders. "I understand that Emry was your friend, and to honor that love, I will help you."

"Truly?"

"Truly."

She threw her arms around him, unable to restrain her tears any longer. He stroked her hair as she sobbed.

"Do not worry, my child," he murmured. "You will not feel this pain any longer." His hand flattened against the back of her head. "Ie memae auferta."

Memae. *I repeated the word in my mind. In Aesin, it meant memory.*

Bellatora stiffened, her brow furrowing as she pulled away from the embrace. "What were we discussing?"

"We were speaking of dinner," Regium said with a smile. "I told you that we are to have lemon tarts as a special treat."

I gasped silently. He'd stolen her memories of my mother's death.

"Oh, how wonderful." Bellatora wiped the empty tears from her eyes, then looked at her hand oddly, no doubt wondering why she had been crying. Shaking her head,

she let out a careless laugh.

The memory forced me to turn, retreating through the dark tunnels while fury burned inside of me. Did Bellatora ever learn what had happened? Or did she remain in that hollow court, blissful and ignorant, believing whatever lies her father threw at her?

A panel opened, and in the mirror across from me, I caught a glimpse of a young Animo. Then, the scene faded into thick swirls of fog.

Aspectu's cavern formed around me. I sat at her desk, a long, white skirt draped over my crossed legs. Animo entered, a bit younger than he was now, a half-packed bag in hand.

"You must stop this." Aspectu's voice rose from my throat.

He ignored her, throwing a roll of bandages into his pack. "I need to find her." He scanned the shelves, his lips moving silently before exclaiming, "Sleeping willow leaves!" He pulled a small, blue bottle from the shelf, tossing it atop the bandages.

Aspectu stood, crossing to stand by his side. "You returned from Vargo last night. You should stay and rest." Her head tilted sharply, and for the first time, I realized how small she was.

"I'll rest once the heir is found."

"You mean when you are dead." Aspectu planted her hands on her hips. "Because that is what you will be if you do not take care of yourself."

He shouldered his bag. "I'll take my chances. And don't forget that you were the one who told me to do this. This is how I save Vaera."

"I never said you should do it alone." She touched his forearm, keeping him in place.

His lips quirked in a smile as he patted her on the shoulder. "I won't be alone. I have Ketch now."

"It was one thing bringing that dwarf here to be healed, but are you honestly bringing him on this quest?"

Animo's hand dropped. "He's my friend."

"Do you trust him?"

"Yes."

"With your life?"

"Yes."

"With the lives of everyone in the Twelve Kingdoms?"

Animo leaned his head back, exasperated. "If you saw something about Ketch, tell me. But if not—"

"This is not about Ketch." Aspectu sighed. "Last night, I had a vision. There is a darkness coming that will shroud all twelve kingdoms. And at the heart of it is her."

"Who? Natalia?"

"No." She leaned in close as if to tell a secret. "Rosara."

"What?"

"Rosara is the cause of the darkness that will overcome the Twelve Kingdoms," she said. "The path she is on could lead to their destruction."

"Rosara is going to destroy the Twelve Kingdoms?"

"It is possible."

Animo shook his head. "No, that won't happen."

"Not if you stop her."

He stiffened. "Stop her how?"

"Find Rosara and lead her down the path of light. Do not let her be enamored by the darkness, not like Natalia was." She shook her head. "You cannot fail, not like I failed with Natalia."

"I won't," he promised.

"Then go."

Animo hugged her and then ran down the hallway, calling Ketch's name.

Aspectu sighed, wandering over to a bookshelf and running her finger along the spines. "Find Rosara Wolfe and make her Queen of Avonshere. That girl could be the savior of the kingdoms. Or their end." Her hand paused on an aged volume of The Epic of Twelve. *"Our world is broken."*

She pulled the book free, thumbing through the pages. "I have seen two futures. One of darkness and one of light. If Rosara leads us down the path into the light, everything will change. She can heal wounds that have burned since the days of Enia." She stopped on a drawing of the High Twelve. They stood in a row, blessed swords grasped in their hands and their divine guardians hovering behind like protective shadows. In the middle stood my ancestor, Tybalt Wolfe, his strength radiating from the ink.

Aspectu's fingers traced the image. "It will be a beautiful sight, indeed, to see them together again."

Setting aside the volume, she walked to the pool in the cavern's center. She knelt, her reflection perfectly captured as she gazed into the still waters. If I didn't know better, I would have said she could see me hiding behind her eyes.

"Do this for me, Rosara," she said. "The time has come once more. A new war will ravage the land, forcing history to repeat itself. But it is what must happen. The First Dark War forged the Twelve Kingdoms, and the Second Dark War will herald a new era." She reached out, her fingers hovering above her reflection. "Please, Rosara. Hear me."

She touched the water, sending a ripple across its surface. In a flash, I was ripped back through every memory I had seen. The cavern, Animo, Bellatora, my mother's death—it pounded through my head like a hammer against steel.

A woman screamed from afar. Another shouted, and fresh pain split my mind. Try as I might to scream, my voice remained silent. Even so, I knew we were past memories.

The screams turned into spells, and everything went black.

I shot up, my scream finally breaking free. Sweat drenched my skin, and my heartbeat pulsed against my chest.

Animo's palm landed on my shoulder. "You're back, you're safe."

"I saw—oh—" I took a deep breath, following his guiding hand to the mattress below me. My brow furrowed as I patted the bed's rim.

"I put you here after you passed out," he explained, taking a seat beside me. "You were meant to be lying down *before* you cast the spell."

"Oh." I probably should have realized that.

"You've been asleep for an hour. At first, you seemed peaceful, but out of nowhere, you began thrashing. Did something happen?"

I swallowed, my dry throat burning. "I saw her. I tried to find out where she was, but she wouldn't tell me. Then she—she showed me memories."

"Memories?"

I nodded. "It was strange… At first, she showed me memories of others. I saw my mother's body and—"

I caught myself. Did Animo want me to know about Regium taking Bellatora's memories?

"—other things," I finished. "Then she took me into her own memory. She said that there is a war coming that will ravage the Twelve Kingdoms. She called it the Second Dark War."

Animo stiffened.

I forced myself to sit upright. "She said that history would have to repeat itself. And she did so while reading the *Epic of Twelve*."

His jaw fell slack. "Do you think that…?"

I nodded again. "Aspectu wants me to reunite the High Twelve."

A QUEEN WORTH DYING FOR

The black gem of the totem glittered in the afternoon sunlight. I held it out over the waves, my fingers spread so that it was barely supported. One little slip was all it would take. The ocean would swallow it, and I would never see it again.

Let it go. Every time I touched it, I heard it calling my name. It begged me to listen, to understand. But I knew it held darkness and nothing more.

I turned my hand to the side, and the totem dropped a few inches, only for the chain to catch on my finger. I clenched my fist. I could throw it. I *should* throw it.

So why haven't you?

"It's a sight, isn't it?"

I stuffed the totem into my pocket as Hertz joined me at the ship's rail, gazing out at the rapidly approaching shore of Nicia.

"Lovely," I replied.

Great ships lined the docks while sailors moved about, unloading cargo. Many of the vessels flew Elwritian flags, but others bore banners from all across the Twelve Kingdoms—save Madoria, Vaera, and the Faelands; Madoria had no need for ships, Vaera had all but cut off contact with the rest of the kingdoms, and the fae were far more likely to utilize fairie circles for transportation. My eyes lingered on the flagless ships sprinkled throughout the harbor. Were they personal crafts here for pleasure or pirate vessels like the one we sailed on?

"Look!" Hertz pointed at a tall spire in the distance. "That's Nicia's temple for Keqec."

"Keqec?" I repeated.

"The Divine Lady of Entremets," he explained. "She's mostly worshiped in Mydor, but there are a few of her followers scattered across the kingdoms."

"I take it you're one of them."

He shrugged. "She speaks to my trade."

I grinned. "So we were right. You really could be a priest at the temple of bread." He smiled softly as I laughed. "Wait until Megs…"

My voice trailed off, our mirth fading. I turned back to the ocean, avoiding his eyes.

Silence hovered between us as *The Dragon's Bane* pulled into port. Sailors adjusted the rigging, raising the sails and pulling us to a stop alongside the dock.

"Lower the gangplank!" Sol called.

The crew moved like a well-oiled machine, pushing a plank of wood through a gap in the gunwale. Camilla emerged from her cabin and, after a quick exchange with Sol, crossed the gangplank and onto the docks.

After directing the sailors on what to unload, Sol came to stand by Hertz and me. "Are you two ready for the sights and smells of Nicia?" he asked, lounging against the rail, his hand draped over his dagger's hilt.

I grimaced. "I think I had enough smells in Medea."

He laughed. "Never fear, Nicia offers a much more pleasant aroma. We've arrived right in the middle of Readwekya, their annual festival of bread."

I raised a brow. "Nicia has a festival of bread?"

"Where?" Hertz blurted, practically trembling with excitement.

"The booths should be set up in the town's square."

No sooner had the words left Sol's mouth did Hertz take off, nearly colliding with a pair of sailors on his way.

"I see he likes bread," Sol said.

"It's his first love," I replied. "And cake is his mistress."

"I see. We'll be docked all day if you'd care to join his potentially illicit activities."

"I'd rather stay here." The totem weighed in my pocket. Though its voice was stifled, the message lingered in my mind. Would it truly be so wrong to listen?

"Suit yourself." He turned at the sound of voices shouting from across the deck. "I have to go."

He departed toward the forecastle, passing Animo.

"Did you talk to Camilla?" I asked as Animo joined me. We had kept my meeting with Aspectu a close-guarded secret, hoping to formulate a stronger plan before telling the captain. Unfortunately, our days of strategizing wielded limited results. As our arrival in Nicia drew near, Animo had offered to speak to Camilla alone in hopes that she would be more amicable.

"I did," he replied. "She rolled her eyes."

"Great." I leaned forward with a huff.

"It will be all right," he said, leaning beside me. "Camilla's only in charge of this ship. Once we determine our course of action, she'll come around."

"I know," I said, though I neither knew nor cared about the pirate's actions. It was the plan that worried me.

According to Aspectu, I was to reunite the High Twelve. That meant bringing together the kings and queens of twelve nations with a history of conflict. And what was I to ask of them? To join me and declare war against a woman who had spent half a decade keeping to herself. Since Natalia had become queen, she hadn't broken any treaties or alienated any allies.

Her single act of violence toward another kingdom was the shade attack in Rudane—something that could be tied directly to me. Why would the other rulers support me when they had nothing to gain *or* lose?

"Are you all right?" Animo asked.

I shook my head.

"Is it Camilla or the High Twelve?"

"The Twelve," I replied simply.

He nodded, falling silent. We both knew what uniting the High Twelve meant: if I did this, I would stand for Avonshere, and if we won, I would be queen. The thought threatened to empty my stomach into the ocean.

I exhaled against the nausea. *Think of something else. Anything else.*

"Aspectu said she failed Natalia," I blurted. "Is that true?"

Animo straightened. "Well… yes. She never told the story in detail, but apparently, Natalia came to Daria seeking help. A cure for a plague, I believe."

Of course.

"It must have been the one that struck Elatire—it's how she came to be betrothed to my father. A mysterious plague spread throughout the dukedom, killing people within days of infection. By the time my grandparents were able to send help, Natalia had already used magic to eradicate it. The way she took charge impressed my grandparents so much they arranged for her to marry my father." I looked up at him. "Did Aspectu give her the magic?"

He shook his head. "Aspectu looked into the future and saw the death that giving Natalia power would cause, so she refused her. I was told Natalia ran off after that, presumably into the Silver Forest."

My eyes widened. *The witch's memory.* Natalia on her knees, sobbing, begging a voice to stop. I touched my pocket, picturing myself by her side.

Natalia had raised her head, changed. Had the voice in her mind won? Would the one in *mine* win? Even now, I could hear it, a soft whisper, twining through my thoughts.

"I can't do this," I said.

"What? Unite the Twelve?"

I forced myself to nod.

Animo shifted, sitting against the railing. "I know it's a lot. But Aspectu saw this in your future. As terrifying as it may seem, she knows that you're capable of it. *I* know you're capable of it."

"But I don't know how to fight a war. I don't even know how to start one. You say that if I reveal myself to be alive, people will rally behind me, but how am I supposed to do that? How do I be the person I'm"—I huffed, struggling to find the word—"*destined* to be?"

"You'll need to make an entrance," he said. "A public return followed by a direct challenge to Natalia. Word will spread, and excitement and adrenaline should be enough to start a movement."

My stomach turned. "A direct challenge? As in a duel? Animo, she has years of training in combat magic. If I challenge her, she will win, and then who will want to follow me?"

He raised a hand. "You don't have to use magic. Natalia may not care about the code of honor, but it still exists. We can use it to our advantage."

"How?"

"We'll lure her into a position where her image is at stake, forcing her to either fight fairly or reveal her true nature to the rest of the kingdoms. If we can make them see her as a threat, they'll be more likely to side with us."

"And if she kills me in this fight?"

"I won't let her."

I folded my arms. "How would that look to the people of Avonshere? A young princess who hid from her duty for five years returns only to lose a duel and have to be saved." The truth of my words burned. That was who I was to them, a weak little princess in need of saving.

Animo held my gaze, his own filled with something on the edge of anger. "It would look like the people finally had a queen worth dying for."

A queen worth dying for. The memory of smoke filled my nostrils as flames flashed through my mind. *A queen.* The crown buried in ashes… The crown I had left behind. The kingdom I had abandoned. The people. They had died for me, but I was not worth it.

My voice shook as I replied, "I am not that queen."

Animo's lips parted, regret flicking across his features. "Rose, I didn't mean—"

"No." I held up my hand only to be struck with guilt. Why did I always push him away? "I'm sorry. Truly. But… I need a moment. Please."

He nodded, although his eyes begged me to stay. "Take all the time you need."

Jaw tight against tears, I turned on my heel and ran into Nicia.

PATHS DIVERGE

Sol was right when he had said Nicia would smell good. The homey aroma of freshly baked bread wafted from the vendor stalls that lined the streets. Pity I was on the verge of throwing up.

No matter how hard I tried, my mind kept circling back to that night and to everything I had done. I had thought I could leave it in the past, but the farther I walked away, the closer it seemed. What I had done would come to light, and when it did, no one would want me to be queen, not even Animo.

My thoughts settled on him. He had remained by my side through arguments and danger. Our beginnings had been rocky, but recently things had shifted. And now… I didn't want to lose him.

But what if I did?

I exhaled, forcing myself to focus on the street before me. Men and women strolled along, carrying baskets brimming with rolls and pastries. The tidiness and warmth Nicia held was impressive, considering its stance as a populated port town.

"Rose!" A beaming Hertz ran up to me, an overflowing basket of bread in his arms. "I thought you were staying on the ship."

I forced a smile to my face. "I couldn't miss Readweyka."

"I'm glad you came. It's incredible."

We strolled side by side, Hertz's eyes darting about, soaking in every last drop of the city. After all the pain of the Silver Forest, his happiness offered me a hint of the comfort I'd missed.

"These people are masters of their craft," he said as we walked. "Their pastries are so light and layered. I never wanted to leave Chess before, but now I want to see every corner of the Twelve Kingdoms and learn everything I can. Then I can bring exotic desserts back to Chess." He paused before saying, "You know, I think it's time."

I raised a brow. "For the Baldwick Family Bakery?"

Ever since I'd known him, Hertz's dream had been to open his own bakery. But before it could become a reality, he wanted a family to help him run it.

He nodded, his smile bright enough to blind. "As soon as we get back, I'm going to propose to Donna. Then, after the wedding, we can set up shop in Torsto. If all goes well, we will have our doors open by the perennial season."

My steps slowed as my smile faded. Perennial began in Marsai, the third month, giving Hertz less than five months to make his dreams come true. Five months that I was about to spend starting a war.

"Rose?" Hertz paused, looking over his shoulder. "Is everything all right?"

"Of course."

His gaze dropped. "Earlier, on the ship, you mentioned Megs. I know that we haven't spoken about her—"

"No. That's not... I'm..."

My excuse faded into a sigh. *He'll find out eventually.*

"The other night, I was able to speak to Aspectu through a dream. She told me that the Second Dark War is coming."

Hertz's jaw fell slack. "That doesn't exist. There isn't a First Dark War. It's *the* Dark War. There's only one."

"Not anymore."

His grip tightened on the bread basket. "I thought you didn't want to start a war. Our quest was to find Aspectu, not *war*."

"I don't *want* to," I argued. "But things have changed, and I think I have to do this."

He shook his head. "What are you doing, Rose? This was never our plan. We were supposed to keep you safe and to keep our families safe. That's why Megs and I left Rudane."

"I know how this sounds—"

"Stop trying to defend this," he snapped, his eyes darkening. "This is madness. You're putting your trust in pirates and elves who only visit you in dreams. You don't even know that she's *real!*" He shook his head again. "I don't know what's gotten into you."

I clenched my fists. "I'm doing what has to be done."

"This shouldn't be your responsibility. You are not made for war."

"You don't know that." My voice wavered on the words. "You don't know what I've lived through. I've seen what real war is like. I have watched men die for their country, and if that will happen again… I can't stand by."

"So you'll throw yourself in front of the sword?" Hertz's brow creased with sorrow. "You deserve better than that. You deserve a life." He took a step closer to me. "We could leave. Run away without telling Animo or the pirates. We'll take Lili and Derek and find our families and escape, exactly like you planned. We don't have to be a part of any of this."

"I do."

"No, you don't." He took my hands in his. "Please, Rose. You never wanted to be queen. And I *do* know you. You don't want to be responsible for the deaths of innocent people. Leaving is our one chance to be happy."

"I can't leave!" I snapped, pulling my hands away. "Five years ago, I ran away, and I've regretted it ever since. Besides, my happiness doesn't matter. I was born to live and die for Avonshere, and that is exactly what I intend to do."

"So you'll start a *war?*"

"If that's what it takes, then yes."

"Are you insane? If you fight a war, you will *lose*. And what if you die?"

"Then I die!" I shouted.

Hertz's eyes widened. Around us, heads turned toward the source of the outburst.

"I will die," I repeated, lowering my voice. "And if my death can save Avonshere, then it will be worth it."

His gaze fell to his feet. "I don't know who it is I'm talking to. I thought… I thought I knew you, but now…" He shook his head. "You're willing to die. You're willing to kill. And I can't be a part of it."

I pressed my lips together, fighting against the swell of rage and sorrow rising within me. "Then go."

His teary eyes met mine. "Stay alive, Rose."

Then, my best friend turned his back on me and walked away.

I sat with my back pressed against the outer wall of a laundry house, facing the quiet street. The sharp scent of lye suffocated me, but it was the only place in Nicia that covered the smell of baked goods. That warm, welcoming scent reminded me of Hertz—the last person I wanted on my mind.

I stared numbly at the thin trail of people walking by. They cast me odd looks as they passed, likely because I was sitting alone in the most undesirable spot in town. But their lingering gazes set my nerves on edge.

I closed my eyes, shutting them out. *He's gone. Hertz is gone.* He had every right to go, but that didn't lighten the ache in my heart.

You're insane… You can't win… You aren't made for this… His words echoed in my head. Was he right? Aspectu had seen *a* future where I succeeded. But that didn't mean there weren't a thousand more where I failed.

She was at the center of the darkness, Bellatora had said.

You're a catalyst for destruction, the ghost at Valintros had told me.

You're a queen worth dying for.

I opened my eyes. Animo was with me. Even if it was only to save Vaera, he was with me.

A bell dinged beside me, and a woman stepped out carrying a basket of freshly folded laundry. As she closed the door behind her, the basket tipped, spilling the neat garments. She cursed, kneeling to pick it up.

"Just my luck," she muttered.

I climbed to my feet and helped her gather the fallen clothes.

"Oh, thank you." Her grateful gaze lifted, only for her smile to fall. Hurriedly, she swept the fallen garments into the basket, ignoring the dirt they collected. "I—I appreciate it. Really." She backed away nervously.

"You're welcome," I replied, offering her a smile, which only seemed to frighten her more.

Unease ran through me as she scurried away. I had done nothing to scare her, yet she ran from me as though I were a hissing skunk. Glancing about, I started in the opposite direction. I slipped down an empty alley—the back streets should run parallel to the main ones, giving me a quiet route to the port.

A poster caught my gaze. My face stared back at me, etched in ink. I snatched it down, my wide eyes roaming across the words. *WANTED: Rose Estmar. Guilty of treason, theft, and murder. Reward: 200,000 mynet. Dead or alive.*

My heart pounded. *Treason, theft, murder.* Natalia. She was the only one who would accuse me of treason. And that reward… two-hundred-thousand mynet was enough to make Camilla question her loyalties.

I have to get back to the ship before anyone else sees this.

I quickened my pace, edging as close to running as I could without drawing attention to myself. At the sight of an approaching figure, I slipped into an adjacent street with clotheslines running between the windows. With a quick glance to ensure no one saw, I snagged a poncho. I swung it over me, lowering the hood and keeping my gaze downcast.

A figure stepped into my path.

"Hello, Miss Estmar."

Ruger Cunningham stood before me, stroking the blade of his curved dagger. I tensed, glancing over my shoulder. Elias Cunningham and the unfortunately muscled Dante loomed behind me.

Straightening my chin, I faced Ruger. "How did you find me?"

He drew a wanted poster from his pocket. Unlike the one I had taken from the alley, this one had no image. "It was really a matter of luck. We were in town when we heard chatter about a wanted woman roaming the streets." A wicked smile curved his lips. "Fate must really want you dead. But alas, we have no choice but to deliver you alive."

"I wouldn't be so sure about that." Drawing all the power I had, I unleashed a burst of magic. All three hit the ground. The wanted poster fell from my grasp as I broke into a sprint.

"Get her!" Ruger screamed.

Heavy footsteps pursued me. I pushed myself harder, ignoring my screaming muscles.

With a shout, someone knocked me to the ground. I struggled against the grasp, kicking wildly. My foot collided with Dante's face, loosening his grip enough for me to slide free.

Elias grabbed at my cloak, so I threw my fist at his jaw. He hollered, stumbling back and gripping his nose while blood streamed between his fingers.

Pain shot through my leg as Dante drove a knife into my calf. I screamed, throwing out my hands and calling upon my magic.

Nothing. I'd drained my well with my first escape.

In a panic, I kicked Dante with my good leg. I took off, running against the agony splitting my bones with every step. Their shouts faded, and I slipped into an alcove. I dropped to the ground, tears streaming down my cheeks. Gritting my teeth, I gripped the dagger protruding from my leg and pulled. Pain seared, and a strangled cry broke free of my throat. I slumped against the wall, tossing the blade aside. With a shaky breath, I placed a hand atop the wound. Blood slicked my palms as I urged my magic to heal. It didn't answer.

I sobbed, pressing both hands against my calf. Blood poured, soaking my leggings and pooling in my boot.

"*Sinet caelai san esede,*" I incanted. My magic sparked weakly, unable to even slow the bleeding.

"No… No." I wiped my cheeks with the back of my hand. It was useless. *I have no choice.*

Closing my eyes, I slipped a hand into my pocket. Fabric met my fingers. Horror slashed through me. I turned out every pocket, to no avail. The totem was gone.

CHANCE

I dragged myself onto *The Dragon's Bane*, relying heavily on the rope rail that had been strung along the gangplank. Every step sent pain flaring through my calf. I'd bound the wound with a strip of fabric torn from my tunic's hem, staunching the bleeding enough to return to the ship.

Shouts rang from the gathered crew at the sight of me hobbling and covered in blood. Animo raced to my side, scooping me up and carrying me to a chair outside the captain's quarters.

"Someone find Ketch and tell him to get the elixir!" he shouted. His hand slid to my neck, and his voice softened. "What happened?"

"The Cunninghams found me," I said through clenched teeth. "The big one—Dante—stabbed me."

Ketch sprinted from belowdecks, elixir in hand. Before he could say a word,

I snatched the bottle and took a large gulp. Tingling spread throughout my leg as the pain faded.

I exhaled slowly, leaning back and returning the bottle to Ketch. "Natalia has a bounty on my head. There are posters all over Nicia."

Animo cursed, turning to Ketch. "Get Camilla. Find out how soon we can leave." He looked back at me as Ketch ran off. "Until then, you should be belowdecks."

"I can't. I have to go back."

"What? Why?"

The concern in his eyes drove a knife into my stomach. "I lost something," I said, my words twisting the blade. What had I lost? The totem was forged with evil. It was a curse. I should have been thrilled to be rid of it, not chasing it down at my own risk. Yet the thought of it being gone forever sent panic through my soul.

"Whatever it is can't be more important than your life," he said.

"It's… I need to do this. Please."

His eyes narrowed. "What did you lose?"

My lip trembled as I held his gaze. *Please don't make me say it.*

"Rose—"

"Fine!" I shot to my feet, pacing a few steps before turning on him. "I lost the totem, and I want it back. I *need* it back."

"Why?"

Why? Because I had no choice. When I had used the totem in the Silver Forest, the beast inside of me had full control. I felt its rage and pain in a rush of power. A part of me longed to give in and accept the beast's power as my own. With it under my control, I could fight any war. I could free Avonshere, destroy Natalia, and *finally* stop running.

Animo stepped closer. "Its power is a lie, Rose. Things like the totem don't just give, they take. It will tempt you and make you give yourself over to it, and then it will betray you, leaving you with nothing."

"I have nothing!" I exclaimed, my fists clenched. "I cast one spell, and I'm spent. I haven't touched a sword in years. All I can do is shoot a bow and throw a punch. That can't win a war." I shrugged weakly. "Hertz was right. This is an impossible task. I'm not a queen or a warrior, but with the totem, I'll have the power to *win*."

Animo's expression darkened. "Whatever Hertz said to you is wrong," he said, his tone fierce. "You cannot win with that thing."

"That's not what he told me." Anger burned within me. Anger at Hertz, anger at Natalia, anger at myself—yet all of it fell to Animo. "He told me I couldn't win at all; that's why he left."

"What?"

"Hertz left," I repeated. "He lost faith in me, so he went home."

Animo sighed, closing his eyes as a soft curse slipped from his lips. "Rose, I'm so sorry."

"Don't be. It's who I am. People trust me, then they come to know me and realize that I'm not who they thought I was. All they can really trust is that I'll fail them."

"What?"

"It doesn't matter," I snapped, my heart pounding as I attempted to brush off my slip. "I'm getting the totem back."

"Rose—"

"What is going on here?" Camilla stalked down from the quarterdeck. She looked between us, her hand resting on the hilt of her cutlass. "I don't like people yelling on my ship if they aren't me."

"Animo is trying to stop me from saving Avonshere," I said, folding my arms.

His brows raised. "That's your move, is it? Well, then, Rose is trying to commit slow suicide in tandem with her people."

Camilla huffed, rolling her eyes. "I know I asked, but I really don't care. Just get your mess together, and stop bothering my crew."

"Let me ask you something, Camilla," I began.

She groaned.

"Am I a good fighter?"

"Not particularly."

"Thank you."

"Camilla has never seen you in combat," Animo argued.

"At least she's honest," I retorted.

"Shut it, both of you!" Camilla snapped. "Stop this useless bickering and find a sword."

"What?" we asked together.

"The only way to know if Rose will last in combat is for her to fight. So let's duel and find your answer."

"He'll throw the match to prove his point," I said.

"Which is why you'll fight me." Steel rang as Camilla drew her cutlass. "And be warned, if you attempt to throw this match, you'll die."

Animo raised a hand. "Enough. Rose is not going to fight you, certainly not with a real blade."

"Natalia wouldn't use a wooden sword," she replied. "She would use every weapon available to carve Rose into pieces."

His jaw clenched.

"I'll fight," I said. His gaze snapped to me. "If I win, we'll leave Nicia at once, and I'll rely on skill and training to defeat Natalia. But I want you to promise me that if Camilla wins, you will not stop me from finding the totem."

He shook his head. "Don't do this, Rose."

"Promise me."

"Fine. I promise to honor the outcome of this duel." His gaze fell, his voice quieting. "No matter how much I hate it."

Sol offered me his sword. I took it and slipped into a fighting stance. The entire crew had circled around us, watching with anticipation as I faced their captain.

Camilla lunged forward. I scarcely had time to block her blow. She stabbed, sending her sword straight through my braid. Pulling my hair free, I knocked her blade aside. I lunged, she parried.

Metal clashed as we fought. Her fervent attacks turned me around, pushing me toward the cabin. My back hit the wall. Steel touched my throat.

"You survived through beginner's luck," Camilla said, lifting my chin with the tip of her sword. "The unpredictability of an untrained fighter has the potential to triumph, but it's a game of chance. You won't win a war with these skills."

"Good."

She laughed. "It really isn't. You won't win with magic, either. No matter what weapons or power you possess, you will lose because you don't want it."

Rage spiked inside of me. I slammed my foot against her chest. She stumbled back, catching herself in a kneel. I raised my sword to advance—she flicked her blade. Pain flashed as it sliced my cheek.

I gasped, halting to touch the wound. Beading blood wet my fingertips.

"Chance," she repeated, climbing to her feet. "That's all you have."

She sheathed her cutlass, stalking toward the ship's bow. The sailors dispersed, returning to their duties and leaving me with Animo.

"There you have it," I said in a hollow voice. "She won."

"Think this through," he begged. "Think about what you could lose."

"I'm willing to pay the price."

His expression hardened. "Don't expect my pity when it destroys you."

"What happened to you being on my side?" I asked with an edge to my voice that I couldn't restrain. "You said that you wanted me to achieve greatness."

"I want you to be the person you were born to be," he snapped. "Not the person you think you are."

I jerked back. "What is that supposed to mean?"

"You've convinced yourself that you aren't enough, that you will bring death and chaos to all you meet. Now you want the totem to fulfill the prophecy you've written for yourself."

"What of Aspectu's prophecy?" I demanded. "Doesn't that say the same thing?"

His eyes widened. "How do you know that?"

"I heard you and Bellatora in Daria."

He closed his eyes, his shoulders sagging.

"She said it again in my last dream. I'm going to destroy them. I am the great darkness in the center of it all."

I'm Natalia.

He lifted his gaze, his deep-blue irises imploring me to listen. "That doesn't have to be true. Aspectu sees potential futures. We can change things."

"I'm not willing to risk it."

"Then don't use the totem."

I bit my lip, fighting to keep it still. "I'm sorry. I don't have a choice."

"You always have a choice," he said sharply. "You can choose not to use it. You can choose not to become the darkness. It's your *choice*, Rose."

"My choice is to save Avonshere. And if I'm going to have any chance at that, I'll need something stronger than myself."

"Don't," he begged. "Please."

"I'm sorry," I repeated.

I turned away, expecting him to take my arm and stop me from finishing the mistake I'd begun. But he didn't lift a finger. Disappointment tangled with guilt as I crossed the gangplank.

It's my choice.

With my face hidden beneath my hood, I searched the streets of Nicia for signs of the totem. But all I found were puddles of blood in the alley where I'd fought the Cunningham gang. An hour passed before I gave up and returned to *The Dragon's Bane*. Animo waited for me by the main mast.

"Did you find it?" he asked.

I didn't respond. My gaze fixed on the wooden ground as I retreated belowdecks.

When someone knocked on my cabin door, I prepared myself for another fight with Animo. There had always been a sort of rift between us—caused by his kidnapping of me and deepened by my infuriating self—and the last argument certainly hadn't done any favors. To my surprise, it was Sol who stepped inside.

"A letter came for you," he said, offering me a crumpled scroll tied with a ribbon. "I'm not sure who the sender is."

"Thank you." I took the letter, and he bobbed his head before exiting.

The door clicked shut as I unrolled the scroll. *WANTED* cut across the page in thick, black letters. A message had been scrawled in the top corner, followed by a rough sketch of a pendant hanging on a chain: *Town's edge, midnight. Come alone.*

"*Uchlet.*" I crumpled the poster into a tight ball, digging my nails into the softened parchment. He had the totem. Ruger Cunningham had my totem, and he was using it to lure me into a trap.

I couldn't go. *But you have to.*

I would die if I went. *But you will never be able to save Avonshere without your power.*

I huffed angrily. *Either way, I lose.*

Sinking down onto my bed, I flattened the poster on my lap. Something wasn't right about it. It had no picture, only a name: Rose Bennai.

Bennai.

The posters lining Nicia labeled me Rose Estmar, a traitor and murderer. But the one Ruger had bore my alias and the description: *wanted for questioning. Ten thousand mynet will be rewarded for her safe return.*

"Safe return," I murmured. Natalia didn't care how I was returned. But if she wasn't the one who placed this bounty, who had?

What am I to do now? If I went after the totem, it wouldn't be to make a deal with the Cunninghams; I would have to find a way to subdue all five of them in order to steal it back. And if I were caught, I would be taken captive and handed over to their unknown benefactor for questioning. But if I remained on *The Dragon's Bane*, I would lose my only hope of saving my kingdom.

I leaned back, letting resolve wash away my doubt. I knew what had to be done. I could only pray that Animo would forgive me.

CHAPTER FORTY-SIX

THE ROCKS BELOW

The night sky closed in around the cabin's porthole. I secured my dagger around my waist, letting it hang over the hunting garb I'd bought in Medea. Though I'd washed them thoroughly, faint stains of goblin blood remained.

This is for you, Megs. Her death would not be in vain. I would take the totem, and I would use it to destroy Natalia. Then it would all be over.

As much as I wanted to take my bow, it would be too suspicious, even covered by my poncho. Instead, I had my blade, and the vial of sleeping willow leaves tucked safely in my pocket. When the opportunity arose, I would drug Ruger and his crew and steal the totem. One fatal swoop for the ghost to take back what was hers.

Tomblike silence hovered as I slipped out of my bedroom. I took a step down the dark hallway, boards creaking softly under my feet.

"Going somewhere?"

I jumped. Animo leaned in the galley doorway, silhouetted in the faint moonlight.

"I wanted a drink." Regaining my composure, I pushed past him and into the galley.

"You weren't sneaking off to meet Ruger?" He struck a match, bathing his knowing face in a golden glow. "I read the letter."

Of course he did. Maintaining steady breaths, I took a pair of cups from the cupboard.

"Please don't do this."

The beg in his voice cut through my resolve. My throat tightened; if I faced Animo, my every thought would be clear to him.

But I have to do this.

"I haven't done anything," I said, pouring two cups of ale.

"But you intend to. I don't believe that you are the darkness Apsectu saw. But if you go after the totem, you may prove me wrong."

I closed my eyes, sliding my hand to my pocket, where the vial of sleeping willow leaves waited. I didn't want to hurt him, but I had no choice.

I slipped the vial free, shaking a small amount into his drink. My heart sank with the powdered leaves dissolving into the ale.

"Very well," I said, sliding the drugged cup to him. "I won't meet with Ruger."

He caught my wrist. "Don't."

"Don't do what?"

"Don't lie to me. If you want to keep secrets, that's fine. If you want to make the wrong choice, that's fine. But after everything we've been through, I deserve more than your lies."

Guilt tightened my chest. "You're right. And I am truly sorry. I don't enjoy lying to you. In fact, I wish I were the type of woman who could be honest with you."

"You are. You are more than the deceit. More than the scars hidden beneath your skin." He took my hand. "Rose, you are more than whatever it is you have hidden in your past. I believe in you."

Tears blurred my vision. His hand slipped away, and he picked up his cup. *No.*

I clenched my fist, fighting against the urge to knock it away. He took a sip and swallowed.

"Forgive me," I whispered.

Animo rose to his feet. His knees buckled, and realization dawned in his eyes. He sank to the ground, his white-knuckled grip tight around the table. "What have you done?"

"Sleeping willow leaves. You'll only be out for a little while."

"Rose—"

"I'm sorry!" I cried. I fell to my knees beside him, holding him upright. His eyelids sagged as his weakening grip dropped to my shoulder.

"Please don't do this."

"It's too late."

His strength failed, and he slumped against me, unconscious. I held him close as shocked tears rolled down my cheeks.

Burn every bridge. Cross every line. That is who I was now: the girl I had sworn I would never be, the girl I had left in the ashes—she was alive, and she was me.

The refreshing chill of midnight air wrapped around me as I walked through the vacant streets of Nicia. It reminded me of Chess but without the warm simplicity I had taken for granted.

It seemed everyone dreamed of their storybook adventure; it was why we told stories. We wanted to live impossible lives. On the page, they were beautiful. Magical. But in reality, the enchantment faded into a black pit of grief for all that had been lost.

There was always a trade: freedom for duty, life for glory, love for power. I knew what Natalia had chosen. Now, it was my turn.

I fixed my gaze on the flickering glow of firelight near the edge of town. Somewhere in that camp lay my totem. My choice had come, and I was nothing if I didn't choose power.

Back hunched, I sneaked toward the Cunningham gang's camp. They gathered around the fire. Ruger lay with his back to a log, one arm around Ali's shoulders and another loosely grasping a small crossbow. Across from them sat Elias and Dante on stumps, while Belinda was nowhere to be found.

Keeping an eye out for the young girl, I weighed my options. I still had some sleeping willow leaves, but my chances of drugging the gang were slim. Even if there were an open pot or bottle, they would have to go inside their tents to give me an opening. My only choice was to fight, but with my ever-weakening magical abilities, I would be forced to rely on my fists and my dagger.

I bit back a huff.

I can't beat all four of them in physical combat. I need some kind of distraction.

The wind picked up, whipping my poncho around me and sending loose hairs in my eyes. I brushed the strands back, my gaze locking on the campfire. *This could work.*

Summoning a bit of magic, I sent a spark skipping out of the fire. It landed on dead grass, igniting the brown blades. The Cunninghams jumped up to douse the flames. I reached for my dagger, preparing to advance, when a small hand grabbed mine.

I spun. Belinda stood by my side, her wide eyes staring up at me. *Don't*, she mouthed.

I drew back, my gaze falling to her hand. A dark-green jewel glittered on her finger—Megs's ring, stolen in Medea.

Anger flared within me. I twisted Belinda's arm behind her back, pressing my dagger to her throat. Keeping a tight grip, I shoved her forward.

"Ruger Cunningham," I called.

Ruger and his gang turned, surprise and anger rippling through their ranks at the sight of me with Belinda.

"You have something that belongs to me," I said. "You will hand it over now, or I will slit her throat."

Ruger laughed, shaking his head. "Oh, dear Rose… you were free, a bird in the wind, yet you returned. For this." He held up the totem, its black gem gleaming in the firelight. "Very pretty," he mused. "And very valuable, or so I'm told. But is your bargaining chip worth its return?"

My confidence wavered. "She's one of yours."

"She's a stray I picked up a year ago," he said dismissively. "I want something better."

"What?"

"Two-hundred-thousand mynet."

"What makes you think I have that?"

He stepped closer, a grin twisting his lips. "Oh, I know you don't. But *he* does."

I whirled. A gloved hand drew the tent door aside, and the Queen's Hunter stepped out.

Horror raced through me. Shoving Belinda away, I flew at the Hunter, only to be jerked back as Elias and Ali pinned my arms behind me. I struggled against their grasp as the Hunter's hidden eyes bore down at me.

"Well done," he said, his deep voice muffled by the mask. "Your queen thanks you." He dropped a sack of coins in Ruger's palm.

"Since when do you work for Natalia?" I snarled at Ruger.

"Since she offered me more than Madame Sconcewood."

My breath caught. *Sconcewood. That's the woman who stole the Staff of Realms.*

"And it was my pleasure," he added, giving the Hunter an exaggerated bow. "Besides, it wasn't difficult to get her here, not with this in my grasp." He dangled the totem before me, clicking his tongue. "So close. Yet so far."

Rage boiled inside of me. I strained against my captors to no avail.

"Poor, poor, child," Ruger crooned.

The Hunter's hand shot out, clamping around Ruger's wrist. "Do not toy with it."

Ruger lowered the totem as the Hunter drew his sword.

"By order of Queen Natalia, you have been sentenced to death for high treason."

"Treason?" My nails dug into my palms. "Am I more treasonous than the woman who murdered my entire family?"

"You know nothing," he growled, raising the blade.

Fury glowed inside of me. Darkness swelled, twisting my stomach and sending sharp tremors racing through my limbs. An invisible hand reached out.

Let me help you.

Ruger stepped back, gripping the totem's chain. "What's wrong with her? Why is she doing that?"

I raised my head, and my pain turned into power.

The totem flew from Ruger's hand, latching itself around my neck. The iron burned, igniting my blood. I screamed, dropping to my knees as the beast awoke inside of me. It clawed at my insides, screaming for freedom. My vision blurred, and my head pounded as my power grew, battling for the limited space within me.

I didn't stop it. I couldn't stop it.

With another scream, I unleashed it all: the pain, the power, and the fire that burned within. The beast roared in furious triumph. Shrill cries erupted.

I fell forward, and the world faded into focus. Dante and Elias lay moaning on the ground while the Hunter had taken shelter behind the tent and now struggled to detangle himself from the collapsed frame and singed canvas. At the center of it all was Ali, sobbing over Ruger's body. His chest had been pierced by a flaming branch, thrown like a spear from the fire. Thrown by *me*.

I had killed Ruger.

"Oh, Kingdoms," I whispered, falling back on my heels. The beast settled, but its fury remained, a quiet flame waiting to be evoked. *I'm here*, it seemed to say. *And I'm not going anywhere.*

"You." Ali jabbed a finger in my direction, her red cheeks stained with tears. "You did this!"

She snatched a dagger and lunged at me. I fell back, dodging her first swipe. She brought the blade around, ready to stab—

A short arrow flew into her throat. With a strangled gasp, she dropped, coughing blood.

"Rose!" Animo slid to a stop beside me. "Are you hurt?"

"The Hunter," I rasped. "He's here to kill me."

Animo nodded. "Can you walk?"

"Of course I can." I stood, only to fall back into his waiting arms.

"I've got you." He caught my legs, scooping me up.

"Let's move!" Camilla shouted from the front of a wagon. Dobbins sat beside her, a crossbow in hand, and Ketch stood in the back, muscles tense as he watched Animo carry me to the cart.

Animo dropped me beside Ketch. "Go!" he shouted, climbing into the back.

A figure leaped onto the wagon. Blood coated Elias's face, peppered with shards of wood. He raised a dagger, his wide eyes flooded with madness.

Before he could attack, he wobbled, then tumbled backward. He hit the dirt, the tip of a blade protruding from his forehead. Belinda stood behind him, her fair skin flecked with cuts.

"Take me with you," she said.

"Traitor!" Dante, the only living member of the Cunningham gang, bellowed. He stumbled to his feet as the Hunter emerged from the tent's remains, thick shards of wood protruding from his arm.

"Failure," he growled, driving his sword through Dante's back. Dante shouted, his limbs tensing, then falling slack as he dropped to the ground. The Hunter's masked eyes rose to us, glowing orange in the firelight.

"Get in!" Camilla shouted.

Belinda leaped into the back of the wagon. Reins snapped, and the horses broke into a gallop. We tore through the field, jostling as the path shifted to cobblestone. Camilla drove us through the streets, jerking the horses to a stop at the harbor's edge.

A battalion of shades lined the wharf, still as shadows with the face of death.

"We'll never make it past them," Belinda murmured.

"Then we retreat," Animo said.

My heart dropped. "My sister is on that ship."

"Natalia doesn't want Lili—she wants you," he argued.

"I'm not leaving her," I snapped.

"If you stay, the shades will too. The only way to keep her safe is to leave her behind."

"What about the crew?" I demanded. "Will they leave without their captain?"

"They're under orders to protect our cargo," Camilla replied. "In this case, that's your sister. If I don't come back, my second mate will take control."

An arrow plunged into the wagon's side. The Hunter barrelled toward us on a dark steed.

"We go now!" Camilla jerked the reins. The horses took off, knocking me onto my back. I gripped the cart's side, struggling to stay upright. The Hunter's cloak billowed behind him as he rode, rage in every pounding hoofbeat. One hand gripped the reins while the other held an empty crossbow. He couldn't reload while riding, but it was only a matter of time before he reached us.

"Ketch!" Animo called, bracing himself as the wagon took a sharp turn. "We need to do something!"

"I've got it!" Ketch drew a large glass vial from his belt. Black powder shifted within. He took aim with his slingshot and fired.

An explosion lit the night as the vial smashed at the foot of the Hunter's steed. The black silhouette of his horse rearing flashed before collapsing into flame. Smoke faded as the Hunter climbed to his feet. His dark gaze followed our cart.

I will come for you, he seemed to say.

I forced my eyes forward, fighting back tears. Flames, blood, death—once again, I was at the center of it all. I closed my eyes. *It's my fault.* I had chosen this, and now, I would have to face the consequences.

PART SIX

SANCTUARY

The wagon rocked as Camilla drove the horses up the rough path. My head rested uncomfortably against the back of the driver's seat, and my eyes ached from the pale dawn light. The treeline blurred beside us, much like the passing days. We'd ridden all through the first night, only stopping to exchange the horses. My awareness of time faded with each rising sun. Silence held our company, broken only by the sporadic screams of shades catching our trail. Though they'd grown fainter since Nicia, the monsters remained far too close for us to make camp.

So we rode on.

The beast slept, a heavy stone in my stomach reminding me of how I'd failed. I had succumbed to its dark power. *Again.*

Five years ago, I had done the same thing. I had known the right choice, yet I'd made the wrong one. I lost everything that night, and in my heart, I knew that the only one to blame was myself.

My unfocused eyes followed the path fading behind us. Against the wagon's back wall, Ketch and Belinda slept, a canvas blanket stretched between them.

That girl can't save us. She's a burden to our kingdom. The words rang in my mind, drawn from a memory I'd fought so hard to bury.

Blinking back tears, I shifted my gaze to the blurred trees. With Animo sitting beside me, it was the only direction I *could* look.

He had warned me that this would happen. He had begged me not to go after the totem, but I hadn't listened. Instead, I'd betrayed him. I betrayed the one person who had never lost faith in me. And for what?

Camilla's voice floated from the driver's seat. "That's the marker. We're eight leagues away."

I wasn't sure where she was taking us, nor did I care. We could go to a palace or pit of muck; it wouldn't change my approaching confrontation. As my companions' fear faded, their anger would return, raining down on me like acid.

And I'll deserve every drop of it.

I rolled to the side, stretching my legs before me. As I shifted, my arm brushed against Animo's. I drew away, risking a glance at him. He gave me no acknowledgment, his eyes fixed on the road behind us.

I crossed my arms beneath my poncho, making myself as small as possible. He moved his leg, letting his knee rest against mine. Guilt ached within me, dulled by exhaustion. I touched my foot to his, then lay back, closing my eyes. At last, sleep came.

The wagon lurched to a stop, jolting me from sleep. I sat up, blinking in the bright sunlight. My vision cleared, and my eyes settled on a golden gate behind which ran a path paved with smooth, white stones. It climbed up the mountain, winding toward an elegant building.

"Where are we?" I asked, standing for a better view. Belinda followed my lead while Ketch joined Camilla and Dobbins in the driver's seat.

"It's one of Emode's temples." Camilla jumped down and pointed at a dove engraved at the top of the gate. "That's her symbol."

Emode. The Divine Mistress of the Arts.

"Can it be shelter?" I asked.

"If the gate opens, then yes," Animo replied, climbing out of the wagon bed.

Dobbins scoffed, joining him and Camilla before the gate. "You really want to trust priestesses to protect you? You'd be better off hiding behind an army of clawless kittens."

A shade screamed in the distance. I dropped to my knees as the horses neighed, bucking and pawing the ground. Animo stepped in front of them, calming them with gentle words. They continued shifting, their hooves carving lines into the dirt. Animo stroked their noses, his touch gentle despite his tight jaw.

"Let's see if we survive, shall we?" Camilla gave the gate a push; it swung open without a sound. She turned back toward the cart and gave Dobbins a shrug.

He rolled his eyes, his arms folded.

"If you wish to remain here, you may," Animo said, his harsh tone laced with exhaustion. "We'll pick up the pieces of your carcass on our way out."

He and Camilla returned to the cart, and she drove the horses forward.

Dobbins glanced back at the road we'd taken. Without so much as a finger touching it, the gate began to close. His eyes widened, and he broke into a sprint, sliding through before it shut.

"Good choice," Animo said as Dobbins climbed back into the wagon, a scowl twisting his lips.

"I must admit that I'm a little skeptical," Ketch said from the seat beside Camilla. "Our last time at a temple didn't end well."

"This time will be different," Animo said. "Emode is peaceful."

The wagon rattled up the winding road, up the mountain, and toward the sanctuary at its peak. Trees thinned as we neared, revealing a white-stone temple. Twisting columns ran along its front, meeting in elegant arches. A priestess clad in a pale-pink gown waited at the door.

She raised her hands as we approached. "Welcome, travelers, to the Aleddai Temple of Emode. I am Sabine. May your spirits be reborn within our walls."

"We need a place to stay the night," Animo said. "And sanctuary from those chasing us."

Sabine nodded serenely. "You will find food and shelter here." She turned, displaying a large tattoo across her back, depicting a dove with its wings spread wide and a lotus flower in its beak.

Gathering our few possessions, we followed her into the temple. The early-morning sun shone through a single skylight, illuminating a massive statue of the divine mistress Emode. A dress, much like her priestesses wore, draped from her smooth, marble skin. Her pounded-gold curls fell atop shoulders so perfect they might have been flesh. In one hand, she held a lotus blossom while the other was raised with a dove poised on her finger.

A large pool of water rippled at the statue's base. Priestesses knelt beside it, their heads bowed and their hands raised, a lotus atop their palms. Each one bore the same tattoo as Sabine.

"This is the Hall of Worship," Sabine said, leading us through the gaping chamber. "Follow me to your rooms."

I stared up at the domed ceiling, adorned with a mural, too distant to properly see—even with my elf eyes. My gaze dropped past the balcony that ringed the hall, and I followed Sabine.

She guided us down an adjacent corridor through a garden courtyard to a long hallway.

Stopping, she gestured to a row of waiting doors. "You may have these six rooms."

"Five," Camilla said, grabbing the collar of Belinda's oversized coat. "This one stays with me."

"As you wish."

Belinda shrugged off Camilla's grip as the priestess retreated down the hall. "I'm not going to run," she snapped.

"I have no reason to trust that," Camilla replied, her glare accentuating the dark circles under her eyes. "You know, you're lucky we didn't leave you to die at the hands of the Queen's Hunter."

"Lighten up Cam," Ketch said. "What's important is that we're alive. Also, food." The growl of his stomach affirmed his words.

"I could eat," Belinda said meekly.

"Excellent." Ketch started down the hall. "Does anyone actually know where the kitchen is?"

Animo caught my arm, holding me back as our companions' footsteps faded. "We need to talk."

My gaze fixed on the floor. "Later."

"Rose—"

"I'm hungry." My voice shook as hot tears welled. "We'll talk later."

He didn't stop me as I walked away, wiping my eyes. I shouldn't cry, not when I was the one in the wrong. But my anger had lost its edge, leaving me a trembling, teary, mess of a girl. I despised it.

I followed my friends' voices down the corridor, stopping before a door. *I will not cry.* Forcing my lips into a firm line, I stepped inside.

Ketch had taken control of the kitchen, and Belinda helped him prepare a stew. Camilla and Dobbins sat at the table, the former stretched out on a bench, her cutlass resting on her legs. They sat in silence, irritation etched on their faces. I leaned against the counter, my hands behind my back.

Animo strode into the room, avoiding my eyes as he used his foot to shove Camilla's legs off the bench. She returned her cutlass to her belt as he sat.

"Stew will be ready in an hour," Ketch said, handing Belinda a basket of bread.

The young girl brought it to the table, only for Camilla's hand to shoot out, clamping around her wrist.

"Since we've got the time, let's have a little chat," she said, her tone vile.

Belinda pulled away, but the pirate's grip held fast.

"Camilla!" Ketch snapped, stalking over to her. "We are not here to fight. We are here to survive. So shut it!" Despite standing at eye level with the table, Ketch's anger cracked like a whip.

Camilla released Belinda, raising her hands in a gesture of goodwill.

"Thank you," Ketch said, composing himself. "Now, let's begin with some bread. Rose, come sit."

I obeyed, dropping beside Dobbins, which, unfortunately, placed me across from Animo. Belinda sat next to me, though she kept her distance, situating herself on the very edge of the bench. Ketch climbed onto the open spot beside Animo, standing to better reach the table.

We ate in silence. Each bite of soft bread seethed in my stomach, tempting nausea. It tasted like home and friendship, two things I had burned to ash.

"So," Camilla began, her eyes fixed on Belinda as she slowly tore a piece of bread in two, "tell us about your previous occupation."

"Camilla," Ketch warned.

"We don't have time for niceties," she snapped. "We are being tracked by an army of shades and the queen's own Hunter. You want to make friends with the stray, be my guest. But I'm getting answers."

Ketch's pupils constricted to slivers, but he didn't speak.

With a hint of victory in her eyes, Camilla returned her attention to Belinda. "Why'd you play turncoat?"

Belinda set her shoulders, meeting the pirate's eyes with her own firm gaze. "I never wanted to be part of Ruger's crew. They picked me up three years ago, and the only way for me to stay alive was to follow them."

"And they led you to the Hunter. Did he tell you to follow us?"

"No," Belinda replied. "And if I go back now, he'll probably kill me."

Camilla laughed. "If you truly helped us escape, he'd torture you for days before letting you die."

Belinda shrank back, wrapping her arms around herself.

Pity swelled within me. She hadn't asked to be part of this. Circumstances led her to Ruger, a man ready to let her die for a payout.

"We're done with this," Ketch said.

"No, we are not." Camilla shot to her feet, stalking around the table to plant herself before Belinda. "How did you contact the Hunter?"

The girl raised her chin. "I'll tell you, but I want something in return."

Camilla's brow arched. "You really want to bargain with a pirate?"

"I want to be kept safe. If that means making a deal with a no-good pirate like you, then fine."

A smirk tugged at the captain's lips. "Not interested. I already have one dead weight to carry." Her eyes flicked to me.

I slammed my fist on the table, rattling the dishes. "Enough!" I stood, placing myself between Camilla and Belinda. "We're not on your ship, and you are not our captain. This is my quest, and I say we make the deal." I turned to Belinda. "You will come with us, and we will protect you until we find a haven for you to stay. But in turn, you will tell us everything you know about the people who Ruger was working for."

Belinda nodded. "I will." She withdrew a satchel from her bulky coat. "This is from Ruger's camp. It's everything he knows about you."

Camilla reached for the bag, but Belinda pulled it away. The pirate rolled her eyes.

"Her Highness has decreed we're on the same side," she said, flattening her palm. Belinda handed over the bag stiffly, her eyes following Camilla as she dumped its contents onto the table. The pirate tossed the empty bag onto the floor and rifled through an assortment of letters, a number of—undoubtedly stolen—jewels, tools, and one large notebook.

Ketch selected a dark-red crystal from the pile. "What is this? It looks evil."

Animo's eyes widened. "That's a witch stone—a magical communication device."

"Ruger used it to talk to the Hunter," Belinda said.

Tension cut the air as our gazes locked on the stone. Its sharp, red angles reflected the candlelight, waving and flickering.

"Could he hear us now?" Even my whisper felt too loud. Sabine had said the name of the temple. If the Hunter could hear us through the stone… I didn't want to think of what would happen.

"I'm not sure," Animo admitted. Ketch dropped the stone like it was a hot coal.

"I'll take it for safekeeping," Dobbins said.

"Keep it hidden," Animo instructed.

Dobbins nodded. He wrapped the stone with his scarf and forced it into a tin before tucking it into his pocket. I would have preferred tossing the stone into a pit, but muffling fabric would suffice.

Belinda picked up the journal. "This is Ruger's notebook. Whatever information he has will be in it."

Ketch held out a hand. "May I?"

Belinda nodded, passing the journal to him.

"Ruger didn't tell me much about his plans," she explained as he thumbed through the pages. "We went to Medea for a heist, but when we met you, he was curious. He wanted to know why you were after the Staff of Realms, so he had me follow you back to the inn to learn more." She spun Megs's ring on her finger. "I couldn't overhear, so I stole. I took some jewelry, a shackle with runes, and a chest with a wolf on it. We couldn't open the chest, so Ruger decided to sell it. His buyer was a woman named Elizabeth Sconcewood. I never met her, but she wanted to know everything about you, Rose. That's why she hired Ruger. To find you."

"Why did your employment with her end?" Animo asked.

"Ruger learned that Natalia had a much larger bounty on your head. He changed sides without a word to Sconcewood." She looked up at me. "Natalia wants you dead, but this Elizabeth's instructions clearly stated that you were to be delivered alive. I've wondered if she was a friend of yours."

"We're familiar with her name," Animo replied. "But even if she wants Rose alive, we can't be certain it's to help."

"Oh no."

All eyes turned to Ketch. A strange sense of repetition swept over me, seeing him stare at a journal with wide eyes. He closed it slowly.

"It would seem that Elizabeth Sconcewood did indeed retrieve the Staff of Realms," he began. "However, it would also seem that she took it to Avonshere."

"Avonshere?" I repeated. My breaths shortened as my heartbeat quickened. "That means—that means she could have it. Natalia could have the Staff of Realms."

"We don't know she has it," Animo said, staring down at the tabletop.

"But we can't get it," I snapped. "We are wanted and hunted and… and we've lost. We've failed."

He finally looked up at me, anger and defeat drowning his gaze. I shook my head, leaving the kitchen before anyone else spoke. I didn't need Camilla's insults or Ketch's desperate attempts to remain optimistic. I needed to be alone.

I retraced my steps, slipping into the first bedroom I reached. Simple furnishings greeted me, but I bypassed them for the mirror.

My hair hung in knots, scant strands forming the end of a braid. Clotted blood formed a line where Camilla had cut me, and ash streaked my cheeks, pale compared to the dark circles under my eyes. Unshed tears lingered, while my downturned lips seemed as though they would never lift.

I ran my fingers through my hair, working out the knots. I remembered a day when I saw my sister's smiling face in the mirror instead of my own hollow gaze. We had laughed back then, fantasizing about our futures. If only we'd known how quickly the tide would turn.

My fingers caught on a knot, and I yanked. Pain shot through my hand and head as I tore off a piece of hair. With a furious wail, I ripped off my leather gloves, throwing them across the room.

My gaze fell to my hands, and I gasped. Blood coated my palms. I ran to the dresser, dunking my hands into the waiting washbasin and scrubbing frantically. The clear water darkened, shifting to scarlet. A metallic stench assaulted my senses. I withdrew my hands, only to find blood flowing from every inch of my skin.

A faint cry slipped out as tears poured. I couldn't breathe. I ran to the bed, wiping my hands and leaving dark red streaks on the snow-white sheets. The blood remained.

My breaths came in short spurts. I retreated, my back slamming against the wall as my gaze locked on the crimson stain.

Murderer.

Flames shot from the sheets. They raced across the floor, engulfing the room. Smoke thickened, smothering my senses. I sank to the floor, squeezing my eyes shut as the flames licked my skin. My heart pounded against the totem that rested on my chest.

I can help you, the beast said, its claws twisting around my mind. *Let me free.*

"No," I whispered. "I can't."

Smoke subsided. I opened my eyes to find an ashen road lined with charred homes. I rose, trembling. My feet moved by memory, guiding me to the only destination I had: the blackened remains of a barn.

Apprehension filled me as I slid the door open, streaking my hand with soot. Moonlight flowed through the broken roof, illuminating the skeleton that lay in the ash. A crown rested by its head, and a ring adorned its finger. Fresh tears welled as I gazed down at it.

I am so sorry.

Before my eyes, pale skin began to reform, wrapping around the bones. Fingers thickened with muscle, and the sapphire ring shifted to an emerald. The skin raced up the body, curving into a neck, then a head with freckled cheeks and lips that only looked right when they smiled. Bright-red curls wound their way out of the head, spreading across the ashen ground.

Megs's eyes opened, her green irises filled with blood.

I screamed. Somewhere in the ashen distance, a woman laughed in triumph.

CHAPTER FORTY-EIGHT

A LIGHT IN THE DARKNESS

A hand stroked my cheek, tucking my hair behind my ear. Warmth enveloped me; a blanket covered my body, and a fire crackled nearby. I dragged my eyes open. Animo sat beside me on the bed, his face cast with the shadows of night.

"Animo?"

"I'm here," he said, concern flowing from his eyes. "What happened?"

"What do you mean?"

"I found you passed out on the floor and shaking. You've been unconscious for hours."

I pushed myself up, leaning against the headboard. "I don't remember falling asleep. But… I had a nightmare."

"What did you see?" The innocent question ignited the anger festering within me.

"I don't want to talk about it."

He shook his head. "We've passed the point where you can say that. You had some kind of uncontrolled vision. Almost as though your magic was manipulating you."

Here we are. I kicked off the blankets and climbed out of bed. "Fine. You want to blame this on my magic, go ahead. But don't forget where that power comes from."

"I think you're the one forgetting that." He pulled the totem from his pocket, its stone glowing with reflected firelight.

"What are you doing with that?" I demanded.

"It was burning your skin. I took it to keep you from being hurt, but I fear I was too late." He held it before me. "*This* is where your nightmare came from. It's controlling you, swaying your decisions and your power. If you don't let go, it will destroy you."

I shook my head. "No. It's a conduit. It doesn't create, it enhances. Whatever darkness it controls has to come from me. It didn't kill Ruger, I did. I was the one who led us into danger time and time again. Everything we've suffered has been because of me. The totem isn't the darkness: *I* am."

His hand fell. The totem slipped through his fingers, dropping to the floor. "How can you say that?"

"Because it's true! I'm the one to blame. They were my choices that hurt us, not my magic's. So please, stop talking about this darkness and accept the fact that it's *me*."

"No."

"Animo—"

"No." He stepped forward, anger burning in his eyes. "I will not stand here and blame you for everything that's happened. Since the day I met you, you have fought. For your family, your friends, and your people. Yes, you have made mistakes, but that doesn't make you the villain."

I shook my head. "You don't know me."

"I know enough."

"No, you don't."

His nostrils flared. Turning sharply, he began pacing before the fire. "What do you want from me, Rose? Do you want me to yell about how much I hate you and how I wished you had died in Darvyn?"

"Yes!" The word broke free as a scream. I gasped, clapping my hands over my mouth.

He froze, his eyes wide, and his lips parted.

Yes. I want you to wish I had died that night because I wish I had died. I want you to hate me because I hate myself.

Lowering my shaking hands, I murmured, "I hurt people. It's as if I'm caught on a wheel, spinning in circles. I try to fix things, to be better, yet every time, I prove myself wrong."

"That doesn't mean you deserve to die."

I pressed my lips together, refusing to respond.

"Rose, please." His gentle voice pushed against my walls. He wanted inside them. He wanted to know. And a part of me wanted that, too.

"I see her," I whispered. "I see Natalia."

"In your dreams?"

"In *myself.*" I took a breath, staring into the fire to keep my tears at bay. "Natalia went to Daria to save her people, only to return as a witch ruled by darkness. I did the same. I'll *do* the same. She and I walk the same path. Perhaps our intentions begin pure, but eventually, they become corrupted. We lead people to death. We destroy. We betray." I bit my lip to stop its trembling. "I'm just like her. If I become queen, all that will do is trade one wicked ruler for another. And I would rather die than make that deal."

"I understand."

My gaze rose to his. A thousand memories of Daria and Regium swirled within his eyes. He stepped forward, taking my hand and guiding it to his wrist.

"Do you feel that?" he asked, running my fingers along the dark rune tattooed on his skin.

At first, I thought he meant his pulse beating steadily—unlike mine, which pounded at his proximity. Then my fingertips touched something hard and plate-like.

My brow furrowed. "What is that?"

"My greatest mistake," he said. "When I ran away from Daria, I swore that I would never be like Reg—like my father. I was so desperate to distance myself from him and his ways, that I fled to Pikbrie. Dwarf blacksmiths are skilled at incorporating runes into designs, so I hired one to forge a shackle that would stifle my magic. He did as I asked, but it wasn't enough."

He gazed down at the tattoo. My fingers remained on his wrist as firelight danced across our skin.

"The cuff didn't eliminate my magic—It would always be there, waiting to be reawakened. But the thought of using it as an escape felt cowardly and too much like him. I needed to be rid of it forever. So I had the smith carve the runes on a small shard of metal and insert it into my wrist."

My jaw fell slack. "That... you... why would you do that?"

"Because I was afraid. That one night—that one reckless decision fueled by my own fear has nearly cost me my life more times than I can count. The runes did more than simply block my magic. They made my body *reject* magic. That's why I never allow you or Aspectu to heal me. The spell would be twisted and instead of repairing damage, it would cause more."

I pulled my hand away, unable to form words. Memories from the past few months flashed through my mind—the magic in Daria, the enchanted liquor, the spells I had cast... they had all hurt him.

"I know I push you," he said. "But it's because I know what it's like to fight these battles. Years ago, I allowed my own fear to destroy my life. I refuse to watch as you do the same."

I shook my head, my lips contorted against a cry. "I don't want to be this person. I don't want to make these choices or take this path. I knew that Ruger's letter was a trap. I knew that using the totem would cause nothing but harm. But most of all, I knew that I would regret betraying you. And I do regret it. I wish I could undo everything or change the course of my future, but I can't. I am trapped in an unbreakable cycle of my own destruction."

Animo's hands slid to either side of my neck. His thumbs brushed my cheeks, gentle yet firm as they guided my gaze to his.

"You are *not* Natalia. And you *can* break this cycle. You created it. You have let your darkest parts write a future that your fear accepts as an unchangeable prophecy. But it's not. You are not doomed to be the villain, Rose. The only thing keeping you on this path is your own fear. This cycle you see only exists because you believe in it. You're dooming yourself."

"If that's true, then why is Megs dead? Why did Hertz walk away from me like I was—?" My voice broke. I turned away, slipping out of Animo's grasp. "It doesn't matter. What's done is done, and there is no going back."

"Stop." All gentleness had drained from Animo's tone. "Stop believing these lies. You're in *pain*. You think you can block it out and fade into an abyss of numbness where nothing can hurt you, but you're wrong. No distance is enough to escape the ache of what you've lost. You have to let yourself grieve."

Let yourself grieve.

I closed my eyes, my breaths coming in rattling spurts. *Dead girls don't cry.* I was a ghost, a dead princess. I didn't cry, and I didn't grieve. I didn't grieve for my father when we left him behind in Del Hera. Nor my grandfather, crushed beneath stone. There was no grief for my mother when she was slaughtered and hung from that bridge or when my best friend abandoned me. I didn't mourn for the people of Darvyn, nor the people of Rudane. Not even for Megs.

I sank to my knees. *Dead girls don't cry.* Why couldn't I be dead? Why couldn't Natalia have driven her blade through my chest and taken all this suffering away from me? Why was I always the one left standing?

Dead girls don't cry, but I wasn't dead. There on the ground, I broke like the shattered reflection of the girl I was. Alive and aching with grief.

Animo knelt beside me, placing a hand on my back as I sobbed. I fell against him, my head resting atop his chest. His rapid heartbeat pounded in my ear, gradually slowing at a comforting pace.

The heat from the fire iced in comparison to the warmth I found safely enclosed in Animo's arms. My tears slowed, and my heartache settled, yet I didn't move. I didn't *want* to move.

Minutes stretched along. We remained on the floor, his arms around me and my tears soaking into his shirt.

Finally, he pulled away, guiding me to my feet. "You should rest."

I nodded, though every part of me wanted to cling to him and beg him to stay. A small *thank you* was all I managed before Animo slipped out the door.

I curled up in the bed. Exhaustion pounded against my head, yet sleep refused to come. I stared aimlessly at the shadows dancing on the ceiling as my last few tears slid down my cheeks.

Music hummed in the distance, its melody rising and falling like gentle waves. I crawled out of bed, following the sound through Aleddai's dark halls. Warm light glowed, guiding me to the Hall of Worship.

Priestesses danced in a circle around Emode's statue, their feet bare and their bodies draped in flowing, white gowns. Golden light swirled around their limbs, running like a spiderweb to where a veiled priestess played an ivory violin. They spun, and the light shifted into orbs, rising and floating about the room like lanterns.

Beautiful.

The music swelled. A golden thread reached out, tugging me forward. I slipped into the circle, mirroring the priestesses's movements. Magic stirred within me as I danced, swaying in time with the rest. My power rose, flooding my chest with its warmth before spilling out in golden spirals along my limbs. The longer I danced, the stronger my magic grew, its strands twining with the priestesses's. Our combined power flowed to the violin, yet it wasn't taken. It wrapped around the strings, blooming with fresh light before returning home.

A smile spread across my lips as tears cascaded down my cheeks. There was no darkness here, only magic like honey and sunlight. Golden and untainted—a healing spell for my soul.

I threw my arms into the air as I twirled, just as I had when I was little. In my mind, Aleddai faded into the empty ballroom with the sun's rays spilling through towering, stained-glass windows. I was ten and innocent. My magic was a friend, and I rested in its embrace.

Hours later, I returned to my chamber. My smile lingered as I slipped beneath the sheets, and my magic guided my mind to peaceful dreams.

ENEMY OR ALLY?

I awoke, the warmth of last night's dance lingering on my limbs. The beast's pull had subsided, leaving me with my own, uncorrupted magic. I still ached from the grief and loss of the past few months, but amid all that sorrow bloomed a light.

I was broken, but not beyond repair. I would end this cycle I had created, freeing myself so I could free my people.

Holding on to the thought, I climbed out of bed and re-braided my hair. The girl in the mirror remained a mess of dried blood and smeared ash. But hope shimmered in her eyes. I tied off my braid, my lips set in a determined line. *I can do this.*

I quickly cleaned my face, then turned—the discarded totem caught my eye. Kneeling, I pulled it into my palm. Cool metal ran along my skin, but that's where the connection ended.

"I don't need you," I said. "After breakfast I will take you to the highest window I can find, and I'll rid myself of you forever."

Like a distant echo, the beast whined in my mind, scrabbling at its door. I didn't listen. I would not be a slave to its darkness any longer.

I met Animo in the courtyard dining hall, where a buffet had been arranged on a long, stone table. A smile flicked across his lips, only to drop as quickly as it came.

"About last night. No one knows about..." He raised his tattooed wrist. "Not even Ketch, and I would prefer to keep it that way."

"Of course. I won't say a word."

"Good." He exhaled, his smile returning. "How are you after everything?"

"I think I'm all right. Truly all right."

We made our way down the buffet, gathering food as I recounted my tale: the priestesses's dance, the way the magic and music flowed as one, and the peace it brought to my soul.

"The Dance of Serenity," Animo said. "I overheard a priestess talking about it. It's a ritual to center their spirits and reignite their connection to Emode's power."

Worry slithered through me. "If I connected with Emode during the dance, was it her magic that I felt?"

"No, not at all," he assured me, spooning quail eggs onto his plate. "Your magic joined with hers, but only for a moment. What you felt last night was *your* power, completely free of the totem's pull."

My fear subsided, and I picked up a fluffy roll. "Well, we won't have to worry about it affecting me again. After I eat, I'm going to throw it out the window."

"That makes me unbelievably happy."

I shared his warm grin. Nerves tickled my stomach once more, this time light and welcome.

"Terrot!" Camilla strode to our sides, her sheathed cutlass earning her sharp glares from the priestesses. "We found something in Ruger's notes you should see. It might be a lead on Elizabeth Sconcewood."

"I'll be right there." Animo stacked a biscuit onto his plate, then touched my arm. "I'll see to this. Once you're done eating, come find us."

I nodded and finished filling my plate as they retreated to the hall. Food in hand, I strolled through the tables. Each was ornately carved of pale stone and depicted scenes of Emode and her followers. I settled on an empty bench held up by a violinist with antlers protruding from his head.

My mind wandered as I nibbled on a roll. If Ruger's notes were correct, Elizabeth Sconcewood had taken the Staff of Realms into Avonshere. Following it there would be a death wish, which left us… where? We couldn't pursue our most promising lead, Aspectu had disappeared from my dreams, and *The Dragon's Bane* could be anywhere in Meridian waters.

I sighed, resting my head on my hand. *What am I missing?*

"May I join you?"

I glanced up. An elderly woman stood before me, aged burns running along her jawline and her silver waves tucked into the hood of her traveling robes.

"Of course," I said, straightening.

The woman took a seat, setting down her plate.

Her brown eyes… They wound through my memory, an unscratchable itch.

"What brings you to Aleddai?" she asked.

"Shelter. We… were separated from our party and needed a place to stay until we could find our way back."

"Most people come in search of something. It's what Emode is known for—guiding lost souls to a new calling."

"Is that why you're here?"

The woman smiled, the wrinkles around her hazel eyes crinkling. My stomach flipped at the familiarity.

"I am here for someone very dear to me. She has been lost for a long time, and no matter how hard I search, I seem unable to find her."

"I am sorry to hear that."

"Your sympathy is kind." She set down her fork to extend a hand. "I am Elizabeth Sconcewood."

If my face betrayed my shock, Elizabeth did not let it show. "Megs Mohler," I blurted, shaking her hand.

Still ignoring my identity, she held down a sausage with her fork, slicing it into bite-sized pieces. Was this a ploy to gain my trust, or did she truly not realize who I was? After all, only *Natalia's* wanted poster showed my face.

"How long have you been in Aleddai?" I asked, taking a bite of food.

"I arrived late last night," she replied.

"From where?"

"Oh, I had a long journey across many kingdoms. As I said before, I have been searching for quite some time."

I forced a smile, but my insides crawled. *She looks so innocent.* But I couldn't allow her gentle appearance to sway my judgment.

"Forgive me, but I must excuse myself." I stood, hoping she wouldn't notice that I'd barely eaten half of my food.

"Perhaps I'll see you again."

"I have no doubt of that," I replied. I all but ran from the courtyard, fighting the urge to look over my shoulder. Was Elizabeth watching me? Would she wait until I had passed through the doorway to rise, prepared to pursue?

I clenched my fists, forcing the mental spiral to an end. This wasn't a misfortune—it was a blessing. Elizabeth Sconcewood sat in the dining hall, leaving her room and belongings defenseless. But first, I had to find it.

I pulled the totem from my pocket and approached a priestess. "Pardon me, but do you know which room Elizabeth Sconcewood is staying in? She left this behind, and I would very much like to return it to her."

"Oh, of course!" the priestess replied. "Her room is in the eastern wing. Come, I will show you."

She guided me down the hall and through another courtyard before arriving at a curved, mahogany door.

"Here we are."

"Thank you." I reached for the knob, then hesitated. "Did she have any companions? I would hate to intrude."

"No, I do not believe so."

Excellent. "Thank you so much."

The priestess smiled, then retreated down the hall. I pushed the door open and slipped into a room much like mine: simple furnishings lined the perimeter, flecked with items that likely belonged to Elizabeth. Closing the door behind me, I began my search.

The staff was too tall to be concealed in any of the drawers, so after checking under the bed, I turned to the small closet. A single worn cloak hung on the rack, and a small pile of garments had been tossed onto the floor. I pulled a dress from the pile, unveiling a wooden chest.

My breath iced in my lungs. An engraved wolf stared up at me, nestled by a crescent moon. *My chest.* The one that had been stolen in Medea along with the restrictor cuff.

The same restrictor cuff the Hunter used against me.

The dress fell from my hand. *Belinda spoke of this… they sold the chest to Elizabeth, but was that before or after they joined forces with the Hunter?* My mind raced, spiraling through fragments of conversation as I fought to find the truth.

The door opened. I whirled around. Elizabeth Sconcewood stood in the doorway, her hand hovering on the knob. I froze like a spotted deer, staring at the woman whose silver guise of innocence had turned black.

Her eyes widened at the sight of me, but she quickly regained her composure, closing the door behind her.

"Rose." The name brought a smile to her lips. "I thought it was you, but after all this time, I couldn't be certain."

My hand slid to my dagger. "You don't know me."

"*You* don't know *me*," she replied. "But you should. Look at me, Rose, and tell me that time has not stolen all of our memories."

My grip wavered on my dagger's hilt. I *did* know her. Age had withered her face, chipping away at her fair features until the remains were all but broken. But it failed to steal her stance. The way she carried herself with her chin raised, trained to support a crown that had long since fallen. All the years and scars of flame could not erase her own spark.

I stepped back. "You're dead. You were ill—you died at the monastery."

"And you burned with Darvyn. But that does not change who we are. You are Rosara Wolfe. And I am Margaret Wolfe, born Margaret Elizabeth Ravenspeer. Your grandmother."

"Stating a name won't make me believe you." I snatched my chest from the wardrobe, brandishing it before me. "You are a liar and a thief. You had this stolen from Medea. You worked with thieves allied with Natalia!"

"I did nothing of the sort!" she exclaimed. "I found a man selling that chest. He had seen you before, so I enlisted him to find you again. Whatever connection he had to Natalia was not shared by me."

My hand lowered. Her words aligned with Belinda's tale, but that didn't make her my grandmother. It was impossible.

"Rosara."

I flinched.

Elizabeth sighed, taking a seat on the bed. "You were born at midnight of the twelfth day of Cisay. Your mother thought it was a gift from Fate—a promise for your future to be great. Your father—my *son*—never truly believed in Fate's power, but he believed in you."

"I will not be swayed by stories."

"Then I will show you proof." She pointed at the chest. "Before it was your mother's, that chest belonged to your grandmother. If I am who I claim to be, the blood lock will open at my touch. If it fails, you may use that dagger of yours to kill me in any way you see fit."

"Fine." I passed her the chest, keeping my distance and a hand on my blade. My heart pounded, caught in my throat as Elizabeth pressed her thumb against the stone.

It opened seamlessly.

She's my grandmother. She's alive.

I threw myself forward, meeting her in a hug. "How?" I asked, my face buried in her shoulder. "How did you survive?"

She drew back. "I *was* ill when I left Del Hera. The sea air did little for my health, and after six months in Sybil, I was convinced my time had come. I sent a letter to James, saying goodbye." Grief dotted her gaze as she continued, "I received his reply in the form of a knight who told me that Del Hera had fallen and that my husband and son were dead.

"I can not be sure what kept me alive. Perhaps it was my heartache seething into rage. Whatever it was gave me enough strength to flee Sybil. The knight who found me helped me escape while the nurses built a tomb that would never hold me. Though I survived Natalia's attack, I was far too weak to be of any use. By the time I was well enough to pursue you and your mother, Darvyn had burned." She tucked my hair behind my ears then cupped my chin. "I am so sorry that I could not be with you these past few years."

I ran my fingers along the burns marking her jaw. "Where have you been?"

"In Avonshere. Even now, we still fight Natalia's reign."

"*We?*"

"No matter how many battles we lose, there will always be someone unwilling to kneel before tyranny." Her lips lifted into a determined smile I had last seen on a girl with red hair and green eyes. "The Ardent Pack remains. Its number has weakened, but not its heart."

"The Ardent Pack survived?" Shock washed over me like ice water. "I thought—I thought after Darvyn..."

"Darvyn was a tragedy, but it was not the end. And the Ardent Pack will always fight until the very end.

Until the very end. Tears pricked at the back of my eyes.

Margaret took my hands. "Now, I ask you, Rose, are you willing to fight with them?"

I drew in a breath. Heartbreak, elation, shock, grief, and a thousand more emotions I couldn't name overwhelmed me. My mind blurred, but my answer rang clear: "I am."

A CAUSE WORTH DYING FOR

W hen I arrived at Camilla's quarters, she, Animo, Ketch, and Belinda were all eagerly waiting to inform me that they had a good idea of where Elizabeth Sconcewood was traveling to. I, on the other hand, gave them Elizabeth Sconcewood *and* Margaret Wolfe, the former Queen of Avonshere.

"In other words, both of you are believed to be dead, but actually faked your deaths to escape Natalia," Ketch said. He sat at the small table beside Animo. "Can we be sure there aren't any other Wolfes running around with a falsified surname?"

Margaret took a seat on the bench opposite the dwarf, gesturing for me to do the same. "Natalia was…*thorough*. When her purge of our line began, she would leave the bodies on display for all to see. If there are any left, their skills of disguise are quite impressive."

"I suppose we'll have to make do with just two of you," Ketch said good-naturedly.

"Two is more than enough," Camilla snarked from the corner, her suspicious gaze fixed on Margaret.

"After so many years of living under Natalia's rule, what can you tell us about Avonshere?" Animo asked.

"It is in ruins," Margaret replied. "Shades run amuck, and soldiers chase even the faintest whispers of rebellion, forcing the Ardent Pack to remain in the shadows. They cannot even disclose their loyalty to their families for fear they will be sold out to Natalia."

"Then how do we convince them to fight?" Animo asked.

Margaret took my hand, her eyes locked with mine. "We give them someone to stand behind."

"As warm as this show of faith is, we have more important things to focus on at the moment," Camilla said.

Margaret's gaze hardened, shifting to the pirate. "Such as?"

"The Staff of Realms."

"I can assure you that it is safe at my home in Avonshere."

Camilla folded her arms. "At what point did you think that bringing a powerful fae relic into Natalia's borders was a good idea?"

"Avonshere is Wolfe territory," Margaret replied icily. "It always has been, and it always will be."

"Besides, Marstaff Manor is practically a fortress," Belinda said from the bed.

Margaret's hand slipped to her pocket, where I could only assume a dagger waited. "How do you know where I live?"

"After he found out Natalia was offering a higher ransom for Rose, Ruger began researching you." Belinda toyed with the cuffs of her long coat sleeves. "I think he planned on stealing from you after we collected Natalia's bounty."

Margaret's eyebrows arched.

"It's a long story," I said. "Belinda is with us now, and Ruger is no longer a threat." My reply didn't erase the suspicion from my grandmother's eyes, but she removed her hand from her pocket.

"The better question is, how are we supposed to get into a kingdom where half of our company is wanted, preferably dead?" Camilla demanded.

"I have a contact," Margaret replied. "He specializes in forged travel documents."

The pirate scoffed. "Rose's face is plastered on every alley wall. The greatest forgeries won't help when the guards see her."

"Do you think me a fool?" Margaret snapped. "I know the dangers of entering Avonshere, and what's more, I know how to enter without being caught. If it is a risk too great for you, I see no need for you to remain."

A smile teased the corner of Camilla's lips. "Risk is one of the few things I trust."

Ketch clapped his hands together. "Well, that's good enough for me. When do we leave?"

"My contact lives in Cavbrooke," Margaret said. "We should reach him in a week or so, depending on the state of the mountain pass. After that, it is an eight-day journey to the border."

My stomach twisted. In a matter of weeks, I would be back in the kingdom I had run from.

Animo drummed his fingers against the table. "Let's say your contact and papers work. We cross the border without arousing suspicion, but what then?"

"We free Avonshere," Margaret replied.

"How?"

"Rose." Her smile lightened her eyes as she gazed down at me. "You are what we have been missing all these years. With you to lead the Ardent Pack, we cannot lose."

Animo frowned.

"Miss Margaret—Your Majesty," Belinda began, "I don't understand why you don't use the Staff of Realms."

"Kid's got a point," Camilla said, somewhat irritably.

I stifled an eye roll. *Kingdoms forbid she say something genuinely kind or encouraging.*

"Natalia has spent the better part of two decades studying the darkest kinds of magic," Margaret explained. "She has discovered ways to track surges of magical energy. If I used the Staff of Realms, she would know in an instant."

My heart sank. "Are you saying we can't use it?"

"Not *yet*," she said. "The detection spells only work within Avonshere's borders—she'll be aware of our departure and arrival locations. I have been unable to use it without revealing myself. However, the time will come when we no longer wish to remain in hiding. That is when we will use the staff."

Camilla's brow raised. "So Natalia can detect powerful magic, and you left said magic alone?"

"There's a difference between active and dormant magic," Animo said before Margaret could. "The Staff of Realms is inherently magical—however, that magic is dormant until it is used, at which point it would release a surge of energy." He glanced at Margaret. "I assume Natalia's spells only detect active magic."

She nodded. "Natalia will only know of the staff's existence in Avonshere when it is used. When we are ready to reveal ourselves, it will be an immeasurable asset. But for now, it must wait."

Wait until war. My plans of a ghostly assassination were long gone, but Margaret's words still landed like a blow to my chest.

It will be all right… You can do this. Break the cycle.

"We should leave tomorrow at first light," Margaret declared. "I'm sure we can scavenge enough supplies for the journey to Cavbrooke."

With that, we dispersed. Camilla followed Margaret, likely to interrogate her further, while Ketch and Belinda headed toward the kitchens. Animo remained in his room, shuffling through documents while Dobbins was… somewhere. I hadn't seen him since yesterday and assumed Camilla would fill him in at some point.

With no belongings to pack, I roamed the halls, finding my way to the balcony overlooking Emode's statue. Her hand hovered before me, while her head loomed high above, gazing out a window. Below, priestesses circled the pool, their soft whispers merging into a hum of worship.

I leaned over the rail. The totem slipped from underneath my collar, swinging above the praying priestesses's heads. I clapped a hand over it, slamming it against my chest.

When did I put it on? I had put it in my pocket so I could throw it away…but before I could, I had used it as an excuse to find Margaret's chambers. I must have instinctively put it back on before searching.

Rack. Why must my subconscious make amplifying my own darkness a reflex?

"Rose."

I shoved the totem under my shirt, forcing a smile as Animo joined me at the balcony rail.

"I wanted to ask you about Margaret," he said. "It must be overwhelming to discover she's alive."

I shrugged. "Perhaps. But it's also wonderful. I'm not alone anymore. There is so much expected of me, and although you have helped me for months, we both know that there are limits. I need someone more qualified than myself to help lead the Ardent Pack."

"If she were more qualified than you, Avonshere would be free."

I raised a brow as he leaned against the rail.

"Margaret doesn't have a plan," he continued. "She has spirit, yes, but no real army and no plan of attack. She's one side of a coin, and you are the other. You may not have the spirit of war, but you've always had a plan."

I leaned beside him. "You hate my plan."

"But you have one. And yes, I believe that long term it would cause more harm than good, but it does accomplish one thing—dethroning Natalia. That's something Margaret is far from achieving."

I chewed the inside of my lip. He was right. My grandmother might be able to sneak across the border, but even that had been described briefly. It was a great risk entering Avonshere, and if we made one wrong move, we could lose everything.

"I'm sorry," Animo said, reading my expression.

"Why? You're right."

"Me being right has a habit of squashing your hope."

"Natalia's the one who killed my hope. All you do is knock the moldy scraps from my hand before I poison myself with them."

He smiled slightly. "Margaret is still an ally. And she's survived all these years, which means there's a strong chance that she *can* help us pass the border guards. That's one step closer to the Staff of Realms."

"Which we can't use."

"*Yet.*"

"Yet." I straightened. "So, how do we begin a war?"

"Allies, troops, a plan of attack." He ticked off each obstacle on his fingers. "And most importantly, a cause worth dying for."

"Is it worth it to you?"

"Yes."

Shock like lightning raced through my chest. Looking into his eyes, I knew he meant it. *But why?*

"I thought Avonshere was just a means to an end," I said, my voice barely a whisper.

"You aren't."

My cheeks flushed, my mind spiraling into a panic trying to comprehend the meaning of his words. *You aren't.* All of this was to help him one day free Vaera. That was why he first went looking for me. When had that changed?

Animo glanced away, his palms flattening against the stone rail. "If I overstepped—"

"No, not at all." I shook my head, turning my attention to Emode's statue. "I have a lot to think about with Margaret and Avonshere. That's all."

"Of course."

Tense silence settled between us. His words echoed in my mind. *You aren't.* I wasn't a quest or leg of a journey. I shouldn't have been surprised he would be willing to die on our mission—he'd proven that time and time again. But hearing him say it aloud was different. It was real and horrifying and evoked feelings I had never before explored.

I suppose there's a first time for everything.

Before I could speak, Ketch's voice reached my ears.

"Rose! Animo!" He sprinted toward us, sliding to a stop at the doorway. "Shades…" he managed, sinking against the wall. "Half a league… Two battalions."

Animo's hand shot to Bathril's hilt. "We can't let them track us. We'll have to take a stand here."

Ketch straightened, breath regained. "The priestesses won't like it. The mean one decided to kick us out two minutes ago."

"Then we leave," I said. "I know that fleeing is risky, but if Natalia discovers Margaret we'll lose our advantage."

Animo's hand dropped. "You're right. Outrunning them is our best option. We'll have to travel light and take horses only—no cart."

"There's a stable out back," Ketch said.

"Good," I said. "Animo, you fetch the horses. Ketch and I will collect the others along with our belongings."

We parted ways, completing our assigned tasks before gathering in the courtyard. Screams floated through the air, but by the time they reached Aleddai, we were already gone.

IMPERIAL DECIET

I sat on the rim of one of Cavbrooke's fountains, sipping hot chocolate while the water's cold spray misted my shawl and hair. We were five days into the twelfth month, Cisay, and already the temperature had forced us to purchase fresh cloaks and gloves, especially since the rime chill would only deepen as we continued north to Avonshere.

Cavbrooke's population trickled like a stream through the neatly cobbled streets. Half-timbered buildings lined the road, each one with beams painted a cheery color. Flowerpots hung from wrought-iron balconies, their blooms still strong despite the frost melting on their petals. I'd never seen a town so lovely before—even the sheep that wandered the street did so as a picturesque little herd.

Animo joined me on the fountain, faint tendrils of steam rising from the mug in his gloved hands. "I spoke to Margaret. She's refusing to tell me anything about her contact."

"Still?"

During our journey, Animo and Camilla had tried every vein of questioning available to no avail. Margaret simply insisted that she had a plan and that we should trust her.

"She's arranging the meeting in *there*." He nodded to a shop on the opposite side of the square. Bright-purple beams ran along the building's face. Above the matching door hung a sign that read, *Nicae's Candle Shop*.

I took a sip of rich, hot chocolate then asked, "What's the matter with it?"

"That shade on the door is imperial purple—it's made of crushed sea snails."

The memory of a Soren ambassador gifting me a gown of purple silk flitted through my mind. Having sole trade rights with Madoria, it was easy for Sorites to gain access to fineries such as pearls or the sea snails needed to make purple dyes. But it was a very different story for the rest of the kingdoms.

"Margaret's contact is wealthy," I realized.

Animo nodded. "And yet, he chooses to live in a small, unassuming town with only a painted frame to mark his status."

"What are you implying?"

"It's only a hunch, but Mydor has an extensive black market, and that shade of purple can be found all around town." He gestured at a hitching post across the street, which, sure enough, bore a small symbol painted in the same shade of imperial. "It could be a signal."

"If it is—if this is the black market we're dealing with, what would that mean?"

He turned the cup in his hand. "I'm afraid it would mean Margaret's contact is far more dangerous than we anticipated."

A chill raced through me, and I pulled my shawl tight.

Animo held out a hand. "Would you like more?" he asked, indicating my empty mug.

"Yes, please."

Taking the cup, he returned to the nearby chocolatier shop, passing Camilla and Dobbins as they exited an alley. Camilla walked a few paces ahead, her hands shoved into the pockets of her long coat and a scowl marking her face.

"I've had it with you," she said. "If I'd known you would be such an infantilized excuse for a man, I would have left you on my ship."

"I'm making a point," Dobbins hissed, grabbing her arm. She spun around, her fist cocked. He released her, retreating to a safe distance.

"Just remember what we're fighting for," he said.

Camilla scoffed, her eyes still rolling when she joined me at the fountain. "Where's your formerly buried granny?"

"*Margaret*, the former Queen of Avonshere, is meeting with her contact."

"Hmph." Her narrowed eyes followed Dobbins as he paced angrily.

"What's the matter with him?" I asked.

"He seems to have forgotten who gives the orders and who takes them."

Animo returned with Ketch, their hands full with mugs of hot chocolate. Sidestepping a wandering sheep, Animo handed me my drink.

"Thank you." I held it close, relishing in the warm steam and chocolate scent.

"Any sign of Margaret?" he asked.

I shook my head.

"So the old woman who shows up out of nowhere isn't entirely reliable," Camilla snarked. "How unexpected."

I pressed my lips together, fighting back a retort. Her hostility had increased since Margaret arrived. Admittedly, my grandmother's blatant distaste for pirates didn't improve the situation, but neither did Camilla's constant jabs.

"You may also notice that a certain little girl isn't here either," she added. "I do hope she isn't off betraying us."

I glanced around the square. Where *had* Belinda gone? She had been with us when we arrived, but I didn't remember seeing her after Margaret left.

"How about a drink?" Ketch offered Camilla a cup of hot chocolate. She took a single sip before frowning and pulling a flask from her pocket, emptying a significant amount of alcohol into her mug.

Ketch watched mournfully. "You really disappoint me sometimes."

She smirked. "You sound like my father."

He shook his head, then wandered off to pet a sheep while she drained her mug. Margaret emerged from the candle shop, followed by a burly man, his glower unsually deep for a candle-maker. He folded his thick arms, planting himself before the imperial door as Margaret approached us.

"My contact is ready to meet," she said.

"Finally." Camilla set her mug down on the fountain rim.

"Ketch!" Animo called.

The dwarf looked up from the sheep he was petting. It nudged him—a plea for attention that ended with Ketch on his back, squirming to avoid further trampling. He scrambled to his feet, sprinting behind Camilla to make her legs a shield. The captain rolled her eyes.

"Where's Dobbins?" Animo asked, scanning the empty square.

"He'll be fine out here," Camilla replied, tossing her red sash—which she now wore as a scarf—over her shoulder.

Animo didn't press. We set aside our mugs, and the four of us followed Margaret past the glowering man and into Nicae's Candle Shop. A strong mix of scents overpowered my senses: floral, seasonal, sharp, warm—they melded together in a powerful aroma, emanating from the candles that lined the shop. Each one was unique with elegant carvings, swirling colors, or twisted wax bodies. Despite the admirable creations and clear prosperity, no one but us occupied the store.

The muscular attendant stopped by the counter, his arms still crossed. "No weapons past this point."

I stiffened. The candles' beauty had made me forget the reason we had come.

"Do as he said," Margaret instructed, handing over a dagger. The attendant placed it in a large, wooden tray numbered *42*.

I caught Animo's gaze. He nodded, undoing his sword belt, and my anxiety faded slightly. I relinquished my dagger as Ketch emptied his pockets of explosives. He handed over his final vial, and our eyes all shifted to Camilla.

She smirked. "This'll take a minute."

CHAPTER FIFTY-TWO

DEN OF BEASTS

I t took Camilla significantly longer than a minute to remove all her weapons. Under the attendant's deep glare, she relinquished her cutlass, sixteen daggers, three small knives, and a piece of sharpened wire she'd braided into her hair. Yet after all that, I still suspected she had something hidden, though I had no interest in knowing where.

Once we were satisfactorily weapon free, the attendant unlocked a door behind the counter and led us into a dimly lit room, hazy with pipe smoke. The scent of candles faded into that of liquor—men and women drank at round tables, their bodies draped in fine silks. Cards lay before them, along with large sums of gold.

My eyes widened. "It's a gambling den."

"Speakeasy," Camilla said. Her narrowed gaze flicked from a man's pipe to

Margaret. "It's not just for drink, is it?"

My grandmother ignored her question, guiding us through the array of tables to a back door. Two men stood guard, their thick arms crossed and eyes boring into us.

"You can only bring one with you," the first guard said.

Margaret stiffened. "Our arrangement was—"

"Boss's orders," the other guard said.

Margaret pursed her lips, her fists clenched at her sides. "Very well. Rose and I will attend the meeting. The rest of you will remain."

Animo stepped forward, placing a hand in front of me. "I'm not sure that's a good idea."

Her sharp gaze landed on him. "I do not appreciate the insinuation that I would intentionally put my granddaughter in harm's way."

"Then let me go instead, and you may prove your intentions."

"Animo, it's fine." I pushed his arm down gently. "I'll go."

"Yes, please," Camilla added, leaning over his shoulder. "I have complete faith that the two of you have the bargaining abilities to secure these vital documents."

Animo shoved her. She easily turned into a spin, landing at one of the bravit tables.

"Well, then, gentlemen, what's the buy-in?" she asked, sliding into a chair.

I stifled an eye roll, blocking out the sound of her bantering voice.

Animo pulled me aside. "You don't have to do this if you don't want to," he murmured.

"It will be all right. One quick meeting, and then we're on our way."

He nodded, stepping back. The men unlocked the door, and I followed Margaret through to a dark hallway. I glanced back, giving Animo a reassuring smile.

Camilla shot to her feet. "You old fool!" she exclaimed, her eyes locked on Margaret.

The first guard ducked through the door, slamming it behind him. "Follow me," he instructed.

I froze, staring at Margaret as unease churned my stomach. *What have you brought us into?*

Doubt flickered in her gaze. She took my arm, guiding me along as we followed the guard down the empty hall. A few turns led us to another door with guards on either side. At the command of the first guard, they opened the door and ushered us through to an office draped in purple velvet.

Imperial purple.

My gaze fell to the man sitting behind a mahogany desk. Snow-white hair shone atop his head, stretching down into a trimmed beard. He leaned back in his chair, his piercing, black eyes watching us.

"Elizabeth Sconcewood," he said, his deep voice rolling over words. "It has been a long time since you graced me with your presence."

"Nelos Caine." Margaret extended a hand which Nelos took, brushing a kiss against its back. "It has been too long."

His gaze shifted to me. "And who is your associate?"

"My granddaughter," she replied, a placid smile on her face.

"Ah, of course." Nelos took my hand and inclined his head. "It is an honor to make your acquaintance, Rosara Wolfe."

My heart dropped with Margaret's smile.

"I'm afraid you are mistaken—" she began.

"Please, Elizabeth. Did you really think I wouldn't know?" He clicked his tongue with disappointment.

Margaret clenched her jaw. "Identity changes nothing," she said stiffly. "Our deal stands, does it not?"

Nelos placed a hand atop his chest. "I am nothing if not a man of my word." Retreating to his desk, he retrieved a small stack of parchment bound with twine. "Falsified credentials for three, and documentation for the transportation of hazardous bodies, signed and stamped with a plague doctor's seal."

Margaret held out her hand, but he pulled the papers back. "Payment first."

She withdrew a sack of gold from her belt. "Five hundred mynet, as usual."

"That was the old price."

Anger flashed in her eyes. "You said the deal had not changed."

"The *deal* has not changed," Nelos said, tucking the papers into his coat pocket. "Merely the price."

"I have no more gold."

"Good. I no longer desire it." He beckoned for us to follow. With no other option, we obeyed, trailing behind him into the hallway. The three guards fell into formation behind us.

"Have their companions been apprehended?" Nelos asked.

"Soon," a guard replied.

Nelos stopped, turning to fix the guard with a deadly glare. "See that it's done."

The guard nodded stiffly, then broke formation, marching in the direction of the speakeasy.

"If you harm any of our companions, our deal will be void," I warned, fighting to keep the fear from entering my voice.

Nelos continued walking as though I hadn't said a word.

"Did you hear me?" I asked, my voice rising. "I said—"

"You should not worry about your friends, Your Highness. Their fate now lies with you."

"With us?" I repeated.

"Shortly before your arrival, I was informed that Elizabeth Sconcewood would bring me a princess with a two-hundred-thousand mynet bounty on her head, along with a wanted elf, dwarf, and pirate. I would collect quite a sum if I handed you over."

If.

"Enough games, Nelos," Margaret snapped. "If you wanted to turn us in, we would be in chains already."

"Indeed. I believe that potential remains for our working relationship, but it is up to you to prove yourselves."

Nelos led us down a steep flight of stairs, stopping before an iron gate with darkness looming beyond its bars. Drawing a key from his pocket, he unlocked it, pushing it open with a grating creak. He waved his hand, and the guards shoved me and Margaret forward. We stumbled through the gate, falling onto a sandy floor. Iron clanged shut, and a key turned.

"Rose?"

I blinked, struggling to discern Margaret's silhouette in the black.

"I'm here." I pushed myself up, dusting sand off my pants. "Although, I'm not sure where *here* is."

She sighed. "Rose, forgive me. I never suspected that Nelos would recognize you—"

"It's fine. Let's focus on escaping."

She let out a low, rattling breath. I felt about the dark until my hands landed on her stiff shoulders.

"Are you all right?" I asked.

"I didn't make that sound," she whispered.

I froze. *Then what did?*

Blazing, orange light cut through the darkness as flames raced around the room in a spiral formation. I threw my hand up to block out the glow. The fire settled to a low burn along the rough stone wall that resembled a cave more than a room.

My adjusted eyes fell to a red stain dried into the sand. Paw prints, bigger than my hand led from it, followed by dragging tracks. Both ended at a barred door opposite us.

"It's an arena," I breathed.

"Welcome, Elizabeth Sconcewood and Rosara Wolfe!" Nelos's voice boomed from above. He stood on a balcony, backed by his speakeasy patrons. They held drinks and slips of paper—were they *gambling* on us?

"You came in search of this," Nelos continued, holding up the papers, "and you were prepared to pay with gold. But now you must pay with blood."

My hand shot to the empty sheath at my waist. *Rack. Why did I agree to hand over my dagger?*

"If you win, you may have your documentation. And if you lose, your bodies will be delivered to Natalia Thornsworth."

"Nelos, you snake!" Margaret shouted, rushing forward.

"You bargained with this snake," he retorted. "So do not cry when you feel its venom." Holding his hands high, he ordered, "Raise the gate!"

Cheers erupted from the balcony. Chains rattled as the gate opposite us rose into the archway. I stepped back, pushing Margaret behind me as my mind raced.

Our blades were gone, and I had no doubt that our fists would be useless against whatever came out of that arch. That left my magic. But would it be enough? My hand slid to my pocket, my fingers taking in the shape of the totem I'd yet to throw away.

Is it worth it to tempt the beast?

A shape shifted in the darkness—graceful despite its bulk. The torchlight fell on its dark-red coat as it breached the gateway. Dried blood coated its whiskers and bared teeth. The head of a lion gazed forward, but from its back protruded the head of a goat. As the creature began to slink around the side of the arena, I saw the hissing snake that was its tail.

My jaw fell slack. A chimera.

"Margaret," I said, my voice uncomfortably high. "I don't know how to kill a chimera."

"But I do—your grandfather faced one years ago. It has three heads but one heart. We must destroy all three heads *and* pierce the heart to kill it for good."

"With *what?*" I practically screeched.

The chimera worked its way around the arena wall, its front haunches lowered. It was stalking us. *Hunting* us. With every step, its claws dug into the sand, leaving flecks of dried blood behind. This wasn't its first time facing Nelos Caine's prisoners, and I feared that it wouldn't be its last, either.

Margaret tapped my shoulder sharply. "Your magic. You have power. Use it."

I closed my eyes, drawing in a deep breath. *It's been days since you used your magic. You have enough built up.* All I needed was a conduit, a tie to my elf heritage that would enhance my spells. One word to throw all of my power into—*fly.*

"*Voli.*"

Warm magic rushed through me, and the chimera flew across the arena, slamming into the wall with a pained yelp. The crowd gasped before collapsing into a mob of cheers and shouts.

The chimera cowered, pacing the edge of the arena like a kicked dog.

"Do it again," Margaret urged as the creature lowered itself, preparing to pounce.

I exhaled slowly, readying myself for another round. "*Voli.*" The same warm magic threw the chimera back against the wall, sending a sickening crack throughout the arena. Cheers, gasps, and boos erupted from above.

A steady ache resonated in my head. I closed my eyes. My arms hung heavy at my sides.

"Rose!"

My eyes snapped open. A red blur struck me, tackling me to the ground. The chimera's lion head roared in my face, smothering me with its hot, coppery breath.

I screamed, throwing up my hands as the monster's claws dug into my shoulders. I caught its neck with one hand, stopping its fangs inches from my face. My arms shook as my muscles weakened. With my free hand, I reached into my pocket, wrapping my fingers around the totem.

Forgive me.

The chimera's claws dug in deeper, sending a flash of pain and adrenaline throughout my body. A spell tore free, knocking it away and washing me in wicked magic. The beast within emerged, ready to destroy that which threatened me.

I wrenched a long claw from my shoulder as I climbed to my feet. Blood belonging to both me and the chimera coated my skin, yet my pain had faded. Without even casting a spell, the beast had healed me.

The chimera growled, struggling to stand. Its back leg hung useless and broken, and blood poured from one of its front paws.

"Keep going!" Margaret shouted above the booing crowd.

I clenched one fist around the broken claw and the other around the totem in my pocket. *We work together,* I told the beast. *You do not control me. You will not corrupt me.*

No, it seemed to say. *I will save you.*

Magic roared within me, flowing into the totem. The chimera collided with the wall, its lion neck snapping. It fell for a moment before slamming back, bone cracking against stone.

Again.

Blood spattered against the rock wall.

Again.

Ruger's body flashed in my mind. I dropped to my knees.

Again.

I couldn't stop the spells. I wasn't the one casting them.

Again.

Dark magic surged through me, so pure yet toxic, as though I were devouring poison meant to save my life. The chimera shrieked, writhing in the air.

The crowd's noise rose as the monster fell into the sand. Its lion head snapped around, twisted and broken yet still staring at me with yellow eyes.

I released the totem, fighting the urge to vomit. In my pocket, it couldn't harm anyone.

Margaret ran to my side. "You have to cast another spell. You have to kill it."

I shook my head as the beast screamed in my mind. "I can't."

Margaret's hand cupped my cheek, her confused and frightened eyes meeting mine. Her fingers closed around the chimera's claw, pulling it from my grasp. "Then I'll do it."

My grandmother stood tall as she faced the monster. It lunged, sharp paws raised. She dropped to the ground, slashing the creature's stomach as it soared above her. It landed with a roar, skidding across the sand as blood poured.

Margaret shifted, brandishing the bloody claw like a dagger. The chimera rose to its feet, its lion head lolling to the side. The goat's head turned to face Margaret, its eyes rabid with hunger and rage.

The chimera rushed forward, spewing flames from the goat's head. Fire licked Margaret's legs. I screamed. She threw herself into the sand, rolling to beat out her flaming dress.

I tackled the chimera to the ground. Channeling all my energy into my fist, I slammed it against the gaping wound Margaret had left on the monster's stomach. The goat's head unleashed another burst of flames that I narrowly avoided.

As the chimera struggled to its feet, the snake head lunged at me. I scrambled back, my elbows and heels propelling me across the sand as it advanced.

An explosion shook the arena. Dust and rock rained down as patrons scattered.

With the chimera distracted, I kicked its broken neck. The remaining two heads howled in pain. I sprinted across the arena to Margaret.

She pointed at the balcony. "Your friends."

My gaze followed hers. Animo's blade clashed with the guards's who formed a wall as Nelos retreated. Ketch dashed to the railing, a small vial loaded into his slingshot. He took aim, firing the projectile at the chimera. Glass shattered against its copper hide, and an explosion ripped it in two.

I clapped a hand to my mouth. The bleeding halves of the chimera smoked, twitching in the sand.

"Heads up!" Ketch's shout warned us mere seconds before two metal objects smacked into the sand—our daggers.

Margaret snatched hers, then approached the chimera's body. With a swift strike, she sliced through the snake's neck. Its jaws opened and closed as blood streamed, soaking into the sand.

Stifling a gag, I grabbed my blade and ran to the arena wall. I shoved my fingers into the cracks, allowing my adrenaline to fuel my climb. At the top, Ketch helped me over the railing while Animo skewered a guard with Bathril.

"Nelos has the papers," I said, sprinting down the hallway. Ketch followed, loading another explosive as he went.

The hall stretched straight, then dropped into a flight of stairs. I took them two at a time, ending at a thick, steel door.

Ketch cursed. "Panic room," he said, rapping the door with his knuckles.

"Can we get through?"

"Maybe. We'll need something stronger than this, though." He held up the vial.

You need me. The beast's voice slithered from my pocket. *I can destroy that door and Nelos Caine. Free me, and I will help you.*

"This should do the trick." Ketch drew a teardrop-shaped vial from his sock, giving it a quick toss before loading it in his slingshot. "You'll want to stand back for this one."

I didn't even question why he would carry dangerous explosives in his sock as I backed away and covered my ears.

The explosion knocked me and Ketch to the ground as it blew the door inward. We scrambled to our feet, sprinting through the smoke. It cleared to reveal an empty room.

My head swiveled on bare, iron walls. "Where is he?"

"I don't know." Ketch coughed, waving away tendrils of smoke. "Could we have gone the wrong way?"

I shook my head. "No, I saw him take this hall…" my gaze fell on a twine-tied stack of parchment on the floor.

I picked it up, flipping through the pages. My eyes widened. "This is the documentation we need. He… he left it for us." I turned back to Ketch. "Why would he do that?"

Ketch stiffened, pulling a slip of paper from the stack. "*Until we meet again,*" he read. "*Nelos Caine.*"

"What does that mean?"

The dwarf shook his head grimly. "Nelos Caine is the single largest black market dealer in Mydor—perhaps even in the Twelve Kingdoms. This note isn't a formality. It's a promise. He *will* be seeing you again, and when he does, you'll owe him."

I released a shaky breath, rattling the beast's cage. We might have defeated the chimera, but we hadn't won anything today. It was a test, and to my dismay, I'd passed.

VENOMOUS PROMISES

"**Y**ou foolish fallen ladies of the court," Camilla snarled, pacing the floor before the abandoned cottage's table. She'd kept her comments to light snark on the way out of Cavbrooke, only lashing out at Dobbins—whom we had found with Belinda outside of the candle shop—but now that we had taken shelter leagues away from any town, her simmering anger was ready to flame.

"You made a deal with Nelos Caine. *The* Nelos Caine. Now do you know why I highlight his name like that?" Camilla didn't wait for a response to say, "Because he has spent the past fifty years building a crime syndicate that stretches halfway across the Twelve Kingdoms." She jabbed a finger at me. "And now you are in his debt."

"I am not in his debt," I snapped. "I defeated his chimera. I paid his price."

"Yes, that's why he threw you in a cage with a chimera—he *wanted* you to kill it." She rolled her eyes, snatching Nelos's note from the table and shoving it in my face. "He will come back for you. It may not be for a month, it may not be for a year, but one day, he will return, and he will demand your services. And for your own sake, you had better hope that it's before you become queen."

I held her gaze. "You're right. Involving myself with criminals would be an awfully large blow to my reputation, wouldn't it?"

Camilla shook her head, taking a seat with a huff. "You played right into Caine's hand. And worst of all, you took a deal without knowing the price. One day, it will come back to bite you, and I'll be there to say I told you so."

"Look," Animo said, his voice unusually harsh. "We have the documentation we need to cross the border. That's what we should be focusing on."

"Animo is right." Margaret entered the living quarters and took a seat beside Ketch, who busied himself preparing fresh explosives. My grandmother had slipped away when we arrived, followed shortly by Dobbins and Belinda, neither of whom I'd seen since.

"But we did more than retrieve the papers." Margaret pulled a bloodstained bundle from her pocket.

"Perhaps you shouldn't—"

Before Animo could finish, she untied the bundle, letting the flaps fall open to reveal the chimera's snake head.

Camilla cursed violently, knocking her chair to the ground as she scrambled out of it and onto a large set of shelves. She drew her cutlass, her eyes wide as she pointed it at the head. "Why would you bring that *thing* here?"

"So I can extract the venom," Margaret explained.

"You'll have to extract my sword from your skull if you don't get that thing out of here!"

"Fine, then." Margaret stood, picking up the bloody head before exiting to a back room.

Only when the door closed behind her did Camilla climb down. "Nice grandmother you've got, Rose," she snapped, stalking away.

I stared at the table for a moment, still processing what I'd witnessed. "So

Camilla doesn't like snakes."

Ketch laughed. He leaned back in his chair, propping up his feet so only the tip of his mohawk peeked above his boots. "That's one way to put it. I have a theory that her fear of snakes is the very thing that drove her to a life of piracy."

"Interesting." I leaned forward, resting my chin on my hands. "Continue."

He straightened, matching my stance. "Have you heard of the siren cult *Hulaka?*"

"No. I didn't even know that siren cults existed."

Ketch extended his hands, his eyebrows raised. "That adds at least forty-five minutes to this story."

Animo chuckled softly, rising from the table. My gaze followed him as he examined the papers retrieved from Nelos Caine. Ever since Aleddai, he had been a constant presence in my thoughts. I wanted his arms around me again—only, this time, under better circumstances.

You're worth it, he'd said. Not Avonshere, not this quest, but *me*. Were his words a statement of solidarity, or did they mean he wanted more?

"Rose?" Ketch snapped his fingers in front of my face.

"What?" I shook my head. "Sorry, I drifted off."

"I gave you a detailed explanation of not one, not two,"—Ketch raised his fingers as he counted—"but *three* bloody murders. How does that not keep your attention?"

I rubbed my eyes. "It's been a long day. But I really do want to hear your theory."

He folded his arms begrudgingly. "All right. But I'll have to start from the very beginning. Twenty-eight years ago, Camilla's father struck a deal with the Divine Master of Wishes, Kinode—"

"Perhaps you should wait to finish the story tomorrow," Animo said. "We could all benefit from turning in early tonight."

"Fine," Ketch said. "But I will finish this story. Just... don't ask about it when Cammie's in earshot." He lowered his voice. "She's not fond of it."

"Got it."

Ketch hopped out of his chair and disappeared up the stairs. Animo took his empty seat. "You certainly know how to dig your own grave."

"He said the words *siren cult*. I have to hear the end of it."

"Trust me, the siren cult is the least ridiculous thing in that story." He glanced out the window at the darkening sky. "I'm going to do a sweep to ensure our perimeter is secure. But you should rest."

"I will." The empty promise left my lips without a thought.

A good night's sleep was sure to relieve my mind and aching body, but I was too awake to settle. Once Animo left, I wandered to the room Margaret had claimed. She sat at a desk, squeezing the snake's head against the rim of a glass vial.

I wrinkled my nose at the sight. "Is that the only way to extract the venom?"

"I'm afraid so."

"It's disgusting." I sat on the dusty bed, the worn mattress sinking beneath my weight. "Why do you even care to have it?"

"Chimera venom is powerful and incredibly rare," she explained. "It can be sold for hundreds, even thousands of mynet per bottle."

"What is it used for?"

"Spells, mostly. I only hope we never have a reason to use it against a person. It's a truly despicable way to die."

"How so?

Margaret gave the head a rest, turning in her chair to face me. "The venom is quite similar to dragon saliva. Both are highly flammable because most of their components are fire-based. I've heard tales of assassins injecting it into a target's bloodstream or slicking their daggers with it. It is said that the sensation is that of fire searing your veins. The victims *burn* from the inside."

I shuddered. "That's horrible."

"Indeed."

The thought of using it against Natalia flickered in my mind. All it would take was a drop of that venom on the tip of my blade, and she would die the death she so desperately deserved.

Why would you think that?

You had planned to murder her, anyway. Who cares how it's done?

I care. I'm not a...

Say it. Lie to yourself. Maybe this time you'll believe it.

But I couldn't believe it. And in my head, the word spun, an unceasing echo: *murderer.*

PART SEVEN

LIVING DEAD

The remainder of our journey through Mydor was uneventful: no sign of the Hunter, shades, or Nelos Caine. After a week, we reached the last village before the border. Margaret and I remained hidden while the rest of our company gathered supplies and traded three of our five horses for a cart. We only rode a few more hours before Camilla pulled the horses to a halt on an empty road.

"Half a league from the border," she declared, jumping down from the cart. "Time to die."

"I don't appreciate the references to death," Ketch said stiffly. He'd been fidgeting the whole ride and casting nervous looks at the coffins stacked in the back of the cart.

"You'll have five hours of air, and it's only a three-hour journey to Brennate," Animo reminded him.

"Of course, if you get scared and hyperventilate, you'll run out of air much faster," Dobbins said, his words carrying just as much of a bite as Camilla's but without the teasing undertone.

Ketch stuck his middle finger out at Dobbins, which was arguably the nicest thing he could have done.

Camilla and Animo removed the top layer of coffins—which had been weighed down with stones—before sliding the tops off the five on the bottom.

"Who's first?" Camilla asked, her sharp gaze sliding over us. Margaret and Belinda stiffened in their seats while Ketch ducked his head, suddenly inclined to pick twigs out of the wagon wheel's spokes.

I sighed. "I'll go."

Animo offered his hand, helping me step into the coffin. Lingering splinters poked through my leggings as I lay down. I gazed up at my friends's grave expressions, my heart pounding against my ribcage.

The lid slid shut. Darkness enveloped me as though I were a disembodied spirit.

The hammer fell, sending shockwaves across the coffin's lid. I tensed, tightening my arms around me. Soon more coffins would be piled atop me. Even if I wanted to, I wouldn't be able to break out. If something went wrong and Camilla and Dobbins were stopped by the border guards, I would die in this box. My body would be found with splinters beneath my bloody nails.

The wagon lurched. I bit back a cry, throwing my hands over my mouth, only to smack my knuckles against the top of the coffin.

I released a slow, shuddering breath. *It's fine, you're fine. This is the plan. Inhale and exhale. Slow and steady.*

I closed my eyes—nothing changed. The same darkness surrounded me, black as pitch and laced with almost hallucinogenic swirls.

We're following the plan. Nothing has gone wrong.

Yet.

I clenched my fists. Our plan was sound: Camilla and Dobbins weren't wanted by Natalia, so the guard would have no reason to stop them. If they were questioned, they had the documentation to prove they were transporting the bodies of Avonsheran citizens who had died from a contagious plague. Old laws allowed these deceased to be laid to rest in their homeland, and the circumstances of our *deaths* would stop any guard from examining the contents of the coffins—the seal of a plague doctor made sure of that.

At this point, it was up to Camilla, Dobbins, and Fate herself. All I had to do was lie in the darkness, breathe in the stale air, and wait for the wagon to stop. And when it did, I would be back in Avonshere. The one place I had promised I would never return to.

I tapped my fingers against my thigh. Was Animo right? Would they accept me as their princess, or would they remember my failures at Darvyn?

Anxiety racked my mind. I couldn't help but wonder if it would be best if the darkness swallowed me whole before the light could burn away my secrets. This was my one chance to make things right. If I failed, I failed for good.

My cycle of self-destruction continued to spin with no end in sight. I knew what had to be done, but I didn't know the first step toward doing it.

But I will. I will be better. I will become the person Avonshere needs me to be.

I held on to that promise, letting it soothe my nerves until the rocking of the wagon finally wore me to sleep.

Aspectu stood before me, pale as a ghost. Her torn, white dress fluttered around her legs. Bruises and clotted cuts speckled her skin, and a fresh gash on her forehead dripped blood.

Panic shot through me. I tried to run to her, but my feet remained rooted in the silver mist that coated the barren ground of my dreamscape.

"Aspectu!" I cried. "Aspectu, can you hear me? Please, say something!"

She stared out into the gray void.

"I know about the High Twelve," I said. "I heard what you said, and I will try to reunite them, but I don't know how or why. Aspectu, please talk to me. I need your help. I need to know how to save my kingdom."

Aspectu opened her mouth, unleashing a sharp, agonizing scream. She fell to her knees. The world flickered around us. Dark stone walls loomed over me. Then, in a flash, the colorless dreamscape returned.

"Aspectu?"

She raised her head, wounds healed. Her gaze found mine, and a smile crossed her lips. "Rosara."

"Aspectu, what—?"

"Please forgive me," she said, stepping forward. The mist swirled as she moved, tendrils twining around her ankles. "The spells I use are tricky. I cannot always control them as well as I should."

"But you were hurt."

"You do not have to worry about me. I will be just fine."

"Can you—can you answer my questions?"

She held out her hands. "Whatever you ask."

I took a deep breath. "How—?"

Aspectu gasped as though she had been stabbed. Her eyes bulged out as her balance wavered.

"Aspectu?"

Her eyes rolled back into her head. Then, like a bird shot down at the peak of its flight, she fell backward into nothingness.

CHAPTER FIFTY-FIVE

HONOR AND SORROW

I awoke, gasping for breath. Hot, stale air met me—breathed ten times too many. My cramped muscles ached, and my mind screamed, fruitlessly searching for relief from the darkness.

The memory of my dream pounded against my head. Aspectu seemed so… deranged. Like an animal trapped in a cage, descending into madness as it clawed at its bars. How could this be the wise and powerful Ancient Elf I had heard so many stories about?

And how am I meant to tell Animo what I saw?

The crack of breaking nails gave me reprieve. A sliver of light cut through the dark, followed by a wriggling piece of metal.

"Rise and shine." Camilla shoved hard on a crowbar, popping the lid off. She kicked the board aside and offered her hand.

I blinked up at her, stunned by the light and my dream. With a huff, she snatched my wrist, dragging me to my feet. I stumbled, my ankle catching on the coffin's lip. A hand caught me before I could hit the dirt.

"Are you all right?" Animo asked me, helping me stand.

"Dazed. But overall, fine." I found it within myself to smile. "And you?"

"Me what?"

"Are you all right?"

"Oh, yes. Of course." He moved on to help Camilla with the next coffin's lid.

He didn't realize I wanted to know he was all right. The thought hung in my mind like a storm cloud raining lead. Had I not asked him before? Did I never show concern? Did *anyone* show concern? Ketch, of course did, but could he be the only one?

Even in my darkest moments, Animo had been there for me. He'd held me as I cried and forgiven me more times than he should have. In my own brokenness, I had taken him for granted.

Never again.

"Finally," Ketch moaned, stretching his limbs while Dobbins and Camilla freed Margaret and Belinda from their wooden confines.

I followed the dwarf's example, rolling my neck to relieve its tension. My gaze trailed along the barnlike ceiling before dropping to the hot glow of a furnace. Leather cloaks and crow-like masks hung from hooks on the walls, along with sturdy gloves—all items made to protect workers from contracting any kind of virus.

"We have thirty minutes before these things are scheduled to be incinerated," Camilla said, nailing a lid back onto one of the empty coffins. "Let's move."

I stepped forward to help, but Margaret caught my arm. "Let them handle it. There is something I must show you."

She guided me to the morgue doors. They slid open with a push, spilling light into the barn. I blinked in the sharp daylight, following her out.

A cold wind stirred the rime-browned grass at our feet. It stretched down a steep hill, interspersed with patches of green, before fading into the cobblestone streets of Brennate. My gaze trailed over the village, soaking in my first look at Avonshere in five years. A single word pressed against my mind: *Ruin.*

Dust covered the town like a blanket. It dirtied the cracked walls of homes and the scrawny dog gnawing on a meatless bone. Men and women walked about, working and farming, yet the fruits they bore were faint, and their bodies were thinned with hunger.

A little girl, no more than four, held on to the frayed hem of her mother's dress as she walked into town. *This is all she has known.*

A thousand emotions tore through me. That girl had been born into a kingdom of ruin, and now she was expected to breathe in this dead air and survive amid the terror of shades stalking the streets.

No. This was my kingdom. These were my people. And I would not let them die this slow death.

But you did. You *allowed this to happen.*

I stepped back, colliding with Margaret. Her steadying hand wrapped around my waist.

Through heavy breaths, I choked, "This can't be it."

Sorrow flooded her eyes. "I'm afraid it is. Natalia's paranoia continues to rage. Every whisper of rebellion tightens her grasp, forcing our people to live in fear. She has limited trading opportunities, cutting off many streams of income. It is a cursed circle that is driving our land into ruin."

A cursed circle….

I stumbled back into the morgue. The coffins had been stacked against the wall, joining nearly two dozen others. My breath caught.

"What are those?" I asked, pointing at the wall of coffins. "This… this morgue is for plague victims. There shouldn't be so many."

Margaret sighed, pulling her shawl tight around her shoulders as she joined me. "Those do not hold the infected. They hold members of the Ardent Pack. Or, as Natalia prefers to label them, traitors."

My head snapped around. "Why are they sent here?"

"Shame. When Natalia's men capture one of our loyalists, they are given a choice: bow before Natalia and die a swift death or refuse and be taken to Malecare to join her army."

My mouth slid open. Natalia had made the Ardent Pack into shades. Men and women willing to fight and die for their homes had had their souls ripped away, and their bodies turned into mangled monsters.

"Why?" I asked.

"She's mad and paranoid," Margaet said harshly. "*Why* does not matter. Motives do not matter. All that matters are the consequences of her actions."

I shook my head, pacing a slow circle. The memory of Natalia cowering on the floor of the witch's hut in the Silver Forest flashed through my mind. She had sought power for noble reasons—she meant to save her home. But the darkness had dragged her down. Had she tried to fight it? Did her life spin in the same circle as mine? Had her hope flickered, like a candle in the distance, only to fade into black? Did she loathe the part of her soul that pushed forward, knowing the result would be the same?

Destruction. Ruin. Regret.

Perhaps we did walk the same circular path. But my path had gone far enough. It would end *now*.

I straightened my shoulders, staring at the coffins stacked atop one another. "We burn them."

"What?" Margaret's brow furrowed. Behind her, the rest of my companions looked at me, confusion clouding their eyes.

"You heard me. We will burn each and every one of these coffins."

"That's why they're here." Camilla spoke slowly as though communicating with a drunken fool.

I shook my head. "Not incinerated. I want them burned on pyres, as we've always done. They will have proper funerals and be bestowed with the honor they deserve."

"I am sorry, Rose, but we can't." Margaret's eyes held sympathy, but it was obscured by the stone walls war had forced her to build.

"Animo—" My gaze bore the desperation I refused to allow into my voice.

He hesitated before nodding. "We can burn them here."

Camilla threw her head back. "Oh, come on. You can't possibly be fool enough to kill us all for the sake of a funeral."

"We won't," Animo said. "We'll do this quickly. No pyres—I'm sorry, Rose, but we don't have time. What we *can* do is incinerate them ourselves. Even if it's not traditional, we'll honor them."

I nodded. "Let's do it."

Camilla scoffed. "You have twenty minutes before I leave," she said. She dropped down into the driver's seat of the cart, propping her feet up.

Me, Animo, Ketch, Margaret, and Belinda worked together, carrying the first coffin to the furnace. At the door's edge, we paused, silence falling over us. The time for respectful words had come, but what was there to say? *Thank you for dying… Your sacrifice was not in vain… I will see justice done…*

What could we say that was not a lie?

"I'm sorry." The words slipped out without a thought.

Margaret's eyes met mine, tears spilling down her cheeks. "I'm sorry."

We pushed the coffin through. Flames consumed the wood, crackling and sparking.

I'm sorry.

I'm sorry for what I did all those years ago. I'm sorry it took me so long to understand. I'm sorry I ever left.

One by one, we gathered the rest of the coffins and slid them into the furnace. I gazed through the smoky door as the final coffin collapsed into embers.

Animo's hand fell onto my shoulder. "Rose?" he asked gently.

I looked up at him, tears blurring my vision. "When we arrive at the manor, I need to tell you something."

He nodded, and together, we joined our company in the back of the cart. Camilla snapped the reins, driving us out of the morgue.

I'm going to tell him. Every dark, loathsome detail would be revealed, and maybe, just maybe, once everything was said, my cycle of destruction could finally end.

I watched as the morgue faded into the distance, thick smoke rising from its chimney. My mind slid back to that night five years ago when Darvyn burned. In a few days' time, Animo would know the truth: it was all my fault.

MARSTAFF MANOR

Marstaff Manor rose against the horizon, a fortress of stone overgrown with ivy. The green growth clung to the old walls, twining around dark, desolate windows. A great moat circled the manor, a soft current shifting its brown waters.

Margaret jerked the reins back. I gripped the driver's seat as the cart lurched to a halt. The bed shifted as our companions rose to gain a better view of the raised drawbridge.

Cupping her hands around her mouth, Margaret called, "Christoph!"

Silence echoed back at us. With a huff, Margaret climbed down from the cart, striding to a large bell standing on our side of the drawbridge. She yanked on its rope, sending the sharp clang of metal ringing across the moat.

"Christoph!" she called again.

"What?!" a man's voice yelled from within the manor walls.

"I'm back, you fool," Margaret shouted.

For a moment, silence fell. Then chains rattled, clanking as the drawbridge lowered.

"Does he know who you are?" I asked as Margaret climbed back into the driver's seat.

"Christoph knows everything," she said. "You may speak freely before him."

She gave the reins a gentle snap, and we clip-clopped across the drawbridge. It raised behind us, followed by movement in the tower window. A dark figure crossed the wall walk, headed toward the manor.

Margaret drove the cart into an overgrown courtyard. Weeds ran rampant, poking through the cobblestone pathway that circled a large, stagnant fountain.

"The stable is out back," she said, passing the reins to Camilla. "Take care of the horses, will you?"

Camilla gave a bitter smile while I fought to contain a grin. That pirate could take control of her ship all she liked, but this was Wolfe territory.

Dobbins remained with her while the rest of us followed Margaret to the manor's looming entryway. She rapped sharply with the brass knocker. Locks disengaged, and the doors opened. An elderly man stood before us, wearing a good-natured smile that highlighted the deep wrinkles worn into his dark skin.

"That took longer than I expected," he said as we filed inside. "Was there trouble?"

"Nothing too serious," Margaret replied, hanging her cloak on an empty peg. "Everyone, this is Christoph Dunmore."

Christoph inclined his head.

"Christoph, I would like to introduce you to my granddaughter, Rosara Wolfe."

"Your Highness." Christoph bowed before me. "It is an honor to meet you at last."

"Likewise."

My reply earned me a soft laugh from him. "She has manners." He glanced at Margaret, his brown eyes twinkling playfully. "Are you sure she is your granddaughter?"

She shook her head, lightly slapping his shoulder with the back of her hand. "Says the knight who did not bow before his queen."

Christoph took her hand, bowing to plant a soft kiss on her knuckles. "I am grateful you have returned safely, My Queen."

"As am I," she replied, a soft smile on her lips. "But now there is much work to be done."

"All of which can wait until after supper," he said. "I have prepared a roast that will be ready in less than half an hour."

"How lovely. Rose, will you help me set the table?"

"Of course."

Leaving Animo, Ketch, and Belinda behind, I followed Margaret first to a washroom and then to the dining hall. Deep-red curtains obscured the tall, arching windows, blocking out the sunlight. The room relied on the light of the crackling fire and the large wooden chandelier that hung over the table for illumination.

Margaret gathered a stack of plates from the china cabinet, passing me half of them. Together, we set the table.

"How did you meet Christoph?" I asked, laying down a plate.

"Oh, we met years ago when I first came to Del Hera," she replied. "He was good friends with James. The three of us were close for a while, but Christoph's duties as a knight led him elsewhere. For decades, we lived our separate lives. Then Natalia took control, and Christoph returned to me. He's the one who smuggled me out of Sybil and nursed me back to health. He is the sole reason I'm alive today."

"He sounds like an honorable man."

"He is. And he will be a good friend to you, too." Margaret placed another plate with a muffled clink. "Christoph was your grandfather's most trusted knight. If we had gone to war while James was king, he would have chosen Christoph to command the armies of Avonshere. He has spent the past three years leading the Ardent Pack from the shadows, and I have no doubt that he will continue to do so under your command."

I set down my last plate, avoiding her eyes.

Camilla strode into the room. "The horses are taken care of," she said, tossing her cutlass on the table as she dropped into a chair. "Now, let's get down to business."

"You and I have no business to discuss, pirate," Margaret replied, gathering silverware from the china cabinet.

"Aww," Camilla crooned mockingly. "You don't trust me. Well, don't worry. I don't trust you, either, which is why I will not be leaving my personal survival in your hands. So tell me, Your Former Majesty—where is the Staff of Realms?"

"Enough," I snapped. "For its own safety, the staff's location should remain a secret, even from our company."

Margaret nodded approvingly, passing me a handful of cutlery. "I will assure you once more: the Staff of Realms is secure. You may search the manor top to bottom, but I assure you that you will not find a thing."

A smile quirked at the corner of Camilla's lips. "Promises, promises."

I gripped a fork, tempted to lodge it in the pirate's flesh. Before I could give in to the thought, Christoph entered, carrying a large roast ringed in vegetables. "Dinner is served."

Animo, Ketch, and Belinda followed him into the dining hall, and we all took our seats at the table. Silence overtook our meal, broken only by the scrape of knives on porcelain. Eventually, Dobbins joined us, scowling as he pulled out the farthest seat from Camilla.

Animo set down his knife, looking at Christoph. "Tell me about your armory."

The other man dabbed his mouth with a napkin before responding. "I'm afraid our supply is low. Natalia suspects all who are seen purchasing new weapons—especially in large quantities. We do have some swords and a fair amount of hunting bows."

"How many could that arm?"

Christoph bobbed his head, thinking. "Twenty. Perhaps a few more."

"What about the rest of the Pack? Are they armed?"

"Well enough." Christoph set down his fork, lacing his fingers together. "It is not weapons that we struggle with. It is finding a battle that we can truly win. Once you are revealed to be a member of the Ardent Pack, you will have no choice but to go into hiding, or else you will be in danger of your neighbors selling you out. Our men are willing to die for their kingdom, but they need to know that their sacrifice will not be in vain."

"Is it not enough to be thanked by a Wolfe?" Camilla's words dripped with snark. "Is that not the *very end* you so desperately seek?"

Margaret glared at her, but Christoph remained calm. "You think that's what those words mean?" He shook his head. "My dear, you have no idea. We do not say that to show our loyalty to a family. We say it so we never forget what we fight for. The end of Natalia's reign of tyranny. The restoration of a noble ruler upon the throne. The Ardent Pack may be loyal to the Wolfe name, but it is our people and our kingdom whom we fight for."

I leaned forward, my gaze fixed on Christoph. Despite his gentle words, fires of determination burned in his eyes. I understood why my grandfather had trusted him as a knight. I, too, wanted this man to lead the armies of Avonshere.

Camilla didn't reply, but something in her gaze had shifted. It wasn't caring—no speech could make her care for a kingdom—but the faintest hint of respect flickered in her eye.

"What happens if Natalia tracks us here?" she asked. "The border guard may not have cared about a few coffins, but if the people here are as loose-lipped as you say, word could easily travel back to Natalia that two Wolfes have returned."

"As you saw, the manor is on an island," Christoph explained. "There is only one way in—through the front doors. The drawbridge can only be opened from the tower, and I check the locks on every window before I sleep."

"Thorough." Camilla toyed with one of her braids. "Of course, if someone *were* to get in, you would all be trapped."

"In that case, we would have no choice but to use the Staff of Realms to flee the kingdom."

"Of course," she said innocently.

Across from me, Margaret's lips were pressed together so tightly that they had lost all color. She sighed, casting her eyes to the ceiling. The wooden chandelier was certainly a more pleasant sight than the pirate.

Camilla pushed her chair back. "Dinner was lovely, Christoph. And thank you, Margaret."

Her smile sent a nervous itch racing beneath my skin. The only reason she had joined us was because she wanted the payout of stealing Avonshere's royal treasures. She could have them, but only once the kingdom was free. And if she planned on starting early, I would kill her myself.

CHAPTER FIFTY-SEVEN

UNFINISHED CONVERSATIONS

"We need to talk." I pulled Animo away as Margaret and Christoph cleared the table. He followed me into a small sitting room and I closed the door behind us.

"Is everything all right?" he asked.

"Yes. No. Are you?"

He furrowed his brow, his lips parted.

I rubbed my temples. "I'm sorry, that was complete nonsense. The first thing I would like to know is if you are all right. We've had several battles recently, and you're always there for me and ensuring that I'm all right. I wanted to do the same for you, which is why I'm asking."

Kingdoms, that was almost as horrific as my first attempt.

To my surprise, Animo smiled. A twinge flashed through my stomach. "Thank you. I am all right. A bit of blood loss, but nothing irreparable."

"Good." A smile flicked across my lips, matching his.

"What did you want to tell me?" he asked.

My smile fell. *So much.* In the days it had taken us to reach the manor, I had practiced this conversation. But now, standing before him, the words crumbled into fragments of nonsense.

Perhaps I should ease into it. If I start with the least awful news, my tongue might loosen enough for the full tale.

"I saw Aspectu," I began. "When we crossed the border, I fell asleep, and she came to my dreamscape."

Animo straightened. "What did she say?"

"Nothing, really. But she was… strange. She was injured—"

"Injured?"

"Yes, but the wounds disappeared. And then she fell. But… there was this mist, and she seemed to be captive."

"That's not possible. Aspectu is the Ancient Elf. She can control any dreamscape she enters."

I shrugged helplessly. "I don't know what to tell you."

Animo turned away, running a hand through his dark hair. "Why would she be hurt?" he asked, seemingly to himself. "Could she—no… I have to see her."

"Can you use the dreamstone?"

"Yes, but I'll need a more powerful spell, considering *this*." He waved his wrist. "The ingredients won't be difficult to find—Christoph may even have them. If not, I can search the forest or go into town to an apothecary."

"Town? Animo, it's nearly nightfall. There will be shades."

I can't lose you to them.

"I'll find a way." He crossed the room, pausing before the door. "I need to do this, but we'll talk when I return."

"I understand," I murmured, my gaze on the floor. "Be careful—"

The door shut, leaving me alone with my secrets.

"It looks like rain." Camilla peered behind one of the sitting room's heavy drapes. The crackling fire reflected off the hilt of her cutlass, along with the faint shadow of Belinda, who sat on the floor, her knees pulled up to her chest.

"The sky seemed fine to me," Margaret said. She sat on a plush chair across from me, a piece of needlework in her lap. It was us four women who had retired to the sitting room. Ketch was refreshing his stash of explosives, Christoph was already preparing tomorrow's meal, and Dobbins had once again disappeared to Kingdoms-knew-where.

"Any sailor worth their salt knows when a storm's coming," Camilla replied, stepping away from the window. "And this one's ready to rage."

"Marstaff Manor is strong," Margaret said, pulling her thread taut. "Not even a hurricane can shake our walls."

Camilla scoffed. "A hurricane would send that chandelier of yours crashing down in a pile of flames."

"The chandelier is secure," Margaret snapped.

A ghostlike smirk flashed across Camilla's features. "If you say so." She strode out of the room, passing Ketch as he entered, traces of black powder smeared on his forehead.

"Is your supply restocked?" I asked.

"Doubled, actually. I have enough to fill both socks." He shook his leg, grinning as glass clinked dangerously. "And now, I can take a moment and relax." He flopped down onto the floor and drew a deck of cards from his pocket. "Anyone up for a game?"

"I suppose." There wasn't anything I could do until Animo returned, and a game might relieve the anxiety burrowing through my brain. I slid to the floor, sitting across from Ketch.

He gave the deck a shuffle. "What about you, Belinda?"

"Sure," she said, crawling over to sit next to me.

"Excellent! Margaret, care to join?"

"I'm quite all right," she replied, rising to take her needlework elsewhere.

"That's just fine." Ketch shifted to an overhand shuffle. "We can have fun, just the three of us." He dealt us each three cards. The game is simple. Each round, you will place a card face down. Your goal is to play a card higher than your opponent. Two out of three rounds wins the game."

"Easy enough," I said, gathering my cards.

"In theory, it is. The trick is strategy. You only have three cards, and there is no trading or redrawing. You can play by chance, throwing down whatever feels right, or you can attempt to predict your opponent's strategy. Will they start with their highest or get rid of their lowest cards first?"

"I'll play by chance." I put down the first card I touched. After a moment of contemplation, Belinda played her own.

"Turn," Ketch instructed. We flipped over our cards, mine the six of shields and Belinda's the king of blades. "Belinda wins."

Seeing as chance had disappointed me, I took a moment to consider my move on the second round. Belinda played a king on the first turn. Was it confidence, or did she have more than one high card? Perhaps she wanted to be certain to win the first round. But I hadn't looked at my card…

"And there's the tricky part." Ketch grinned, looking between us. "You try to figure the other one out, sending your mind into an endless circle of possibilities that you can never truly understand."

"I'm not sure I like this game," I said, laying down the nine of crowns.

Ketch shrugged. "At its heart, it's chance. There's always a chance you'll stop playing. But if you stop now, there's no chance you'll win."

We played his game for nearly an hour, victory bouncing between me and Belinda. Ketch was right: I was never able to discern her thought pattern. After I won three full games, Belinda and I were tied and down to the final round. She turned her final card over in her hand.

"If I win," she began softly, "I have to tell you something. But if I lose, I don't."

I glanced at Ketch. He shrugged slightly—he didn't know her mind any better than I did. "All right," I said. "I'll take your deal."

She played her card.

"Turn."

Two kings.

"It's a tie," Ketch declared.

Belinda stared at the cards, her face twisted with indecision.

"Belinda?" He leaned forward, meeting her eyes. "If something's wrong, you can tell us."

She bit her lip. "I… I've heard things. Talk."

"What sort of talk?" he asked.

She opened her mouth to speak, but the door swung open. Camilla strode inside, followed by Dobbins. Belinda's mouth snapped shut, her eyes tracking them across the room.

"Belinda?" Ketch asked gently. "What is it?"

"Never mind." She rose, hurrying to the stool by the fire.

"What was that?" I whispered, my gaze flicking to the pirates pouring glasses of whiskey by the fire.

"I wish I knew." Ketch packed up the cards, his shoulders tense. "She doesn't seem to trust them, though."

I watched Camilla and Dobbins as they tossed back the liquor. Narrowed eyes, hushed voices, hands on cutlasses—I couldn't blame Belinda's wariness.

CHAPTER FIFTY-EIGHT

BLACK SANDS

The storm struck in the middle of the night just as Camilla had predicted. I awoke, well after midnight, to rain thrumming against the window, occasionally cut by the clap of thunder.

With a sigh, I dragged myself out of bed. I hadn't bothered to change before falling asleep, simply unbraiding my hair and letting it hang in tangled waves. I tugged at a thick knot. *What I wouldn't give for an elf comb right now.*

I stared absently at my chest, sitting on the shadowed dresser. Like lightning striking the sky, it hit me. *It's the twelfth of Cisay. It's my birthday.*

A nervous smile crossed my lips. Perhaps this new age could be my new beginning.

A sharp knock came at my door. My hand flew to my dagger.

"Rose?"

I relaxed at the sound of Animo's voice. "Come in," I called, lighting a candle.

He stepped inside, a satchel slung over his shoulder.

"What took you so long?" I asked, scanning his body for any sign of injury. To my relief, none were visible.

"I had to find the ingredients for the spell," he explained, pushing the door shut. "That shard in my wrist keeps me from properly navigating my dreamscape, so I need you to be my compass."

"By using magic?" Unease flickered within me. "I thought that would kill you."

"*Could* kill me."

I laughed sharply. "Oh, well, that changes things."

"Rose—"

"No, Animo. I won't risk your life for this."

"You won't have to." He raised his wrist. "The shard's restrictions are… complicated. From what I've learned, it rejects magic, twisting it into the opposite, almost. That's why healing spells fail. The magic is corrupted, so instead of healing, it harms. But this spell isn't affecting my body—it's reaching into my mind."

"I don't want to hurt your body *or* your mind."

"I promise you won't."

I shook my head. "I'm not willing to take that chance."

"But I am. This is a risk I have to take."

I sighed, pacing the room's length. "Even if I agreed, there's no guarantee it would work. A few weeks ago, I failed to perform a simple healing spell."

"A few weeks ago, you doubted yourself," he replied. "Your power is not limited—it's untapped. You believed that the totem is what gave you strength, but it cannot create magic, only amplify what already exists."

I wrapped my arms around myself. "That proves that what exists inside of me is dangerous. It shattered the restrictor cuff in the Silver Forest. For all we know, it could do the same to the shard. It could cut your veins, and you would bleed to death internally."

He stepped forward, taking my hands in his. "I know it's dangerous. But I *need* you to do this."

"I want to help you, but…"

"No, no buts." A beg drowned his voice. "Please, Rose, Aspectu is all I have."

I clenched my jaw. "Fine. I'll do it."

His shoulders relaxed with a relieved sigh. He took a seat on the floor, withdrawing an intricately carved candle from his satchel. "The spell is to be performed over a flame."

"Is that one of Nelos's?" I asked, settling on the hard wood.

Animo nodded, pulling a pair of linen-wrapped bundles from his satchel. "Ketch did a bit of shoplifting when he retrieved our weapons."

"Hmm." I picked the candle up, taking in a deep breath of its floral scent. For a criminal mastermind, Nelos was a surprisingly talented candlemaker.

I set it down, and Animo struck a match, lighting the fresh wick. He untied the bundles, revealing mugwort and rosemary.

"These herbs will help protect me from the magic and make the spell dormant. The final step is, well…" His hand slipped to the dagger on his belt. "I'm sorry, Rose, but the spell requires blood."

"It's fine." I offered him my palm. He placed the cold blade against my skin. Pain flashed as he sliced, before settling into a sharp sting.

He wiped the blade on a fresh cloth before using the tip to break open the nearly healed cut he had sustained in Daria. Blood bubbled as he placed the mugwort and rosemary atop his palm. Drawing the dreamstone from his pocket, he added it to the assortment.

"Lie down," he instructed. I followed his lead, lowering my body to the floor. The candle burned between us, its golden light flickering in Animo's eyes. He reached out, guiding my hand atop his. My cut stung against the dreamstone's smooth surface.

He handed me a piece of parchment. "Whenever you're ready, read this spell."

I recited the words in my head, familiarizing myself with the syllables' rhythm before speaking. "*Arnui te aruni, iman te entai, erhae en somunus.*"

The totem burned in my pocket. The Beast stirred inside me, its voice twining through my mind. *I'll help you.*

I squeezed my eyes shut. *No… no, I don't need your power.*

The beast's presence faded. Had I quelled it, or had the spell? I opened my eyes; Animo lay before me, his hand covering mine.

Disappointment settled over me. "It didn't work. Why didn't it work?

"I think it did." Animo examined his palm—completely healed.

My gaze shot to my own. Not even a drop of blood sullied my skin. But if we were in a dream…

"Why does it still look like the manor?" I asked.

Animo stood and helped me to my feet. "Dreamscapes are formed based on a person's subconscious. Since we both entered awake, it must have used a common thought: this room."

"How do we find Aspectu here?"

The bedroom door creaked open, pulled by an unseen hand. Beyond the frame loomed a sky, red as blood. It stretched as far as the eye could see, its horizon meeting a plane of black sand. Silver lightning sliced through the dark clouds, landing with a sharp crack and spitting granules of sand into the air.

I shrank back. "What is this place?"

"It's *wrong*." Animo stepped through the door, leaving me with no choice but to follow.

Rocky sand crunched beneath our feet as we walked across the barren land of red and black. The open door to my room grew smaller and smaller in our wake until it was nothing more than a dot on the horizon.

"I think we should go back," I said. "We can retry the spell if we need to."

"No," Animo said firmly.

"We haven't seen even a hint of Aspectu."

"She's here," Animo argued, his eyes fixed on the unending sea of dark sand. "She'll be here."

I dashed in front of him, forcing him to stop. "That's what you said in Medea. Why won't you admit that she's not coming?"

"I can't."

"Why not?"

"Because—" His shoulders sagged as his voice softened. "Because she can't have left me." He pulled away, his gaze falling to the ground. "When I went to find Aspectu's note in Medea, it wasn't addressed. She had left it with a man who was instructed to give it to me sixteen minutes after the fourteenth hour. She knew the *exact* moment I would come looking for her. She had seen the future, and she knew that she wouldn't be there to meet me."

Oh. "You don't know that for sure. The future is always changing."

"That's what I've been telling myself for months." He turned back to me, tears glittering like stars in his eyes. "It's not true. She knew she would be attacked. She saw that future, and she accepted it."

"If that's true, then she had to have had her reasons."

"She had her reasons when she told my mother to make a stand against the goblins." Grief clawed at his voice. "She is the reason I'm here, Rose. She gave me this quest. She told me that if I followed her orders, I would find everything I've ever wanted. But all I've found is *nothing.*

"When Aspectu took me in, I thought I would finally have someone who wouldn't leave me. She could see the future—she could protect herself from any harm. But now… She *knew*, Rose. And if she dies—" his voice broke. "She didn't even bother to say goodbye."

He turned away, covering his mouth to stifle his tears. I closed the distance between us, wrapping my arms around his shaking shoulders. "I am so sorry, Animo."

He leaned into my embrace, his head falling on my shoulder. His arms slid around my waist, and his tears grew silent.

I closed my eyes, tightening my hug. *You're not alone*, I tried to say through my touch. *I'm here.*

Sand crunched. I opened my eyes, and there she was.

"Animo." I turned him so that he could see the woman in white standing before us.

"Aspectu!" He rushed forward, but her hand raised sharply.

"Don't," she warned.

He stopped in his tracks, hurt flashing across his face.

"You had a mission," Aspectu said, pointing an accusatory finger at him. "Your path was clear, yet somehow, we are at the brink of destruction. And you,"—her finger shifted to me—"*you* will be the one to drag us down." Her voice rose hysterically. "We're doomed!"

"What are you talking about?" I demanded.

"The kingdoms." Aspectu waved her arms wildly. Blood seeped through her sleeves in fine lines. "Look at them! When I look forward, I see *death*. No light, no hope, only flame."

She swayed, her gaze clouded, and her mouth hanging open. "I'm drowning… I'm gone."

Animo watched her, horror twisting his gaze. I took his hand—the only thing I *could* do.

Aspectu dropped to her knees, scooping up the black sand. Her eyes followed as it slipped through her fingers, falling like a waterfall. "The Twelve Kingdoms are a pot of black powder, and you are the candle teetering on the edge." Her stone-cold gaze flicked to me. "When you fall, they will burn. Just. Like. That."

Aspectu snapped her fingers, and the world exploded in a flash of white.

I shot up, my heart racing. Relief flooded me as wooden walls came into focus. Wax dripped down the still-burning candle, pooling on the floor. Animo sat up, his expression masked with blank shock.

"Animo?" I winced, accidentally using my cut palm to prop myself up.

"Fine," he said numbly. "And you… are you all right?"

I nodded. "I'm fine."

He pulled his satchel to his side, withdrawing a clean cloth. "Let me see your hand."

I held it out, and he gently wrapped the cloth around my cut palm.

"Do you want to talk about it?" I asked.

He shook his head.

I bit my lip, falling silent as he tied off the bandage, carefully tucking in the ends. He gathered a second cloth from his bag and moved to set it on the floor. I took it from him, pulling his hand forward to bandage it.

"Thank you," he murmured.

I nodded, my attention fixed on the rough callouses worked into his palm. One might mistake them for the hands of a laborer, but I knew the truth: they came from years of wielding a sword.

Years of blindly following Aspectu's command.

"I'm sorry I made us go there," he said. "My—this—"—he held up his wrist—"it was likely what confused the spell."

"It's not your fault, Animo. And neither is what's happening to Aspectu."

He sighed. "I… I wish there was a way I could help her. She sees everything. If there is a way to save her, she should have told me instead of… *that*."

"Do you think she meant it?" I asked, tying off his bandage.

"No." He gripped my hand. "She's *broken*. Whatever vision she had of the future isn't true. You are not the darkness she has seen."

I sat back, releasing a slow breath. "I want that to be true. I want to break my cycle and free myself from following Natalia's path. In order to do that, I have to tell you the truth; you need to know what really happened that night in Darvyn."

THE NIGHT HOPE
BURNED

"**I**'ve never told anyone what happened that night," I began, my knees pulled to my chest. Animo and I sat on the floor, facing one another. Firelight danced across our faces, the warm crackles louder now that the storm had subsided.

"People think they know, but..." I forced myself to take a breath before continuing. "A week had passed since my mother left Darvyn. She had followed a rumor that my father had been seen, alive. Of course, it was a trap. The Pack knew it would be. They warned her, but she was so sure... the way she spoke to them—the way she *led* them—she had their trust. She promised to return, and they believed her. Time proved her wrong." I swallowed hard, my gaze dropping to my feet.

"I didn't believe them," I whispered. "There was no body, so it seemed impossible. But they were certain she was gone and terrified they'd lose me as well. They locked me in my home and had me guarded at all times because if they lost me, they would have no claim. No kingdom would help rebels overthrow a seated queen."

Tears welled, blurring my vision with the reflected glow of the fire. "I was twelve, and my mother had disappeared. I didn't think about the consequences, only that I needed her with me. One night, I slipped past the guards, stole a horse, and journeyed to Malecare."

Animo closed his eyes. "You saw her, didn't you?"

I nodded. "She hung from the bridge. Her body had been torn apart. And when I saw her, I crumbled. I sobbed in the streets for everyone to see. Everyone, including Natalia."

Realization flooded Animo's eyes. "That's why her body was left on display. It was a trap for you."

I nodded again. "I was so lost in my sorrow, I didn't realize I was being tracked. I led sixteen battalions of shades straight to the Ardent Pack."

I picked at my fingernail, gazing into the fire to avoid Animo's eyes. "When I returned to Darvyn, the Pack was meeting, scrambling for a new plan. They had already written me off as dead, so one might have expected joy upon my arrival. Instead, I was met with fury. They told me I had endangered them by leaving. They said I was meant to be their hope, but all I had done was make things worse. I was a burden to Avonshere, and they would be better off with me gone."

Even after five years, the words stung like nettle.

"I know now that it was a moment of anger on the part of the Pack. But at the time, I believed every word. I ran away, ignoring their calls for me to return. I made it all the way to the forest's edge before I looked back. That was when I saw them."

I tightened my arms around my knees as if making myself small would truly allow me to disappear. "Shades swarmed the village. Like shadows at first. Then they struck." I clenched my fists against my leggings. "I hid in the forest, covering my ears to block out their screams. It didn't help. I heard each and every one of them die because of me. *I* had led Natalia to the Pack."

Animo took my hand. "You were a child trying to save her mother. Anyone would have done the same."

"I'm not finished."

He drew back, his gaze asking *what more could there be?*

"After a while, I knew I had to act. I was the heir and one day I would be queen, so it was only right that I protected my people from Natalia. I crept from the forest to a barn on the edge of town. It was full of straw, and I thought that if the shades saw me enter, they would follow. I could light it on fire and leave them to burn."

Animo watched me, pity seeping into his eyes. *He still doesn't realize.*

"I went to the barn. As anticipated, the shades followed. They swarmed it, clawing at its sides. It was what I wanted, but... I didn't realize she would follow me." I wiped a tear from my cheek. "Her name was Ilsa. She was my age. She... she wanted to follow her parents' lead and protect their future queen. She barred the door behind us and told me to run. I tried to make her leave, but she wouldn't listen, and I had already begun the spell."

"A spell of flame," Animo murmured, the realization finally settling over him.

My vision glazed over as I stared into the crackling fire. "My mother had taught me how to focus my magic and draw more power from myself. Before, I had used it to heal, but on that night, I summoned fire meant for destruction. I wanted to destroy the shades, but Ilsa... she wanted me to stop. She saw the power I held, and it *scared* her. She begged me—fought me. I had never held such powerful magic, so when she distracted me, it all..."—I waved my hand before me—"released."

The ghostlike scent of Ilsa's flesh charring tickled my nose. My spell had consumed her in seconds, leaving only her skeleton behind.

"Rime had struck, and the ground was dry, so the flame had nothing to stop it. It spread throughout Darvyn, destroying not only the shades but everything it touched." My tears spilled, flowing freely down my cheeks.

"It burned for hours. Ilsa was the first to die by my hand, but she wasn't the last. I heard so many screams. They shouted *fire*, but it was useless. They couldn't stop it. *I* couldn't stop it. It moved so fast and burned for *so long*."

Squeezing my eyes shut, I hung my head. "I thought I could save the Pack. I thought I could save my mother. Both times, I was proven wrong."

"How did you survive?" Animo asked.

I scoffed lightly. After everything I had told him, that was his question?

"The flames didn't burn me. Just like in the Silver Forest—I killed the goblins, yet we remained unharmed. Only, in Darvyn, it was only me who was protected."

I wiped my cheeks, smearing tears into my skin. "Once the fires died down, I found my ring and crown, and I left them by Ilsa's skeleton. Then I ran." Finally, I met his gaze. "Not very queenly, was it?"

"You were a child, Rose," he said. "You tried to do the right thing. It's not your fault the spell failed."

"It didn't *fail*," I argued. "It was powerful and uncontrollable, and *I* created it. I create darkness. That is why I feel trapped in the fate of destruction—it's all I've known."

He shook his head. "You don't deserve that. You deserve a throne and a kingdom and the chance to *lead*, not the weight of wars on your shoulders."

"Maybe I didn't before, but after Darvyn—"

"That doesn't change a thing," he snapped, taking my hand. "Fate gave you a life you don't deserve. She forced you to endure horrible things, but maybe, just maybe, there is a reason. Avonshere can't have peace, not without war first. The people will need someone to bring them through that war. A leader who knows what it's like to suffer, who has felt pain at Natalia's hand. A leader who won't recoil at the touch of the flames but will urge them higher until they burn down everything that's corrupt. They need a queen who won't abandon them when all that's left is ruin. Someone who will rebuild and restore their homes. Someone who will stay until the very end."

He leaned in, his grip tightening around mine. "I see all of this in you. I wish you could see it, too."

"So do I." No matter how hard I looked, I couldn't see past the little girl standing amid the flames she had created.

"What do I do now?" I asked.

"That's your decision. But it seems to me that if your guilt stems from destruction, the only way to ease it is through restoration."

"Do you think saving Avonshere will really set things right?

"I don't know." He sighed, shaking his head. "I haven't... I've never been able to save anyone I failed."

"You will. Once I free Avonshere, it will be your turn."

"I hope so."

A sad smile curved my lips. We were both broken. Perhaps that was why I cared for him—because I understood him in a way few could. I understood why he fought so hard for a cursed kingdom, and I understood his hypocrisies because they were my own. At the end of the day, we wanted the same thing: freedom.

My gaze fell to our still-joined hands. I adjusted my grip, twining our fingers together. *Maybe I want more than freedom.*

A young girl's scream split the silence. Animo and I shot to our feet, weapons in hand. There was only one person in this manor who could scream like that.

Belinda.

A TRAITOR REVEALED

Animo and I burst into the sitting room, blades at the ready. A candlestick sat on the ground, casting ghastly shadows on Christoph's face. He hovered over Belinda's bleeding form, a dagger in his hand.

"Stop!" I cried.

He paused, shifting so his hands raised in surrender. "I am not the one who hurt her. I am trying to see if she's breathing."

I lowered my dagger, but my nerves remained high as Christoph placed the silver blade before Belinda's nose. It fogged ever so slightly.

"She's alive, but her breaths are weak," he said, sheathing the dagger. Lifting Belinda's coat, he examined her wounds. "She was stabbed once. She hasn't lost much blood yet, but if we don't do something to quell the flow, she will die."

"Let me try." I knelt by Belinda. Placing my hands atop her stomach, I called on my magic. It fluttered like smoke from a blown-out candle, doing little to stop the bleeding. I sighed and turned to Christoph. "We put the wagon in the stables—you can take her into town and find a healer."

"Be careful," he warned as he gathered Belinda's limp body in his arms. "I checked our security before I went to sleep—all the windows and doors were locked. That means the attacker came from *inside* the manor."

Animo and I exchanged a wary look. He had been with me when Belinda screamed; it was impossible for him to have committed this act. Ketch seemed to have forged a connection with her, and even if he hadn't, I couldn't imagine him attacking her—not without a good reason, anyway. Christoph was by her side when we entered... but Margaret trusted him, and I trusted her. That left only two people, and I had a strong suspicion about which one was our attacker.

"Whoever did this knows we're onto them," Animo said as Christoph left the room.

"*Whoever?*" I asked. "Animo, it's not a mystery. This was Camilla."

Animo opened his mouth to speak, but I cut him off. "Listen to me. Belinda had something she wanted to tell me, but the moment Camilla entered the room, she stopped talking. And all night Camilla was asking about the Staff of Realms. This is her making her move to take it."

"I trust Camilla," he said. "And I know what it looks like when she kills someone. She either makes a scene or wipes away all traces of the body. This is too messy and rash to be her."

"Then who did it? Dobbins? Because the last time I checked, he *worked* for Camilla."

"Check again."

I spun around as Camilla entered the sitting room, her cutlass drawn and blood dripping from her forehead and lip.

"What happened?" Animo asked.

"Dobbins and I had a hugging contest." She pressed her palm against her split lip. "That sult tried to kill me."

"Why?" I asked.

"He got tired of almost dying and decided to chase two-hundred-thousand mynet."

My stomach dropped. "He's working for Natalia?"

She nodded. "The good news is he doesn't know where the Staff of Realms is. Knowing the fool, he'll be looking in all the obvious places. Terrot, come with me. Wolfe, you'll want to find your grandmother before he gives up the pixie chase and goes after her."

I pushed past Camilla, dashing through the manor's dark halls. Margaret had shown me around earlier and pointed out her bedroom. If I could only remember the way…

A crash echoed from the dining hall. I turned sharply, throwing open the door and rushing in just in time to see a bloody Margaret slash Dobbins's forearm with a knife.

Dobbins shouted, slamming her into the china cabinet. Her head banged against the wood, and she fell to the ground with a moan.

"Get away from her!" I shouted, rushing toward Dobbins, my dagger raised. He grinned at the sight and drew his cutlass.

He slashed, and I ducked, scampering away. I cut downward, my short blade slicing nothing but the air before him. Dobbins grabbed me by the neck and shoved me against the table, the tip of his cutlass pressing against my chest.

"Let's try this again," he growled as Margaret struggled to her feet. "Where is the Staff of Realms?"

"Let my granddaughter go," she commanded, her fists balled at her sides.

"Give me the staff, and I will," Dobbins replied. He grinned down at me. "You will be free to roam an entire cell in Malecare's dungeon."

A shoe flew through the air, smacking him in the head. He stumbled back, his grip loosening enough for me to slip free.

"Next time, I send an explosive," Ketch warned, loading a glass bottle into his slingshot. Animo and Camilla rushed into the room, swords drawn.

Fury flashed in Camilla's eyes. She pushed past the dwarf, charging at Dobbins. Their cutlasses met with a clash of metal, leaving a sharp ring echoing in my ears. A volley of curses erupted as the pirates exchanged angry blows.

"Camilla, get out of the way!" Ketch shouted, his slingshot lowered.

The pirate ignored him, knocking Dobbins's blade aside. She moved to stab, but he turned, leaving her attack harmless.

I raced to Margaret's side, helping her to her feet. "Are you all right?"

"I'll live," she replied, sinking into a chair.

Camilla slashed Dobbins's chest. He fell with a howl, blood blooming on his shirt. She planted one foot on his wrist and kicked his cutlass away with the other. The tip of her sword settled against Dobbins's throat.

"If you have any drop of sense left in your moldy brain, you will not move," she warned.

Dobbins glowered, his hand sliding inside his coat.

"Camilla!" Animo's warning came just in time. Dobbins drew a handheld crossbow. Camilla threw herself to the ground beside him, shoving his arm toward the ceiling. The bolt flew through the air, slicing through the rope that held the chandelier aloft.

I yanked Margaret aside as the chandelier fell. Wood cracked as it collided with the table, candles spilling across the floor. A long, golden object fell from the chandelier's frame.

The Staff of Realms.

Camilla kneed Dobbins in the ribs. She climbed on top of him, only to be thrown off as he scrambled to his feet. He drew a thin bolt from his pocket, sliding it into the crossbow.

Animo planted himself between Dobbins and the staff. "You're not getting it."

Dobbins raised the crossbow. "I've burned too many bridges to stop now."

Animo ducked, and the bolt passed right through where his head had been mere seconds before.

Ketch fired an explosive at Dobbins. The pirate dodged, and the bottle exploded against the wall.

Camilla rushed to Dobbins before he could reload. He pushed her sword to the side, elbowing her in the nose. I drew my dagger and plunged it into Dobbins's shoulder. With a scream, he threw Camilla into me. We tumbled to the hard floor.

"Next time, aim for something useful, like the throat," she snapped, dragging me to my feet.

Animo grappled with Dobbins, Bathril discarded on the ground.

"Take him down," I told Camilla, rushing past the fighting pair to the broken chandelier. From the wreckage, I pulled the gleaming Staff of Realms.

This was the real one; the moment my fingers touched its surface, the fairie magic awoke, its thrum warm, like a calescent afternoon.

Dobbins knocked Animo to the ground and raised his crossbow, aiming for my head.

"Camilla!" I threw the staff into her waiting arms. Dobbins fired. The bolt grazed my neck, just deep enough to draw blood.

Dobbins loaded another bolt, but Camilla had already thrown the staff to Margaret.

"Animo!" Margaret called, tossing it to him.

"Ketch!" Animo threw the staff.

"Rose!" Ketch threw it back to me.

"Camilla!"

"Animo!"

"Rose!"

"Margaret!"

We threw the staff around in an ever-changing loop. Dobbins spun about like a compass's needle, aiming his crossbow at anyone who moved, his eyes growing wilder by the second.

Unleashing a furious scream, he fired. The bolt flew past us, lodging into the drapes' support rod. The curtain floated as though time had slowed, settling on the candle-strewn ground.

Camilla sighed. "Rack."

The curtain burst into flames. They reached up, igniting the rest of the drapes. Smoke brewed as fire raced across the floor, lapping at the table legs. I leaped off the table, rushing to avoid the flames.

Ketch frantically emptied his sock, desperate to free himself of black powder. The bottles exploded in the air, emitting a flurry of glass and sparks.

Dobbins drew another bolt, but Animo tackled him to the ground. The pirate threw the elf off of him, sending Animo crashing into Camilla and knocking the Staff of Realms from her grasp. It landed in the middle of the floor, reflected flames dancing across it as though it were made of molten gold.

The six of us lunged forward, our outstretched hands grasping at the staff. Dobbins's fingers closed first.

Ocean blue flashed before my eyes. The ground fell out from under us, and we dropped into darkness.

PART EIGHT

A DARK QUEEN ON A DARK THRONE

I fell through the black. Darkness pressed against me, shifting and swirling like wind as I tumbled. A portal glowed in the distance, its blue energy rippling like ocean waves.

I threw out my hands as I fell through the portal. My chin smacked against the stone floor, the sharp tang of blood blooming in my mouth.

I coughed, reaching out to brush my fingers along the weblike strands of silver that cut through the black marble. The blood froze in my veins—I had been here before.

Trembling, I lifted my gaze.

Before me sat a woman, her black skirts nearly disappearing against the throne beneath her. Faint hits of silver ran through her dark hair, matching the twisted ring on her finger.

"Natalia." The name slipped out like knives on my tongue.

She stared down at me, her gaze as cold as the steel crown she wore. *My crown.*

I pushed myself to my feet, my eyes scanning the room. Armored guards lined the throne room like dark statues. Among them stood the Hunter, his hand poised on the broken hilt of his sword.

Ketch and Camilla struggled to their feet, their gazes darting between the guards and their weapons strewn just out of reach. Margaret remained on her knees, her face twisted in a sharp grimace while Animo lay on his back, struggling to catch his breath.

His body is rejecting the staff's magic. I longed to run to him, but any sudden motion would end with a sword thrust through my chest. My eyes snapped back to Natalia.

"Take them," she commanded.

The guards moved as one, snatching Ketch and Camilla as they dove for their weapons. The pair kicked and shouted to no avail. More guards hauled Margaret and Animo up, but only Margaret found her footing. Animo sagged between captors, helplessness radiating from his eyes.

The Hunter himself grabbed me, squeezing my arms so tight that my fingers tingled, rapidly numbing. I threw my head back, thoughtlessly slamming it against his mask. Pain burst through my skull as my vision darkened. I wobbled, barely staying upright as I fought the urge to vomit.

Camilla swore, struggling against her captors. Ketch yowled, held aloft by a guard who was just out of reach of the dwarf's kicking feet. Their weapons, along with Bathril, my dagger, and a satchel belonging to Ketch, were collected by another guard. With a bow to Natalia, he exited the throne room, leaving us defenseless.

Dobbins stepped forward, dropping to his knee before Natalia. Inclining his head, he presented the staff. "The Staff of Realms. As promised."

"Traitorous pig," Camilla growled. Murder glinted in her eyes as a guard took the staff from Dobbins, carrying it to Natalia. "Just wait until I get my hands around your throat."

A guard kicked the back of her knee. She fell with a shout, her lips twisting into a grin of rage. If she'd had a blade, she would have massacred every one of us.

Bowing, the guard offered the staff to Natalia. She took it delicately, a smile slithering across her lips as she ran her hands along the twining gold.

"Pay him," she declared, her lustful gaze drinking in the staff's curves.

Another guard stepped from the elliptic ranks, escorting Dobbins toward the door.

"Run, little piggy," Camilla taunted.

He paused by her side. "I have no reason to run. Your life ends here. Mine, however, is only beginning. Soon, I will sail as the new captain of *The Dragon's Bane*."

Camilla threw herself toward him, nearly knocking over her guards.

"Enough!" Natalia bellowed. The room froze; only Camilla's muscles twitched.

"Farewell, *Miss* Hawkins." Dobbins's coat fanned behind him as he strode out of the throne room.

Natalia propped the Staff of Realms against the ornate arm of her throne. "Well, I am sure you have much to discuss with your turncoat, but I am afraid that we have no time for you to attain closure, Captain. Perhaps it is for the better—he had the intelligence to accept my offer, something you seemed to have no interest in."

Camilla glared up at her. "I'm not in the business of taking orders. Or being a witch's lapdog."

"And that is why you will die." Natalia nodded to a guard. "She may go."

At the command, the guards dragged Camilla away.

"Now, then, let's move on to our dear, deceased Lady Margaret."

Margaret raised her chin, her unwavering gaze meeting Natalia's.

"I had my doubts about your death, but I must admit that I'm surprised nature has yet to snatch you away."

"I refuse to die while my kingdom remains in this broken state," Margaret replied. "I have spent five years fighting you, and I will spend a hundred more clawing my way through the trenches if that is what it takes to end your reign."

A deep frown cut Natalia's face. "You blame me for Avonshere's brokenness, yet the cracks were there before me. I rule the same crumbling kingdom you left me."

"I left you *nothing*," Margaret snapped. "Your birthright made you a duchess, yet you demanded more."

"You stole my birthright when you cast me aside!" Natalia shot back, her grip tight on the throne's arms. "I was promised the crown. When you broke that promise, I had no choice but to uphold it myself."

"You abandoned your people to seek a title you are unfit to bear," Margaret said, her voice steady. "The proudest moment of my life was when my son requested his betrothal be annulled."

Natalia's expression darkened. She rose slowly, her skirts dragging behind her as she approached Margaret. "Do you know what the proudest moment of my life was?" she asked, her voice an amiable facade. "It was watching your husband's corpse twitch as it was crushed beneath stone. Because I truly believe that he was still alive, and he felt it."

Margaret's lips trembled, sending a smile across Natalia's.

"We'll have such fun, you and I." She turned her attention to Ketch and Animo. "The dwarf and the elf… a fascinating pair. One, an outcast from his own family, and the other, a forsaken prince." Her focus locked on Animo; he stood tall, his fists clenched at his sides. "Your father begged me to spare the lives of your sisters, yet when it came to you, he merely asked I send him proof of your death. Tell me, how does it feel to have spent years searching for someone only to help guide her to the hands of death?"

Animo's jaw tightened. "She won't be the one to die tonight."

"You truly think you can protect her, don't you?" Natalia shook her head. "You are not the first to try, but you will be the last to fail."

"Natalia—" Margaret began.

"When I want your opinion, crone, I will ask for it!" Natalia flicked her fingers. My grandmother gawked, opening and closing her mouth like a fish on land.

She stole her voice.

Natalia's attention returned to Animo. "More powerful elves than you have stood against me, and now they remain with me in spirit and in power." Magic formed in her outstretched palm, twining into a sphere. "Do you know the spells locked away in the Great Library of Daria? Because I do."

The blood drained from Animo's face. With a screamed curse, he threw himself forward, breaking free of the guards' grasp. Natalia's sphere flew, slamming against his chest. He fell with a shout, gripping his singed side as blood dripped from his cut hand.

Ketch cursed, thrashing against the guards' hold. One clamped a hand over the dwarf's mouth, leaving him wide-eyed and kicking.

Natalia drew her sword, stalking toward Animo. "Your father tells me your power is weak, which means I have no need for you, especially now that Rosara is in my grasp."

He struggled to rise, barely supporting himself on his hands and knees. Natalia drove her foot into his back, pinning him down as she raised her sword.

"No!" I screamed, straining against the Hunter's grasp. He forced me to my knees, twisting my arm behind my back. My other hand slipped free, and I reached out aimlessly.

Panic raced through me. Animo, helpless on the ground. Natalia's glinting blade, seconds away from falling… she was going to tear away another person I cared for.

Unless we stop her. The totem burned in my pocket.

I shifted my free hand, brushing it against the dark stone. The beast purred, its wings lifting at the touch. Closing my eyes, I searched within myself and the totem, shattering the chains I had fought so hard to forge.

Finally.

The beast surged within me, breaking free in a wave of joyful anarchy. My magic flowed, blazing brighter than ever before. It swelled and raged—raw like the jagged edges of broken glass, yet there was no cruelty in its cut. My magic wasn't running through the totem. *I* was enhancing the totem's power. The beast used *me* as a conduit, exacerbating the power I had stored in the totem as it surged in a fresh wave of destruction.

We'll save them, it said. For the first time, I doubted calling it *beast*.

Its invisible hand closed around mine; our powers combined. The Hunter dropped me as though I were molten. All around me, the guards began to crumble, their mouths open with the silent screams Natalia had stolen from them.

Fingers closed around my wrist—Natalia dragged my hand from my pocket, snatching the totem from my grasp.

No! The word tore through my mind like a scream as the power drained from me. I collapsed to the floor, my body cold and empty, without a single spark of magic to warm me.

"What have you done?" I whispered, looking up at Natalia.

She loomed over me, stroking the totem's jewel, only to jerk her hand away as though she'd been burned. With her glare fixed on the totem, she waved a hand at Animo. "Take him away. The dwarf too. Put them in the dungeon with the pirate—I'll deal with them later."

The guards dragged Ketch and Animo away. The latter looked back at me, his shoulders tight as fury as terror split his gaze. Ketch clenched his fist as he was carried through the door, his fingers working subtly at something wedged in his leather bracelet.

The tiniest splinter of hope pierced me. They could escape. All they had to do was leave me behind.

Please, whoever is out there listening, let them leave me.

The Hunter dragged me to my feet. My head spun; I fell against him as my vision swam, a dull ache radiating throughout my head. Natalia settled on the throne, her sword resting against its arm and the totem lying in her palm.

"Rosara Wolfe." She tried out the name as if it had never been spoken. "You wear the name of dead kings."

I met her brown eyes. The eyes of a woman who had been there every day of my childhood, a scowl buried in the shadows, now sat as a cold face on a dark throne. She gazed down at me, almost bored.

"Well?" she asked. "After all the trouble I went through to bring you here, will you not speak?"

"I have nothing to say to you."

She sniffed. "You always were a spineless brat."

"What do you want of me?" I asked. "You have Avonshere. The Twelve

Kingdoms believe that I'm dead—why bother hunting me down?"

"I won't let my loose ends run amuck. Lesser queens have done so, and it has led to their undoing."

Anger sparked within me. "I wasn't a threat to you. I would have spent an eternity hidden away, but *you* dragged me back into the fight. You're no queen. You're a tyrant."

"Tyrant, queen, either way, it is I who wears the crown." Her icy gaze pierced through me. "Your existence threatens to oppose me. You will fall as your ancestors did, but there will be no parade or gowns of mourning. You will not be mourned, for you are already forgotten. You, Rosara Wolfe, are a sliver of the past. It does no good to mourn the past. And it does less to mourn the loss of a dead girl."

"The people will rise against you," I said, sudden fury driving my words. "You can wear that crown, and you can sit on that throne, but that doesn't make them yours."

"Why not? These things are passed down by blood, are they not?"

"They are passed by the bond of blood, not by the shedding of it."

"How do you think the Twelve Kingdoms were forged?" she asked. "Through kindness and love? No. Your ancestor won a kingdom by killing a man."

"An evil man," I reminded her. "And that's exactly how I will win my kingdom back."

Natalia's glare deepened. "You think you can kill me and everyone will accept you? You left. You hid while Avonshere fell to me. Tell me, Rosara, what gives you the right to come back now?"

I raised my chin in defiance. "I do."

She leaned back. "Well, it seems you've grown a spine, after all."

"And you've fallen from a corrupt queen to a full-on sult."

She smirked. "Call me whatever you wish. But never forget the most important thing about me—I always get what I want."

"Not this time. You sit on the throne, but that doesn't make it yours. Tell me, do you think of my family when you set that crown on your head?"

She stiffened. "Perhaps if you had fought for this crown, your claims would mean something."

"Why must I die?" I demanded.

"Your death gives me power. When you are gone, I will be the most powerful queen Avonshere has ever seen, and I will live on in history."

"You will go down as the pathetic witch that you are."

"*Pathetic?*" Her bottom lip pooched out as though offended. "Oh, dear girl, I am many things, but pathetic is not one of them."

"You chide me for hiding, yet you have spent seven years locked away in your fortress," I said, my confidence climbing with every word. "You hide behind your magic and let your shades do your dirty work. I have more respect for pirates than for you."

"Oh, if you only knew… magic is a beautiful thing, Rosara. And I used it to craft the perfect disguise that would lead any naive little princess to confess *everything* to me."

Unease twisted my stomach. "What do you mean?"

"*Tell me where you are, Rosara*, I said. *On my way to Nicia*, you replied."

"No." My dreams flashed before my eyes. Every word I had said, every word I had *trusted*—it was all a lie.

"How do you think I found you? Those hapless thieves?" She shook her head. "You told me everything, Rosara. And all because you trusted the face of Aspectu Demore."

"Where is she?"

"Safe and sound, kept under lock and key. Not that it matters. You'll all be dead soon enough."

I clenched my fists, digging my nails into my palm. Any harder, and I might have drawn blood.

Natalia sighed. "It didn't have to be like this, Rosara. If you had surrendered all those years ago, then your friends would not have to die today. Remember that. You chose this path. You chose death."

"I chose survival," I snapped.

"Your survival cost the lives of thousands. Their blood is on your hands." She rose from her throne, collecting her sword with a heavy scrape of steel against stone. "You see, death is a simple thing. A quick slash and it is all over.

But if you really want someone to suffer, you must break their soul before destroying their body."

Her gaze fell to Margaret, who looked on in silent horror. "Bring her forward," she commanded.

I bit back a whimper as the guards shoved Margaret to the ground, forcing her to kneel at the witch's feet.

"Margaret Elizabeth Ravenspeer Wolfe," Natalia began. "If you have any final words, say them now, or let them follow you to the pyre." She flicked her fingers, undoing her spell.

Margaret swallowed hard before speaking. "You were a daughter to me, Natalia. You came to me broken, but kind. Your struggles made you stronger, and I thought that we could provide shelter and a home and guide you to be a leader. But nothing we gave was ever enough for you."

Natalia shook her head. "I was not a broken doll for you to mend. You never truly cared about what I endured—all you wanted was to be the one to save the lost, orphaned duchess. But I found my own way, and it is my turn to guide *you.*" She lifted her sword, running her fingers along its sharpened edge.

Margaret raised her chin. "Like my husband and my son before me, I will die at your blade." Regality radiated from her as if a crown awaited her instead of a blade. "Let my blood be the river that brings your destruction."

"Let it flow." Natalia swung her sword, slicing clean through Margaret's neck.

I screamed, falling to my knees as Margaret's body toppled over. Her head rolled across the floor, stopping before me. Her eyes remained open, yet they held no sight. Tears ran down my cheeks as the puddle of blood spread, soaking into my pants.

Drip... drip... drip... Margaret's blood ran down the blade of Natalia's sword, dropping onto the marble in a heavy, rhythmic pattern.

I was wrong. It sounded nothing like water.

Natalia placed the tip of her sword beneath my chin. I grimaced at the hot stick of Margaret's blood against my skin. The point dug into my neck as Natalia forced my head upward—my gaze meeting hers.

My voice trembled as I spoke. "How does this end? You've had me here long enough to kill me a thousand times. Why won't you do it?"

She knelt before me on the bloodstained floor. Adjusting her blade, she let it rest against my cheek. I shuddered, imagining the scarlet mark it would leave.

"I do not kill without reason, Rosara. You will die, but not before I have taken everything I can from you."

"What's left to lose? You strung my mother up like a hog at market and left my father to die as Del Hera crumbled."

Natalia laughed. "Oh, my dear, I did nothing of the sort. I may not have loved your father, but I was not blind to his potential."

My heart pounded as she stepped away, that awful, wicked smile curving her lips.

"Leon!" she called. "Say hello to your daughter."

The Hunter released my arms, marching to Natalia's side. Frozen, I watched as he removed his mask and pulled back his hood. Green eyes gazed down at me, framed by fair skin and golden waves. I'd known that face since the day I was born.

"Father!" I cried, dashing to throw my arms around his neck. I squeezed my eyes shut, longing for him to return the embrace. His arms remained at his side as though I were hugging a statue.

I drew back. He stared into the void, his eyes as glassy and unseeing as Margaret's.

"What have you done to him?" I asked, fighting to keep the tears from stealing my voice.

"I made him into a machine of war."

My father turned toward Natalia. She extended a hand which he took into his own, sinking to his knee before her. Her fingers traced his cheek, satisfaction glittering in her gaze.

"He is my assassin. My hunter."

My mouth hung ajar. "He's a shade." I stumbled back, but my feet slipped out from under me. I fell face-down into the puddle of Margaret's blood.

Letting out a desperate cry, I scrambled away, but the blood had latched onto my lips. Every move I made carved a crimson trail. I collapsed, curling into a ball of tears and blood.

"He's not a shade," Natalia said, ignoring my sobs. "He follows my every word, but his soul remains."

I raised my head as my father kissed the knuckles of the woman who had murdered his own family. Somewhere within that hollow shell of a man, my father was surely screaming. It was beyond cruelty. What reason could Natalia have for this?

"Now, I think it's time you rejoin your friends," she said. "Take this time to say goodbye and think about all the life they will miss because of you."

The remaining guards stepped forward, hauling me to my feet.

"You'll pay for this," I spat as my tears ran dry. "I will *make* you pay for this."

Natalia swept her skirts behind her, settling on the throne. "You're seven years too late. Oh, but before you go,"—A thin smile slid across her lips—"happy birthday."

CHAPTER SIXTY-TWO

WHO I AM

Natalia's guards led me through the dark halls of Malecare, two before me, two behind, and two gripping my arms. If they expected me to run, they were wrong. There was nowhere to flee to and no way to fight my way out. I had hours left to live. Natalia had told me to say goodbye, but there wasn't enough time to express how much the people at the end of this road meant to me, nor my agony over what she would do to them.

My head drooped as a tear slipped down my cheek. *I am so sorry.*

A glass projectile flew through the air, shattering against the leading guard's head. Flames spiked, climbing down his hair to ignite his uniform. The other guards drew their swords. I dove to the side, covering my head as a second, larger vial landed in the middle of them. Roaring fire engulfed the guards and singed my hair.

"Rose!" Animo swept me into his arms. He carried me down a side corridor, past Ketch and Camilla, who rushed to disarm the guards.

Animo hurried down a winding staircase and into a dim storeroom. Dusty barrels and crates lined the room—provisions unused by Natalia's lifeless army. He set me on a crate, then turned, bolting the door behind us.

"It's only a matter of time before Natalia realizes we're loose," he said. "We need a plan, fast."

His gaze landed on me. The blood drained from his face as his eyes crawled over every inch of my blood-soaked body. "What did she do to you?"

I opened my mouth to speak, but no words came. I shook my head as fresh tears welled.

"Rose." Animo cupped my cheek with one hand, his thumb stroking the bloody mark. His other hand held my own.

I squeezed my eyes shut.

"Rose," he repeated. "Tell me what happened."

A tear slipped out.

"Rose, please," he begged. "Look at me."

I opened my eyes.

He dropped my hand to brush the hair away from my face. "I need you to be okay."

I shook my head. "No, Animo, it's—" My throat tightened on the words. "It's not mine."

Understanding filled his gaze. Wordlessly, he pulled me close, letting me sob against his shoulder.

"She killed her," I cried. "She didn't have to, but she did. And my father—" My words fell apart into a sob. "He's alive. He's *enslaved* to her. Possessed. It's all her game. She tortured him by making him her Hunter, and she manipulated me." I drew back, wiping away my tears. "It's been her in my dreams. *She* was Aspectu. And I trusted her, and I told her exactly how to find us. I gave her everything she wanted, even the Staff of Realms."

Animo's gaze fell to the ground, defeat settling over him. "The dreamscape," he murmured. "It was broken. *She* was broken."

I bit my lip, staring at the dark sky visible through the thin, barred window.

"Everything is broken," I whispered. "Natalia drags me through pain for the pleasure it brings her. That's why she showed me all those memories."

"Memories?"

"Memories about Daria and my mother. She showed me my mother's body and Regium erasing Bellatora's memories of it."

Animo's eyes widened. He clutched my hand. "Rose, I don't think it was all a lie. Natalia didn't see Bella lose her memory, making it impossible for her to show you. And you can't change your appearance in dreamscapes—magic doesn't work that way. But it *is* possible she used Aspectu as a vessel."

A memory surfaced. "Natalia said Aspectu was being kept under lock and key. It wouldn't make sense to keep her alive that long unless she had a use for her."

His expression hardened. "She has a use. In the throne room, Natalia spoke of Daria's grimoires. In them are the spells I once told you of, the ones that have spells to… take an ekeider's power."

"Wait, do you mean…?"

He nodded. "She took your mother's magic, Rose."

"No. That—that's not how it works. It can't be. Magic is part of our blood, you can't—"

"She did. Natalia took your mother's blood and used dark magic to steal her power as well."

Horror shot through me. I gripped Animo's arm. "She has my mother's blood. *My* blood. The totem was forged with blood magic—"

"She controls it." His voice reflected my dread. "The totem and all the magic you stored in it."

No… kingdoms, no.

"I gave it everything. And now…" I searched within myself to find a bone-dry well. "I can't feel my magic."

Animo closed his eyes. I slumped against the crates. The strongest weapon we had—the darkest power I had ever seen—was now in the hands of my greatest enemy. The image of my mother's body hanging from the bridge, her skin in tatters, and her crown shattered in a pool of blood, seeped through my mind.

"She *mutilated* my mother for the sake of power."

Fury licked my chest, rising from pummeled coals. It was her magic. My *mother's* magic, my mother's *blood,* ran through the veins of my enemy.

"I wanted to be rid of her," I whispered. "To be rid of this crown, this weight on my shoulders. I wanted it gone. I wanted to go home. But what home is there to return to? Everything… it's gone. I've lost Margaret twice now. My best friends in the world are either dead or have no faith in me, and at the end of the day, Avonshere is no closer to freedom."

Animo gazed down at me, his broken edges ringing his irises. "Then say the word. Say that you want to leave, and I swear I will get you out of here and hide you where no one will ever find you again."

You will die, but not before I have taken everything I can from you. Natalia's words echoed in my mind.

"No." I slid to my feet. "I refuse to hide because I have spent the past five years hiding and mourning my losses—what losses? I didn't lose Margaret. I didn't lose my parents, and I certainly didn't lose Avonshere. They were *stolen* from me. But now it's my turn to take back what is mine." I paced the small storeroom. "I want to see Natalia broken on the ground. I want to force her to her knees and see the look in her eyes when she realizes that she's lost." I clenched my fists, my anger rising and morphing into power. It wasn't magic, but it was all I needed. "I want a war."

"Are you sure?" Doubt didn't prompt Animo's question; it was a final offer for my escape.

I met his eyes, determination settling over me like armor. "I am."

I had fought so hard against this. But Natalia had built a kingdom of suffering that could only be destroyed through war. What I was about to do would shake the foundations of the Twelve Kingdoms, but it had to be done.

You should have killed me, Natalia. For too long, I'd lived as a frightened little girl haunted by flames. I had thought my wheel of destruction was a cursed fate, but I was wrong. Destruction would be my salvation because it would no longer hurt me. From now on, it would rain down upon the head of Natalia Thornsworth.

As dawn lit the sky, I caught my reflection in the window pane. The girl who'd haunted me for years was gone. For the first time since Del Hera fell, I saw myself for who I truly was. *I am Rosara Wolfe, Crown Princess of Avonshere, and it is time to claim my throne.*

CHAPTER SIXTY-THREE

THE PLAN

A knock rapped on the storeroom door. Animo froze; the cloth he had been using to clean away Margaret's blood hovered above my arm. Our gazes locked on the door. It could be Ketch and Camilla—or it could be my father, the possessed Hunter of Queen Natalia.

"Open this door right now, or else Cammie and I are going to be executed." The sound of Ketch's dark sarcasm had never brought me so much joy.

Shoulders dropping with relief, Animo opened the door. Camilla and Ketch hurried in, arms filled with swords, hands smeared with blood, and only three shoes between the two of them.

"We tossed the bodies out the window, but there's a lot of blood," Ketch said while Animo barred the door behind him.

"*We* tossed the bodies?" Camilla stared down at the dwarf, her brow raised.

"Fine, take the credit." He propped his armful of swords against the crates and then dusted off his hands. "The good news is that we didn't see any more guards. What happened while we were gone?"

Over the next ten minutes, Animo and I recounted the events in the throne room and all we had uncovered about Natalia and her magic.

Camilla huffed, a tight, joyless smile on her lips. "So, to summarize, Natalia has the Staff of Realms, the totem, your father, and an army of shades waiting to kill us."

"Yes," Animo said.

"Well, then, I vote we search for some rope and climb out the nearest window. Worst-case scenario, we fall into the canyon and die on impact—which is still preferable to having our lungs clawed out by shades."

I straightened, meeting the pirate's irritated gaze with one of strength. "We're not leaving like this. We're fighting back."

She rolled her eyes. "Natalia has the Staff of Realms—you don't even have magic."

"Then we'll have to steal it back."

Ketch grimaced. "Rose, I want you to know that I will follow you even if it kills me—but stealing the staff from Natalia seems impossible. She has all the power here."

I shook my head. "Not all of it. She has magic, yes, but she didn't hunt me down just for my magic. She knows that if I reveal myself, the people will turn on her."

"That doesn't get us out of here," Camilla muttered, leaning against a barrel.

"If it distracts Natalia, it might."

"*Might*," she repeated.

"It's better than falling to our deaths," Ketch pointed out. "How do we do it?"

"We need something big and bold," I said. "We're not simply telling Avonshere that I'm alive. We're declaring war, and we need the Twelve Kingdoms to know it."

"And therein lies the problem." Camilla folded her arms. "Ghosts can't declare war. Why should the people believe it's you? Why should the kingdoms even care?"

"I don't know," I admitted. "I don't know how to persuade the Twelve Kingdoms to join me, and I don't know how to spread this message. But we have to find a way."

Ketch snapped his fingers. "We burn it into the sky."

My eyes widened. *I want them to be able to see this in Vargo.* Our message… a declaration of war, carved in flame. The answer had been in our possession the entire time.

"Megs, you brilliant girl," I murmured. "Ketch, please tell me you have the messaging sphere."

"I do—well, did. It was in my satchel, which the guard took."

Animo tapped his fingers against his knee. "Since the guard took it with our weapons, it's likely he stowed it in the armory."

"That's where we'll look," I said. "This place was meant to be a refuge for royals. I know the layout, and I guarantee you I can bring us there without running into any guards."

Ketch held up his hands. "Wait, wait, wait—It won't work. The messaging sphere doesn't have any ignition. It needs something that burns like dragon fire."

My mouth slipped open. "Dragon fire… Margaret said that the chimera's venom was made of the same flammable compound found in dragon saliva. Biaht! Why did we leave the venom behind?"

Camilla laughed, a vengeful smile slithering across her lips. "At the manor, when the girl screamed, I went looking. Instead of a body, I found Dobbins stealing the venom from Margaret's chamber."

Hope lifted my heart. "He brought it through the portal?"

She nodded. "If we find him, we'll find your ignition."

"Do you think he's still here?"

"He won't leave until he's counted every single coin," she replied. "And he's a slow counter."

Animo glanced between me and Ketch. "How much venom do you think it would take?"

"I doubt a lot," Ketch said. "Why?"

"I'm thinking we need a bit more than a message to knock Natalia off her feet. Unfortunately, our supply of black powder is severely lacking."

I raised a brow. "Is a bit of venom enough to recreate one of your prison breaks?"

A grin spread across Ketch's face. "I can put something together."

My gaze shifted to the window. The morning light illuminated the path winding through Devil's Canyon, ending in a long bridge that stretched over a chasm, connecting it with Elatire.

An idea sparked in my mind. I faced my companions. "I have a plan."

True to my word, I guided us through cobwebbed servants' stairwells, free of Natalia's men. We soon reached the armory's door without any sign of the enemy.

"Shouldn't it be guarded?" Ketch asked, his wary eyes scanning the hall.

I shook my head. "No one comes near Malecare, and the only people who live here are controlled by Natalia. She has no fear of uprising and, therefore, no need for guards."

"It may be a good sign," Animo added. "The fact that she hasn't sent anyone here could indicate she isn't aware we've broken free."

"Or she's simply not afraid of us," Camilla said.

That will change.

I tried the handle only for it to click securely. Locked. I glanced over my shoulder at Animo. "Do you still have your picks?"

"I left them on *The Dragon's Bane*. But I don't think there's any need for subtlety, do you?"

"I'm hoping for the opposite."

"Good. Then stand back."

We scooted away as Animo readied himself to kick. His foot slammed into the door, knocking it off its hinges with a sharp bang.

We filed into the dusty armory. Cobwebs draped over the hilts of swords and hung from the tips of halberts, while rust dulled the edges of every piece of steel.

"This place is a dump." Camilla kicked a rack of swords, sending a cloud of dust into Ketch's face. He coughed, glaring up at her.

"Here." Animo crossed the room, stopping before a crate. Fresh handprints marred the dust on its lid. It creaked open, revealing our belongings piled atop old chainmail. Ketch snatched his satchel as Animo distributed our weapons.

The dwarf sighed in relief, withdrawing an unassuming bronze sphere from the bag. "It's here."

"Are you sure you know how to work it?" I asked.

He nodded, tucking it away. "Megs showed me. Once I get the venom, we'll be set."

"And you remember the message?"

He tapped his temple. "Fully committed to memory."

"Are we ready to go?" Camilla hovered by the door, her hand on the hilt of her cutlass.

"Not yet," Animo said. "We need armor."

I mentally slapped myself for not thinking of it first. "Everyone, find something that fits."

We spread out, rummaging through trunks of dented armor dotted with dark specks of what I wished were rust. Animo found a breastplate and metal arm bracers while I settled for the smallest chainmail shirt I could find. I discarded my vest, letting the cold mail rest over my short-sleeved shirt. It hung all the way down to my elbows, the rings primed for pinching. It'd be uncomfortable but far preferable to being stabbed.

Ketch let out an awe-filled curse. He turned slowly, brandishing a great longsword. My jaw dropped.

"It was in the crate," he said, his wide eyes meeting mine.

My fingers closed around the hilt, and I drew it from its scabbard with a furious ring of steel. The blade glimmered in the warming sunlight. Age had not diminished its pristine silver, nor had it dulled the sparkle of the egg-sized sapphire set into its hilt.

"Is that what I think it is?" Animo stood beside me, his gaze fixated on the blade.

"Anasir," I breathed. The sword of my family, wielded by every ruler since Tybalt Wolfe himself. Blessed by the divine maiden Cisin and used in the Dark War when the High Twelve fought against the evil that had cloaked the land.

I brushed my thumb against the steel wolf's head that protruded from the cross guards. *This* was the sword of a queen.

Fury blazed within me. This ancient symbol of my family's power had been left to rot amid rusting blades and bloody uniforms.

Animo caught my darkened expression. "Are you all right?"

"Fine," I replied, sheathing Anasir. "I'm simply imagining the satisfaction I'll feel when I kill Natalia—but not tonight."

A smile raised the corners of his lips. He reached into his pocket, withdrawing a small, silver ring set with a sapphire. "I think this belongs to you."

He offered me the ring as he had months before. Only this time, I accepted it.

CHAPTER SIXTY-FOUR

MAKE THEM RUN

Fully armed and protected by armor, we made our way to Malecare's dungeon. Aged splatters of blood sullied the walls and floors of the empty cells, yet once again, there was no guard.

Unease filled me as we searched. Natalia held the most powerful elf alive as her prisoner. Why would she not post a guard?

The barred cells ended in a hallway of thick, vaultlike doors with only thin slits permitting a view. Animo peered through the first one.

"It's her!" he exclaimed, tugging on the handle. It didn't budge. "Ketch!"

The dwarf shook his head. "I don't have any explosives."

Animo yanked, then pounded on the door. "We have to get her out of here."

"We need the venom," I said. "If it burns like dragon fire, then all it would take is one spark." I paused, running through the plan in my head. "We need

Dobbins."

Camilla grinned. "Come with me, Princess."

I led Camilla through the abandoned halls to Malecare's treasury. The door stood ajar, torchlight spilling out as the clinking of coins resonated from within.

We slowed, slinking alongside the wall. No voices. That could mean Dobbins was alone, but the more likely answer was simply that there was no good conversation to have with Natalia's possessed guards.

Camilla tapped my shoulder. "Stay here." She slid past me, positioning herself in front of the door, cutlass drawn. A smile lifted her lips, and she kicked it open. "Hello, piggy."

"You—!"

Camilla's enraged scream cut off Dobbins. She surged forward, her blade held high.

Shouts ensued, then coins clattered, and bodies thumped on the floor.

Camilla called, "You can come in now, Your Highness."

Ignoring her condescending tone, I entered the treasury. Three bodies lay on the ground, two of them guards with blood soaking their chests. Dobbins himself bore a gaping wound between his eyes, leaking brain matter.

I gagged.

Sheathing her cutlass, Camilla rifled through Dobbins's coat, pulling out small knives and the unwrapped witch stone—*that must be how he contacted Natalia*—before finding the vial of chimera venom. She held it up to the torchlight, then tossed it at me. "Catch."

My heart nearly stopped as I dove forward. The vial landed safely in my palms, and I tucked it into my pocket.

"Are you out of your mind?" I snapped. "You could have ruined our entire plan."

"Ugh, it's fine. You caught it." She grabbed a bag, filling it to the brim with coins.

"Are you actually focusing on gold at a time like this?"

"What? Someone has to pay me, and I doubt it will be you."

I pursed my lips, anger simmering within me.

"Take a torch," she said, tying the bag shut before securing it to her belt. "We'll need something to ignite the venom."

I slid one of the torches from its sconce, careful not to hold it too close to my pocket; I wasn't sure of the venom's sensitivity to heat, and I certainly wasn't going to risk finding out.

Armed with the venom, Camilla and I returned to the dungeon. Animo and Ketch waited, shade corpses littered at their feet.

"Trouble?" I asked, hurrying over.

"A bit," Animo replied. Splatters of dark blood flecked his cheek. "But nothing we couldn't handle."

"Did you get the venom?" Ketch asked.

I carefully passed him the vial.

"Perfect." He poured a small drop on the handle of Aspectu's cell, then gestured for us to back away. Standing off to the side, he tapped the torch against the handle.

Fire flashed before us, washing us in a wave of heat. Animo pulled me behind him, shielding me with his body.

The heat died as quickly as it had come. A smoldering hole gaped where the door once stood, flames lapping at the edges.

"Rack," Camilla said, impressed.

Animo raced through the hole to Aspectu's side. She lay on a stone slab, her wrists and ankles secured with leather straps. The same wounds I had seen in my last few dreams marked her skin along with fresh cuts down her arms.

Animo searched for a pulse while Camilla and I freed her limbs. "She's alive," he said, fear battling the relief in his tone. "But she's cold. Whatever Natalia did... it's caused more than unconsciousness."

"Not to be overly crass, but *who cares?*" Camilla asked, undoing the final restraint. "She's alive. We can deal with her general health later."

Animo nodded, his brow still creased with worry.

"We need a way to transport her," Ketch said. "Camilla, I think I saw a cart by the stairwell."

She ducked out of the room, heading toward the cells.

Ketch looked up at Animo. "She'll be all right."

Animo's jaw tightened. I placed my hand atop his.

"Ketch is right. As soon as we're free of this place, we'll take her to a healer."

He covered my hand with his, taking a deep breath. "Thank you. Both of you."

Camilla returned to the hole, pushing a cart long enough to fit Aspectu. "Load the elf up."

With me at Aspectu's legs and Animo at her shoulders, we maneuvered our way through the burning doorway, setting her down on the cart.

"You hop on too," Camilla instructed Ketch. She held up a hand when he began to protest. "I'm not slowing my pace, and I'm certainly not turning around."

"Fine," he said bitterly. He reached for the cart, then paused, turning back to me. "Rose, you are better than Natalia, and you are stronger than Natalia. You can win this."

I swallowed hard, nodding. "Thank you, Ketch."

His gaze lifted to Animo. "Please, don't die." The simple statement carried all the weight it needed.

Animo nodded. "The same goes for you."

Ketch exhaled heavily, then clambered onto the cart, settling by Aspectu's legs. "Venom, sphere, torch"—he patted his pockets, then raised the flickering torch—"Let's topple a regime."

I laughed softly. "Let's."

Camilla's brows arched. "Well, if I don't see the two of you within a week's time, I will assume you're dead and sell your belongings."

"Good luck to you, too," Animo said.

She gave the cart a shove, rattling down the hall toward a back door.

My eyes met Animo's. It was down to the two of us now.

"She sent shades," I said. "She knows we've escaped."

He nodded. "The question now becomes whether or not she realizes we're coming for her."

"Let's hope the answer is no."

He nodded, laughing slightly. We both knew the answer, and it most certainly wasn't *no*.

WRITTEN IN THE SKY

*A**t least we were right**, I thought, peering around the corner. The hall before the throne room loomed, lined with shades. They stood like the wooden pieces of a board game—only this game was unevenly matched. "Do you think we can take them?" I asked, despite knowing the answer.

Animo shook his head. "There are too many. They'll tear us apart."

"Then how do we get past them?"

"I don't think *we* do."

I stepped away from the corner's edge, turning to face him. "You can't take them on your own."

"Maybe not, but I can draw them away."

"They'll kill you!"

"I'll be running, not fighting."

I opened my mouth to protest, but he cut me off. "You need to face Natalia. Once you have the staff, you can come back for me. I'll barricade myself in the storeroom so they won't be able to reach me."

I sighed reluctantly. "Fine. But once you are in the storeroom, you do not leave, no matter what. Wait for me to get you."

Animo nodded. "I swear it."

I pressed my back against the wall as he slipped past me, pausing at the corner's edge.

"Stay out of sight," he instructed. "Give them plenty of time to chase me before you make your move."

He reached for his sword, but I caught his hand. "Thank you for being here," I whispered. "For never leaving me no matter how foolish I was and for pushing me when I was too afraid to take a stand. You have been there for me every day since we met, and that means more to me than you will ever know."

Animo laced his fingers with mine, giving my hand a squeeze. "I'm not going anywhere, Rose."

I gazed up into his starlit eyes. Something about the looming shadow of death washed away my inhibitions, replacing them with a reckless desire for life. My fingers closed around his collar, and I lifted myself onto my toes, pressing my lips to his.

His arms wrapped around my waist as he returned the kiss, the adrenaline of battle surging between us. We broke apart, his warmth lingering on my lips.

His hands traced the curve of my waist. "I'm not going anywhere," he repeated. He took my hand, giving the back of it a soft kiss before drawing Bathril.

I turned away as he stepped out into the hallway. Leaning against the wall, I closed my eyes, bracing myself for an onslaught of shade screams.

But none came.

"Rose," Animo called. "I think you should see this."

With a hand on Anasir's hilt, I stepped out. The shades remained standing, still as statues.

"What is the matter with them?" I asked.

"I'm not sure…" He stepped forward, pressing the tip of his sword against the closest shade's chest. Slowly, he drove it through the monster's flesh. The shade's eyes bugged out, but it didn't move until Animo pulled his blade free. It collapsed onto the ground, a black pool forming beneath it.

"They're not here to fight us," Animo said, his tone doubting every word.

"No… they're guards." I stepped forward. The sea of shades parted, clearing a path to the doors. "Natalia *wants* me to face her."

"That means it's a trap."

"I am well aware," I replied, taking another step. Animo trailed after me, his gaze sharp on the shades. They remained, frozen sentinels as we passed.

At the path's end, I took a slow breath. *We made it through her first trap, but who is to say whether or not there's a second?*

I squared my shoulders, facing the throne room doors. Whatever lay before us, we would handle it.

A shade screamed behind me.

I spun—their path had closed, trapping Animo in its center. The pale monsters circled him, their claws hungry for spilled blood. From an adjacent hallway stepped the Hunter—my father. He placed himself opposite of me, the swell of shades between us.

"Animo!" I cried, drawing Anasir.

"Don't!" he shouted. "This isn't your fight. You take Natalia—I'll handle this."

"But—"

"Just go!"

My heart pounded. His gaze ran along the ever-tightening ring of shades as he prepared for battle.

He can't take them. But he had to. *But if he doesn't…*

No. He would survive.

Tearing my eyes away from the deadly scene, I faced the double doors. I threw them open, striding into the throne room as they slammed shut behind me.

Natalia stood in the center of the room, sword in hand. Eathraze, I recalled. *The Punisher.* Behind her, the Staff of Realms rested against the arm of her—*my*—throne.

"You have something of mine," I said. "Several somethings, actually."

"You think you can intimidate me?" she asked condescendingly. "I have you exactly where I want you. Tell me, what do you think of my plans for your elf protector?"

My stomach twisted at the thought of Animo alone against her army, but I refused to allow my fear to reach my face.

"Do you think he'll survive?" Natalia asked. "I certainly don't."

I forced my voice to remain calm. "You won't be able to kill him. His own father tried and failed for years."

"Hmm… confident," she mused. "*Confidence* is really another word for *pride*, which is just a pretty way to say *woefully misinformed about one's importance*."

"You would know—you're a witch wearing a stolen crown."

She scoffed. "I'm much more than a witch, darling. I have power beyond your imagination." She touched the totem glittering around her neck, stroking its black gem. "Beautiful, isn't it? I really must thank you for bringing it to me."

My jaw tightened, my teeth grating together. Like a knight falling on his own sword, so could my own weapon destroy me.

Natalia laughed at my fury, an evil gleam shining in her eye. "You can't even begin to comprehend the power it wields. Shall we give it a try?"

My abdomen exploded with pain. I screamed, gripping my stomach as unseen knives slashed through me. My vision blurred—I searched the ground, waiting for my skin to rip open and my guts to spill onto the shining, black abyss that was the floor.

Only the pain disappeared.

Natalia cried out, stumbling back and clutching her own stomach. "You…" she growled. "You don't control me. *I* am the one in control!"

Her vacant eyes stared through me. Realization flooded me like morning sunlight.

"It won't let you hurt me." My beast… it was protecting me.

I pushed myself to my feet, snatching Anasir from the floor. "Even with stolen blood, the totem's power belongs to me."

"Not anymore," Natalia snarled. "I drained your mother of her magic. It's mine, and yours will be too."

I shook my head, circling her. "You can't control anything."

"You know nothing of what speaks to me. One word from it would send you crawling back to the shadows."

"Sounds like it has the power—not you."

Natalia screamed, hurling a wave of magical energy at me. I ducked, covering my head. The magic struck, sizzling against my skin before dying out.

"No!" Natalia cried. She ripped the totem from around her neck, hurling it across the room. "I can still kill you without magic," she snapped, raising her sword.

I readied Anasir. "Try."

She flew forward, bringing her blade against mine in a clash of metal. Natalia fought with fury and skill that I couldn't hope to match. More than once, her sword scraped against me in what would have been a death blow had I not been wearing chainmail.

I struggled to stay upright against her force. From the other side of the doors echoed the dying screams of shades. A man's shout followed them.

Animo.

Natalia used my distraction to slam the pommel of her sword against my head. I fell with a cry, Anasir slipping from my grasp. Her heel bit into my back, pressing me against the floor.

"Foolish girl. Your magic may be flawed, but my own power is not."

With a muttered spell, she sent me flying through the air. My body slammed into the throne so hard that it toppled. I tumbled across the floor, colliding with the wall. Groaning, I pushed myself onto my elbows.

Natalia stalked across the room. She gripped my hair, forcing my chin up as she pressed her blade to my neck. "Any last words?" she hissed in my ear.

I squeezed my eyes shut, fighting a whimper. *This can't be how it ends.* Not when Megs had given her life for another, and my grandfather had been slaughtered for the kingdom he adored. Not when my mother's body was strung up like an ornament, and my grandmother had met death with strength in her eyes. Not when my father had stared at me without a trace of recognition. Their sacrifices meant nothing if Natalia went free.

"Very well," she said. "Goodbye, Rosara."

An explosion shook the ground. Tremors raced up the walls, rattling the window panes. Faint screams erupted, overcome by the echo of crashing stone.

Natalia's gaze snapped to the open balcony. Flames carved through the sky, curving into letters:

Tyranny has held you hostage for too long.
Your heir has returned, and she brings war with her.
Join us and fight—until the very end.

A laughing sob slipped out. *It actually worked.*

The device had been carried from Rudane, with Megs tinkering with it practically every night. Through high and low, it had somehow found its way with us. And now it was the final spark. The fire had been lit, and there was no turning back.

I drew my dagger, driving it into Natalia's soft, unprotected side. She let out a cry, releasing my hair. I rolled away, blade still in hand.

"This doesn't mean you win," she snarled, her hand pressed against her bleeding side.

I stood, my dagger poised for defense. "The people know they aren't alone anymore. I am coming for my throne, and if you continue to stand in my way, I will destroy you. However, if you surrender now, I will allow you to live. You'll be imprisoned, but I can ensure that your confines will be respectable."

She straightened despite the blood pouring down her side. "You think you're strong. *Worthy.* But you have no idea what I have lived through."

"I think I do." *I think you and I are alike. And if I fell as far as you have, I think I'd want someone to stop me before I hurt anyone else.*

Natalia shook her head. "Goodbye, Rosara." She thrust her blade forward, but I dove out of the way, snatching Anasir from the floor.

I threw my sword up just in time to block her next blow. She slammed her blade into mine again and again, pressing me against the ground.

Kingdoms, I'm going to die.

Natalia loomed above me, her sword held high. Pure madness twisted her face as her arms tensed, ready for the final strike. Before her blade could fall, a crash resonated from the hall. A pained shout followed.

That didn't sound like Animo.

Natalia froze. Her gaze locked on the door, the blood draining from her cheeks. I rolled out of the way, scrambling to my feet and brandishing both my sword and dagger.

The doors burst open. Animo stumbled in, his armor tattered and hanging off of his shoulder. Crimson blood coated his skin, flowing freely from the long claw marks that ran across his chest and arms.

My heart dropped. *But he's alive,* I reminded myself. *He survived.*

Animo limped forward, the doors slamming shut behind him. Blood dripped from his fingertips, leaving a trail in his wake.

"Where is my Hunter?" Natalia snapped.

Animo raised Bathril, backing away from her. "Why do you care?" He cut a wide circle, aiming for the Staff of Realms, discarded by the toppled throne.

Quietly, I sheathed my blades, preparing to run.

"Tell. Me."

The doors banged open. My father stepped in, his unmasked face splattered with blood. A smile stretched across Natalia's lips.

"Rose!" Animo broke into a sprint toward the staff.

I dove to meet him.

Natalia shouted an order at my father. Before he could move, Animo's arms were around my waist. The world collapsed into rippling blue, then darkness.

EPILOGUE

I stood on the balcony of Marstaff Manor, watching the sunrise. A week ago, Animo and I had escaped Malecare. We'd reappeared several leagues away from the Manor and left a number of rumors and false leads for Natalia to chase. It was still a risk returning, but it was the only place we could rely on for a rendezvous. If our calculations were correct, Ketch and Camilla should be arriving today with Aspectu in tow. Christoph and Belinda were still gone when we had arrived, leaving us to do nothing but hope they were alive.

A cool morning breeze rustled my loose hair and the long, puffy sleeves of my dress. Being Margaret's, it was a bit long on me—but for the first time in months, my clothes were completely free of blood.

Animo joined me on the balcony, his shirt lumpy from the many bandages wrapped around his limbs. He might have won the fight with the shades, but it hadn't been without consequences. They had torn through his armor, shredding his chest. When we fell through the portal, the magic had affected his ability to heal, leaving him unconscious and bleeding out.

I could live a thousand years and never forget the terror I had felt as I struggled to keep him alive.

"Any sign of them?" he asked, leaning against the railing with a stifled grimace.

"Not yet. But they'll be here."

Rumor had it that Natalia had yet to emerge from Malecare. Nor had she attempted to repair the bridge, leaving her forces all but trapped in Devil's Canyon.

Since our escape, something had shifted in Avonshere. Whispers ran like lightning, igniting the coals of rebellion. *Until the very end* remained a deadly phrase to utter, but it was beginning to regain the strength and honor it had once carried.

There was one thing that still bothered me: "I can't stop thinking about the fight with Natalia. She should have killed me, but there was something holding her back." I drummed my fingers against the railing. "Her madness… I think it comes from her totem."

"You think she's possessed?"

"Not possessed. Corrupted, perhaps. But even that… I don't know. It doesn't match what I felt with the beast."

I'd told Animo about the way my totem had fought against Natalia. His confusion matched mine, although he was doubtful that its loyalty would last. Sooner or later, Natalia—or her own beast within—would break it.

Animo's arm slipped around my waist. I leaned against him, careful not to press too hard on his wounds. His closeness brought comfort but also reminded me of the one subject we'd yet to broach—our kiss.

"If there's something stopping Natalia from killing you, we should be grateful," he said, redirecting my attention. "She's furious now, and we'll need all the help we can get to stop her from ripping you apart." He paused. "Have you thought about it?"

I nodded. "This has always been Natalia's war. She silenced all who could oppose her, forcing the fight into the dark. We can't win that way. For us to win this war, we have to fight it in the light of day." I twisted, leaning back against the rail so I could meet his eyes. "Aspectu once gave me a vision about the High Twelve. I believe that this war will bring unity between the Twelve Kingdoms and create an army great enough to topple whatever power Natalia can summon."

"If we succeed, it could be the start of a new age for the Twelve Kingdoms."

"And if we fail, all twelve will be destroyed." I sighed. I hadn't forgotten Aspectu's warnings.

He brushed his thumb against my cheek. "Hope is stronger than fear. Wait, and you'll see."

"Margaret had hope," I said. "Even when she died. She wasn't sad or afraid—she was ready. I think it's because she had faith we wouldn't leave Avonshere like this. And we won't."

"Then where do we begin?"

"By gaining an army. We'll find *The Dragon's Bane*, then return to Chess. I think I have enough connections to receive an audience with Queen Astrid." I shook my head. "Kingdoms, that's strange to say."

"I think it suits you," Animo replied. He took my hand, raising it so we could see the ring on my pinky. The sunlight shone into the sapphire, illuminating the Wolfe family crest carved within. "We're going to win this. And if we don't, the kingdoms will remember us as the ones who spent every last breath fighting."

"Good."

A smile lifted his lips. "Look."

I followed his gaze to the wagon cresting the hill. A woman with braided hair sat in the driver's seat, a single-shoed dwarf by her side.

I laughed, leaning back against Animo. His arm settled around my shoulders. "We're going to win this. Especially now that we have the rest of the war effort."

I grinned up at him. "For now."

Chess was only the beginning. From there, we would travel to each of the Twelve Kingdoms, gathering allies until nobody, not even Natalia, could challenge us. War would not be easy or quick, but my people would endure.

But for now, we had a message to spread to every corner of the Twelve Kingdoms: the Second Dark War had begun.

524

THE STORY ISN'T OVER YET...

Scan this QR code and learn how to unlock exclusive bonus scenes featuring your favorite characters!

GLOSSARY

AESIN DICTIONARY

This dictionary includes the Aesin words and phrases found in The Twelve Kingdoms along with their closest English counterparts (not all translations are exact).

Accipeum (ah-sehp-EE-um): dismissed/you may go

Ambai ne omniin cu illa (ahm-BYE neh ohm-nihm): may the one I seek be found in the land of sleep

Arnui te aruni, iman te entai, erhae en somunus (ah-ROO-nee tay ah-ROO-nee EE-mahn tay ehn-TIE er-HAY in sohm-NUS): Mind and mind, meld and twine, join us in dreams

Eian (EE-ahn): Princess

Eian Cray (EE-ahn kray): Crown Princess

Emea tu (eh-may too): Look there

Iblitha (ihb-lith-yah): library

Ie memae auferta (eye mem-AY ahf-WEAR-tah): Take the memory away

Itrae (ih-tray): again

Lumaia vaccerae (loo-MY-ah VAH-sear-ay): bring forth sunlight

Marcix (mahr-sicks): murderer

Navu (nah-voo): coward

O cis Viria. O cis ei, tes sotip ei (oh cihs veer-EE-ah oh cihs AY, tay SO-tip AY): you killed Viria. You killed her, yet you claim to love her

Oei (oh-EYE): queen

Oesin los solrae (oh-sin lohs sohl-ray): throne room balcony

Oex (oh-AY): king

Ospetie (ah-speh-teh): You may

Ov eure sahl aei erden sive. Lav daes icha uthae ertas il de heliv orvu. Lav mavine erdas (ohv YUR sal AY-ah ER-den SEEV. lahv days ITCH-ah OOH-they ER-tahs ill day HEEL-ihv or-VOO. lahv MAH-veen ER-dahs): the spell used to forge a Reyth totem—the exact translation is unavailable

Qi fectie (kay fee-tay): what is this?

Rumif aella (ruh-mihf ay-lah): watch where you're going

Saete (say-tay): Enough

Sinet caelai san esede (sihn-eh say-lie san eh-sehd): a healing spell—the exact translation is unavailable

Tempe unar (tehm-pay uh-nahr): One moment

Ustos (uhs-toss): Guards

Voli (voh-lee): Fly

CHARACTER GUIDE

Ali Jesser (a-LEE jeh-SUR): the blonde member of the Cunningham Gang who's in a relationship with Ruger

Animo Terrot (ah-NEE-moh TEH-roh): the mysterious elf who guides Rose on her quest.

Anne Crowborne: Derek's mother, Rudane's local healer

Aspectu Demore (ah-SPECK-too DEH-more-ay): a powerful elf dubbed the 'Ancient Elf' who sent Animo to find Rose

Belinda Seib (beh-LEND-ah SEEb): young, dark-haired girl, part of the Cunningham Gang

Bellatora Regiis (bell-ah-TOR-ah): daughter of Regium and Viria and the Crown Princess of Vaera

Bette Mohler (bet MOLE-er): mother of Megs and sister of Anne, a successful seamstress

Camilla Hawkins: Captain of *The Dragon's Bane*

Cerise Estmar (sur-EESE ehst-MAR): mother of Lili and wife of Ronan

Christoph Dunmore: a former knight of Avonshere and ally of Margaret.

Cisin (SIHZ-in): Avonshere's divine guardian

Count and Countess Triani (tree-ah-nee): a wealthy couple in Lucia with a large collection of artifacts

Dante (dahn-TAY): the Cunningham Gang's "muscle"

Derek Crowborne (dare-ick): a dear friend of Lili's and Meg's cousin

Desmin (dehs-men): a librarian at the Great Library of Daria

Donna Branburn (dohn-nah): Hertz's long-time flame

Duaex (doo-AY): the first elf who is believed to guide the spirits of fallen elves to the Everlands

Ekkshu (ehck-shoo): the leader of a goblin campaign located in the Silver Forest

Elias Cunningham (EE-lie-iss): brother of Ruger and member of the Cunningham Gang

Elizabeth Sconcewood: the mysterious woman who stole the Staff of Realms from the Trianis

Emode (EE-moh-day): the Divine Mistress of the Arts

Emry Avron (em-ree ahv-ron): Rose's mother

Fate: a name associated with a divine being who is said to control

Garblesh (gahr-bleh-sh): the right-hand goblin of Ekkshu

Hertz Baldwick (hurts bald-wick): Rose's gentle and protective friend

James Wolfe: Rose's grandfather, killed during Leon's coronation

Ketchnoori "Ketch" of Family Runix (catch-nor-EE rune-icks): Animo's dwarf companion

Keqec (keck-WEE): the Divine Lady of Entremets

Layona (lay-oh-nah): the Divine Maiden of Harvest

Leon Wolfe (lee-on wolf): Rose's father and brief King of Avonshere

Liliana "Lili" Estmar (lih-lee-ah-nah est-mahr): Rose's adoptive sister

Mahori (MA-hor-ee): the Divine Commander of the Storm and Seas and the Divine Guardian of Madoria

Margaret Wolfe: Rose's grandmother

Megara "Megs" Mohler (meg-AR-ah MOLE-er): Rose's spunky and inventive friend

Natalia Thornsworth (nah-tall-ee-ah): the witch who overthrew the Wolfe reign

Nelos Caine (neh-LOS cane): a notorious drug lord who operates out of Nicia

Olstaff Hestr (ohl-STAHF heh-STIR): the local innkeeper and life of the party

Percival Branburn: the town master of Rudane and father of Donna

Pura Regiis (poo-rah rehg-ihs): daughter of Regium and Sapientaie and Princess of Vaera

Regium Regiis (REG-ee-um REG-ihs): the King of Vaera, an enemy of Aspectu and Animo

Ronan Estmar (roh-nahn ehst-mahr): father of Lili and husband of Cerise

Rosara "Rose" Wolfe (row-SAR-ah wolf): the Crown Princess of Avonshere, believed to be dead

Ruger Cunningham (ROO-gur): the leader of the Cunningham Gang

Sabine (sahb-EEN): a priestess at Aleddai

Sapientiae Regiis (SAH-pee-in-tay): The second wife of Regium Regiis, Queen of Vaera, and mother of Pura

Sol (sahl): Camilla's first mate on *The Dragon's Bane*

The Queen's Hunter: A masked soldier who serves Queen Natalia

Tybalt Wolfe (tie-bahlt): the first King of Avonshere and member of the High Twelve

Zevre (zehv-ray): the white wolf companion of James Wolfe

FANTASY RACES AND SPECIES

Brownie: a fluffy creature about the size of one's fist known for causing trouble despite its general adorableness

Chimera (KIE-mer-AH): a creature with the body of a lion, a goat's head protruding from its back, and a living snake as its tail. Its venom is valuable and highly flammable

Divine Beings: immortal and immensely powerful beings worshiped as gods throughout the Twelve Kingdoms. Each kingdom has its own divine guardian, held in the highest regard because of the guardian's aid in ending the Dark War (blessing the sword wielded by that kingdom's original ruler)

Dwarf: a non-magic, humanoid race with an extended life span

Ekeider (eek-eye-dehr): an umbrella term for beings born with natural magic (elves, fae, etc.)

Elf: an immortal, ekeider being with a passing resemblance to a human

(primary distinctions come in the form of pointed ears and uniquely multi-
ticolored eyes)

Fae: a magical race of beings tied to the elements (includes fairies, nymphs,
and pixies)

Fairie: winged fae subspecies

Goblin: a non-magical race with distinct green skin and pointed ears

Liposa: a magical, butterfly-like creature

Nixie: a forest spirit known for luring children by playing the violin

Nymph: a fae subspecies deeply connected to nature

Pixie: a small and mischievous fae subspecies

Shade: twisted monsters created by severing a human's soul from their body
and contorting their appearance through dark magic. Created by Natalia
Thornsworth

Tree Elf: a cursed goblin/elf hybrid native to the Silver Forest

Vitus (VEE-tuhs): a race of trees brought to life through magic (plural: viti)

HISTORICAL EVENTS & HOLIDAYS

Readwekya (red-week-YAH): Nicia's festival dedicated to bread and other
baked goods

The Dark War: a brutal war fought over a thousand years ago

The Dance of Serenity: a ritual that reconnects Emode's priestesses with her
magic

The Goblin-Elf Wars: an on-and-off series of battles fought between the
goblins and elves that inhabited Vaera. The primary source of conflict was
over the goblins' desire to obtain magic

The Harvest Festival: a celebration in Chess that occurs on the first day of
Primnen, the night before farmers begin harvesting their crops

The Reign of Enia: the period of time in which the land was one

The Reign of Twelve: the period of time in which the land has been divided
into twelve kingdoms

LANGUAGES

Aesin (AY-sihn): The language of the elves

Ancient Elarian (EE-lah-REE-in): a dead language spoken during the Reign of Enia

Common: a colloquialized name for the 'Common Tongue,' an established language spoken throughout the Twelve Kingdoms

Dwarvish: a language spoken by dwarves that has its own, runic alphabet

LOCATIONS

Aleddai (ah-leh-DIE): a temple dedicated to Emode, the Divine Mistress of the Arts

Avonshere (ay-vohn-share): the northernmost kingdom

Biaht (BYE-ht): a commonly accepted afterlife for those who lived evil lives

Brennate (brihn-ate): a town not far from Avonshere's border

Cavbrooke (CAHV-brook): a picturesque town in Mydor**Chess** (chess): a kingdom ruled by Queen Astrid Varangot

Daria (dahr-ee-ah): Vaera's capital city where most elves live

Del Hera (dehl hair-ah): the now-fallen capital city of Avonshere

Devil's Canyon: a dangerous part of the mountain range that runs through Avonshere

Elatire (el-ah-TEER): a dukedom in Avonshere formerly governed by Natalia Thornsworth

Elwrite (ell-rite): a kingdom filled with blooming meadows year-round

Eterios (EE-teer-EE-ohs): a commonly accepted afterlife for those who lived noble lives

Everlands: an afterlife believed in by elves

Faelands (fay-lands): the fae kingdom, thick with enchantment

Holfetine Wood (holf-tine): a forest that borders Rudane

Idycen (ih-DEE-sin): a commonly accepted afterlife for those who lived ordinary lives

Lucia (loo-SHE-ah): a warm and wealthy kingdom where swamps and canals are common

Madoria (mah-door-ee-ah): the ocean kingdom ruled by mer clans. On poor terms with all kingdoms except Soren.

Malecare (mal-EEK-air): Natalia's fortress nestled in the rocky heights of Devil's Canyon

Marstaff Manor (mahr-staff): the residency of Elizabeth Sconcewood

Medea (meh-DEE-ah): a wealthy city in Lucia, rife with crime

Mydor (MIE-door): a northern kingdom ruled by the Fenwick family

Nemeth (neh-mith): a kingdom known for its dense jungles and skillful warriors

Pikbrie (pick-bree): the mountainous kingdom where dwarves and dragons live in harmony

Rudane (roo-dane): the village in Chess where Rose made her home after fleeing Avonshere

Shieldore (shEEL-door): a prison built within an active salt mine

Soren (soar-in): a barren wasteland of a kingdom where class tensions run high

The Evishal Palace (EE-vee-shal): the castle where the royal family of Vaera lives

The Great Library of Daria: a massive library that houses ancient works of literature and powerful grimoires. Located within the Evishal Palace

The Silver Forest: The nearly impenetrable forest that surrounds Vaera. Filled with curses, goblins, witches, and more dark creatures than one can count

Vaera (vay-rah): the elf kingdom ruled by King Regium Regiis and surrounded by a cursed forest

Valintros (vahl-in-tross): The former capital of Vaera and stronghold of Salvator Regiis. Now in ruins

Vargo (vahr-go): a desert kingdom with a history of treachery

MISCELLANEOUS

Bravit (brah-viht): a popular card game similar to poker

Grimoire (grim-WAHR): a book of magic and spells

Halias (HA-lie-ahs): a burial shroud used in Avonsheran funerals

Mahori Light: a candle sailors light to earn the protection of Mahori, the Divine Commander of the Storms and Sea, during their voyage

Mynet (mihn-yeht): a common form of currency. Standard mynet is a gold coin but can also be found in silver (half-mynet) and bronze (quarter-mynet)

Ocit el Saira/The Epic of Twelve (oh-sit ehl SIE-AR-ah): a book outlining the formation of the High Twelve and the creation of the Twelve Kingdoms

Pyrix Crystals (PEER-icks): magical, fire-like crystals from Pikbrie

Reyth Totem (RAY-ith): a blood magic totem forged through darkness and human sacrifice

The Ardent Pack: a group of rebels loyal to the Wolfe bloodline

The Staff of Realms: an ancient fae relic with the power of teleportation

Town Master: a leadership role reminiscent of a mayor

MONTHS OF THE YEAR

Calam (CAL-am): the first month

Sacay (sah-KAY): the second month

Marsai (mar-SIE): the third month. This marks the beginning of the perennial season

Arsind (ahr-SEND): the fourth month

Akendae (AH-keen-DAY): the fifth month

Cassan (KAH-san): the sixth month. This marks the beginning of the calescent season

Fanrae (fahn-ray): the seventh month

Cellin (sell-in): the eighth month

Primnen (prim-nihn): the ninth month. This marks the beginning of the harvest season.

Nictam (NICK-tahm): the tenth month

Gelan (gehl-an): the eleven month

Cisay (sihs-AY): the twelfth month. This marks the beginning of the rime season.

NAMES OF SWORDS

Anasir (an-ah-SEAR): a sword blessed by Cisin and wielded by Tybalt Wolfe in the Dark War

Bathril (bath-REEL): Animo's blade

Eathraze (EETH-rays): the punisher. Natalia's blade

Inbane: Leon's blade sporting a cracked griffin claw on the hilt

PHRASES & TERMS

Biaht (BYE-ht): a curse referencing the afterlife for evil souls (commonly heard in the Kingdom of Chess, where belief in Biaht is most prevalent)

Cleming (cleh-ming): a rude term referring to an insufferable person

Craven (cray-vihn): coward

Modir (moh-dehr): a term for "mother" in Chess

Nettled/Nettling: irritated/irritating. A reference to the stinging nettle plant

Pixie Chase: a useless goal or journey

Rack/Racking: a vulgar exclamation of distaste

Sult: a rude or unappealing person

Uchlet (oosh-let): a particularly vulgar dwarvish term for a despicable being

ACKNOWLEDGEMENTS

These will possibly be the worst acknowledgments you've ever read. I don't really do the whole sappy, overflowing-with-emotions sort of thank yous, so this will be short and to the point. Let's get into it!

Thank you to Mom, who will probably complain if she isn't the first person mentioned. Thank you to Dad, who would *definitely* complain if he didn't make the acknowledgments cut. And thank you to Gigi for helping with final grammar edits (along with Mom) and basically funding the entire publishing process.

Thank you to my line editor, Ariana Tosado, for helping me clean up my prose and use words wisely (and spell them correctly).

Thank you to my beta readers: Kat, Sabrey, Danielle, Makaela, and Brenda. Your comments were priceless and helped change this story for the better.

Thank you to my street team—the First Reader's Club. You guys have been so encouraging and supportive; it's amazing. I'd also like to thank the Instagram writing community, who have also done a fantastic job of hyping up me and my release.

Thank you to Lauren Graves and Chelsea Pawer for helping me rename the beloved (albeit short-lived) innkeeper formerly known as Clipclop.

A second thank you goes to my parents, who are admittedly wonderful, loving people who have always supported me (my mother wasn't exactly fond of my roast in the second paragraph).

Finally, I'd like to thank God. I consider this book to be proof of a higher power because if time has proven anything, it is that I'm not nearly smart enough to connect all these plot points on my own.

ABOUT THE AUTHOR

Dana A. Caldwell is an independently published author from South Carolina. Ever since she was a little girl, Dana has loved daydreaming and coming up with stories. She started pursuing writing seriously when she was fourteen and went on to publish her debut novel, *The Twelve Kingdoms,* at age nineteen, shortly after graduating from Liberty University with an Associate's degree in Creative Writing. Now that her first book is published, Dana is ready to leap fully into her career as an author and invites you to follow along on her journey.

Connect with Dana:
Instagram: @author.danacaldwell
Website: www.danaacaldwellbooks.com
Email: authordanacaldwell@gmail.com

www.ingramcontent.com/pod-product-compliance
Lightning Source LLC
Chambersburg PA
CBHW020332010826
48970CB00010B/27